Frank Moore

Heroes and Martyrs

Notable men of the time. Biographical sketches of the military and naval heroes,

statesmen and orators, distinguished in the American crisis of 1861-62

Frank Moore

Heroes and Martyrs
Notable men of the time. Biographical sketches of the military and naval heroes, statesmen and orators, distinguished in the American crisis of 1861-62

ISBN/EAN: 9783337213763

Printed in Europe, USA, Canada, Australia, Japan

Cover: Foto ©Raphael Reischuk / pixelio.de

More available books at **www.hansebooks.com**

Heroes and Martyrs:

NOTABLE MEN OF THE TIME.

BIOGRAPHICAL SKETCHES

OF THE

Military and Naval Heroes, Statesmen and Orators,

DISTINGUISHED IN THE AMERICAN CRISIS OF 1861–62.

EDITED BY FRANK MOORE.

With Portraits on Steel, from Original Sources.

NEW YORK:

G. P. PUTNAM, 532 BROADWAY.

C. T. EVANS, GENERAL AGENT.

CONTENTS.

iv. CONTENTS.

NOTABLE MEN.

WINFIELD SCOTT.

WINFIELD SCOTT was born near Petersburgh, Virginia, June 13th, 1786, was the youngest son of William Scott, Esq., and was left an orphan at an early age. He was educated at the high-school at Richmond, whence he went to William and Mary College, and attended law lectures. He was admitted to the bar of Virginia in 1806. The next year he went to South Carolina with the intention to take up his residence there; but before he had acquired the right to practise in that state, Congress, in view of imminent hostilities with England, passed a bill to enlarge the army, and young Scott obtained a commission as captain of light artillery.

General Wilkinson was then stationed in Louisiana, and Captain Scott was ordered to join the army at that point in 1809. In the next year Wilkinson was superseded, and the young captain then expressed what was a very general opinion: namely, that his late commander was implicated in Burr's conspiracy. For this he was tried by court-martial, and sentenced to one year's suspension from rank and pay. Probably this suspension was a fortunate event; for the whole of that year was employed in the diligent study of works on military art.

War was declared against Great Britain June 18th, 1812; and in July of the same year Captain Scott was made a lieutenant-colonel in the second artillery, and was stationed at Black Rock with two companies of his regiment. With this force he covered Van Rensselaer's passage of the Niagara River on the expedition against Queenstown, October 13th. Later in the day, when Van Rensselaer was disabled, the command fell upon Scott, who, after a gallant fight, deserted by the New York militia, and outnumbered very greatly by British reinforcements, surrendered his whole command, two hundred and ninety-three in all, prisoners of war.

While a prisoner, he saw the British officers select from the American soldiers taken with him such as appeared to be Irishmen; and these men, they declared, were to be sent to England as British subjects, there to be punished for treason. Scott then, in the presence of the British officers, assured the soldiers that the United States government would not quietly see them suffer, and would certainly retaliate upon British prisoners the treatment they should receive. Exchanged in January,

1813, he immediately made a report of this matter to the secretary of war. Laid before Congress, this report originated the act by which the President of the United States was invested with "the power of retaliation;" and from prisoners subsequently taken by himself, Scott chose a number equal to the number sent to England to abide their fate. For this purpose he was careful to choose only Englishmen.

Immediately after the capture of York, Upper Canada, Scott rejoined the army on the frontier as adjutant to General Dearborn, with the rank of colonel. He took part in the expedition against Fort George; landed his men in good order, and scaled a steep height in the presence of the enemy, who was finally driven from his position at the point of the bayonet. Fort George was then no longer tenable, and the British abandoned it, having placed slow matches to all the magazines. Only one of them exploded, and from a piece of timber thrown by it, Colonel Scott received a severe wound in the left shoulder. Disaster and disgrace marked the close of this campaign, and for another it was necessary to form a new army.

In March, 1814, Colonel Scott was made a brigadier-general, and immediately thereafter established a camp of instruction at Buffalo, where his own and Ripley's brigades, with a battalion of artillery, and some regiments of volunteers, were drilled into thorough and accurate discipline.

Brigadier-General Scott crossed the Niagara River with his brigade July 3d, 1814; on the fourth skirmished for sixteen miles with a detachment under the Marquis of Tweedale; and that night encamped upon Street's Creek, two miles from the British camp at Chippewa. Between the two camps lay the plain upon which the battle was fought next day. East of this plain was the Niagara River, west was a heavy wood; and on the northern side from the wood to the Niagara ran the Chippewa River, while Street's Creek ran in a similar direction on the southern side. Behind the Chippewa was the British army under General Riall, well provided with artillery.

About noon of the fifth, a bright, hot summer's day, there occurred a skirmish of light troops in the wood. Some Indians and British militia were there engaged by General Porter, with volunteers, militia, and friendly Indians, and driven back until they came upon the main body of the British army, which was seen to be in motion when Porter's irregulars broke and fled. Major-General Brown, in the wood with Porter, thus first learned of the British advance; and Brigadier-General Scott, also ignorant of it, was leading his brigade into the plain to drill. This was at four P. M. Brown hurried to the rear to bring up Ripley's brigade, and Scott's force passed the bridge over Street's Creek in perfect order under the British fire. The action soon became general. Major Jessup, with a battalion in the wood, for some time checked the enemy's right wing, whereupon the enemy left one battalion with him, formed a new right, and continued to advance. The British line was now drawn nearly square across the plain. Opposed was a battalion under McNeill, which faced his right obliquely, and another under Leavenworth, which opposed his left in the same manner. Scott's line, thus formed, and supported by Towson's artillery on the right, continued to advance, fire, and halt, until it was within eighty paces of the enemy, when McNeill's and Leavenworth's battalions, almost simultaneously, charged with the bayonet. This shock was decisive; the British army broke and fled, pursued nearly to its intrenchments, in complete rout. The American loss was three hundred and twenty-seven, the enemy's five hundred and three; while the Americans engaged numbered only one thousand nine hundred, and the British two thousand one hundred. Three of the enemy's regiments, the Royal Scots, the Queen's Own, and the Hundredth regiment, were esteemed the best troops in the British army.

Much gloom was cleared from the public mind by this battle; it atoned for many disasters, and the country was taught, when it needed most to know it, that American soldiers, in proper hands, were equal to those whose skill and discipline had been acquired in the hard-fought fields of the Peninsular war. "Brigadier-General Scott," said General Brown in his official report, "is entitled to the highest praise our country can bestow."

With Scott's brigade still in the van, the American army passed over the Chippewa two days after the battle, and the British army retreated before it. But to mask a movement against Burlington Heights, a feigned retreat was almost immediately made. Should this fail to draw the enemy out, it was intended to use the 25th of July as a day of rest, and force an action on the 26th; but on the 25th word came that a portion of the enemy's force had crossed the Niagara, and Scott was sent forward to attack the remainder thus weakened. His force consisted of four small battalions of infantry, Towson's battery, and a detachment of cavalry, one thousand three hundred men in all. About two miles from camp he came upon the enemy drawn up in line of battle on Lundy's Lane. No British troops had crossed the Niagara, and Scott was now in front of the same army he had beaten on the 5th, swelled with a heavy reinforcement which had come up unknown to him only the night before. Retreat must have a bad effect on the force behind him: to stand fast was impossible, as he was already under fire; he therefore advanced, determined to hold the enemy in check, if possible, till the whole American army should come up. The battle began a little before sunset, and continued into the night. Major-General Brown arrived upon the field, and assumed command at nine P. M. Then the enemy's right, in an attempted flank movement, had been driven back with heavy loss; his left was cut off and many prisoners taken: his centre alone remained firm, covered by a battery on a hill, which was finally carried by the bayonet.

Scott received a severe wound in the side early in the night, and at eleven o'clock was disabled by a musket-ball in the left shoulder, and borne from the field.

For his gallant conduct in these two battles, Scott was breveted major-general, received a gold medal from Congress, and was tendered a position in the cabinet as secretary of war, which he declined in favor of his senior. While yet feeble from his wounds, he went to Europe by order of the government, for the restoration of his health and for professional improvement. He returned home in 1816, and in March of the following year was married to Miss Maria Mayo, daughter of John Mayo, Esq., of Richmond, Virginia.

Ordered to the command of the forces intended to act against the savages in the Black Hawk war, in May, 1832, General Scott reached Prairie du Chien the day after the battle of Bad Axe, which ended the war, and in time only to assist in the preparation of the treaties thereupon made with the various tribes. From the western frontier, he arrived in New York in October, 1832, and was at once ordered to Charleston, S. C. Nullification had there agitated the community since the passage of the revenue act of 1828, and in 1832 a state convention provided for resistance to the objectionable law. President Jackson pronounced the resistance thus proposed incompatible with the existence of the Union; and the governor of the state called out twelve thousand volunteers. General Scott's duty at Charleston was to examine the forts in the harbor, and strengthen and reinforce them if he deemed it necessary; and he was ordered to act subordinately to the United States civil authorities in all that he did, but to prepare for any danger. Every part of this duty was discharged with an admirable forbearance and delicacy, which tended greatly to soothe, and did much to allay the angry excitement; and South Carolina, thus firmly met, rescinded her nullification ordinance.

In January, 1836, Scott was ordered to Florida, and opened a campaign against the Indians there, which, from the nature of the country, the climate, inadequate stores, and the insufficiency of his force, proved entirely fruitless. Greater success crowned his efforts against the Creek Indians in the same year, and all went on well until, in July, he was recalled, that inquiry might be made into his first failure. Upon full deliberation, the court of inquiry pronounced his Seminole campaign "well devised, and prosecuted with energy, steadiness, and ability." Yet he took no further part in the Florida war, though it employed the government for six years longer.

Canada became, in 1837, the scene of great political excitement, and all along the northern frontier the American people sympathized with the patriot party over the line, and their sympathy became active. Navy Island, in the Niagara River and within the British line, was occupied by some hundreds of Americans, who kept up communication with the American side by the small steamer Caroline; and this steamer, while at the wharf on the American side, was cut loose at night by a British force, fired, and sent over the Falls. Great excitement spread through the whole country with the news. General Scott was ordered to the point January 4th, 1838. Through the remainder of the winter he was occupied in the organization of a regular and volunteer force; but at the same time he exercised everywhere a great influence for peace, and mainly through his noble exertions in this direction the war-cloud passed by.

Again he was ordered to the Canada line in the next year. Hostile movements were then on foot in the Maine boundary dispute. Congress had appropriated ten millions of dollars, and authorized the president to call and accept volunteers. British troops were in motion toward the disputed territory; the Maine militia was ready to move, and correspondence between the two governments had come to an end. Yet Scott, from his first appearance, became a mediator. He was met in a similar spirit on the other side by Sir John Harvey, of the British army, with whom he had had not dissimilar relations in the campaign of 1814; and the correspondence begun between the two veterans brought about a peaceful solution of the whole difficulty.

In June, 1841, upon the death of Major-General Macomb, General Scott became commander-in-chief of the entire army of the United States.

War with Mexico having resulted upon the annexation of Texas, General Scott was ordered to that country in November, 1846, and reached the Rio Grande in January, 1847. The battles of Palo Alto and Resaca de la Palma, had then been fought, and the town of Monterey taken.

General Santa Anna was at San Luis Potosi, with twenty thousand men. Taylor was at Monterey with eighteen thousand, and Scott had with him only a small portion of the force with which it had been arranged that he should act against Vera Cruz. Government, busied only with the attempt to supersede him by the appointment of a civilian to the post of lieutenant-general, virtually abandoned Scott to his fate. Santa Anna knew that Vera Cruz was to be attempted, and how he would act was doubtful. Scott, in this juncture, drew from Taylor's force enough regular infantry to swell his own force to twelve thousand. With this number he moved forward and invested Vera Cruz March 12th; on the 22d the bombardment was begun. Arrangements were made to carry the city by storm on the 26th, but on that day overtures of surrender were made by the governor, and were completed on the 27th. Ten days later the army, eight thousand strong, took the road to the city of Mexico, defeated the Mexican army, fifteen thousand strong, under General Santa Anna, at Cerro Gordo, April 18th, entered Jalapa the day after, occupied the strong castle and town of La Perote, April 22d, and the city of Puebla May 15th. Only thirty-four days had elapsed from the investment of Vera Cruz, and there were already taken ten thousand prisoners of war, ten thousand stand of of arms, seven hundred cannon, and thirty thousand shells and shot.

When he reached Puebla, Scott had left capable of the march on the city of Mexico but four thousand five hundred men; but at Puebla he was detained by negotiations for peace, which proved futile. Meantime reinforcements arrived, and the army, increased by these to the number of ten thousand, again moved forward August 7th.

Every practicable road to the city of Mexico, within the valley in which that city lay, was now held by parts of the Mexican army, and fortified with great skill. Contreras, San Antonio, and Churubusco, with ten batteries in all, must of necessity be carried, as they could not be turned, nor with safety left behind. General Valencia held Contreras with seven thousand troops, and twenty-two pieces of artillery, and Santa Anna had twelve thousand men in the woods behind it. After an indecisive action of three hours, August 19th, the United States troops stood to their arms all night in roads flooded by heavy rain that fell incessantly, and at daylight on the 20th carried the place by storm. So rapidly was the latter attack made, that the division ordered to mask it by a diversion had not time to arrive; and the actual fight lasted only seventeen minutes.

By the capture of Contreras, Churubusco was taken in flank, and San Antonio in the rear. The troops were immediately moved forward to attack the latter place, when the enemy evacuated it. Churubusco only remained; its defences were a tête-de-pont on the main causeway, and a convent strongly fortified. After a fierce struggle, both these defences were taken, the tête-de-pont at the point of the bayonet. Upon this day the Mexican loss alone exceeded, by three thousand, the whole American army.

To the military possession of the city of Mexico, it was yet necessary that the castle of Chapultepec should fall. Molino del Rey and Casa de Mata, dependencies of Chapultepec, were carried by assault September 8th; heavy siege-guns were placed in battery September 12th, and by the 13th had made a practicable breach in the walls of the military college, which was stormed the same day. From Chapultepec, Mexico city is within range, yet it still resisted, and two divisions of the army skirmished all day at the city gates; but the same night Santa Anna marched out with the small remnant of his army, and the city of Mexico lay at the mercy of Major-General Winfield Scott.

About daylight of the 14th, the city council waited upon the General to demand terms of capitulation for the church, the citizens, and the municipal authorities; to this the general replied, that the city was already in his possession, and that the army should be subject to no terms not self-imposed, or such as were not demanded by its own honor, and the dignity of the United States.

Winfield Scott, with his small and heroic army, had accomplished the object of the war; peace was concluded February 2d, 1848, and very shortly after he received from Washington the order, dated previously to the conclusion of peace, by which he was suspended from command, and a court of inquiry was ordered upon charges preferred against him by brevet Major-General Worth. This court consisted of brevet Brigadier-General N. Towson, paymaster-general, Brigadier-General

Caleb Cushing, and Colonel E. G. W. Butler; thus a paymaster-general, a brigadier of volunteers, and a colonel of dragoons, were ordered to examine the conduct of the veteran commander upon the charge of a subordinate.

General Worth's charges were, that Scott "had refused to say whether he was the person referred to in a certain army order, and refused to forward charges against him to the war department." Secretary Marcy virtually admitted that the conduct of the government needed defence in this matter, by making an argument in its support. But the whole country was astonished, and the people did not sympathize with the cold indifference of formality. Scott relinquished the command, and appeared before the court, which sat, first in Mexico, and subsequently in Washington; but meantime the war terminated, the transactions of the court were allowed to fall out of view, no decision was ever given, and General Winfield Scott resumed his position at Washington as commander-in-chief of the army.

In June, 1852, Winfield Scott was nominated a candidate for the office of president of the United States, by the Whig National Convention, at Baltimore. By a great portion of the people, this nomination was received with sincere joy, but it was reserved for the hero to receive his first great defeat at the hands of his countrymen.

Government, in 1859, with the desire to confer some additional mark of honor, bestowed upon the gallant veteran the brevet rank of lieutenant-general; and to make it the more clearly a personal distinction, and not a mere addition to army grades, the brevet was purposely so framed that it should not survive him.

When the Southern rebellion began in 1860, General Scott adhered earnestly and uncompromisingly to the constitution and government of the United States, with whose history his life was identified, and for whose honor he had ever so consistently labored. With what pain he saw those dear to him for many years fall away from their allegiance, may be conceived; but he, a son too of that Virginia that has given so many soldiers to the country, felt that he was not so much a southerner as a citizen of the United States. From the commencement he saw that the true course was to meet the trouble firmly, and his suggestions, made while James Buchanan was still president, were such as, if followed, would have crushed rebellion in its very birth. But they were all unheeded. Twenty-eight years before, and in the same city of Charleston, Winfield Scott had been present at the rehearsal of this drama of secession—yet all the experience then gained, was not only not permitted to be of service to the country, but the old soldier was even compelled to abandon to its fate, a brave garrison in an insufficiently provided fort. Despite, however, the inactivity forced upon him by weakness, or crime, General Scott secured to the government the possession of Washington city, which it was openly asserted could not be saved, and also secured the safe inauguration of President Lincoln.

General Scott's experience, and great knowledge of the American people, were of infinite value in the organization of the army destined to act against the rebels. To an early movement of that army he gave a reluctant consent, and disaster followed the departure from his advice. Many differed with him, honestly no doubt, as to the method most likely to crush rebellion; yet every American must bitterly regret that neither his honorable and great services, nor his age, could, upon that point, preserve the veteran from the gross vituperation of an intemperate and ribald press.

Finally, feeling himself no longer equal to the proper discharge of the important duties of his position; and that the best service he could render his country would be to make room for a younger man, Lieutenant-General Scott retired from the army, November 1st, 1861. No act of history is marked by more of simple dignity and truth, than this withdrawal of the man who felt that in the decay of age his faculties were no longer equal to the requirements of his country. Upon his conclusion to retire, General Scott wrote thus to the secretary of war:

"HEADQUARTERS OF THE ARMY,
WASHINGTON, *October 31st*, 1861.

"TO THE HON. SIMON CAMERON, Sec. of War:

"SIR:—For more than three years I have been unable from a hurt to mount a horse, or to walk more than a few paces at a time, and that with much pain. Other and new infirmities, dropsy and vertigo, admonish me that repose of mind and body, with the appliances of surgery and medicine, are necessary to add a little more to a life already protracted much beyond the usual span of man. It is under such circumstances, made doubly painful by the unnatural and unjust rebellion now raging in the southern states, of our so lately prosperous and happy Union, that I am compelled to request that my name shall be placed on the list of army officers retired from active service. As this request is founded on an absolute right, granted by a recent act of Congress, I am entirely at liberty to say it is with deep regret that I withdraw myself in these momentous times, from the orders of a president who has treated me with much distinguished kindness and courtesy, whom I know, upon much personal intercourse, to be patriotic without sectional partialities or prejudices; to be highly conscientious in the performance of every duty, and of unrivalled activity and perseverance; and to you, Mr. Secretary, whom I now officially address for the last time, I beg to acknowledge my many obligations for the uniform high consideration I have received at your hands, and have the honor to remain, sir, with high respect,

"Your obedient servant,
"WINFIELD SCOTT."

In response the Secretary of War wrote as follows:

"War Department,
Washington, *November* 1*st*.

"General :—It was my duty to lay before the President your letter of yester-day, asking to be relieved, under the recent act of Congress. In separating from you, I cannot refrain from expressing my deep regret that your health, shattered by long service and repeated wounds, received in your country's defence, should render it necessary for you to retire from your high position at this momentous period of our history. Although you are not to remain in active service, I yet hope that while I continue in charge of the department over which I now preside, I shall at times be permitted to avail myself of the benefits of your wise counsels and sage experience. It has been my good fortune to enjoy a personal acquaintance with you for over thirty years, and the pleasant relations of that long time have been greatly strengthened by your cordial and entire co-operation in all the great questions which have occupied the department and convulsed the country for the last six months. In parting from you, I can only express the hope that a merciful Providence, that has protected you amidst so many trials, will improve your health, and continue your life long after the people of the country shall have been restored to their former happiness and prosperity.

"I am, general, very sincerely, your friend and servant,

"Simon Cameron, Secretary of War.

"Lt.-Gen. Winfield Scott, Present."

General Scott's request, it was decided in a special cabinet council, held November 1st, could not be declined in view of his age and infirmities ; and in the afternoon of the same day, the President, attended by all the members of the cabinet, waited upon General Scott at his residence, and there read to him the following order :

"On the first day of November, A. D. 1861, upon his own application to the President of the United States, brevet Lieutenant-General Winfield Scott, is ordered to be placed, and hereby is placed upon the list of retired officers of the army of the United States, without reduction in his current pay, subsistence or allowance.

"The American people will bear with sadness and deep emotion that General Scott has withdrawn from the active control of the army ; while the President and unanimous cabinet express their own and the nation's sympathy in his personal afflic-tion, and their profound sense of important public services rendered by him to his country during his long and brilliant career, among which will be gratefully distin-guished, his faithful devotion to the constitution, the Union, and the flag, when as-sailed by parricidal rebellion.

"Abraham Lincoln."

General Scott, thereupon rose, and thus addressed the President and cabinet, who had also risen:

"President, this honor overwhelms me. It overpays all services I have attempted to render to my country. If I had any claims before, they are all obliterated by the expression of approval by the President, with the remaining support of his cabinet. I know the President and this cabinet well. I know that the country has placed its interests in this trying crisis in safe keeping. Their counsels are wise, their labors are as untiring as they are loyal, and their course is the right one.

"President, you must excuse me. I am not able to stand longer to give utterance to the feelings of gratitude which oppress me. In my retirement I shall offer up my prayers to God for this administration and for my country. I shall pray for it with confidence in its success over all enemies, and that speedily."

The President and the members of the cabinet then severally took leave of the general.

Upon the same day Major-General George B. McClellan was appointed General Scott's successor in command of the army, and issued the following general order:

"HEADQUARTERS OF THE ARMY.

WASHINGTON, *November 1st*, 1861.

[GENERAL ORDERS No. 19.]

"In accordance with general order No. 94, from the war department, I hereby assume command of the armies of the United States.

"In the midst of the difficulties which encompass and divide the nation, hesitation and self-distrust may well accompany the assumption of so vast a responsibility, but, confiding as I do in the loyalty, discipline, and courage of our troops, and believing as I do that Providence will favor ours as the just cause, I cannot doubt that success will crown our efforts and sacrifices. The army will unite with me in the feeling of regret that the weight of many years and the effect of increasing infirmities, contracted and intensified in his country's service, should just now remove from our head the great soldier of our nation, the hero, who in his youth raised high the reputation of his country in the fields of Canada, which he sanctified with his blood; who, in more mature years, proved to the world that American skill and valor could repeat, if not eclipse, the exploits of Cortez in the land of the Montezumas; whose whole life has been devoted to the service of his country, whose whole efforts have been directed to uphold our honor at the smallest sacrifice of life; a warrior who scorned the selfish glories of the battle-field when his great qualities as a statesman could be employed more profitably for his country; a citizen who in his declining years has given to the world the most shining instance of loyalty in disregarding all ties of birth, and clinging still to the cause of truth and honor. Such has been the career and character of Winfield Scott, whom it has long been the delight of the nation to honor, both as a man and as a soldier. While we regret his loss, there is one thing we cannot regret—the bright example he has left for our emulation. Let us all hope and pray that his declining years may be passed in peace and happiness, and that they may be cheered by the success of the country and the cause he has fought for and loved so well. Beyond all that, let us do nothing that can cause him to blush for us. Let no defeat of the army he has so long commanded embitter his last years; but let our victories illuminate the close of a life so grand. "GEORGE B. McCLELLAN,

"Major-General Commanding U. S. A."

Eight days later General Scott sailed from New York for Europe, there to join his family and seek repose from the labor and excitement that, added to his years, had so nearly borne him down.

President Lincoln in his message of December 3d, 1861, to Congress, thus refers to the retirement of General Scott:

"Since your last adjournment, Lieutenant-General Scott has retired from the head of the army. During his long life the nation has not been unmindful of his merit. Yet, on calling to mind how faithfully, ably, and brilliantly, he has served the country from a time far back in our history, when few of the now living had been born, and thenceforward continually, I cannot but think that we are still his debtor.

"I submit, therefore, for your consideration what further mark of recognition is due to him and ourselves as a grateful people."

These words, a noble tribute in themselves, have hitherto called out no response from Congress; and it remains to be seen what action will be taken to express the full sense of the nation's gratitude toward the great man who has for so long a period so faithfully and faultlessly served it.

JOHN ELLIS WOOL.

JOHN ELLIS WOOL was born at Newburg, in the state of New York, in the year 1789. He received, in early life, only a rudimentary education, and for the greater part of his youth was employed as clerk in a store in the city of Troy. Dissatisfied with this condition in life, he began the study of law, continued it for one year and then gave it up. This relinquishment of his first ambition fell just in that period when the country began to prepare for the war that soon ensued with Great Britain, and when Congress stormily debated the increase of the military force. Fired with a patriotic spirit, and an earnest desire to serve his country, Wool's ambition at once sought a more extensive sphere, and upon the enlargement of the army he obtained, April 14th, 1812, a captain's commission in the Thirteenth Regiment of Infantry. He soon after joined the army under General Van Rensselaer, on the Niagara frontier, and there passed the summer of 1812 in the drill and discipline of his men, and other technical duties of his rank.

Captain Wool's command was part of the force in the expedition against Queenstown, and in the brilliant struggle at Queenstown Heights, the young officer won his first distinction. After Colonel Van Rensselaer was carried from the field, and previous to the arrival of General Van Rensselaer, the command, for a time, rested with, and was held conjointly by, Captains Wool and Ogilvie. Wool received a severe wound in this fight, and by the eventual surrender, became a prisoner of war; but his gallantry was recognized, and he was promoted to be a Major, and upon his exchange assigned to the Twenty-ninth Regiment of Infantry, April 13th, 1813. Stationed at Plattsburg, he participated in the successful resistance offered at that point to the British army under Prevost, and again became conspicuous for his gallantry. He was especially efficient in harassing the march of the British army, and in the various minor struggles that for five days preceded the principal battle on the Saranac. For his gallant conduct in the battle of the 11th September he was breveted Lieutenant-Colonel.

In September, 1816, he was appointed Inspector-General of the army, with the rank of Colonel; in February, 1818, Lieutenant-Colonel of infantry; and for "ten years of faithful service," he was breveted Brigadier-General, April 29th, 1826.

In 1832 General Wool was sent to Europe in government commission to obtain information on military matters, and in the discharge of that duty, travelled through

all of France and Belgium, and was present at the siege and bombardment of
Antwerp by the French. In 1836 he assisted in the removal of the Indians from
the Cherokee country to Arkansas, and in two years after was placed in command of the troops posted on the Maine frontier. He was appointed a Brigadier-
General, June 25th, 1841.

Brigadier-General Wool, in the war with Mexico, commanded the "centre division" of the United States army, organized to act against Chihuahua, in pursuance of the primary plan of the United States government to cut off from Mexico its
more northerly provinces. Though thus in command of a separate division, General
Wool was subject to the orders of General Taylor. Taylor, however, only named the
point of destination, and left all beside to the discretion of Wool. His command
assembled at San Antonio de Bexar, in Texas, and comprised three thousand men.
Washington's battery of light artillery formed part of it. General Wool began his
march September 26th, 1846, and in eleven days reached the Rio Grande, near to
San Juan Bautista, better known as Presidio. At that point the river is two hundred
and seventy yards wide, and has an exceedingly rapid current; but a flying bridge,
brought with the army, was thrown across, and the whole command and an immense
train of stores were safely landed on the opposite shore by the night of October
11th. Thus within the Mexican territory, General Wool published an order in
which he stated that the army of the United States would act only against the
Mexican government; that all who did not take up arms, but remained peaceably
in their homes, would not be molested either in their persons or property; and that
all who furnished supplies' would be treated kindly, and paid for whatever was
taken. From Presidio the division marched by San Juan de Nava, San Fernando
de Rosas, and Santa Rosa to Monclova. The authorities of the latter place protested
against General Wool's advance upon it, and on November 3d he entered with the
army, and took formal possession of the town. Orders were here received from
General Taylor for the "centre division" to remain at Monclova until the end of the
armistice, and it consequently rested twenty-seven days. Meantime the troops were
incessantly drilled, and stores were collected for the establishment of a depot. Two
hundred and fifty men were detached to guard the depot, and on the 24th November
the division took up the line of march for Parras, one hundred and eighty miles distant.
At Parras it was intended to take the great road from Saltillo to Chihuahua, but
upon its arrival there the division was held to co-operate, if necessary, with General
Taylor then threatened by Santa Anna, and weakened by the withdrawal of troops
for Scott's line of operations. While the "centre division" still remained at Parras,
General Taylor learned of an intention upon the part of the Mexicans to surprise
Saltillo, and massacre the small body of American troops stationed there, and im-
mediately sent word with marching orders to General Wool, and also to General
Butler at Monterey. "Wool, who had been marching from Port Lavoca to Parras

in search of a battle," says Ripley in his History of the War, "and who, in his desire of adventure and fame, had only wished to abandon the Chihuahua expedition
in order to penetrate, with his single corps, still further south in the direction of Du-
rango and Zacatecas, hailed the news as the harbinger of glory to be acquired. He
at once broke up his camp at Parras, and marched with the greatest celerity toward Saltillo, pushing his artillery and cavalry at the rate of forty miles a day."
General Butler also hurried forward; and General Taylor marched upon Saltillo
with Twiggs's division; and the Mexicans consequently made no attack. From this
time, however, the "centre division" was merged into the "army of occupation,"
and joined General Taylor's command at Agua Nueva, December 21st; and from that
time until the battle of Buena Vista was fought, the whole American camp, and
the instruction and discipline of the soldiers, were placed under General Wool's
command and direction.

Upon the second day after Wool's arrival at Agua Nueva, an incident occurred
to which the subsequent battle gave importance. Accompanied by several gentlemen of his command, and his aide-de-camp, Lieutenant Irwin McDowell, he rode
from his camp at Agua Nueva, December 22d, to visit Generals Butler and Worth
at Saltillo, and upon his return next day, and while in the pass or narrows near
the Hacienda of Buena Vista, he said, "This is the very spot of all others I have
yet seen in Mexico, which I should select for battle, were I obliged with a small
army to fight a large one." He then described the various advantages of the position, and rode on. General Taylor at this time intended, if attacked, to fight at
Agua Nueva, and General Butler opposed the wish of General Wool to form his
encampment near to Buena Vista, and even compelled the removal of the camp
after it was formed there. General Taylor, however, upon examination, agreed
with General Wool as to the advantages of the position at Buena Vista, and
when it became certain that Santa Anna would attack with a large army, determined
to meet him there. General Wool has thus the honor to have chosen the field
upon which the American army was enabled to struggle so gloriously and victo-
riously.

General Taylor was at Saltillo on the morning of the 22d, and the command
of the army fell upon General Wool, as next in rank. He accordingly ordered
the advance from camp to the field, and disposed the army in its first order of
battle. Previous to the commencement of the fight, however, General Taylor arrived, and General Wool again took the command of his own division. But on
the night of the 22d, by Taylor's return to Saltillo, General Wool was again left
in command of the army, and retained the command for a part of the next day,
when the battle was fought. Of the small army in the field on the 22d, General
Taylor took with him to Saltillo, a squadron of dragoons, and Colonel Davis's regiment of Mississippi riflemen. General Wool was thus left with four thousand two

2

hundred men; and with this small force he held Santa Anna's army of twenty thousand in check until General Taylor came up and assumed the command. For "gallant and meritorious conduct" in this battle, General Wool received the brevet of Major-General in May, 1848.

Upon the close of the Mexican war, General Wool was assigned to the command in the Eastern Military Department of the United States, and this position he held until some time after the present war broke out. Previous to the recent creation of several new departments, his command embraced the states of South Carolina, Georgia, Florida, Alabama, and Mississippi.

When the treasonable agitation began in South Carolina, General Wool urged strongly the support of Major Anderson in Fort Sumter, and as early as December, 1860, declared that the surrender of that post would put two hundred thousand men in arms in defence of the Union. During the same month he wrote: "Before South Carolina can get out of the jurisdiction or control of the United States, a reconstruction of the constitution must be had, or civil war ensue." * * * He also declared himself as, "now and forever in favor of the Union, its preservation, and the rigid maintenance of the rights and interests of the states, individually as well as collectively," and in a letter to General Cass he expressed the desire that "the President would command his services" if he could be of any aid.

Immediately after the surrender of Fort Sumter, one of those great Union demonstrations that were made all over the country was made at Troy, N. Y., and a great concourse of citizens adjourned from their place of meeting to the house of General Wool, who there addressed them, and in the course of his remarks used these words: "I have fought under the stars and stripes that were carried in triumph by Washington, and under which Jackson closed the second war for independence at New Orleans in a halo of glory. Will you permit that flag to be desecrated, and trampled in the dust by traitors now? Will you permit our noble government to be destroyed by rebels, in order that they may advance their schemes of political ambition, and extend the area of slavery? No indeed, it cannot be done. The spirit of the age forbids it. Humanity and manhood, and the sentiments of the civilized world forbid it. My friends, that flag must be lifted up from the dust into which it has been trampled, placed in its proper position, and again set floating in triumph to the breeze. I pledge you my heart my hand, all my energies, to the cause."

Yet despite this known devotion to the cause, and the general's great experience and capacity as an officer, he was, at a time when the country's greatest need was experienced and able officers, kept for several months, through some unaccountable cause at the war department, in virtual retirement at Troy; and assured that it was done "for the benefit of his health," though he publicly declared that his health had never been better.

Great dissatisfaction with the course of the government in this matter was publicly expressed through the newspapers and otherwise, and at length, August 12th, 1861, the veteran received from the war department the order to proceed to Fortress Monroe, and take command of the forces there. On his way thither he arrived in New York, August 15th, and that night was serenaded at his hotel. In response to the calls of the assembled multitude, he appeared upon the balcony and spoke as follows:

"Fellow-citizens: I thank you for this unexpected honor. Nothing is more gratifying to a soldier's feelings than the good opinion of his fellow-citizens. I do not, however, regard it merely as a compliment personal to myself, but on behalf of my country, my bleeding country, which is now contending for the most precious of rights. But yesterday we were a great people, commanding the admiration of the world, with an empire extending from the frozen regions of the north to the tropical regions of the south, and with a population of more than thirty-one millions, enjoying a prosperity unparalleled in the history of nations. Every city and hamlet was growing rich, and none so much so as those at the South. But this is not so to-day. And for what reason? For nothing under God's heavens but because the South wants to extend the area of slavery. Nothing else but that. The only question with you is, whether you will support free speech, free government, free suffrage, or extend the area of slavery. This was the happiest country on the face of the globe a few months since, with a government more kind than any other in existence, where man could walk abroad in his own majesty, and none to make him afraid. Never sacrifice that government, but maintain it to the last. I thank you, gentlemen, for the honor you have done me."

After several patriotic airs were given, another pause was made in the music, cries were renewed for the appearance of General Wool, and he came forward and said :—

"Gentlemen, a few words more: though I am too hoarse to speak, I have only to say to you, let us have liberty and union, the whole Union, and nothing but the Union now and forever. Good night."

General Wool reached Fortress Monroe two days later, and assumed command of the army assembled there. The force was mostly made up of volunteers, and had since the war began been under the command of Major-General Butler. General Wool immediately began the institution of a more perfect and thorough discipline, and, by holding every colonel and line officer responsible not only for the good conduct but for the efficiency of their respective commands; by exacting specific reports from them of every thing; by insisting upon their being personally acquainted with the facts they state; and by the infusion of good activity into every branch of the service, he is rapidly fitting the men of his command for any emergency.

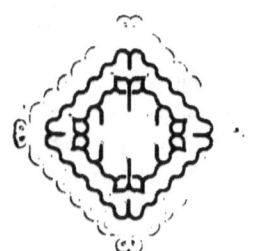

WM. H. SEWARD

WILLIAM HENRY SEWARD.

WILLIAM HENRY SEWARD was born in the town of Florida, Orange county, New York, May 16th, 1801. He was the son of Dr. Samuel S. Seward of that place; a gentleman who held the office of county judge in Orange for seventeen years, and who was distinguished for more than ordinary business ability, and for practical philanthropy. From childhood the son exhibited a love of knowledge, and an earnest inclination and taste for study. Books were his favorite companions, and he ran away—*to school*. When nine years of age, he was sent to Farmers' Hall Academy, at Goshen, in Orange county. There, and at an academy subsequently established in his native town, he pursued his studies until his fifteenth year, when he entered Union College, at Schenectady. "Thin, pale, sandy-visaged," as he is said to have been, there was perhaps no great promise in his appearance, for he was persuaded to enter the sophomore class, though upon the examination he was found qualified for the junior. His favorite studies in college were rhetoric, moral philosophy, and the ancient classics. In the year 1819, when eighteen years of age, and while in the senior class, he withdrew from college for about a year, six months of which were passed as a teacher at the South. Slavery was not altogether strange to him, for he had seen some remnant of it in his native state, and even his own nurse had been a negro slave; yet his experience of life at the South tended to confirm and deepen a natural hostility to that form of oppression. Seward returned to his college, and graduated with high honors. He was one of three commencement orators chosen by the college society to which he belonged, and the subject of his oration was, "The Integrity of the American Union." Thus, before he had attained the age of manhood, he felt his way instinctively to that cause which was to employ the ripened abilities of his later life.

Soon after his graduation, Mr. Seward entered the office of John Anthon, in New York city, as a law student; completed his preparation with John Duer and Ogden Hoffman, in Goshen, New York, became associated in practice with the latter, and was admitted to the bar of the Supreme Court in 1822. In January of the next year, he took up his residence in Auburn, where he formed a business connection with the Hon. Elijah Miller, whose youngest daughter he married in 1824. By severe industry he soon became possessed of an extensive and successful practice. He gave also considerable attention to politics, and as his father had been an ardent Jeffersonian Democrat, his first prepossessions were in favor of that party; but during the struggle incident to the admission of Missouri into the Union, he saw that subserviency to Southern influence ruled in the Democratic party, and he left it. At the same time he first expressed his convictions in opposition to the extension of slavery. In October, 1824, he drew up the "Address of the Republican Convention of Cayuga County to the People," which was an exposure of the origin and designs of the Albany Regency. General Jackson's election to the presidency in 1828, dissolved the national Republican party of Western New York, and thus the only opposition left to the Regency was the anti-Masonic organization, and from that party Mr. Seward received the nomination to represent the seventh district in the State Senate. He was elected by a majority of two thousand votes, and took his seat in January, 1831, probably the youngest member that ever entered the New York Senate. Against the formidable power of the Jackson party and the Albany Regency, the opposition was necessarily feeble; but young Seward fearlessly entered it, and became its acknowledged leader. He took part in all the debates; supported the common-school system, the abolition of imprisonment for debt, and the melioration of prison discipline. He was one of the earliest friends of the Erie Railroad, and supported the Jackson administration in regard to Southern nullification. His first speech was on a militia bill, and he then proposed to substitute for the general performance of military duty, the formation of volunteer uniformed companies—substantially the system now (1862) in use in the State of New York. During the second session of his term, Mr. Seward spoke in favor of a resolution, which declared the necessity of a national bank. His speech was an elaborate criticism of Jackson's objections to the renewal of the Bank Charter. This speech, with others of the same nature, concentrated an opposition in the Senate, and thus gave rise to what subsequently became known as the Whig party. In 1833 Mr. Seward visited Europe in company with his father, and travelled through parts of the United Kingdom, France, Holland, Germany, Switzerland, and Sardinia. From those countries he wrote home the series of letters subsequently published in the Albany Evening Journal.

Mr. Seward was nominated in September, 1834, by the Whig State Convention, as candidate for governor of New York. But the party was immature; it had not yet won popular confidence, and its young candidate was defeated, by the re-election of William L. Marcy. Upon the conclusion of the canvass, Mr. Seward resumed the practice of his profession, and in 1836 settled in Chautauque county, as the agent of the Holland Company. In 1838 he was again nominated for governor by the Whig party, and was elected by ten thousand majority. Governor Seward's administration was one of great mark in the history of the state. The Anti-Rent Rebellion occurred, and was quelled; through the threatened trouble of the McLeod case the state, and with it the country, was safely brought without the loss of honor; the Erie Canal was enlarged; imprisonment for debt was abolished, and every vestige of slavery removed from the statute books; the State Lunatic Asylum was established; important election reforms were effected, and reforms were also made in prison discipline, in bank laws, and in the law courts. Governor Seward took ground also against the rendition of fugitives from justice in connection with slavery, and maintained his position in a correspondence with the Governor of Virginia, in what has since been known as the "Virginia Case." He declined a renomination, and upon the expiration of his term resumed the practice of his profession. For six years he devoted himself with great assiduity to business, and obtained, in addition to an extensive practice in the state courts, also a large and lucrative one in patent cases in the national courts, and was thus brought into association with the most distinguished jurists in the United States. During this period, he appeared in many celebrated cases, and very conspicuously in the case of the negro Freeman, indicted for the murder of the Van Nest family. He also pleaded gratuitously the case of John Van Zandt, before the United States Supreme Court, charged with aiding certain fugitives in their attempt to escape from slavery.

In 1848 Mr. Seward earnestly supported the election of General Taylor as President of the United States, and canvassed in his behalf the states of New York, Pennsylvania, Ohio, and Massachusetts. Connected with Taylor's election, a Whig majority was returned to the New York legislature, and thus Mr. Seward's name was brought up for the vacancy soon to occur in the United States Senate. There was no serious opposition; he was elected, and took his seat in the thirty-first Congress.

General Taylor's administration was opposed by the Southern members in the apprehension that he would adopt a decided antislavery policy. Identified to some degree with such a policy, and very decidedly with the support of General Taylor's election, Mr. Seward became recognized as the foremost advocate of government measures; and for a consistent resistance to the ever-hungry encroachments of the slave-power, he was denounced by the makers of public opinion as an agitator and a dangerous man. In the debate on the admission of California, March 11th, 1850, he spoke thus: "It is true indeed that the national domain is ours. It is true it was acquired by the valor, and with the wealth of the whole nation. But we hold, nevertheless, no arbitrary power over it We hold no arbitrary authority over any thing. whether acquired lawfully, or seized by usurpation. The Constitution regulates our stewardship; the Constitution devotes the domain to union, to justice, to defence, to welfare, and to liberty. But there is a Higher Law than the Constitution, which regulates our authority over the domain, and devotes it to the same noble purposes. The territory is a part, no inconsiderable part, of the common heritage of mankind, bestowed upon them by the Creator of the universe." While the law of God is here actually named as in agreement with the "noble purposes" of the Constitution—one phrase has been dragged from this passage, the most material interpretation given to it, and the senator made to appear before the world as if he had urged against the Constitution certain conscientious scruples and ideas of his own. How false this is all can see. Yet Senator Seward has thus been made the author of the phrase, "The Higher Law," which, in the party contests in which it has been employed, has not certainly been without its value. Governor Seward took part in all the more important debates of the Senate, and spoke upon the compromise measures of 1850, on the public domain, on Hungarian affairs, apropos to his own resolution of welcome to Kossuth, on the motion to declare the sympathy of Congress with the exiled Irish patriots O'Brien and Meagher, on the survey of the Arctic and Pacific Oceans, on the fisheries, and various other topics of national interest. Upon the close of his first senatorial term in 1855, Mr. Seward was re-elected, though persistently opposed by the "American" or "Know Nothing" party, to whose doctrines he could in nowise bend; and by the Democratic party, for his desire to restrict slavery. Toward the election of Colonel Fremont to the presidency in 1856, he labored zealously and effectively, as he had also done for the election of General Scott in the previous canvass. In an address to the people of Rochester, New York, made in 1858, Mr. Seward, in reference to the collision between the two systems of labor—free and slave—in the United States, said:—"Shall I tell you what this collision means? They who think that it is accidental, unnecessary, the work of interested or fanatical agitators, and therefore ephemeral, mistake the case altogether. It is an irrepressible conflict between opposing and enduring forces, and it means that the United States must and will, sooner or later, become either entirely a slaveholding nation, or entirely a free-labor nation." For this phrase also, "An irrepressible conflict," Mr. Seward has been not less bitterly reviled and contemned than for that other of the "higher law," though it contained clearly enough a great truth; and by a strange confusion of ideas and things, he who saw and gave expression to this truth, was held responsible for what he had not caused but only pointed out.

In 1859 Mr. Seward made a second visit to the old world. In the presidential canvass of 1860, he supported Abraham Lincoln, and spoke in his behalf in nearly all the Western states. Mr. Seward's second senatorial term expired March 3d, 1861. Only a short time previous to its conclusion, and when the Southern rebellion had become fully manifest, he boldly entered the contest in these words:—"I avow my adherence to the Union—with my friends, with my party, with my state, or without either, as they may determine; in every event of peace or of war, with every consequence of honor, or dishonor, of life or death."

Immediately after President Lincoln was officially informed of his election, he tendered the chief place in his cabinet to Mr. Seward, who accepted it, and entered upon his duties, as Secretary of State, March 4th, 1861· Since that time his course has been marked by the strictest integrity and patriotism, especially prominent in the very able and satisfactory settlement of the international difficulty consequent upon the capture of the rebel commissioners, Mason and Slidell.

NATHANIEL LYON.

NATHANIEL LYON was born at Ashford, Windham county, Connecticut, in the month of June, 1819. He was the son of Amasa Lyon, a farmer. He entered the United States Military Academy at West Point, July 1st, 1837; was graduated in 1841, and appointed a second-lieutenant in the second regiment of infantry. He served in Florida, in the latter part of the Seminole War, was subsequently stationed for several years at different posts on the Western frontier, and was promoted, in February, 1847, to be first-lieutenant. Upon the commencement of the war with Mexico, Lieutenant Lyon was ordered to active service in that country. He joined General Taylor at Monterey, and accompanied his regiment when it was detached from the command of General Taylor to that of General Scott. He served at the bombardment of Vera Cruz, and in the battle of Cerro Gordo. In the battles of Contreras and Churubusco, he commanded his company, and in the report of the officer who led the regiment on that day was recommended to the special notice of the brigade commander. He also participated in the capture of the city of Mexico, and was wounded by a musket-ball in the assault on the Belen gate. For "gallant and meritorious conduct" in the battles of Contreras and Churubusco he received, in August, 1848, the brevet of Captain.

When the war with Mexico was ended, Lyon was ordered to California. He reached that country soon after its acquisition by the United States, and remained there several years, chiefly employed against the Indians. The full rank of Captain was conferred upon him June 11th, 1851. From California, Captain Lyon was again ordered to the Western frontier, and served in Kansas and Nebraska in the height of the political troubles there. While upon this duty he took great interest in the various questions which divided the people, and became strongly opposed to the position of the Democratic party, though previously he had always believed and acted with it. Several articles written by him during the summer and fall of 1860, and published in a Kansas newspaper, express his hope for the country in the election of the Republican candidate for President in the pending canvass. These articles are written with manly vigor, and indicate in every line an earnest patriot and a bold, energetic thinker.

Captain Lyon was the United States officer in command of the arsenal at St.

Louis, Missouri, when, on May 6th, 1861, the police commissioners of that city formally demanded the removal of the United States soldiers from all places occupied by them outside the arsenal grounds. Captain Lyon declined compliance with the demand, and in reply to the charge of the commissioners, that such occupancy was in derogation of the constitution and laws of the United States, required to know what provisions of the constitution and what laws it violated. Thus rebuffed, the commissioners referred the matter to the governor and legislature of the state. Not long before, the governor of Missouri had authorized the formation of camps of instruction in various parts of the state, and on May 4th such a camp had been formed under the supervision of General Frost at Lindell's Grove, near St. Louis. Taken with the action of the commissioners and the general tendency of affairs, Captain Lyon regarded the concentration of this force near him as directly hostile, and on May 10th, suddenly surrounded the camp known as Camp Jackson, with a large force of the state "Home Guards," the then newly organized volunteer regiments under Blair and Siegel, and twenty-three pieces of artillery, planted his guns on the heights around the camp, and sent in to General Frost the following letter :

"HEADQUARTERS U. S. TROOPS,
ST. LOUIS, MO., *May 10th*, 1861.

"GEN. D. M. FROST, commanding Camp Jackson :

"SIR:—Your command is regarded as evidently hostile toward the government of the United States. It is for the most part made up of those secessionists who have openly avowed their hostility to the general government, and have been plotting at the seizure of its property and the overthrow of its authority. You are openly in communication with the so-called Southern Confederacy, which is now at war with the United States, and you are receiving at your camp from the said confederacy and under its flag, large supplies of the material of war, most of which is known to be the property of the United States. These extraordinary preparations plainly indicate none other than the well-known purpose of the governor of this state, under whose orders you are acting, and whose purpose, recently communicated to the legislature, has just been responded to by that body in the most unparalleled legislation, having in direct view hostilities to the general government and co-operation with its enemies.

"In view of these considerations, and of your failure to disperse in obedience to the proclamation of the President, and of the eminent necessities of state policy and welfare, and the obligations imposed upon me by instructions from Washington, it is my duty to demand, and I do hereby demand of you, an immediate surrender of your command, with no other conditions than that all persons surrendering under this demand shall be humanely and kindly treated. Believing myself prepared to enforce this demand, one half-hour's time, before doing so, will be allowed for your compliance therewith.

"Very respectfully your obedient servant,

"N. LYON, Capt. 2d Infantry, commanding troops."

General Frost, upon consultation with his subordinate officers, found his command unable to resist the force of General Lyon, and he accordingly surrendered his whole command prisoners of war. This quick and severe blow at rebellion in Missouri awakened great joy in the hearts of all the Union men in that state, and when, four days later, General Harney arrived at St. Louis and assumed the command there, Captain Lyon was elected to the command of the first brigade of Missouri volunteers. On May 15th, he effected the occupation of Potosi, whence a body of rebels was driven, and also caused in rapid succession several important seizures of war material in various parts of the state. No other United States officer exhibited equal activity in the discharge of his duty.

By agreement with General Price of Missouri, General Harney committed himself to a course of inaction, and was removed, and General Lyon was thus left in command of the department, May 31st. But Harney's agreement with General Price had contemplated the disbandment of the state troops in arms upon the governor's requisition; they refused to disband, and the governor declared that the interests and sympathies of Missouri were identical with those of the slaveholding states, and that they necessarily united her destiny with theirs, and the legislature passed a military bill, which General Lyon pronounced "so offensive to all peaceable inhabitants, and so palpably unconstitutional, that it could be accepted by those only who were to conform to its extraordinary provisions for the purpose of effecting their cherished object—the disruption of the Federal government." Lyon therefore announced to the people, by proclamation, that his duty required him to act against the so-called state forces, and he accordingly moved from St. Louis, June 17th, toward Jefferson City, with a force of the Missouri Home Guard Volunteers, and some United States troops. Governor Jackson, upon Lyon's approach, endeavored to impede his march by the destruction of Moreau bridge, abandoned Jefferson City, burning the bridges behind him, and retreated to Booneville. Lyon pursued in boats up the Missouri river, and on the same day landed four miles below Booneville, found the rebels posted in the road near that place, immediately opened fire upon them, and drove them from their position. They fell back and formed again in the woods, whence they kept up a sharp fire upon the national forces. General Lyon then ordered a feigned retreat, and when the rebels were well drawn from their cover in pursuit, he opened upon them a severe fire of artillery and musketry, and they were dispersed in complete rout. Lyon's force was about two thousand, and his loss was very small. The rebel force was about four thousand, and their loss in killed and wounded was nearly one hundred. A great many of their men were made prisoners. General Lyon then issued a proclamation from Booneville, in which, after a statement of the facts in relation to the battle, he said : " I hereby give notice to the people of this state, that I shall scrupulously avoid all interference with the business, right, and property of every description recognized by the laws of the state, and belonging to law-abiding citizens. But it is equally my duty to maintain the paramount authority of the United States with such force as I have at my command, which will be retained only so long as opposition makes it necessary, and that it is my wish, and shall be my purpose, to visit any unavoidable rigor arising in this issue upon those only who provoke it."

General McCulloch, with a large force, was at this time in the south-western part of the state, and was soon joined by General Price with some portion of the Missouri rebels, and subsequently by Parsons and General Rains. Lyon left Booneville to march against them July 3d. His small force swelled as he advanced, and when he reached Springfield, July 20th, he had under his command ten thousand men ; but this force had again decreased to six thousand by August 1st. On that day at five P. M., General Lyon marched to look for the rebels, who were said to be in motion toward Springfield, and not finding them, bivouacked ten miles south of the town. Early the next day the march was resumed, and about noon, at a place called Dug Spring, the rebels were reported in sight. A halt was ordered, and while a reconnoissance was made, two companies of regular infantry were thrown forward as skirmishers, supported by a company of cavalry. This force encountered a body of about five hundred rebels, and a warm fire was exchanged. The national infantry was hard pressed, when this advanced body of the rebels was entirely scattered by a brilliant charge of the cavalry. The rebels rallied, however, engaged the infantry again, and having received support formed a line to advance, but at this juncture Captain Totten's artillery was brought to bear, and after a few discharges scattered them for the day. Next morning, August 3d, the march was continued six miles further, but the enemy made no stand, and, unable to bring on a general action, and being out of provisions, and with many of his men ill, Lyon marched his force back to Springfield, which he reached August 5th. Generals McCulloch, Price, Rains, and Colonel Parsons, were then known to be in motion toward Springfield with a combined force variously reported at eight, twenty, and twenty-four thousand men, well-armed and effective. They reached Wilson's Creek, ten miles south-west of Springfield, August 6th, and encamped there. General Lyon, thus vastly outnumbered, and left without reinforcements, saw but little hope for success, and a council of his officers advised the abandonment of Springfield and a further retreat: he determined, however, to attack the rebels in their camp, and for that purpose marched from Springfield on the 9th, at sunset, with but little over five thousand men. His force was disposed in two columns. The right or main column comprised four regiments and a battalion of volunteers, five companies of regular infantry, one company of artillery recruits, and two batteries of artillery, and was commanded by General Lyon in person. The left column was commanded by Colonel Siegel, and was made up of two battalions of volunteers and six field-pieces. The rebel camp stretched along Wilson's Creek for three miles, and it was intended that the two columns should attack it at nearly opposite extremities. Lyon's column encountered the rebel pickets near the northern end of their camp at five P. M., and one of his volunteer regiments was soon warmly engaged with the rebel infantry, whom they drove from an eminence, on which the national artillery was immediately posted and opened fire. Repeated attempts of the rebels to carry this position were repulsed, and the battle merged into this endeavor on the part of the rebels, until Siegel made his attack in the rear and fired their baggage train, when they desisted from their attempt against the batteries and the battle was virtually relinquished.

From the first attack General Lyon had actively assisted and encouraged his men where the fight was thickest, and was thrice wounded. Near nine A. M., when the enemy was about to make one of his several attempts against Totten's battery, the first Iowa regiment was brought up to relieve, in its support, the Kansas first and second. This regiment had lost its colonel, and when Lyon ordered it to prepare to repel the enemy with the bayonet, the men called upon him to lead them. He had been standing by his horse, but now mounted to lead the charge, and gave the word. The rebels did not stand, but delivered their fire and broke. General Lyon was struck by a rifle-ball in the breast. He fell into the arms of his body-servant and expired almost immediately. His fall was not generally observed, and the battle continued for several hours after it.

Four months after General Lyon's death, on the 20th December, 1861, the following resolution was introduced into the United States Senate from the House of Representatives, and unanimously concurred in:

"*Resolved, by the Senate and House of Representatives of the United States of America in Congress assembled,* That Congress deems it just and proper to enter upon its records a recognition of the eminent and patriotic services of the late Brigadier-General Nathaniel Lyon. The country to whose service he devoted his life will guard and preserve his fame as a part of its own glory. *Second,* That the thanks of Congress are hereby given to the brave officers and soldiers who, under the command of the late General Lyon, sustained the honor of the flag, and achieved victory against overwhelming numbers at the battle of Springfield, in Missouri; and that, in order to commemorate an event so honorable to the country and to themselves, it is ordered that each regiment engaged shall be authorized to bear upon its colors the word 'Springfield,' embroidered in letters of gold. And the President of the United States is hereby requested to cause these resolutions to be read at the head of every regiment in the army of the United States."

Previous to its adoption, however, Senator Pomeroy, of Kansas, delivered an eloquent tribute to the general's memory as follows:

"Mr. President: The resolutions which have just been read to the Senate were introduced to the House of Representatives by the distinguished member from St. Louis, and passed the House very unanimously. I trust they will in like manner pass the Senate. But to me there is one reason why they should receive at least a passing notice. The state of Kansas was largely interested in that battle at Wilson's Creek, near Springfield, and the country and mankind have a large interest in the fame of the immortal Lyon, who fell in that battle. Such a man and such a general is not often found, and very rarely combined in one person. Perhaps I may be pardoned here for saying that I had the pleasure of a personal acquaintance with General Lyon for years; and it was an acquaintance formed and matured under the most impressive circumstances. The early struggles for the freedom of our own state were not unlike in their nature the present struggles of the nation. The same questions, to a great extent, entered into the one that now convulse the other. The same interests, passions, and barbarity, so disgraceful to our age and humanity, entered as largely into that struggle as in the present.

"General Lyon, whose deeds and fame now belong to the whole country, was then Captain Lyon, of the regular army, stationed at Fort Riley, in Kansas. He had for ten years served the country in that capacity, and without promotion. He was as true a soldier as ever stood in the line of battle; a sagacious officer, strict in habit and discipline, and an honest man.

"His attention to me, on an occasion of great personal fatigue and exposure— taking me to his quarters, welcoming me to all his comforts, and then loaning me his own horse, fresh and strong, and taking in charge mine exhausted and worn, were acts of generosity and kindness that I shall never forget. The elements of a friendship cemented by unity of sentiment and principle, in an hour of great extremity, are the most enduring attachments of this life.

"As Captain Lyon, he sympathized with the free state men of Kansas, espoused their cause, and vindicated their rights in the presence of superior army officers and government appointees, who were, even there, as false to their country, to freedom, and to God, as secession itself. He was then, as always, an earnest man, true among the false, faithful among the faithless, devotedly attached to the Union that he loved, the constitution that he vindicated, and the flag of his country for which he died.

"Comparisons are odious, and I hesitate to draw them. Still, amidst the general inactivity so prevalent on the Potomac, and so discouraging to live men, it is refreshing to notice that when the order was for Captain Lyon to take and capture General Frost's command at Camp Jackson, the ink was scarcely dry on the order before that work was accomplished.

"The 10th day of May will be forever memorable in St. Louis as a day when one decisive blow, struck by one decided officer, forever freed that city from subjection to the rebellion. And there she remains to-day a proud monument, her edifices standing in towering magnificence, vindicating that policy, and safe amidst surrounding desolation.

"One Friday morning in June last, Claib. Jackson, the so-called governor of Missouri, issued his proclamation, declaring war against the United States forces in Missouri. That very afternoon, before the sun went down, General Lyon commenced moving his little army of two thousand seven hundred men upon steamboats, at St. Louis, and was soon under way for Jefferson City, the capital. On the following Sabbath evening, he took possession quietly of that capital. The rebels, governor, and officers, and soldiers, had fled, burning bridges, and spreading destruction in their train. Before Monday morning, he commenced moving a portion of that little invincible army to Booneville, fifty miles further up, where he engaged the enemy and dispersed them, taking the city. Thus, I say, it is refreshing to see that there was one general who could move his army three hundred miles in three successive days, and have a battle and a victory! General Lyon moved south from Booneville toward Springfield, in the wake of the fleeing rebels, who were retreating into Arkansas. After several successful skirmishes about Springfield, restoring order and quiet, he halted there for reinforcements. On his way there, he was joined by one regiment from Iowa and two from Kansas.

"And now may I be allowed to pause in my argument a moment to say that these two regiments were only the first generous offerings of our young state to the cause of the country? But the flower and pride of our young state were in them. These were of the kind of men who spring spontaneously to their arms in an hour of danger. They mustered in as infantry in the month of June, and were ordered immediately into Missouri. Thank God there were no wretched traitors in Kansas left unhung to rise up against their country, and to seek the overthrow of the government. So our troops were ordered into Missouri—many of them without one day's notice. The first day's march of one regiment was forty-five miles in twenty-two successive hours, without baggage-wagons or ambulances. And before they could

3

be provided with clothing or shoes, they were ordered onward and still onward into Missouri; and when they had joined General Lyon at Springfield, they had marched over three hundred miles; and one of the regiments had only seven baggage-wagons! A part of the Kansas and Iowa regiments, under an order from General Sweeney, were marched in two days from Springfield to Forsyth, sixty miles, and had a battle; and after dispersing the rebels, returned to Springfield in two and a half days; and during this unparalleled marching, over two hundred of these brave men were entirely destitute of shoes.

"But the memorable day about which cluster all the interests of that southwestern campaign was the 10th day of August, 1861. Upon the evening of the 9th, as darkness quietly settled down into the valleys, and light lingered blushingly upon the hill tops, this little army of five and a half thousand men set out to meet twenty-five thousand and engage them in conflict. They marched by two different routes all night, and at daybreak came upon the enemy encamped upon Wilson's Creek. Immediately, without waiting on points of etiquette, General Lyon formed the line of battle. And here began, at five o'clock in the morning, the conflict of arms—more terrible and destructive, according to numbers, than ever engaged men on this continent before. From the beginning to the close, for six and a half hours, the firing was incessant and terrific. At half-past ten o'clock the man of all men there—the general of all generals in this war —fell at the head of one of our regiments, leading them gloriously onward to victory. He placed himself there in a moment, in response to the call of these men as unconquerable as himself. General Lyon had before, that day, been twice wounded, and had one horse shot under him. He resisted all entreaties for refreshments, willing to hazard every thing himself, anxious only for his men and their cause. He neither faltered nor complained, until the fatal shaft entered the life fountain, and the 'golden bowl was broken.' He thus sunk quietly to rest, amidst the din of battle and the smoke of the contest—the Warren of this war. The battle went on, though its leader had fallen. Few of either officers or men knew what had occurred. The enemy being repulsed, returned with fresh regiments, again and again, but returned only to retreat in confusion, leaving their trail strewn with the fallen. Our troops advanced and took possession of the field. The rebels, in fear, now burned their own baggage-wagons. Volumes of smoke rolled up from every side of the battle-field, and concentrating above them, hung the heavens in a drapery of mourning. The rebels were receding, and the firing ceased altogether. *   *   *   *   *

"Thus ended the 10th day of August, 1861; evening shadows, cooling the heat of both sun and fire; our troops marched regularly to camp. And I now say, in contradiction to much that has been written and said, that that battle was a triumph. It was a costly one; nevertheless a victory. What other battle-field was ever won more triumphantly? I do not allow the fact that there were not reinforcements on hand sufficient to hold that whole country, to detract from the brilliant triumph of our arms that day. It was a battle of five thousand five hundred men against twenty-five thousand; and a victory of the few over the many; showing again that

"'Thrice armed is he who hath his quarrel just.'

"The hero of that battle sleeps beside other graves, in his dear native valley. He has been literally 'gathered to his fathers.' There need be no monument of marble or granite for him. All the way from St. Louis to Connecticut his remains were honored by tributes of respect from a grateful people. I had the melancholy pleasure of seeing the almost spontaneous gathering of his old friends at Hartford. They honored suitably the noble dead. In that they honored themselves. From Hartford to Eastford, where he now sleeps, the way was all marked by tokens that were becoming to a returning conqueror. The dear old people at home have garnered up his memory; it shall be to them as endearing as liberty and life."

WILLIAM LOWELL PUTNAM.

WILLIAM LOWELL PUTNAM was born in Boston, Massachusetts, on the 9th day of July, 1840. He fell, mortally wounded, at the battle of Ball's Bluff, on the 21st of October, 1861, and died the following day.

Seven years of his short life were passed in Europe. We can in no other way give, in a small compass, so just an impression of what he was, and what were his leading tastes and pursuits during the period of his absence from his own country, as by extracting the following pages from the memoir recently published in France by Dr. Guépin, of Nantes:

"Lowell Putnam was brought at eleven years old to Europe for his educa-tion. Two years in a school at Paris, journeys in France and in other countries, prolonged residence in Paris and in some of the principal cities of Germany and Italy—these were the means employed to give him a knowledge of languages, and to enable him, at the same time, to acquaint himself with the history and works of art of the ancients and moderns.

"Lowell Putnam was thirteen years old when we saw him for the first time. He was then charming in person, full of life and movement, and of so remark-able a loyalty that he did not think falsehood possible. The vivacity of his first emotions, the expression of his joys, had something very original. But he be-came calm, he was all eye and ear, when he found himself in the presence of serious men, and especially of eminent writers.

"Michelet was then at Nantes, studying on the spot the civil wars of which Brittany and La Vendée were the theatre in 1790–1795. William was strongly moved by the conversation of this great painter, who has thrown such vivid lights on the most important pages of our history. He found his own vocation revealed to him.

"We made a tour through Brittany with William and his parents. During the whole excursion, he inspired us with the liveliest interest. The picturesque and the reason of things interested him in turn. One asked one's self, which would, at last, take the ascendency in him, love of art or the spirit of investiga-tion, imagination or philosophy. This child was so interesting, his young intel-lect was so eager, that we could not resist the desire of planting in it some germs for his future of serious study. We became his cicerone. We did not let any thing pass, whether of Druidism, of the events of the Reformation, of the more recent events of the Revolution, without telling him what we knew about it. We also showed him whatever there was to interest him in the department of art.

"A year later, Lowell Putnam passed some months at Nantes, already giving promise of future eminence by his brilliant intellect and firm will. On this second visit he asked us for more detailed explanations of all that his journey of the preceding year had left in his memory.

"Lowell Putnam left France for Germany very well prepared—already knowing several languages, and acquainted with the origin of the European peoples and their migrations. His studies in Germany were serious, as also in Italy. The letters which he wrote to us from this latter country, upon the Etruscans, upon Rome and the Campagna, upon Naples and the devotion paid to Saint Januarius, were very much beyond his years. He could not live in Italy, which was then groaning under the yoke, without being continually struck by the ignorance, the misery, and the superstitious prejudices, engendered by despotism ; and as often his mind necessarily reverted to the little republic of Massachusetts.

"He returned to us in October, 1857, a young poet, a serious thinker, under the form of a tall, handsome youth, as modest and reserved in society, as firm and courageous in the practice of his duties. His dream for the future had not changed : it was still that of serving the interests of his country and of humanity as historian. That nothing might interfere with the fulfilment of his desires, he determined, in the first place, to fortify his constitution. He drank only water, took every day a very long walk, went to bed betimes, and rose very early. The cold was rude in the winter of that year, but he never allowed a fire to be made in his room ; if he suffered too much from the temperature, he went out to skate. He was fully aware that a necessity for comforts takes from our physical and moral liberty ; that the factitious wants of a too refined civilization are the evil of our age. And besides, as he had studied the Etruscans in Etruria, so he desired to study Egypt and India in their own monuments. For this, long voyages and journeys were necessary, requiring great physical strength, and the habit of living on little.

"Physiology and jurisprudence were the necessary complement of his studies. Postponing to a later period the study of American and of comparative legislation, he profited by his residence in France to initiate himself into the science of life. Never, in our twenty years of professorship in the School of Medicine at Nantes, have we met with a more perceptive or a more sagacious intellect. . . . .

"Very exact in following the courses of our Superior School of Science and

Letters, he heard with especial interest the lectures on history and literature, although they did not always fully correspond to his desires. . . . .

"While in the west of France, Lowell Putnam visited the principal battle-fields of the wars of La Vendée. He talked with some of the old witnesses of the events of that time, and was ardent in searching out the truth.

"Before returning to Paris and thence to America, he made a last excursion to La Rochelle. He thought this pilgrimage due to those noble martyrs of another time who have revived, so great and so worthy, in their writings and even in their familiar letters. An ardent faith inspired their language and their acts, but this vivifying faith was united to a profound respect for human reason.

"A few days after his arrival in Paris, Lowell Putnam wrote to us. Persuaded that much is to be learned from the lessons of persons whose opinions are opposed to ours, he had begun to attend several courses of lectures in which views were maintained of a different tendency from his own: among others, the lectures of M. Flourens. In the autumn of the same year (1858), he left France for the United States.

"The principal features of the character of this young man were very marked. What we chiefly observed and esteemed in him was his firm will to govern his impulsiveness, to bring all his impressions under the control of his rational faculties before taking a determination and acting upon it. The duties which had been given him by nature and those which arose from his projects for the future, seemed to occupy his life. Very generous, very devoted, always ready to succor the unfortunate, whoever they might be, he yet knew how to be on his guard against himself. He especially dreaded being drawn out of the line he had marked for himself. But when a desire agitated him, when it was found in accordance with his duties, when Reason said to him, 'Forward!' there was then in him an ardor impossible to subdue. The moral and the rational faculties had in him a complete ascendency over the lower. He had a horror of blood and of war, and despised those great vanities which fill the trumpet of false glory. His modesty and his reserve overlooked raillery addressed to his own person, but he was easily drawn out of his habitual calm by an attack on the great laws of morality, on the men who have made glorious sacrifices for humanity, or on the manners and institutions of his country. The confusion, often malicious, which some of the Paris journals constantly made between the slaveholding and the free states of the great American confederation, made him suffer keenly."

After his return from Europe, Lowell Putnam set himself to acquiring a knowledge of his own land with the same zeal and the same method with which he had studied foreign countries. He listened to its leading orators; visited its battle-fields and other scenes of historical interest; delighted himself with its grand or beautiful scenery. He also applied himself to several branches of

instruction which he had hitherto postponed for others more conveniently cultivated in Europe. After two years thus spent in alternate study and travel, he
began the reading of law, and, in March, 1861, became a student in the Cambridge Law School.

In the mean time he had continued to correspond with his friends in France.
We quote once more from Dr. Guépin:

"Soon after his return from America we received a long letter from him,
in which he enlarged with great pleasure on the number and the nature of the
public lectures in Boston, and the large audiences that attended them. He was
happy to be able to tell us with how much more esteem and consideration his
country treated men of learning than old Europe, even than France herself. . . . .

"Another letter gave us his travelling impressions. We received a third
from Kentucky, whose caves he had just been visiting. It was accompanied by
some eyeless fishes, caught in ponds which never receive any other light than
that from the torches of visitors. His last letter but one inquired into the state
of science as regards the nervous system. Then he remained a long time without writing. His silence surprised us, for his country was already the scene of
grave events. We had begun to be anxious, when arrived this last letter, a
simple note:

"'CAMP MASSASOIT, READVILLE, *August 4th*, 1861.

"'DEAR AND REVERED FRIEND,*

"'I am second Lieutenant in the 20th Regiment of Massachusetts Volunteers. We are encamped a few miles from Boston. I do not think we shall
leave for the South for thirty or forty days. When we are there, I hope to have
time to write you long letters.

"'Good-bye! Remember me to Madame Guépin, and thank her very much
for M. Charton's History of France which she has sent me. Remember me also
to Auge.

"'I think very often of you and of Madame Guépin, and I shall never forget the time I passed at Nantes.

"'Again, good-bye. Your friend, WILLIAM LOWELL PUTNAM.'

"How explain this transformation? How had William, with his tender
heart, been able suddenly to sacrifice all his affections and all his projects, to
become a soldier? Nothing more simple. That which governed in him was
sense of duty. The law was in danger; the constitution had been violated by
the South, and he immediately made himself the armed defender of the right,
and of the institutions consented to and sworn to by the rebels themselves."

* The original of this letter is in French.

On the 4th of September, one month after the date of his last letter to Dr. Guépin, Lowell Putnam left Camp Massasoit, with his regiment, for the South. In less than seven weeks from that time, his earthly career was closed. The beautiful mortal form was brought back to his native city. The funeral services were held in the West Church. On this occasion, the following address was made by the Rev. Dr. Bartol, pastor of this church:

"My friends of this funeral company: You, whose still flowing blood claims kindred with these ashes; you, whom sympathetic sorrow has drawn to-day to these courts; you, who pay the respect of constituted authority, the civil and military power of the state, and, by official and federal relationship, of the United States—not unsuitable to its object, let me say, is the tribute you all render. With a full heart, with an earnest soul, with a communing spirit, I join you in that tribute. This altar, this sanctuary, this old church, which I represent, unites in the honor to the lifeless remains, to the living soul, of our brother.

"But, in discharging my part of this service, I must be excused from following any prescribed form. Few are even the informal words I am moved to utter. Little, perhaps nothing, need I say. The scene itself, with the well-known incidents that have produced it, speaks to you. The story of our brother's blameless life speaks. The devotion with which he went, and his parents and kindred offered him, to the strife that afflicts our land, betwixt government and anarchy, union and secession, freedom and slavery—speaks. The humanity with which he rushed forward on the field to support a wounded comrade, speaks. The disinterestedness with which, after receiving his own mortal wound, he desired others to be cared for rather than himself, speaks. The smiling calm in which he bore his weakness and pain, speaks. Out of the hiding-place in which he kept his anguish of body and mind, his patient self-denial speaks. The gentleness with which he received the angel of death as the angel of sleep to his pillow, speaks. All these things speak loudly of and for our brother. They speak emphatically, as the Spirit itself, to the human soul; and God speaks to us all, admonishing us, in all the way and warfare of our life, to imitate the example of such fidelity to the highest laws of his being and our nature.

"But, though I have nothing on this occasion to say as of myself, I may be permitted to remember another funeral,* nine months ago, in its relation to this, in this same spot. That was of an aged man of nearly fourscore; this is of a youth of hardly more than one. The gray hair, turning to white, lay placidly on the manly beauty of that furrowed brow; silken locks curled over this forehead and about these temples. The lines of much thought and long experience of the deepest feelings were printed all over that countenance; how smooth and

---

* That of Rev. Dr. Lowell, grandfather of Lieutenant William Putnam.

6

fair are these cold cheeks! Amid apparent contrasts was, however, the same essential worth. The mingled benignity and resolution of that eloquent and holy mouth are repeated in the sweet firmness of these tender lips which I looked at yesterday. A great company of intimate friends participated in those former obsequies; while few, I suppose, of this great congregation, had the personal intimacy it would have been any one's privilege to enjoy with this dear boy, just budding into manhood. Yet, cordial as was the honor offered to the aged minister of the church, my own venerated colleague, there is as utter absence of all scruple, qualification, or reserve, in that paid to the grandson as to the grandfather. They are associated as respects the place where their bodies have lain in death. As there is a God who lives, and a heaven for his filial servants, their spirits are already joined in the fellowship of saints in everlasting light and bliss.

"The sword lies motionless, unwielded, here across the coffin. Amid fading blossoms of the garden and the field, a fairer flower within withers away. But something, not of the dust, which cannot be borne out on this bier, which the funeral procession cannot marshal, nor the mighty state precede, nor the whole earth, whose mouth is open, soon to close again, swallow up, has escaped, beyond the bonds *we* yet wear, into the region where *is* liberty, unity, peace, and light, with no need of the sun, for the Lord God doth lighten it and the Lamb is the light thereof.

" 'The beauty of Israel is slain upon thy high places.' Our brother gave himself, and his friends gave him, to country, to liberty, and to God. He is not dead. He is not lost to country and liberty and God. Country and liberty and God will keep his name and memory precious on earth, will keep his soul alive forever and blessed in heaven.

"O God, to whom the swords and shields of the earth belong, bless to the cause of truth and right, not only the blood that runs in the veins of thy children, but that which is shed and poured out like water on the ground. We thank thee that, with all we mourn, there is so much we must rejoice in as long as we live and recollect. Help us to see him, cut down as a plant in its bloom, and him, coming to his grave like a shock of corn fully ripe in its season, alike and together in thy kingdom. May the short career of our brother, in obedience to thy will, show to us 'the wisdom which is the gray hair to man, the unspotted life which is old age,' and be sanctified to influence and usefulness as great to his native land and mankind as though he had filled out the allotted measure of threescore and ten."

The Rev. James Freeman Clarke then gave a sketch of the life and character of Lowell Putnam, from which we take these extracts:

"Born in Boston in 1840, he was educated in Europe, where he went when eleven years old: and where, in France, Germany. and Italy. he showed that he possessed the faculty of easily mastering languages, and where he faithfully studied classic and Christian antiquity and art. Under the most loving guidance he read with joy the vivid descriptions of Virgil, while looking down from the hill of Posilippo, on the headland of Misenum and the ruins of Cumæ. He studied with diligence the remains of Etruscan art, of which, perhaps, no American scholar, though he was so young, knew more.

"Thus accomplished, he returned to his native land; but, modest and earnest, he made no display of his acquisitions, and very few knew that he had acquired any thing. When the war broke out, his conscience and heart urged him to go to the service of his country. His strong sense of duty overcame the reluctance of his parents, and they consented. A presentiment that he should not return alive was very strong in his mind and theirs. But he gave himself cheerfully, and said, in entire strength of purpose, that to die would be easy in such a cause. And, in the full conviction of immortality, he added: 'What is death, mother? It is nothing but a step in our life.' His fidelity to every duty gained him the respect of his superior officers; and his generous, constant interest in his companions and soldiers brought to him an unexampled affection. He realized fully that this war must enlarge the area of freedom, if it was to attain its true end; and, in one of his last letters, he expressed the earnest prayer that it might not cease till it opened the way for universal liberty.

"These earnest opinions were connected with a feeling of the wrong done to the African race, and an interest in its improvement. He took with him to the war, as a body-servant, a colored lad named George Brown, who repaid the kindness of Lieutenant Putnam by gratitude and faithful service. George Brown followed his master across the Potomac, into the battle, nursed him in his tent, and attended his remains back to Boston.

"In the fatal battle a week ago, Putnam fell, as is reported, while endeavoring to save a wounded companion—fell, soiled with no ignoble dust—'non indecore pulvere sordidum.' Brought to the hospital-tent, he said to the surgeon who came to dress his wound, 'Go to some one else, to whom you can do more good; you cannot save me'—like Philip Sidney, giving the water to the soldiers who needed it more than himself.

"Brave and beautiful child! was it for this that you had inherited the best results of past culture, and had been so wisely educated and carefully trained? Was it for this, to be struck down by a ruffian's bullet, in a hopeless struggle against overwhelming numbers? How hard to consent to let these precious lives be thus wasted, apparently for naught, through the ignorance or the carelessness of those whose duty it was to make due preparation before sending them to the field! How can we bear it?

"We could not bear it, unless we believed in God. But believing in God and Christ, we can bear even this. It is not any blind chance, nor yet any human folly, which controls these events. All is as God wills, who knows what the world needs, and what we need, better than we can know it. He uses the folly and sin of man for great ends; and he does not allow any good and noble effort to be lost. . . . .

"Farewell, then, dear child, brave heart, soul of sweetness and fire! We shall see no more that fair, candid brow, with its sunny hair; those sincere eyes; that cheek flushed with the commingling roses of modesty and courage. Go, and join the noble group of devoted souls, our heroes and saints. Go with Ellsworth, protomartyr of this great cause of freedom; go with Winthrop, poet and soldier, our Körner with sword and lyre; go with the chivalric Lyon, bravest of the brave, leader of men; go with Baker, to whose utterance the united murmurs of Atlantic and Pacific Ocean gave eloquent rhythm, and whose words flowered so easily into heroic action. Go with our noble Massachusetts boys, in whose veins runs the best blood of the age. Go gladly, and sleep in peace. Those who love thee as much as parents ever loved child, give thee joyfully in this great hour of their country's need."

On the Sunday after the funeral, Dr. Bartol preached from the text—"*The beauty of Israel is slain on thy high places.*" His sermon, afterward published under the title, "Our Sacrifices," contained a tribute to Lowell Putnam, with which we complete this memoir:

"Familiar events prove that to property and happiness we must personally like the Jews in old Canaan, for ourselves or those dearest to us, add the sacrifice of life. To one, among many such noble and widely-commemorated sacrifices, I wish, in closing, to refer, not to gratify myself or any others peculiarly concerned, but, through the public attention, already fixed on it by circumstances of thrilling interest, for the benefit, as great as can be derived from any sermon, of delineating what I must consider a model of human worth.

"WILLIAM LOWELL PUTNAM, born July 9th, 1840, lieutenant in a Massachusetts company, fell bravely fighting for his country, in the act probably of at once leading on his men and making a step to the relief of a wounded officer, in the battle of Ball's Bluff, October 21st, 1861, and he died, at the age of twenty-one, the next day. The state that gave him birth, and to which he gave back honor, joined with his kindred and friends in celebrating his obsequies in this church, last Monday, October the 28th. The coffin lay on the same spot occupied nine months ago, by that of Dr. Charles Lowell, his maternal grandfather. The corse of the soldier and hero, surmounted with the sword unwielded and motionless in its scabbard, was not unworthy to succeed here that of the preacher and saint; for spiritual weapons were no cleaner in the hands of the first than carnal ones in those of the last. Striking was the contrast made by the youth's silken locks and smooth, fair cheeks, cold in death, with the white hair on the furrowed brow that had also reposed at the shrine so long vocal with well-remembered tones of an eloquent and holy mouth. But there was more union than separation. The benignant resolution of the elder's expression was repeated in the sweet firmness of the young man's lips. They seemed as near together in spirit as circumstantially wide apart. The two venerable names of Lowell and of Putnam—the eminent jurist, as beloved as he was distinguished*—were well united in that of the youth; for he justified every supposable law of hereditary descent by continuing in his temper and very look, with the minister's loving earnestness, the singular cordiality, the wondrous and spotless loving-kindness, which in his paternal grandfather's manner was ever like a warm beam of the sun. . . . . A worthy grandchild William was. He bore out in action, in danger and death, every rising signal and promise of his brief but beautiful life. In the conflict, he cared more for others' peril than for his own. He sank, from all his forward motion, under one mortal wound. But, while he suffered, he smiled. He deprecated any assistance to himself as vain; he urged all to the work before them, and even forbade his soldiers to succor him. 'Do not move me,' he said to his friend; 'it is your duty to leave me; help others: I am going to die, and would rather die on the field.' With noble yet well-deserved support, however, he was borne nearly a mile to the boat at the fatal river's brink by Henry Howard Sturgis, of Boston, who left him only to return to fight in his own place, and afterward watched him like a mother in the hospital, hoping for his restoration. As he lay prostrate, knowing he could not recover, he beckoned to his friend to come to him, that he might praise the courage of his men in the encounter, rather than to say any thing of himself. With such patient composure he endured his anguish and weakness, probably no mortal but himself could suspect how far he was gone. He sent home the simple message of love. Brightly, concealing his pangs, he wore away the weary hours. Cheerfully, on the Tuesday morning, which was his last on earth, he spoke to his faithful servant, George. He closed his eyes at length, and did not open them again—presenting, and perhaps knowing, no distinction between sleep and death. He 'is not dead, but sleepeth,' might it not have been said again? But, like the child raised by our Lord, he slept but a little. The greatness of his waking, who shall tell?

"I looked often and earnestly on that young man's face, in the house and by

---

* Samuel Putnam was born 1768, and died 1853. At the bar he was particularly distinguished for his knowledge of commercial law, a chivalric sense of honor and duty, and uniform amenity of manners. On the bench of the Supreme Court, where he served for twenty-eight years, the exhibition of these powers of mind and elements of character gained for him universal affection and respect; and his opinions in that branch of the law are esteemed among the most valuable contributions to jurisprudence to be found in the Reports of the State of Massachusetts.

the wayside; and now that I can see it in the flesh no longer, it still hangs and shines conspicuous in the gallery of chosen portraits in my mind. I would fain put into some photograph of words what it expressed, and what the likeness fortunately taken of him largely preserves, respecting others' testimony, while I render my tribute, and blending their views with my own; for I find in all estimates of him a notable uniformity. The first impression which any one beholding him would have received, was of a certain magnanimity. The countenance was open, and, as from an ample doorway, the generous disposition to meet you came out. There was a remarkable mixture of sweetness and independence in all his aspect and bearing. From his very gait and salutation you would perceive that his mind was made up, and he meant something by his glance or utterance; as one who knew him said, there was *character* in whatever he did. I am not sure a discerner of spirits might not have gathered, before he elected his part, from his effective carriage and fine physical development, signs of a military taste. Yet, if the martial inclination were in him, it was combined with a strong aversion to take life or inflict distress. He proved once more, as it has been proved ten thousand times, that the brave is also the tender heart. But above all mortal considerations of pleasure or pain was his regard for justice and truth. He had a rare native rectitude. He never deviated from sincerity. If any thing could grieve him, or, even in his childhood, move him for a moment from the admirable felicity of his temper, it would be any calling in question of his word. But the sensibility in him that felt all forgave all too; and without the sensibility that measures our forgiveness, our forgiveness is nothing worth. Beyond any passion, he evinced the reason in which his passion was held. Coolness in him covered enthusiasm; the gravity of deep though early experience repressed the sparkles of natural humor; a heart wistful of affection attended self-reliance; the modest and almost diffident was the courageous soul; by ready concession to another's correctness in any debate, he curbed a mounting will; and he suited the most explicit clearness of opinion to the perfect gentleman's ways. With his seriousness went along a keen sense of the ludicrous, by which almost every highly moral nature is quick to observe what is outwardly awry, as well as what is intrinsically wrong; but he was more apt, when he laughed, to laugh at himself than at other folks. He could contend also, but never from love of contention. He would fight only for a great object; he went to the war in his country's emergency, at the outset proposing to go as a private; and he intended to return to the study and practice of the law if he survived. *If he survived:* but no sanguine thought of surviving did he entertain. He had no reserves; he was a devotee in arms. He offered himself as though less to slay than be slain were his end. No more of hero than martyr was in his mood, as in his doom. He threw his life in without scruple, with the ancient judging it sweet and decorous to die for one's country; and the parental presentiment, that die he would, was matched in the entire readiness for such an event with which the always fearless son, under no shadow of his own apprehension, marched on to the fatal fray. In every extremity he was self-possessed. If by one word I must mark the quality most prominent in his deportment, I should call it *balance.* Did this unqualified courage, in one extraordinarily conscious of existence, and with constitutional tenacity rooted in the present life, spring from the faith he so vividly had in immortality? and did that faith in turn spring from a profoundly religious trust in God? I believe it! I believe even the exuberant, vivacious, frolicsome boy had in him the germ, afterward to open, of all this faith and trust. Impulsive, he did not act from impulse, but from that contemplation on the truth of the universe which told him on what impulse to proceed, and marked his way over the earth into the heavens.

"Precious intellectual gifts, mostly philosophic, though with no want of imagination, were in our brother, so that his friend abroad, Guépin, expected in him great scientific attainments; while he spoke French, German, and Italian, in the style of the common people, whom he loved, as well as the dialect of the refined circles. He was fond of reading, but only of the best works in composition of any kind; and he left an exciting romance half finished, at the hint of something not wholesome or altogether lofty in the author's tone. His mind and heart were in unison; and on his young companions, as well as elders, he made the same stamp of a superiority permitting only one idea of him. It were hard to tell whether the reflective or executive faculties prevailed, so exact in his very nature was their poise. But the moral in him ever presided over the intellectual. Not for distinction, but duty, he lived, as he died. I know how the dead are eulogized, and what a eulogy I give; but out of the sincere thoughts of my heart I give it—that those who knew him best, while they admired his talents, were never able to discover his faults.

"Such is one of our sacrifices of life. A dawn predicting individual excellence through a long career, as plainly as the yet beardless Raphael's picture of the holy marriage was said to be prophetic of all his subsequent fame, has suddenly withdrawn its lustre from the earth. Is the sacrifice too great? I ask his kindred, is it too great? Would you have your boy back? Under the old dispensation, when a sacrifice God would surely accept was to be made, a firstling of the flock, a lamb without spot or blemish, was singled out for the altar. A firstling of the flock, a lamb without spot or blemish, has been selected now. God himself, for this very purpose, as I think, of a measureless blessing to enliven the common heart, has chosen a victim from our beloved fold. No, we would not have him back. We would have him where he is! In the victim may we see the victory too. In the follower, as in the master, may the twofold lesson of triumph with sacrifice be seen. May the Divine wisdom, that loses life more certainly to save it, and gives up to gain all, shown so well in a new example, have imitation everywhere and continuance without end. Be humbly proud, be sacredly envious of the dead in the pattern displayed; for imitation and continuance it has! The enlistment, at the public need, of educated young men is not damped, but inspirited, from a companion's or kinsman's expiring breath. That breath passeth far through the whole air, into their nostrils! 'I must go,' said one of them to his father; 'I feel like a poltroon here at home.'— 'Go with my blessing,' was the father's reply. As the father himself told me this yesterday, he could talk no farther, for tears, but turned away. May the spectacle, so frequent among us—the most beautiful spectacle now beneath the sun—of boyhood tearing itself from mothers' embraces and fathers' arms, and happy homes, and loving dissuasives, to consecrate itself to country's good, prefigure another spectacle, of a country purged of its errors and renewing *its* youth. May Heaven bless to our redemption every vicarious sacrifice—of the wounded and still exposed, as well as the dead; and so may all loss and self-surrender be sanctified in a perpetual resurrection, from the Most High, on earth and in heaven, of 'the beauty of Israel,' slain upon *our* high places, till the blood of the martyrs, which is the seed of the Church, shall be also the life of the State. Standing, for us and ours, 'as on life's utmost verge,' at the edge of whatever may come to mortals, so to the Eternal we pray;—and may the Eternal to what even on earth is immortal in us too, answer our prayer! Then we shall not have sacrificed on his altar in vain. All our sacrifices will redound alike to his glory, our country's welfare, and our own final gladness and peace. It is no sacrifice of truth, justice, freedom, or any human right, that we make. Only lower and cheaper things we sacrifice to these principles which are the attributes of God. Fixed be our faith that something, not of the dust and not laid low on the field, something which the funeral procession cannot marshal, nor the mighty state precede, nor the whole earth, whose mouth opens for the dead, swallow up, has escaped alive above the bonds we yet wear, into the region where is liberty, unity, peace, and light, with no need of the sun, for the Lord God doth lighten it, and the Lamb is the light thereof."

MICHAEL CORCORAN

Michael Corcoran

MICHAEL CORCORAN.

IN conformity with a custom, to which the wisest and best men have given their sanction, it will not be deemed inappropriate, in giving a biographical memoir of the heroic colonel of the famous sixty-ninth regiment of the New York state militia, to preface it with a glance at his genealogy. While it affords solid gratification to the friends of Colonel CORCORAN to know that he is the founder of his own good name, it certainly detracts nothing from his record to learn that, according to testimony still preserved in his family, he is, on the female side, descended from a celebrated Irish hero, who, like the subject of the present notice, nobly fought to uphold the flag of his adoption when exiled from his native land. While presenting a flag to the Irish brigade, and alluding to that previously presented to the old sixty-ninth, the Honorable Judge Daly touchingly and significantly called up the relationship between those gallant exiles, and the faith of an Irish soldier, as illustrated by both. "At the head of it" (the sixty-ninth), said Judge Daly, "was the noble-minded, high-spirited, and gallant officer to whom so much of its after-character was due. A descendant by the female line of that illustrious Irish soldier, Patrick Sarsfield, Earl of Lucan, whose name is identified with the siege of Limerick, and who fell fighting at the head of his brigade upon the bloody field of Landen, Colonel Corcoran, in the spirit of his noble ancestor, received that flag with a soldier's promise, and kept that promise with a soldier's faith. It was not brought back from the field of Manassas, on that day of disastrous rout and panic, but he at least, and the little band who stood around him in its defence, went with it into captivity. I need say no more when presenting this splendid gift with which these ladies have honored your regiment, than to point to this Irish example of the faith and fidelity that is due by a soldier to his flag. Colonel Corcoran is now within the walls of a rebel prison, one of the selected victims for revengeful Southern retaliation; but he has the satisfaction of feeling that he owes his sad though proud pre-eminence to having acted as became a descendant of Sarsfield." At the same fight—the siege of Limerick—which made Sarsfield immortal, the O'Corcorans of Sligo were not without a representative who has inspired the muse of Carolan. In the second volume of the *Irish*

4

Minstrelsy (Hardiman) will be found a hearty song, translated from the Irish commencing—

> "O Corcoran, thy fame be it mine to proclaim"—

in honor of one of the heroes of that memorable struggle. Thomas Corcoran, one officer in the British service, returned from the West Indies, and, having retired on half-pay, was married to Miss Mary M'Donogh, in the year 1824. From this union Colonel MICHAEL CORCORAN sprang. He was born on the 21st September, 1827, at Carrowkeel, the seat of the M'Donoghs, in the county Sligo. After receiving a plain English education, he spent some three years in the Irish constabulary establishment, resigned his place in August, 1849, and emigrated to America. Gifted with a keen, clear intellect, and having nothing to rely on but his own exertions, he would not allow himself to be long idle. He was almost immediately employed. He exhibited directness of purpose, unimpeachability of action, and strong natural talents. The former made him friends, and the latter kept awake an honest ambition, which ultimately found a noble outlet in the patriotic support of the Union. Besides being engaged in business in New York, he was appointed to an official situation in the post-office, and was clerk in the register's office just previous to his departure for the seat of war.

The military career of Colonel Corcoran in America may be dated from his entrance into the sixty-ninth, as a private in Company I (which has since been changed to Company A). Here the passion which has been so strongly developed was not dormant. He soon was elected orderly sergeant, and rose by the voice of his comrades to be successively first-lieutenant and captain, receiving from the company, during his upward progress, several substantial testimonials to his fitness and ability in every position.

Captain Corcoran was a faithful servant of the state in what is known as the "Quarantine War," being then senior captain of the sixty-ninth; and the inspector-general's return pays a distinguished tribute to his military character. In this official recognition of true and modest merit, the inspector said: "What I might say of Captain Corcoran, commanding Company A, as to his military knowledge, would not add to his already well-known reputation as among the best, if not the very best officer, of his rank in the first division." This was high praise, and occurrences since and recently show that it reflects not less credit on the officer who conferred than on him who received it.

Captain Corcoran was elected colonel of the sixty-ninth, August 25th, 1859, to fill a vacancy caused by the death of Colonel Ryan. Since that time, his name and that of the regiment have been synonymous. He was especially brought before the public on the occasion of the visit of the Prince of Wales. Colonel Corcoran deeply sympathizes with the cause of Irish nationality, is a personal friend of several gentlemen who were prominent in the Irish movement of '48, and a leading member of one of the most extensive Irish societies in America. He declined to parade the Irish-born citizen, in his command, to do honor to the son—however harmless—of the sovereign under whose rule those whom he believed to be the best men raised in Ireland for half a century were banished. He was consistent with the history of those heroes of Limerick with whom tradition associates his blood, not less than with the feelings of the corps he commanded, and his own theories and principles. His court-martial and de-fence—ably delivered by Mr. Richard O'Gorman—are now matters of pride, not only among hundreds of thousands of his adopted fellow-citizens, but those who deem the subsequent conduct of England any thing but a fair or grateful requital for the hospitality extended to her heir-apparent.

Colonel Corcoran's action at the breaking out of the rebellion was quite characteristic of his patriotic character. Great hopes were built upon the Irish Democrats by sympathizers with the leading traitor. This was enhanced by the treatment Corcoran and the sixty-ninth received in the conduct of the court-martial. It is not too much to say that Corcoran's upright and unselfish course at this juncture was one of the most severe and deadly blows the sympathizers with secession in the North could have received. Many of the officers of the sixty-ninth were doubtful of the propriety of "turning out" while their colonel was undergoing a court-martial for an act which they completely justified. Im-mediately Colonel Corcoran, in a public letter, implored them not to take him into any account, but to stand by the flag of the Union and the sacred principles involved in its sustainment. The result is known. The court-martial was quashed; the Union sentiment of the Irish rushed like a torrent into the ranks of the army; and the sixty-ninth left for the seat of war, attended by one of the most enthusiastic multitudes ever chronicled in our city history.

In the progress of the arduous labors which were assigned to his command, Colonel Corcoran won the esteem of the heads of the war department, and the enthusiastic applause of the United States officers with whom he served or co-operated. As the bulwark and *avant garde* of the brigade having in special charge the defence of the principal avenues from Virginia into the capital, the sixty-ninth won enduring honors. Fort Corcoran—a name conferred by the war department—will remain a lasting monument of its zeal and energy. All through its service—at Annapolis; along the railroad to the junction; at Georgetown; during the building of Fort Corcoran, along Arlington Heights; at the relief of the Ohio troops at the railroad near Vienna; the various midnight alarms and preparations in and out of camp; and the subsequent movements at Centreville, ending in the battle at Bull Run—the indomitable colonel gave his regiment un-ceasing examples of courage and patriotism. He greatly distinguished himself at Bull Run, and we believe is the only one officially chronicled (see General

Sherman's report) as having brought his regiment off the field in a hollow square. A soldier's letter, which found its way into the papers at the time, gives a graphic glimpse of the fact. "Sherman," says the writer, "told the bravest of colonels (Corcoran) to form square. The gallant colonel said, 'I have not as many as I like to do so, but we'll do the best we can.' The brave and determined colonel formed us into square, and so we retreated, receiving a fresh flanking fire from our adversaries as we went along." It was in this fire Colonel Corcoran was wounded, which led to his capture. For some time he was held prisoner in Richmond; subsequently sent to Castle Pinckney, Charleston harbor; and in anticipation of an assault on the city of Charleston by the Port Royal expedition, was removed to Columbia, in the interior of the state of South Carolina. Soon after his capture, he was offered his liberation if he would not again take up arms against the traitors. He indignantly repelled the overture, avowed his enthusiastic faith in and devotion to the cause of the Union, and declared his intention to take up arms for it as soon as circumstances would permit.

Upon Colonel Corcoran probably more than on any other of the Union prisoners has public attention been fixed and public sentiment aroused. His conduct as a prisoner has reflected credit upon the Union soldiery, and the treatment he has received from the traitors has appealed deeply to the hearts of the whole community. The announcement that he was chosen as one of the hostages for the safety of the privateers condemned to death as pirates, sent a thrill of indignant pity and shame throughout the North, and fixed more intently and impatiently the minds of thinking men on the subject of a general exchange of prisoners. The matter was ardently and in the main privately agitated; and a commission, composed of Hiram Barney, Esq., collector of New York, Judge Daly, and Messrs. Richard O'Gorman and John Savage, Esqs., was induced to proceed to Washington to confer with the cabinet and Congress on the immediate and humane necessity of such a proceeding. For several days the committee were actively engaged canvassing the leading minds at the seat of government, and on the 10th December they were invited by the President to attend a full cabinet council. Their efforts were satisfactory in an eminent degree. The military committees of both houses of Congress, as well as General M'Clellan, met their proposals with eager and humane statemanship, and they were encouraged by many eminent men. In a recent letter, Colonel Corcoran thus warmly alludes to these efforts in his case: "Be pleased to present the expression of my warmest thanks to Judge Daly, Hiram Barney, Richard O'Gorman, and John Savage, Esqs., and the other friends who have so kindly devoted so much time, labor, and expense, in their endeavors to obtain my release, and assure them I feel just pride in the knowledge of having such friends; and if a shade of gloom shall at any time darken the hours of my captivity, a recollection of their services shall be sufficient to dispel it." The great popularity of Colonel Corcoran in the North renders him an object of particular attention on the part of the rebels; and the influence of his name with the Irish population is doubtless the chief reason why he has been in more than one instance selected as the subject of Southern retaliation. The "government" of the "Confederate States" seem to bitterly appreciate and acquiesce in the force of the remark made by Mr. John O'Mahony—the Gaelic scholar and a leading Irish exile of '48—at a public meeting in Philadelphia, when he said: "May they everywhere prove, as Corcoran has done, that the Irishman who is most faithful and devoted to his own land, is also the best and loyalest citizen of America—that the best Irishman makes the best American. I have no hesitation in saying that so far as he has gone up to this, Colonel Corcoran has done more to assert the dignity and importance of the Irish citizens of the Union, and to elevate their position in this country, than any Irishman who has yet visited the American shores."

ABRAHAM LINCOLN

A. Lincoln.

ABRAHAM LINCOLN.

PRESIDENTS must first be candidates, and candidates are public property, for all the great purposes of defamation and personal abuse; when one is named for the Presidency, a large section of the press, and a great portion of the people, find a direct interest in the propagation of whatever may tend to render contemptible the person named, and to make him appear unfit for any position of dignity or trust. Hence the present President is known over a great part of the country as "the baboon," and respectable writers in Europe have lamented the result of universal suffrage in his election; though perhaps no man ever occupied the same position who in himself and in his personal history was more truly representative of all that is best in the American people.

ABRAHAM LINCOLN was born in Hardin county, Kentucky (at a place now included in La Rue county), February 12th, 1809. • His ancestors were Quakers, and migrated from Berks county, Pennsylvania, to Rockingham county, Virginia, whence his grandfather Abraham removed with his family to Kentucky, about 1782, and was killed by the Indians in 1784. Thomas Lincoln, the father of Abraham, was born in Virginia, and the President's mother, Nancy Hanks, was also a native of that state. Thomas Lincoln removed with his family in 1816 to a district now included in Spencer county, Indiana, where Abraham, then large for his age, assisted with an axe to clear away the forest. For the next ten years he was mostly occupied in this and other equally hard work on his father's farm, and in this period he went to school a little at intervals; but the whole time of his attendance at school amounted in the aggregate to not more than a year. He never went to school subsequently. His first experience of the world beyond home was acquired on a flat-boat, upon which he made the trip to New Orleans as a hired hand, when nineteen years of age. The advantages of travel under these circumstances are not great. Flat-boats it is true have been made the centre of a certain kind of free, western romance, and to float down the Ohio and the Mississippi in happy companionship with the "jolly flat-boat man," looks very pretty in a picture; especially if the picture be well painted, like Mount's. But unfortunately all flat-boat men were not jolly, and flat-boats didn't always float, flat-boat men were not the chosen of the human race, except perhaps for roughness, and flat-boats had very often to be poled along; there was much of coarse association for a boy to struggle against, and a deal of hard work to be done. On the other hand such travel is not delusive, it does not permit life to look the least like a holiday affair, nor unfit the wanderer for a sober return to the quiet-ness of home. Young Lincoln at the least travelled in a practical American man-ner, saw something of the world, and got paid for it.

Settlers are a most unsettled generation, and in March, 1830, Thomas Lincoln migrated again; this time to Macon county, Illinois. Abraham accom-panied his father to the new home, and there helped to build a log-cabin for the family, and to split enough rails to fence ten acres of land. From this he has been called the Rail-splitter. Now, to split rails has been a necessary piece or labor since the days of Milo of Crotona, who was a rail-splitter in his time; and while that occupation may not qualify a man for statesmanship, the name of Rail-splitter is a better one than Hair-splitter; moreover, while a man's career and the words he has spoken show his brain to be a good one, it is no harm to him before the people to be able to show a good muscular record. Young Lincoln's flat-boat trip soon proved to be an advantage, and in 1831 he was engaged, at twelve dollars a month, to assist in the construction of a flat-boat, and subsequently in its navigation down the river to New Orleans. He acquitted himself to the satisfaction of his employer, who upon his return put him in charge of a store and mill at New Salem, then in Sangamon, now in Menard county, Illinois. But these peaceful successes were soon lost sight of in the excitement of the Black Hawk war, which broke out in 1832. Lincoln joined a company of volunteers, and was elected their captain, an event which gave him a great deal of pleasure. He served through a campaign of three months, and on his return home was nominated by the Whigs of his district as a candidate for the state legislature; but the county was Democratic and he was defeated, though in his own immediate neighborhood he received two hundred and seventy-seven votes, while only seven were cast against him. These indications of personal popularity flattered and stimulated to future effort, and were thus not without their effect upon a young man looking for a career. His next venture was the establishment of a country store, which did not prove prosperous, and which he relinquished to become postmaster of New Salem. While in this position he began to study law, and borrowed for that purpose the books of a neighboring practitioner; the books were taken at night, and returned in the morning before they could be needed in the lawyer's office. Upon the offer of the surveyor of San-gamon county, to depute to him a portion of the work of the county surveyor's office, Mr. Lincoln procured a compass and chain and a treatise on surveying, and did the work. In 1834 he was again nominated as a candidate for the legislature, and was elected by the largest vote cast for any candidate in the state. He was re-elected in 1836, and in the same year was licensed to practise law. From New Salem he removed in April, 1837, to Springfield, and there opened a law office in partnership with Major John F. Stuart. Mr. Lincoln was re-elected to the state legislature in the years 1836 and 1840, and meanwhile rose rapidly to distinction in his profession, becoming especially eminent as an advocate in jury trials. He was also several times a candidate for presidential elector, and as such canvassed all of Illinois and part of Indiana for Henry Clay, in 1844, and made speeches before large audiences almost every day.

Mr. Lincoln was elected a representative in Congress from the central district of Illinois in 1846, and took his seat on the first Monday in December, 1847. His congressional career was consistently that of one who believed in freedom and respected the laws. He voted forty-two times in favor of the Wilmot proviso. He voted for the reception of anti-slavery memorials and petitions; for an inquiry into the constitutionality of slavery in the district of Columbia, and the expediency of abolishing the slave-trade in the district; and on January 16th, 1849, he offered to the House a scheme for the abolition of slavery in the district, and for the compensation of slave-owners from the United States treasury, provided a majority of the citizens of the district should vote for the acceptance of the act. He opposed the annexation of Texas, but voted for the loan bill to enable the government to carry on the Mexican war, and for various resolutions to prohibit slavery in the territory to be acquired from Mexico. He voted also in favor of a protective tariff, and of selling the public lands at the lowest cost price. In 1849 he was a candidate for the United States Senate, but was defeated. Upon the expiration of his congressional term Mr. Lincoln applied himself to his profession; but the repeal of the Missouri compromise called him again into the political arena, and he entered energetically the canvass which was to decide the choice of a Senator to succeed General Shields. The Republican triumph, and the consequent election of Judge Trumbull to the Senate, were attributed mainly to his efforts. Mr. Lincoln was ineffectually urged as a candidate for the vice-presidency in the national convention which nominated Colonel Fremont in 1856. He was unanimously nominated candidate for United States Senator in opposition to Mr. Douglas by the Republican state convention at Springfield, June 2d, 1858, and canvassed the state with his opponent, speaking on the same day at the same place. In the course of this canvass, and in reply to certain questions or statements of Mr. Douglas, Mr. Lincoln made the following declarations: "I do not now, nor ever did, stand in favor of the unconditional repeal of the fugitive slave law. I do not now, nor ever did, stand pledged against the admission of any more slave states into the Union. I do not stand pledged against the admission of a new state into the Union with such a constitution as the people of that state may see fit to make. . . . I am impliedly, if not expressly, pledged to a belief in the right and duty of Congress to prohibit slavery in all the United States territories."

In explanation he said, "In regard to the fugitive slave law, I have never hesitat-
ed to say, and I do not now hesitate to say, that I think, under the constitution of
the United States, the people of the Southern states are entitled to a congressional
fugitive slave law. . . . . In regard to the question of whether I am pledged to the
admission of any more slave states into the Union, I state to you very frankly that
I would be exceedingly sorry ever to be put in a position of having to pass upon
that question. I should be exceedingly glad to know that there would never be
another slave state admitted into the Union ; but I must add that, if slavery shall
be kept out of the territories, during the territorial existence of any one given
territory, and then the people shall, having a fair chance and a clear field, when
they come to adopt their constitution, do such an extraordinary thing as adopt a
slave constitution uninfluenced by the actual presence of the institution among
them, I see no alternative, if we own the country, but to admit them into the
Union." Assertions like this should be a sufficient answer to those who pro-
nounce Mr. Lincoln an abolitionist. The Republican candidates pledged to the
election of Mr. Lincoln received one hundred and twenty-five thousand two hundred and seventy-five votes ; the Douglas candidates received one hundred and
twenty-one thousand one hundred and ninety votes ; and the Lecompton candidates five thousand and seventy-one. Mr. Lincoln had thus, on the popular
vote, a clear majority over Mr. Douglas of four thousand and eighty-five ; but
Mr. Douglas was elected Senator by the legislature, in which his supporters had
a majority of eight on joint ballot.

Mr. Lincoln acquired a national reputation mainly through his contest with
Senator Douglas, and it consequently excited much surprise when, in the Republican national convention assembled at Chicago, his name was put forward in
connection with the Presidency. Many prominent Republicans did not hesitate
to declare their further support of the party conditional upon the nomination of
Mr. Seward ; but the availability of Mr. Lincoln was persistently urged by those
who considered his most prominent opponent too conspicuously committed to
the unpopular opposition to slavery interests. The whole number of votes in
the convention was four hundred and sixty-five, and two hundred and thirty-
three were necessary to a choice. Mr. Seward led on the first two ballots ; and
on the third, Mr. Lincoln received three hundred and fifty-four votes, and his
nomination was declared unanimous. His opponents for the Presidency in other
parties were brought forward in such a manner, that the country was geographically divided, and the contest was made almost exclusively sectional. By the
extreme course of the Southern press, the sectional feature of the contest was
more clearly brought out, and it was forced upon the North that Mr. Lincoln was
exclusively its own candidate ; and the disruption of the country was openly
threatened in the event of his election. From this it resulted that Mr. Lincoln

received at the North a support that he could never have received on his party account, and with three other candidates in the field his popular vote was one million eight hundred and fifty-seven thousand six hundred and ten. His vote in the electoral college was one hundred and eighty, against one hundred and forty-three for all others; and the gentleman who had received the largest opposing vote, John C. Breckenridge, declared from his place as president of the Senate, February 13th, 1861, that "Abraham Lincoln, of Illinois, having received a majority of the whole number of electoral votes, was duly elected President of the United States for the four years commencing on the 4th of March, 1861."

Mr. Lincoln arrived in Philadelphia, on his way to the capital, February 21st; and he there received full and accurate information, through the detective police, of the particulars of a plan for his assassination in the streets of Baltimore when he should reach that city. On the next day he visited Harrisburg, spoke before the legislature of Pennsylvania, and that night returned privately, but not disguised, to Philadelphia, whence he took the regular night train for Washington, and, without change of cars, arrived in the capital shortly after six, A. M., of February 23d. He was duly inaugurated on the 4th of March, and upon that occasion he said: "Apprehension seems to exist among the people of the Southern states that, by the accession of a Republican administration, their property and their peace and personal security are to be endangered. There has never been any reasonable cause for such apprehension. Indeed, the most ample evidence to the contrary has all the while existed, and been open to their inspection. It is found in nearly all the published speeches of him who now addresses you. I do but quote from one of those speeches when I declare that 'I have no purpose, directly or indirectly, to interfere with the institution of slavery in the states where it exists.' I believe I have no lawful right to do so, and I have no inclination to do so. . . . . I consider that, in view of the constitution, the Union is unbroken, and to the extent of my ability I shall take care, as the constitution itself expressly enjoins upon me, that the laws of the Union shall be faithfully executed in all the states."

For some time previous to the election, resistance to the laws had been determined upon in the event of Mr. Lincoln's success; and on December 20th a convention assembled in South Carolina had declared that state out of the Union. During the months of January and February, 1861, the states of Mississippi, Alabama, Florida, Georgia, Louisiana, and Texas, had been also declared out of the Union in a similar manner; and a congress of representatives from those states had convened at Montgomery, in Alabama, February 6th, had chosen a President, and proceeded otherwise to organize a new government. Such was the position of affairs at the time of Mr. Lincoln's inauguration. Only a day after it,

Peter G. T. Beauregard, an officer of the United States army, but involved in the rebellion, was ordered by the rebel President to the command of the forces assembled for the investment of Fort Sumter, and on March 9th, the so-called Confederate Congress passed an act for the establishment and organization of an army. Yet Mr. Lincoln did not entirely despair of a settlement of the trouble without war, and the policy chosen by him, to use his own words, "looked to the exhaustion of all peaceful measures before a resort to any stronger ones." He therefore "sought only to hold the public places and property not already wrested from the government, and to collect the revenue, relying for the rest on time, discussion and the ballot-box. He promised a continuance of the mails, at government expense, to the very people who were resisting the government, and gave repeated pledges against any disturbances to any of the people, or to any of their rights. Of all that which a President might constitutionally and justifiably do in such a case, every thing was forborne, without which it was believed possible to keep the government on foot."

But this was of no avail, and in a little more than a month after Mr. Lincoln's accession to office, Fort Sumter in Charleston harbor was attacked, and "bombarded to its fall." The bombardment and surrender were concluded on the thirteenth of April, and on the fifteenth the President issued his first proclamation—by which he called out "the militia of the several states of the Union to the aggregate number of seventy-five thousand, in order to suppress rebellious combinations, and to cause the laws to be duly executed;" and convened both houses of Congress in extra session. By subsequent proclamations he declared the complete blockade of all the ports of the United States south of the Chesapeake; increased the regular army by twenty-two thousand, and the navy by eighteen thousand men, and called for volunteers to serve during three years, to the number of five hundred thousand. "These measures, whether strictly legal or not, were ventured upon under what appeared to be a popular demand and a public necessity; trusting that Congress would readily ratify them."

Congress readily did so. Further reference to these affairs was made by the President in his first message to Congress in these noble words: "It was with the deepest regret that the executive found the duty of employing the war power in defence of the government forced upon him. He could but perform this duty, or surrender the existence of the government. No compromise by public servants could, in this case, be a cure—not that compromises are not often proper; but that no popular government can long survive a marked precedent that those who carry an election can only save the government from immediate destruction, by giving up the main point upon which the people gave the election. The people themselves, and not their servants, can safely reverse their own deliberate decision. As a private citizen, the executive could not have consented that those institutions should perish, much less could he in betrayal of so vast and so sacred a trust as these free people had confided to him. He felt that he had no moral right to shrink, nor even to count the chances of his own life in what might follow. In full view of his great responsibility he has so far done what he has deemed his duty. You will now, according to your own judgment perform yours. He sincerely hopes that your views and your action may so accord with his, as to assure all faithful citizens who have been disturbed in their rights of a certain and speedy restoration to them under the constitution and the laws, and having thus chosen our cause without guile and with pure purpose, let us renew our trust in God and go forward without fear, and with manly hearts."

No truer estimate of the President's career, and no higher panegyric of it has ever been uttered, than the assertion of Mr. Wendell Phillips, that "Lincoln is led astray by his idolatry of the constitution." These words, uttered in derogation of the President's course, are his best praise with every lover of his country.

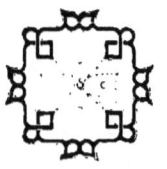

LOUIS BLENKER.

HISTORY does not give its unqualified admiration to the soldier of fortune; but the soldier of fortune, luckily, can do without it. Satisfied to
"drink delight of battle with his peers"—to fight and win, whether in one land
or another—he comes and goes; and while the world may perhaps be something
the worse for him, it is doubtless very often the better. And we certainly should
find but little fault with a disposition in men that so often gives our country's
battles the benefit of experience gained in other lands and in other causes; and
far from the manifestation of an orthodox and pious horror at the mention of his
name, we ought rather to consider "soldier of fortune" an honorable title.

LOUIS BLENKER was born in the city of Worms, in the grand-duchy of
Hesse-Darmstadt, in the year 1812. His father was a jeweller in respectable
business there, and had no more ambitious views for his son than to see him in
the future a worthy jeweller also, earning an honest livelihood in his native city.
Louis was accordingly instructed in the manipulation of fine gold, and in the
general art and mystery of his father's craft, duly "served his time," and suddenly found himself arrived at the age of manhood, a journeyman jeweller, with
the world before him. Disposed to "look about" rather than to settle immediately into the inevitable routine of a workman's life, the juncture was a favorable one. Just then a large share of the attention of Europe was turned toward
Greece. That country was in a state of indescribable anarchy. Every individual, apparently, who had assisted in the war of independence, then recently concluded, desired to govern the country on his own account; and the various
mountain-chiefs, with bands of wild, brave fellows at their heels, who in the war
had stood fire like salamanders, fought one another, massacred the people, pillaged
the cities, and in every way kept up a tumult. One congress and government
assembled at Napoli di Romania, when another, in opposition, was immediately
convened at Megara, overran the country with its forces, and drove out the first.
No sooner did this revolutionary body become thus the established government,
than all the elements of disorder arrayed themselves against it, and it was in
a fair way to be driven out in turn, when a change for the better took place
through the decision of the three great European powers. They agreed in May,
1832, upon the election of Prince Frederick Otho, of Bavaria, as king of Greece,

and Greece acquiesced in the choice. But a crown prince was not all that Bavaria was called upon to furnish, for with the Prince was to go a Bavarian legion of three thousand five hundred men; and immediately the drum went round for recruits, and all along the Rhine stout fellows desirous to see the world, and tempt the Lady Fortune in their favor, were in brisk demand.

Louis Blenker was just then free from an apprenticeship served in a dull German city, and an adventurous life must necessarily have seemed to him possessed of every charm that fancy could give it; so he became one of the thirty-five hundred, and entered the Bavarian legion in the capacity of a private soldier. Otho, accompanied by the legion, embarked at Brindisi, in the kingdom of the Two Sicilies, January 24th, 1833. And there is our soldier fairly started in life. What destiny could offer higher promise of the romantic than this? And how it must have winged the young German's aspiration to be thus a soldier, afloat on that blue sea, in the train of one on his way to receive a throne, and with his face turned toward Greece, that parent-land of heroism and poesy—that

> "Clime of the unforgotten brave,
> Whose land from plain to mountain-cave
> Was freedom's home or glory's grave!"

Otho and his train arrived in Greece without mishap, and the legion was debarked at Napoli, February 6th, 1833. There seemed a magic in the touch of German feet upon the classic soil. Tumult and schism were universally stilled, and there was a happy calm. It lasted, however, only till midsummer, when Colocotroni, a mountain chief and a universal agitator, began again to make trouble, and formidable combinations against the government appeared among the Maïnotes and Roumeliotes. Against these the Bavarian legion was employed in various directions, and in its ranks young Blenker saw four years of peculiarly hard and almost incessant service. From a private he became sergeant, and upon the disbandment of the corps in 1837 he received with his *congé* the honorary rank of lieutenant. Lieutenancies, it should be remembered, are not thrown around in European countries as we have recently seen them in America. They are the rewards (when bestowed upon men who are in the ranks) only of valuable and efficient service, and they consequently carry with them a legitimate distinction. Thus honored, and, in European eyes, elevated in the social scale, Blenker returned to Worms in 1837. Of course, it was no longer possible to settle in life as a jeweiler, and from Worms he went to Munich, where he attended medical lectures with the view to the adoption of that profession—either to kill or cure he evidently thought his destiny. But his intention toward a profession was relinquished very soon in favor of commerce, and he returned again to Worms, was married, and became established in the wine trade; such was his position when the troubles in 1848 began. His business, hitherto prosperous, then declined, and he was eventually declared bankrupt; but this was not in any sense a commercial failure, and was the inevitable consequence of the stormy times. From its commencement, he was conspicuous in the popular movement. He became commander of the national guard in Worms, and also burgomaster of that city, and upon the actual outbreak of the revolution, he took an energetic part in it, and was of great assistance in the organization of the revolutionary forces. When the revolutionary army was threatened by the imperial army and the Prussians under their Prince, he joined it at the head of a considerable body of men, and shared its subsequent fortunes throughout 1848. Several skirmishes which he had in the next year, with the royalist forces, approach very near the proportions of battles. On May 10th he defeated a corps of the Baden army and made prisoners a number of officers, while many of the royal soldiers joined his own force. Seven days after he occupied Worms, which he abandoned for a useless movement against Landau. Master of Worms for a second time, he left in it three hundred men, and marched into the Palatinate. His three hundred men were driven out the next day by the government troops—while he himself, near to Boblenheim, encountered and defeated, after a hard fight, an equal force of Prussians. He then re-entered Baden, and took the command of that portion of the revolutionary forces destined to cover Carlsruhe, and to sustain Mieroslawski, whose forces occupied the line of the Neckar. After the combat of Durlach, he occupied the posts of Muhlbourg and Knielingen. Driven from these posts, though not without a severe struggle, he lost his last opportunity in the revolution through his failure to seize Baden-Baden, by the posssesion of which, it was thought he could have covered the disastrous retreat of the revolutionists. Upon the departure of Mieroslawski, he joined the forces of Sigel, Mieroslawski's successor. But the popular movement was effectually crushed, and he retired into Switzerland. Throughout his irregular struggle the forces under Blenker's command had behaved remarkably well—and that more was not done with them, was perhaps the fault of their leader, who, in the opportunity afforded, exhibited no conspicuous quality of soldiership, if we except the one (that he unquestionably possessed) of cool and resolute courage.

Blenker was ordered to leave the territory of the Helvetic confederation in September, 1849. He was permitted to travel through France, and embarked at Havre for the United States, where he landed near the end of the year. Arrived here, he purchased a small farm in Rockland county, New York, and began life as a farmer. But his farming did not prove prosperous, and he abandoned it for more active business in New York city, in which he continued until the war began. Then he immediately took the proper steps for the organization of a

9

regiment of his countrymen in New York city, in which he was completely successful, and the regiment received the designation of the eighth regiment of New
York volunteers, or first German rifles. Both this regiment and the German
regiment of Colonel Max Weber were originally, by some confusion, designated
the twentieth regiment. Colonel Blenker's regiment was among those most
promptly organized for the war, and left New York city May 27th, 1861, only
twenty-five days after the promulgation of President Lincoln's call for men to serve
for three years. It had then already attained a fair degree of discipline and considerable proficiency in drill. From New York the regiment proceeded to Washington, where it arrived May 28th, and was quartered in various parts of the city
until June 9th, when it went into camp on Meridian Hill, about two miles from
the capital. During all the period from the first enrolment of his men, Colonel
Blenker labored earnestly to make them perfect in every detail of soldiership;
and when they went into camp, this endeavor was pursued by him even more
rigorously still.

Shortly before the advance to Centreville, Colonel Blenker's regiment was
ordered into Virginia, where, with the twenty-ninth New York, the Garibaldi
Guard, and the twenty-seventh Pennsylvania regiment, it formed the first brigade of the fifth division, and Colonel Blenker was placed in command. Upon
the day when the battle of Bull Run was fought, the fifth division was in reserve, and Blenker's command was formed upon the heights east of Centreville.
Here it continued, necessarily inactive, until the retreat of the United States
forces began, when, at about four, P. M., it was ordered to advance upon the road
from Centreville to Warrenton—an order executed with great difficulty, as the
road was blocked up by baggage-wagons and the whole confusion of the retreat.
Nevertheless, owing to the coolness of the officers and the discipline of the men,
the passage through the village was successfully executed, and the further advance made with admirable precision, and Colonel Blenker took a position
which would have enabled him to prevent the advance of the rebels, and protect
the retreat of the Union forces, had the rebels made any pursuit. Blenker's
own regiment, the eighth, was posted one mile and a half south of Centreville, on
both sides of the road to Bull Run; the twenty-ninth regiment was half a
mile behind the eighth; and the Garibaldi Guard was in reserve in line, behind
the twenty-ninth regiment. While in this position, the regular lines of the brigade were a pleasant sight to the distressed fugitives from the lost field. "The
suffering of a hundred deaths," says a witness of the scene, "would have been as
nothing compared with the torture under which the few brave soldiers writhed,
who were swept along by the maniac hurricane of terror. But suddenly their
spirits were revived by a sight which, so long as God lets them live, they will
never cease to remember with pride and joy. Stretching far across the road,

long before the hoped-for refuge of Centreville was reached, was a firm, un-swerving line of men, to whom the sight of the thousands who dashed by them was only a wonder or a scorn. This was the German rifle-regiment; and to see the manly bearing of their general, and feel the inspiration which his presence gave at the moment, was like relief to those who perish in a desert. At least, then, all was not lost; and we knew that, let our destiny turn that night as it should, there was one man who would hold and keep the fame of the nation un-sullied to the end." And in this position Blenker held his men throughout the evening, and spread a sure protection over the multitude who fled disordered through his columns. Toward eleven o'clock, several squadrons of the enemy's cavalry advanced along the road, and appeared before the outposts of the eighth regiment, but were driven back without difficulty. At midnight the order to re-treat was received, and the brigade moved on to Washington, which it reached in safety nineteen hours after. For these services, Colonel Blenker was com-missioned a brigadier-general of volunteers, August 9th, 1861.

In the various re-arrangements of corps that were made some time after the accession of General M'Clellan to the post of commander-in-chief, Blenker's command swelled to the proportions of a division; and, on the grand review of November 20th, it mustered eleven regiments of infantry, two batteries of artil-lery, and a regiment of mounted riflemen. Although his command was thus as large as the other divisions of the army on the Potomac, various regiments of his countrymen, on their arrival at Washington, desired to be attached to Blen-ker's division. He also desired that all his countrymen should be made subject to a single command, and addressed General M'Clellan upon the subject. General M'Clellan replied that the division was already sufficiently large. To this, Gen-eral Blenker responded in a letter which was probably written in some heat, and the tone of which was not what the etiquette of the service requires. General Marcy, as chief of General M'Clellan's staff, wrote to General Blenker in reproof of his note; and General Blenker immediately penned a resignation of his posi-tion, and, it is said, sent it in, but subsequently withdrew it.

General Blenker is now, therefore, in command of the fifth division of the army of the Potomac. His command extends geographically from the Potomac to the most westerly limit of the national lines in Virginia; and is divided from General M'Dowell's division on the north by a line drawn a little to the south of Fort Runyon and Munson's Hill; and from General Franklin's division on the south by a line drawn a short distance to the north of Alexandria.

FRANZ SIGEL.

NEVER engaged in any battle where the side upon which he fought could fairly claim an unqualified victory; and never engaged in a separate command where he was not compelled to retreat, Franz Sigel yet keeps a sure hold upon public confidence, and a perusal of his career compels the acknowledgment of his thorough soldiership, and his ability as a general. This can only be the result of some real power in the man, for the world—and especially our world —is too fond of success to overlook disaster; and unless fully impressed with the conviction that a better chance than he has hitherto had would show a better result, it would not hesitate to cry down the soldier whose only fault has been an utter want of luck, that great constituent of military fame.

FRANZ SIGEL was born at Zinsheim, in the grand duchy of Baden, November 18th, 1824. His father held the important position of Kreisumtman—the highest magistrate in the county of Bruchsal. Franz received a liberal education, and was graduated from the military school at Carlsruhe, whence he entered the regular army of Baden. Rapid advance is not common in that service, yet the young lieutenant had reached the post of chief-adjutant in the year 1847, and in this perhaps, we may see the benefit of his father's position. But when the revolution broke out in Southern Germany, young Siegel openly sympathized with it and was even said to have been compromised in Struve's premature attempt to revolutionize his native state; through these difficulties he lost his commission in the Badish army. All Germany was at that period divided upon the great question of a central government—with a liberal constitution, and the cashiered lieutenant at once cast his fortunes with the liberal party. He entered the contest with the natural ardor of a young soldier already martyred in what he believed to be the cause of his country and of freedom. Various journals agitated the cause on the part of the liberals, and for these Sigel wrote earnestly against the government, and in favor of a new one. He thus acquired a considerable influence with the people, and became prominent among the leaders of the movement. In March, 1849, a preliminary parliament was held at Frankfort, which issued a call for a National Assembly to meet in May, and to submit a plan of government. Disturbances in Rhenish Bavaria anticipated the action of the assembly thus called, and were denounced by the opponents of the liberal movement, as only the trickery of the agitators, intended to make changes in the government appear more necessary, and to commit the people in advance to whatever revolutionary measures might be brought forward at Frankfort. Prussian soldiers were immediately marched into Rhenish Bavaria. Scarcely had the Prussians moved than the liberalists in the grand duchy of Baden made common cause with those in Rhenish Bavaria, and about twenty thousand persons publicly assembled at Offenburg in Baden, passed a series of resolutions, to the effect that the movement in Rhenish Bavaria should be supported, that the constitution voted by the National Assembly should be acknowledged, and that officers in the army should be chosen by the private soldiers. Many soldiers were in attendance, and one of the resolutions that referred to them secured their adherance. On the same day the fortress of Rastadt was seized by the soldiers of the garrison, and disturbances broke out at Carlsruhe. By ten o'clock that night, the grand duke and his ministers were in full flight, and the state was in the hands of the liberal party A "National Committee" assumed the powers of government. Lieutenant Eichfield was made minister of war, and Lieutenant Sigel became prominent among the young officers whose fortunes were in the movement, and who were ready to organize and lead a popular army. With the state itself there had fallen into the hands of the liberals, seven millions florins in coin, two and a half in paper, and seventy thousand muskets, besides those in the hands of the army. The army numbered seventeen thousand men. Some energetic measures were taken by the new government; but, in accordance with the revolutionary idea, the army was ordered to choose its officers anew. Doubtless, this was the death-blow of the revolutionary cause, for it virtually deprived the state of its army. Discipline was destroyed, and all organization entirely lost. "Soldiers appeared on parade," says an eye-witness, "in what they had indiscriminately plundered from the stores at Carlsruhe. Shakos, helmets, caps, great-coats, frocks, full-dress and undress uniforms, all figured in the same ranks. . . . . Officers and privates, arm-in-arm, and excessively drunk, reeled through the streets." Raw recruits rose to the rank of major in a day, and a similar disproportion between service and position prevailed throughout. Head-quarters were established at Heidelberg, and there Lieutenant Sigel arrived May 19th.

Five days later, a meeting of liberals near the frontier, in Hesse-Darmstadt, was dispersed by the Hessian soldiery, and Lieutenant Sigel was ordered to lead the revolutionary army of Baden across the frontier. Four battalions of the line, with about six thousand volunteers, were reviewed at Heidelberg previous to the march; and Sigel, as commander of the troops, issued a manifesto, in which was set forth the reasons why he prepared to enter the territory of Hesse-Darmstadt. But Mieroslawski, a Pole, who had been called to the chief command, arrived before the troops moved, and Sigel lost this early chance of distinction.

The revolutionary force, between ten and twelve thousand strong, marched May 28th. On the 1st of June, the "National Committee" was superseded by a "Provisional Government"—formed of the same men as the committee had been —and Sigel was made minister of war. From that period he necessarily exercised a controlling influence upon the struggle; but, though no serious blow had yet been struck, the strength of the cause was gone. Bad counsel had prevailed; the army was already ruined; the volunteers who came forward to fight fell into the radical German error, confounded personal with political freedom, and were consequently impossible to control; and the confidence of the people was lost. Moreover, the leaders themselves appeared to have lost faith in the movement. Yet, under the administration of the young minister, a far from contemptible resistance was made to the united imperial and Prussian armies.

Active operations against the revolutionary forces began about the first of June; and an imperial army, under Peucker, advanced from Furth in two columns, and came up with the army under Mieroslawski, near Weinheim, on the 14th. Mieroslawski attacked Peucker's front and right flank, posted in the village of Grossacken, at six, A. M., on the 15th, and obtained some advantage, but was repulsed, though the battle continued till night. Peucker renewed the battle on the 16th, and suffered severely from Mieroslawski's artillery, but drove the latter from his position. Both sides claimed the victory, and Mieroslawski regretted his inability to pursue, through want of cavalry; but each fell back to the position occupied previous to the fight on the 15th.

Peucker was superseded in command of the imperial army by the Prince of Prussia, who proclaimed the grand-duchy of Baden in a state of war, and that all offenders against military law should be tried by court-martial, and, if deemed necessary, punished with death. Mieroslawski withdrew his forces from his position near Weinheim to Waghausel on the Rhine, whither he was followed by the Prince of Prussia, whom he attacked, June 22d. He was again beaten, however, and retreated to the upper Neckar and the region of the Black Forest. Sigel, though minister, was present, and took an active part in these battles. After their victory at Waghausel, the Prussians crossed the Neckar, came up with the revolutionary forces at Ettlingen, beat them again, and drove them across the Murg. Mieroslawski now abandoned the cause and fled, and Sigel assumed the chief command. With his broken and demoralized forces he made a splendid retreat, and reached the fortress of Rastadt without loss of a gun. Here the most considerable portion of the revolutionary army was now left, while Sigel endeavored to rally further resistance in other quarters, and concentrated a force at Salem, in the Badish lake district. But the members of the provisional government were already fugitives, and Rastadt was invested; and, though some further resistance was offered, it was at best but a guerilla warfare, and was soon abandoned by Sigel, who entered Switzerland, July 11th. Driven from the Swiss territory, in common with all other fugitives from Baden, by the decree of the government of the Helvetic confederation, he was compelled to seek a further refuge, and reached the United States in 1850. He took up his residence in New York city, became associated in the conduct of an academy in Market street, and married the daughter of the principal of that academy, Dr. Dulon. He also took an active interest in the volunteer militia organization, and even held the position for some months, under Colonel Schwarzwaelder, of major in the fifth regiment.

In September, 1858, Sigel removed from New York to St. Louis, where he was employed as a teacher in the German-American Academy, when the present war became imminent. Peace had perhaps become *ennuyante* after ten years, and Sigel immediately determined, in the event of war, to take an active part. Known as a soldier of experience, he obtained a colonel's commission, and, upon the first call of the President upon the people, he organized a regiment of his countrymen, which, under the designation of the third Missouri, was incorporated, May 15th, in General Lyon's first Missouri brigade. This regiment was one of those enlisted for three months. Under Sigel's command, it participated in the seizure of Camp Jackson, where, posted with Blair's regiment, and four pieces of artillery, on the ridge to the north of the rebel position, it guarded the main approach to it, and prevented the possibility of assistance being received by the rebels from St. Louis. This movement was effected with a celerity and precision that spoke highly for the degree of discipline to which the regiment had already attained. After the capture of this rebel force, Governor Jackson was known to be very active in the organization of another at Jefferson City, and General Lyon apprehended that the intention was to make a sudden movement upon St. Louis. He therefore posted the several regiments under his command at the various avenues of approach to the city, to guard against this movement, and also to intercept supplies and munitions of war which it was endeavored to send from St. Louis to the rebel governor at the state capital. In discharge of this duty, Colonel Sigel with his regiment was posted to the west of the city, in Lindall's Grove, and performed efficient service there.

Just previous to the battle at Booneville, Mo., rebel military organizations became very active toward the Arkansas border, and Ben M'Culloch was known to be in motion with forces for the assistance of Jackson and Price, then at Jefferson City. Rather to watch, perhaps, than to fight these forces, Colonel Sigel was ordered for active service in the extreme south-western part of Missouri, and left St. Louis with six companies of his regiment on the night of June 11th, followed on the next day by the other four companies. Colonel Salomon's regiment, the fifth, was subsequently added to his command, which also included the various home-guard organizations of the district. Squads of men were detached all along the Pacific railroad, to guard the bridges, and keep open communication; and from Rolla, the terminus of the road, Colonel Sigel marched his force to Springfield, and thence extended his line of operations westward to Sarcoxie. After the battle of Booneville, and when the forces of Jackson and Price were in full retreat toward the Arkansas border, all eyes were turned toward Colonel Sigel, then the only man in a position to intercept them, and news from his command was breathlessly expected from day to day. Throughout the state more was likely to be expected from him then than a calm review of his force would justify; for his whole command numbered less than three thousand men, and his line of operations was nearly three hundred miles in extent. Yet the bulk of his force was gathered to the west of Springfield, for there was evidently the critical point, and toward that point Major Sturgis pressed hurriedly forward with his Kansas men; and with his face turned that way, the earnest Lyon hurried the preparations for his march from Booneville. From Booneville, Jackson had retreated to Lexington, and every day contradictory reports of his movements reached Sigel. Now he had formed a junction with Price, with Rains, with Parsons, or with M'Culloch, and his force was reported at every number from six hundred to ten thousand. Moreover, this united force was represented at various times to be upon every road by which it could possibly reach the Arkansas line. Sigel's duty to watch or intercept this body with such a part of his own command as he could have at any one place, was thus no light one; and still Lyon did not move, and Sturgis was heard from very far away.

Sigel, with only his own regiment, arrived in Sarcoxie on Friday, June 28th, at five P. M., and there learned certainly that Price, with between eight and nine hundred men, was encamped to the south of Neosho, twenty-two miles west of Sarcoxie; and that Jackson's troops, under command of Parsons, and another body, under General Rains, were to the north, near Lamar. He determined to march against Price, near Neosho, and to attack subsequently those to the north. He accordingly marched from Sarcoxie on the morning of the 29th; but, on the same morning, the rebel camp at Neosho was broken up, and the troops there stationed fled. Sigel then ordered the battalion of the fifth regiment, at Mount Vernon, under Colonel Salomons, to join him at Neosho; and as soon as they had arrived, he moved forward, leaving one company in Neosho, and on the evening of the 4th of July encamped on Spring River, one mile to the south-east of Carthage, the county seat of Jasper county. The troops had marched twenty miles that day. Colonel Sigel ascertained that Jackson, with four thousand men, was only nine miles distant, encamped on the prairie. His own force consisted of nine companies of the third regiment, seven companies of the fifth regiment—in all nine hundred and fifty men—with two batteries of artillery, of four field-

13

pieces each. With this force he moved, on the morning of July 5th, to attack the rebels. Dry Fork Creek was passed six miles north of Carthage, and after a further march of three miles, Jackson's force was found drawn up in order of battle, on an eminence which rises gradually from the creek, and is about a mile distant. Jackson's front presented three regiments, one regiment of cavalry being on each wing, and the centre being formed of infantry, cavalry, and two field-pieces; other field-pieces were posted on the wings. The force in this line was computed at two thousand five hundred men. Behind it was a large force in reserve. Colonel Sigel detached one cannon, and an infantry company, to pro- tect his baggage, three miles in the rear, and at about nine, A. M., opened fire with his artillery. The fire was promptly answered, and the rebel cavalry moved for- ward on his flanks, and threatened to turn them. Notwithstanding this move- ment, Colonel Sigel continued his fire until that of the enemy was sensibly weak- ened, when he ordered the guns to be advanced. Captain Wilkins, commander of one of the batteries, at this moment announced that his ammunition was exhausted. Both wings were also engaged with the rebel cavalry, and the loss of the entire baggage became imminent. A retreat toward Dry Fork Creek was accordingly ordered; and at that point, after a junction with the baggage-train, a stand was made for upwards of two hours, and a heavy loss inflicted upon the enemy. Meanwhile, the rebel cavalry had completely surrounded Colonel Sigel's command, and formed a line in his rear, on Buck Branch, a little creek which it was necessary that he should pass. At this point a feint was made toward either flank of the enemy's line, which drew his whole force into the road, and exposed it to the fire of the national artillery. One round was fired, and the infantry charged at double quick, and completely routed these two regiments. From this point the march was undisputed, until Sigel's command reached a ridge to the north of Carthage, on the Springfield road, where the enemy again took position. Here a severe fight occurred, the hardest of the day. The enemy was driven from his position, and the Union force obtained cover in a wood, which rendered the enemy's cavalry for the time useless. After the men were somewhat rested in the wood, the march was continued to Sarcoxie, which they reached at two, A. M., on the 6th. Reliable accounts represented the rebel loss on this day at three hundred and fifty men, while the whole loss in Sigel's command was but thirteen killed and thirty-one wounded.

Soon after the battle near Carthage, the whole Union force in Missouri sub- ject to the command of General Lyon was concentrated at Springfield. While they remained there, the three months for which Colonel Sigel's regiment was enlisted expired, and he began to reorganize it for the war. Inspired by their whole association, and especially by the recent fight, with high admiration of and entire confidence in their colonel, six hundred of his men re-enlisted, and the regiment was soon filled up by recruits from the neighborhood of Springfield and from St. Louis. When, in the beginning of August, General Lyon left Springfield upon his first march in search of the rebel army, Colonel Sigel accompanied him with a battalion of the third regiment, was present at the Dug Spring skirmish, and returned to Springfield with the general.

Lyon determined, on the 9th of August, to attack the rebels in their camp on Wilson's creek, and with this purpose divided his force into two columns: the right he commanded in person, and the command of the left was intrusted to Colonel Sigel. Sigel's division consisted of a battalion of the third regiment, under Lieutenant-Colonel Albert; a battalion of the fifth, under Colonel Salomon —only nine hundred men in the two battalions; six pieces of artillery, and two companies of cavalry of the United States army. It should be remembered that the men of the fifth regiment were on this occasion volunteers in a double sense, as the term of their enlistment had expired eight days before ; and that the third regiment was composed in a great degree of recruits who were imperfectly drilled, and had never been under fire. Moreover, the field-pieces were not served by practiced artillerymen, but by men taken from the infantry regiments. Sigel's command left Camp Fremont, south of Springfield, at sunset on the 9th, and at daybreak on the 10th was within a mile of the south-eastern extremity of the enemy's camp. Here the advance was very slowly and carefully made, and a large number of prisoners was taken before the rebels had discovered the proximity of the Union forces. Four pieces of artillery were planted on a hill in sight of the rebel camp, a line formed to support them, and when the firing announced that Lyon's attack had begun, the four pieces opened a very destructive fire. Under cover of this, the infantry advanced, drove out the enemy, and formed nearly in the centre of his camp ; whereupon the artillery was also moved forward, and, after some minutes, the enemy was driven into the woods in confusion. In order to render all possible assistance to Lyon's attack, Colonel Sigel now advanced still more to the north-west—further, it is said, than had been contemplated in the plan of attack—and even received a very destructive fire from Totten's battery. Taking a position near a farmhouse, he formed his men across a road that he supposed the enemy would follow in retreat ; and meanwhile the firing in Lyon's direction almost entirely ceased, and it was supposed that the attack had been successful. This was the state of affairs at half-past eight o'clock, when it was reported to Colonel Sigel by his skirmishers that "Lyon's men were coming up," along the very road which he had supposed the rebels would take, and the infantry and artillery were notified not to fire on men coming in that direction. Lyon's men were thus momentarily expected, when a strong column of infantry appeared ; two batteries simultaneously opened fire on Sigel's men, and the infantry also. Great confusion spread in the national ranks, and the cry was raised that Lyon's men were firing on them. Order could not be restored in time to avail, and the rebel infantry advanced to within ten paces of Sigel's guns, and killed the horses. Salomon's regiment broke, and could not be rallied; Sigel's also broke, but was partially rallied, and brought away one gun. Thus repulsed, Sigel could only make the best of his way to Springfield, which he did, and there formed a junction with the other column, learned of Lyon's death, and assumed the command as next in rank. Preparations were made the same night for a further retreat, and at daybreak on the 11th the whole command moved toward the Gasconade River, which, contrary to expectation, was reached without a fight. But before that river was passed, some question as to his actual rank was raised; and, though it was known that Sigel had then been confirmed a brigadier-general, the fact that he had not received his commission was insisted upon, and the command was assumed by Major Sturgis, of the United States army, who conducted the retreat to Rolla.

Franz Sigel received his commission as a brigadier-general of volunteers, August 17th. On the 19th he arrived in St. Louis, where he was enthusiastically received by his German fellow-citizens, upon whom his recent achievements had made a great impression. He remained in St. Louis several weeks, conferring with the commander of the department upon the various measures necessary for the march southward of a large force, and left that city to take command of the advance—the largest division of Fremont's army—then posted at Georgetown and Sedalia. He arrived in Sedalia September 28th, and on October 13th marched from that place for Warsaw, "with sufficient force to open the way;" passed the Osage at Warsaw on the 16th, and reached Springfield, to the great joy of its inhabitants, October 27th. Sigel's command was at this time in splendid condition. To all the wants and grievances of his men he gave personal attention, mingled with them on the march and in camp, and cheered them through every difficulty. He was consequently a great favorite, and they were enthusiastically eager to follow him in the actual strife. But while the advance still remained at Springfield, General Fremont was removed from the command, his plan of campaign was abandoned, and Sigel with his brigade retraced his steps to Rolla. New measures were now inaugurated. General Hunter assumed the command, and we hear of activity in every part of the state, upon both sides; and the rebels are roughly handled in several places; Price again advances to the Osage, and again retires; but in all these movements we hear but little of Sigel. And thus it continued for the remainder of October, for November and December; and while all was movement, life, and triumph around him, he fretted in compulsory inactivity, till it seemed that he was forgotten, or that there was an intention to ignore his past services. From this state of affairs a rumor easily spread that it was his intention to resign his commission, and general credence was given to it. "For a long time," said one of his friends, "things have looked as though the intention were to trifle with him. Where he sowed, where he was first in the field and was the first to strike, and while his name rang, like that of Mars, from every German lip throughout the Union, and helped to fill the camps, others are now to reap the harvest."

General Sigel did indeed feel that injustice had been done to him, and that he had been improperly interfered with in his command. Finally, it appeared to him impossible to retain his position under the circumstances and with a proper regard to his self-respect; and on the 31st of December, therefore, he tendered his resignation. General Halleck, to whom the resignation was sent, at St. Louis, did not, it is said, immediately forward it to Washington. General Sigel, when informed of this, reiterated the tender, January 14th, and demanded the immediate dispatch of his letter to head-quarters. He was, however, compelled on January 27th to tender his resignation for a third time, which was not accepted.

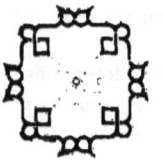

HENRY W. BELLOWS, D. D.

DR. BELLOWS has for many years been quite prominent as a writer and preacher, but of late he has risen to a new and national position as head of the Sanitary Commission, and of course as chief adviser in that great work of saving the health and life of our troops, which is quite as important as leading them to victory. He is still a young man, for one who has accomplished so much. He was born in Boston, June 11th, 1814, thus being under forty-eight years of age. He received his early education there, and completed his preparation for college at the famous Round Hill School at Northampton, Massachusetts, while it was under the charge of George Bancroft and Dr. Cogswell. He entered Harvard College in 1828, and graduated in 1832. Spending the two subsequent years in teaching, part of the time in Louisiana, he returned to Cambridge to study theology at the Divinity School there, and completed his course in 1837. A few months afterward (January 2d, 1838), he was ordained pastor of the First Congregational Church in New York city, where he still continues to labor. His church stood first in Chambers street, where he remained until a new edifice was built for him in Broadway, where Dr. Chapin now preaches; and in a few years, on account of the rapid change in the centre of residences, the present All Souls' Church was erected for him, at the corner of Fourth avenue and Twentieth street.

Dr. Bellows has made his mark upon the age, not only by the boldness of his positions and the fervor of his eloquence, but by prominent acts of executive force. He was the principal originator of the "Christian Inquirer," the Unitarian newspaper of New York, in 1846, and for several years he was chief editor. He was the moving power in the rescue of Antioch College, Ohio, from extinction, and in putting it upon a footing of usefulness and hope. He has been known to the country at large, however, by the original and eloquent sermons, orations, and addresses, that have been put forth from time to time upon topics of popular interest. A volume of twenty or thirty of these productions will make an important chapter of our literary and social history, as well as an excellent illustration of the many-sidedness of the man. The most conspicuous of these were his discourse at Cambridge on the suspense of faith, 1859, and his noted defence of the drama in 1857. This latter was really an act of great bravery; and while his performance was a profound and brilliant one, its heroism was even more memorable.

Probably the most careful studies that he has given to the public are his lectures before the Lowell Institute, Boston, on the "Treatment of Social Diseases," in 1857. These lectures were very patient, practical, and sagacious, and undoubtedly prepared the author for his present task as President of the Sanitary Commission. The organization of this commission was in great part his work; and they who were with him throughout the first struggle of its friends to secure to it a firm foundation, testify to the boundless courage, versatile talent and practical sagacity, with which he carried his point, and won over to his cause the heads of the nation, and discomfited the red-tape procrastinators who are such masters of the art "How not to do it." His labors for nearly a year in this commission have been very great. He has conducted a large correspondence, given many addresses, had personal interviews with important persons, travelled east, west, and south, to inspect the camps and hospitals in person, and actually rendered the service of a major-general in the corps of militant benevolence. Meanwhile, he has kept his ministerial charge, and maintained the high intellectual and devotional character of his pulpit labors.

Dr. Bellows is a versatile man, and, by a necessity of his nature, as well as from the opportunities of his position, he has taken a warm interest in subjects of the most diverse kind. Thus, shortly after astounding the old priesthoods by his defence of the drama before an association of actors, he came out with his famous discourse at Cambridge on the suspense of faith, and alarmed his old friends in freedom and progress with fears lest he were taking the back track, and would be soon at the Vatican, kneeling for the pope's blessing on his penitent head. But they who look to the springs of his convictions discover the interior unity of the man, and can see that he may be a warm champion of a new and purer Church Universal, and be all the more ready to give the beautiful arts, the drama among them, a place within its benediction. We should, perhaps, be sorry to be obliged to reconcile all Dr. Bellows' utterances through a term of years with each other, for he writes and speaks from the spur of the moment, pushing his fiery steed on at full gallop, apparently without looking behind him. Yet it is very remarkable how well his various positions illustrate and complete each other; and even when he runs counter to himself in appearance, as in his attitude at one time as a teacher of transcendentalism, and again as a champion of an authoritative Church, it will be found, as in his recent volume of sermons of various dates, that his course is cumulative, and that he is travelling over different parts of the same great domain, and now ranging in the open pasture and now resting in the safe fold. If, however, he had the same power in setting forth and urging a complete system of truth or practice that he has shown in dealing with specific ideas and measures, he would take a place among the great constructive minds of the age. As yet he has not brought his convictions and powers to bear organically upon his work, and his brilliant thoughts sometimes flash more in lines of impulsive force, like the lightning, than shine together like the constellations. Yet it is not difficult to conceive of him as combining his views, experiences and plans into one method, and bringing his electric power to bear upon some great and permanent work of social or religious construction. He has some great gifts as a religious teacher and organizer; and if he lives twenty years, he ought to do something to meet the great want of our time, which he has so ably set forth, the want of a broad and effective and truly catholic church system, that shall be at once generous and strong. As it is, however, he has done little in this direction; and with gifts that in some respects rival Wesley's or even Loyola's, he has been apparently little ambitious of church influence, and depends mainly upon his rare personal power as preacher for the success of his ministry, without any help from the methods of edification and administration which he so powerfully discusses and advocates as needed to unite and strengthen the generous minds of our day. As yet, he talks catholicity, and practises extreme individualism.

Dr. Bellows is an acute and original thinker, a shrewd observer of men, a lover of the best books, especially of the day, a ready and brilliant writer and eloquent speaker, a cordial friend, a humane and devout Christian. His main gift that marks him above most other men is a certain force of character that gives him direct influence over others. He has contemporaries more learned, more philosophical, more constructive than he, and quite as brilliant in style and eloquent in speech. But no man can carry a given point where enthusiasm and moral power are needed so well as he; and he has a certain princely quality in his temper and presence that gives him remarkable sway. Were he not eminently public-spirited, and full generally of humane purposes, his tone might often seem presuming; but in leading movements he rides his hobby or his knightly steed not for himself, but for the good cause of patriotism, or humanity, or faith; and while the superannuated dignitaries of the faculty, or the staff, or the pulpit, whom he starts from their sleep, may curse him for his insolence, the patriots and philanthropists of the land will honor him as a brave and sagacious reformer, and wish him God-speed in his campaign of mercy and heroism.

These stirring times have evidently had a decided effect on Dr. Bellows' ways of thinking. He has long been a leader in the liberal school of thought, and has given a large part of his life to vindicating the rights of the human soul against ancient prescriptions and priesthoods, dogmas and dignities. In this he has followed in the track of Channing, and sometimes he has approached the extreme individualism of Emerson, and tended to slight the power of positive

14

institutions and constitutional laws. Of late years he has been more conservative, and since his public position has connected him more closely with national affairs, and shown him the difficulty of carrying out abstract ideas, and the importance of uniting men as far as possible upon some standard of authority, he has taken a bold stand with the constitutional party. He is now, as ever, an emancipationist, but he trusts mainly in the power of social and moral causes to free the slave; and, while favoring the rigid enforcement of law against rebel slaveholders, he is for leaving to all loyal states and men their full rights of local jurisdiction under the constitution.

In person, Dr. Bellows carries dignity and suavity, and has an air of experience and age beyond his actual years. At heart, however, he is very young, and can be as merry and amusing as any of the solid old fathers of the Church, like Luther and his compeers, who thought an honest laugh sometimes no unseemly preparation for a sincere prayer. Perhaps the doctor's prayers are the best thing that he does; and the fair inference is, that if so much unction drops so readily from his lips, there must be a deep fountain within. It is well that he is thus a devout man, and earnest to subdue his will to the Supreme will; for his temperament is of the impulsive, commanding kind, such as tends, not from calculation but from instinct, to take the lead, and to submit with great difficulty to any other position. If the army has thus lost a brave and somewhat exacting general, or the Senate a brilliant and imperious leader, the Church has gained a commanding preacher, and humanity a fearless and faithful friend.

JOHN TROUT GREBLE.

A MONG the events which give a peculiar sadness to the early history of the
war, was the ill-advised attempt to drive the enemy from Great Bethel, on
the 10th of June, 1861, and especially the fall of the gallant young artillery officer, the sacrifice of whose own life on that occasion saved the main body of the
attacking force from entire destruction.

The memory of this brave soldier is now a part of his country's inheritance.
His name will hereafter find an honorable mention in every history of the great
North American republic. The following brief sketch of his life will show that
the deeds which made his end illustrious, even amid defeat, were not the result
of chance, but the legitimate fruits of right principles and of long and patient
culture.

JOHN TROUT GREBLE, the oldest son of Edwin and Susan Virginia Greble,
was born in Philadelphia, January 19th, 1834. The traditions of the family
were all patriotic. His great-grandfather on the paternal side, Andrew Greble, a
native of Saxe Gotha, who came to this country in 1742, and settled permanently
in Philadelphia, enlisted warmly in the cause of the War of Independence. He,
with his four sons, joined the American army, and fought at the battles of
Princeton and Monmouth. The ancestors of Lieutenant Greble on the mother's
side were from Wales. They settled in Philadelphia in 1689. Though belonging to the Society of Friends, and professing the principles of non-resistance, they
also espoused actively the cause of independence; and two of them, Isaac Jones
and William Major, great-grandfathers of Lieutenant Greble, were in the continental army.

The earliest aspirations of young Greble, so far as they are known, were all
in keeping with these early traditions of the family. Though living in a home
where all the avocations and interests were peaceful—though delicate in physical
constitution, and possessed of a singular gentleness of disposition and manners,
which followed him through life—he yet among his earliest dreams fondly contemplated the career of a soldier; and when the time for decision came, he made
a soldier's life his deliberate choice.

In tracing the history of one who has given to the world proofs of goodness, wisdom, and valor, it is instructive and interesting to know the influences
which contributed to the formation of his character. No formative influences

compare with those which cluster around one's home. A man's father, mother, brothers and sisters, beyond all other human agencies, help to make him what he is. No one could have had even a passing acquaintance with young Greble, without feeling an assured conviction that the home which had nurtured him was the abode of the gentler virtues. Next to home, in its influence upon the character, is the school. In early childhood, Greble attended for a short time a private school kept by a lady, where he learned the first rudiments of knowledge. With this exception, all his education, outside of his home, was received in public schools; first in those of his native city, and afterward in that of the general government at West Point. He entered the Ringgold Grammar School of Philadelphia at the age of eight, and remained there four years. At the age of twelve having passed a successful examination, he was admitted to the Central High School. There he remained another four years. Having completed the course in that institution, he graduated with distinction in June, 1850, receiving the degree of bachelor of arts at the early age of sixteen.

Up to this point, his education had been conducted without reference to a military career. It had been his father's expectation, in due time, to receive him as a partner in his own business; but when the time for selecting a profession drew near, he was so clear and decided in his preferences, that his parents wisely determined not to thwart him. The decision, when made known, created some surprise in the mind of the principal of the High School, between whom and himself relations of more than usual kindness had grown up. There was nothing in the appearance or manners of the youth to point him out to the mind of an instructor as one likely to choose the life of a soldier; there was nothing in his disposition in any way combative or belligerent. He was never known to have a quarrel with a schoolmate. He was gentle almost to softness; pacific even to the yielding of his own will and pleasure, in almost every thing that did not imply a yielding of principle. His military taste seemed to be the result of some peculiar inclination of his genius, leading him, as if by instinct, to his true vocation.

The Honorable L. C. Levin, at that time representative in Congress from Mr. Greble's district, having heard of the young man's desire for a military life, and knowing him to be a youth of fine promise, generously and without solicitation, tendered him a cadetship at West Point. Having received the appointment, he entered the academy in June, 1850, the very day but one after his graduation at the High School. The letter of recommendation which he bore with him to the professors of the academy is thought worthy of record here, because it shows the impression he had made on the minds of his earlier instructors, and because he himself always set a peculiar value upon it as coming from one whom he had learned to love almost as a father:

"CENTRAL HIGH SCHOOL, PHILADELPHIA, *June 11th*, 1850.
" *To the Professors of the Military Academy at West Point.*
"GENTLEMEN : Mr. John T. Greble having been appointed a cadet in your institution, I beg leave to commend him to your kind consideration. As he has been for four years under my care, I may claim to know him well; and I recommend him as a young man of good abilities and amiable disposition; punctual in the discharge of duty, and seldom off his post. In these whole four years he has lost, I believe, but two days—one from sickness, and one to attend the funeral of a classmate. He leaves the High School with the unqualified confidence and respect of every professor in it. \
" Your obedient servant,   JOHN S. HART, *Principal.*"

The career of the young cadet was not marked by any thing worthy of especial record. At West Point, as at the High School, his habits were studious, while his amiable manners and soldierly conduct won for him the friendship of his fellow-cadets and of his professors. After graduating with credit in June, 1854, he at once entered the army, and was attached to the second regiment of artillery as brevet second-lieutenant. He was ordered first to Newport barracks, and shortly afterward to Tampa, Florida, where part of his regiment was stationed, to keep the Seminoles in order. While there, he made the acquaintance of the celebrated chief Billy Bowlegs. The latter took a great fancy to the young lieutenant, and, in testimony of his admiration, promised him that, in case of war between the Seminoles and the whites, the lieutenant should not be slain by any of his young warriors, but should have the honor of being killed by the chief, Billy Bowlegs himself!

The arduous duties detailed to Lieutenant Greble, in scouring the everglades and swamps in search of the Indians, brought on a violent fever. The disease not yielding to medical skill, he was ordered home, with the hope that a change of climate might effect a cure. From the effects of this illness he never entirely recovered. Having remained with his parents for a short time, and before his health was really sufficiently established to justify a return to active duty, he again took charge of a detachment of recruits, and proceeded with them to Fort Myers, in Florida, in March, 1856. He remained in Florida until December of that year, engaged in the same uninviting duties which had already imperilled his health—searching swamps and everglades for stealthy and vindictive foes, who were always near, yet never to be seen by a superior force; hiding themselves in the water, with a leaf to cover the head, or wrapped up in the dark moss of a cypress or live-oak, ready to shoot any unwary white man who might be so unfortunate as to cross their hiding-place. The young lieutenant escaped at length the perils of this inglorious warfare, and was transferred to a field of duty less dangerous and of much more importance.

15

In December, 1856, at the request of the professors of West Point, the secretary of war ordered Lieutenant Greble to report himself at the post for academic duty. He was made assistant to the Reverend John W. French, D. D., chaplain of the post, and professor of ethics. It became the duty of the assistant professor to instruct the cadets in *international and constitutional law*, and in the constitution of the United States. He applied himself at once to the task with his characteristic constancy and zeal. Finding that the confinement and sedentary life incident to his new duties were impairing his health, he twice made application to be placed again in active service; but the request was not granted, and he remained in that position until the end of the term for which he had been appointed, a period of four years.

The comparatively tame and inactive life at the academy was not without its compensations to the ardent young soldier. In the refined and cultivated domestic circle which graced the home of Professor French, the assistant found congenial society. On the 4th of August, 1858, he was married to Sarah B., eldest daughter of Professor French. Two of the happiest years of his life followed this union. In October of 1860, Lieutenant Greble was relieved from duty at West Point, and ordered to join his company at Fortress Monroe. His wife and children joined him in November. In anticipation of their coming, he had fitted up the homely apartments appropriated to their use, in the casemates of the fortress, with that exquisite delicacy of taste which was one of his prominent characteristics, so that the grim old walls looked quite gay and picturesque when the youthful family were assembled beneath their shadow.

About this time a circumstance occurred, of no great magnitude, perhaps, but worthy of record as showing Lieutenant Greble's generosity of disposition, as well as his sincere, unostentatious loyalty to the government. An officer, who had been his friend and classmate, had resigned his commission, with the view of joining the ranks of the rebel army. The lieutenant, hearing of this circumstance, sought his friend, and remonstrated with him with such force and urgency as to induce a reconsideration. But a difficulty existed. It would be necessary for his friend to go immediately to Washington, and perhaps remain for some time attending to this business, and he had not the means necessary for the journey. Lieutenant Greble had himself barely enough for his family expenses. Nevertheless he determined that want of funds should not ruin his friend, and occasion the loss of a skilled officer to the government. He was fond of books, of which he had a fine collection; and he was about to add to their number a handsome copy of the "Encyclopædia Britannica," having already ordered the work. But he now countermanded the order, and, putting the sum which the work would cost into the hands of his friend, saw him off with joy on his repentant errand.

The domestic happiness of Lieutenant Greble was soon to be interrupted, never to be renewed. In April, 1861, the whole nation, at the call of their patriotic President, sprang suddenly to arms. Large numbers of troops were expected at Fortress Monroe, and of course all the quarters would be needed for their accommodation. Orders were given, therefore, for the women and children to be removed. On the 19th of April, Mrs. Greble, with her two little ones and nurse, left the fortress for Philadelphia. They arrived at Baltimore in the midst of that fearful riot in which the soldiers of Massachusetts and Pennsylvania were fired upon by the mob. All means of conveyance northward being cut off, the unprotected family made their way westward through Maryland and Virginia to Ohio, and thence, by way of Pittsburg, finally reached Philadelphia in safety.

On the 26th of May, Lieutenant Greble was detailed with twenty-two regulars to proceed to Newport News as master-of ordnance, and to instruct the volunteers, who numbered about three thousand, in artillery practice. An officer on General Butler's staff, in a letter written after Lieutenant Greble's death, gives the following account of his conduct at Newport News:

"I found him with his tent pitched nearest the enemy, in the most exposed position, one of his own selecting, living and sleeping by his gun—the gun which he used so faithfully a few hours later. His pleasant, open face, and kind, gentle manner, won me from the first. We exchanged many little courtesies, and I was his guest and the object of his thoughtful and kind attentions. I never met with a more high-minded, honorable gentleman. If, in this rebellion, we met with no other loss, one such man is enough to render it an execration throughout all time. He was intent on robbing war of half its horrors, and was deeply interested in and co-operated with me manfully in plans for checking the depredations about the camp at Newport News. In this he displayed a firmness and moral courage that satisfied one of his manly character, and made a strong impression on the general. He spoke of the possibility, even probability, of his speedy fall, with perfect coolness, and seemed entirely prepared to meet all the dangers of sustaining the flag. I need not say to you how proud I should have been to have stood by his side on that fatal day; to have seconded his efforts; to have aided his friends in bringing off his body, as I am sure he would have brought mine."

The following extract from a letter to his wife, written from Newport News, Sunday, June 9th, the very day before his death, shows how calm and serene was his mind in the midst of the fearful excitement around him:

"It is a delightful Sunday morning. It has a Sabbath feeling about it. If you had lost the run of the week, such a day as to-day would tell you it was the Sabbath. The camp is unusually quiet; and its stillness is broken by little except the organ-tones of some of the Massachusetts men, who are on the beach, singing devotional airs. Last Sabbath the men were in the trenches. To-day is their first day of rest. A great deal of work has been done during the past week, under unfavorable circumstances—rainy days. With very little additional labor, our whole line of intrenchments will be finished. There is a little trimming off to be done, and a magazine to be built; a little earth to be thrown up in front of some heavy columbiads that have been mounted, and some storehouses to be built. But enough has been done to allow the rest to be completed by general details, and to give a chance for drilling. Colonel Phelps has appointed me ordnance officer of the post. We do not fear an attack; the position is too strong. I hear that Davis has given the federal troops ten days to leave the soil of Virginia. The time is nearly up, but we are not quite ready to move away. . . . . I hope that I may be given courage and good judgment enough to do well my duty under any circumstances in which I may be placed. As far as I can see, there is not much danger to be incurred in this campaign at present. Both sides seem to be better inclined to talking than fighting. If talking could settle it by giving the supremacy forever to the general government, I think it would be better than civil war. But that talking can settle it, I do not believe."

Little did Lieutenant Greble suppose, while writing this letter, that an expedition was then planning, to move in a few hours, and that he would be sent with it. As ordnance officer of the post, and the only regular artillery officer there, he did not expect to be ordered on an expedition, leaving the armament in charge of those not qualified to use it if attacked by the enemy. But such was the case. An expedition against Great Bethel had been determined on; and, although well qualified to take command of it, he was not even made aware of it until a few hours before the order was given to march. When informed of the plan of attack, he said to a brother-officer: "This is an ill-advised and badly-arranged movement. I am afraid that no good will come of it. As for myself, I do not think I shall come off the field alive."

Unwell and at midnight, and with these gloomy forebodings on his mind, he did not hesitate, but with the promptitude of a soldier made preparations to obey the orders of his superior. The only available guns at Newport News were two small six-pounders, and for these he had no means of transportation. He succeeded, however, in borrowing two mules to draw one of the pieces, and he detailed one hundred volunteers to draw the other. With eleven regular artillerymen to serve the guns, he started off with the rest of the forces on the expedition at night, to attack an enemy of whom no reconnoissance had been made, either in regard to their force or position.

The particulars of this ill-starred expedition are but too well known, and need not be repeated here. Lieutenant Greble, being considerably in advance of the main body, with one of his guns, heard firing in the rear from the other

gun, which was in charge of his sergeant. Knowing that there could be no enemy there, he galloped back, and found, as he had suspected, our own forces by a
fatal mistake firing on each other. He immediately ordered the firing to cease,
and when he saw the dead and wounded around him, exclaimed that he would
rather have been shot himself than that such a disaster and disgrace should have
befallen our arms. The result of this fatal error it was easy to conjecture. The
enemy were notified of the approach of the federal troops, and, hastily retiring
from Little Bethel, which it was intended to surprise, prepared for a vigorous
defence of their works at Great Bethel.

Order being restored, the attacking party again began to move forward.
Lieutenant Greble returned to his gun, which was in the advance with Duryea's
Zouaves. As they approached Great Bethel, a concealed battery opened fire
upon them. Lieutenant Greble immediately unlimbered his guns, and took
position in the open road, about one hundred and fifty yards from the enemy,
firing his guns alternately, and moving them forward at each discharge, until he
was within one hundred yards of their battery. In this firing, he sighted the
pieces each time himself, remaining as cool as if on parade. So accurate and
effective was his firing, that he succeeded in silencing all of their guns but one, a
rifled cannon. The Zouaves, and Bendix's regiment, by whom he was supported,
were lying close to the ground in the woods, waiting the order to storm the enemy's work; but no general was to be found, to give the order. In the other part
of the field our troops had been repulsed, and were in full retreat. It was a
critical and awful moment. There, in full view of the enemy, and within a hundred yards of their intrenchments, stood this young artillerist with his two guns
and but eleven men, keeping the entire hostile force at bay, and by his cool intre-
pidity and skill preventing a general rush upon the retreating ranks. For two
whole hours he kept up his fire, and whenever the enemy attempted a sortie,
drove them back with a shower of grape. One of his guns, having expended all
its ammunition but a single discharge of grape, was ordered into the rear; and
the volunteers, who were to have been his support, were scattered by the enemy's
grape and shell, so that he was left with but one gun and five men. Still the
brave artillerist held his ground. Seeing the battle virtually lost, an officer went
to him and begged him to retreat, or at least to *dodge* as the others did. His
reply was characteristic: "I NEVER DODGE! *When I hear the bugle sound a retreat, I will leave, and not before.*" Not many minutes after these noble words
were spoken, as he was standing by his gun, a ball from the rifled cannon before
mentioned struck him on the right side of the head, when he fell, exclaiming,
"O my God!" and immediately expired.

Thus ended the earthly career of one of the most promising officers in our
national service. His death, just at the time when courage, patriotism, and mili-
16

tary skill were most needed, was a public calamity, and was mourned as such. During the whole of the engagement, his conduct was the admiration of all who saw him. An officer, who was in a position to observe him, remarked: "He kept up during the entire action a galling and successful fire upon the enemy's battery; and, although grape, shell, and solid shot rained all around him, he was as quiet and gentle in manner and spirit as if in a lady's drawing-room." *He never, under any circumstances, was otherwise.*

Upon the fall of Lieutenant Greble, the guns were abandoned, and the whole remaining force retreated. But Lieutenant-Colonel Warren and Captain Wilson, rallying a few men, placed the body of the brave young officer on the gun which he had served so well, and brought them safely off to Newport News. On reaching Fortress Monroe, the body was placed in a metallic coffin, which had been procured for the purpose by the officers at the fortress, and was thence sent by boat to his friends at Philadelphia.

The narrative of this fatal battle leaves no doubt that Lieutenant Greble deliberately sacrificed his own life to save the lives of a large number of his countrymen. His practised eye saw at a glance the position of affairs; he saw our forces defeated and in full retreat, and an exultant foe eager to pursue and cut them to pieces. Once, indeed, they made the attempt. As soon as he saw them outside of their intrenchments, he quickly remarked to an officer of the Zouaves, "Now I have something to fire at; see how they will scamper!" Deliberately aiming his gun at them, loaded with grape, he discharged it full among them. So precise was the shot, that they instantly disappeared behind their intrenchments, and were not seen a second time. Had Lieutenant Greble retreated, or "dodged," as he was requested to do, the effect would have been to intimidate the few troops that remained with him, and to allow the enemy to cut off the retreat.

Lieutenant-Colonel Warren, who was with him in this action, bears the following testimony to Lieutenant Greble's conduct: "I was near him during much of the engagement between the two forces, and can testify to his undaunted bravery in the action, and to the skill and success with which his guns were served. *His* efficiency alone prevented our loss from being thrice what it was, by preventing the opposing batteries from sweeping the road along which we marched; and the impression which he made on the enemy deterred them from pursuing our retreating forces, hours after he had ceased to live."

In his pocket was found a paper, written apparently after he had started on this ill-fated expedition. It was scrawled hastily in pencil, and intended for his young wife. It was in these words: "May God bless you, my darling, and grant you a happy and peaceful life. May the good Father protect you and me, and grant that we may live happily together long lives. God give me strength, wisdom, and courage. If I die, let me die as a brave and honorable man; let no stain of dishonor hang over me or you. Devotedly and with my whole heart, your *husband.* What a priceless heir-loom must that scrawled paper be to the widowed mother and her babes! A letter, also found in his possession, ran thus: "It is needless, my son, for me to say to you, be true to the stars and stripes. The blood of Revolutionary patriots runs in your veins, and it must all be drawn out before you cease to fight for your country and its laws." So wrote a loyal father to a loyal son, not many days before that bloody 10th of June. Well might the native city of such a sire and such a son ask as a privilege that the body of the young hero be laid in state in the Hall of Independence!

Lieutenant Greble was buried in the beautiful Woodland cemetery, to which place his remains were escorted by the city authorities, the faculty and students of the High School, a large body of military and naval officers, and an immense concourse of citizens. The character of this young man stands out so clearly in his life, that it needs no separate delineation. It was thus beautifully summed up on the occasion of his funeral, by his pastor, the Rev. Dr. Brainerd:

"Few have passed to the grave whose whole life could better bear inspection, or who presented fewer defects over which we have need to throw a mantle of charity. In his family circle, in the Sunday-school, in the High School where he graduated, as a cadet at West Point, and as an officer in the service of his country, up to the very hour when he bravely fell, he has exhibited a life marked by the purest principles and the most guarded and exemplary deportment. In his nature he was modest, retiring, gentle, of almost feminine delicacy, careful to avoid wounding the feelings of any, and considerate of every obligation to all around him. Indeed, such was his amiability, modesty, and delicacy of temperament, that we might almost have questioned the existence in him of the sterner virtues, had not his true and unshrinking courage in the hour of danger stamped him with an heroic manliness. In this view of qualities seemingly antithetical, we discover that beautiful symmetry in his character which marks him as a model man of his class."

Among the many official testimonials to the services and the worth of Lieutenant Greble, none would seem to form a more fitting conclusion to this brief memoir than the following:

"At a meeting of the officers of the army at Fortress Monroe, Virginia, on the 11th of June, the following resolutions were adopted relative to the lamented death of John T. Greble, late a first-lieutenant of the second regiment United States artillery, who was killed in battle at County Creek, near this post, on the 10th instant:

"*Resolved,* That the heroic death of this gallant officer fills us all with admiration and regret. Standing at his piece, in the open road, in front of the enemy's battery, till shot down, he served it with the greatest coolness and most undaunted courage.

"*Resolved*, That, while deploring his untimely end, and feeling that his loss to his country is great, and to his family and friends irreparable, still a death so glorious can but tend to lighten the burden of grief to all.

"*Resolved*, That, as a mark of respect to the memory of the deceased, the officers of the army stationed at this post wear the usual badge of mourning for thirty days.

"*Resolved*, That a copy of the foregoing resolutions be furnished to his family.

"J. DIMICK, *Colonel U. S. A.*"

NATHANIEL PRENTISS BANKS.

AS bobbin-boy, machinist, editor, lawyer, and representative, studious, energetic, and aspiring; as Congressman, and governor of his native state, statesmanlike and comprehensive; as major-general, clear, earnest, and practical —the life of N. P. Banks exhibits a career peculiarly American in every feature, and is well worthy of study by the American people themselves as a "representative life," and also by all who have any desire to understand that riddle of all foreign writers, "the American character."

NATHANIEL PRENTISS BANKS was born in Waltham, Massachusetts, January 30th, 1816. Waltham was even then a busy place, and the roar of engines and the whirr of looms and spindles were the familiar circumstances of daily life to its people. Nathaniel was the son of an overseer in a cotton factory; and when he had years enough—a very few suffice—he became himself a "bobbin-boy" under his father's direction. Some few months' early attendance at a common school had instilled into him, however, a thirst for knowledge: and all his hours "not occupied in the factory were devoted to the grave and important studies of history, political economy, and the science of government." From the factory he went to the forge, and learned the machinist's trade. Literary aspirations came upon him in connection with the representations of a dramatic company formed among his associates, with whom he played the principal parts with great success; he lectured before lyceums, temperance societies, and political assemblages; became editor of the village paper of his native place, and subsequently of a paper at Lowell, in which he advocated the principles of the Democratic party. Through this means he entered somewhat advantageously upon the field of politics, and received an office, under the Polk administration, in the Boston custom-house. For six years he was a candidate for a seat in the Massachusetts legislature, and was defeated every successive year; but in the seventh year, 1848, he was elected representative for Waltham. His first speech, delivered February 23d, 1849, was on the presentation of certain resolutions on the slavery question; and its purport was, that the Democratic party, in the extension of territory, was not influenced by any desire for the extension of slavery. A wide publicity was given to this speech, and the Democrats of Massachusetts were so impressed by it, that Mr. Banks was recognized as a leader in that party. Honors followed fast. In 1850, he was simultaneously elected to the state senate by the Democracy of Middlesex county, and to the house by his constituents of Waltham. He decided to remain in the house, and was chosen speaker by a large majority on the first ballot. He held this position for two successive sessions. Upon the rolls of the house, for his first year in it, Mr. Banks is entered as a machinist, but in the next year as a lawyer.

In 1852, Mr. Banks was elected to Congress, by an affiliation of the Democrats of his district with the American party, or "Know-Nothings." Upon this canvass the American party was very largely in the majority, and Mr. Banks "avowed his sentiments freely and fully." In the summer of 1853, he was chosen president of the convention called to revise the constitution of Massachusetts. Apparently he had been mistaken in the Democratic party, for he soon transferred his allegiance to the new Republican organization. He was twice re-elected to the national House of Representatives, and served in the thirty-third, the thirty-fourth, and part of the first session of the thirty-fifth Congress. He very strongly opposed the Nebraska-Kansas bill, and argued against it that wherever the government obtained the right to acquire territory, there they got the right to control it. Mr. Banks also came somewhat conspicuously before the country by the part he took in the debate brought on by a resolution in reference to the society of "Know-Nothings," as to whether or no the pope claimed a temporal power over the members of the Roman Catholic Church.

Upon the meeting of the thirty-fourth Congress, parties were pretty well broken up and complicated, and a great difficulty was found in the choice of a Speaker. For nine weeks the organization of the House was delayed by the obstinacy of party men. Finally, it was determined that the recipient of a plurality of votes should be declared Speaker; and, in accordance with this rule Mr. Banks was chosen to the position. Mr. Banks presided over the deliberations of the House with marked ability and fairness; or, in the words of a Southern member, he "stood so straight, that he almost leaned over to the other side." On the adjournment of Congress, a vote of thanks was passed, upon the acceptable manner in which he had discharged the difficult duties of his position.

In 1856, Mr. Banks was elected governor of his native state, and resigned his seat in the House on the 24th of December. To his new position he did such honor, that he was re-elected in 1857, and again in 1858. During three terms he administered the government of the state of Massachusetts with eminent wisdom, and finally retired from that position crowned with the high respect of his fellow-citizens of all parties throughout the state; a more striking example than any other chapter of our American history furnishes, of the dignity and honor to which native energy and genius may attain.

Soon after the expiration of his third gubernatorial term, Mr. Banks determined to abandon the field of politics, and with that view removed from his native state to that of Illinois, where he became associated in the conduct of a railroad. In that sphere he continued until the war actually broke out, when he again became "a public man."

He was appointed a major-general in the United States army, May 30th, 1861, and his appointment was confirmed by the Senate on the 3d of August. Major-Generals M'Clellan and Fremont were confirmed on the same day. Previous to his confirmation (June 10th), General Banks was ordered to the command of the department of Annapolis, with his head-quarters at Baltimore. In this command he superseded General Cadwallader, who was appointed to a division destined to co-operate with General Patterson toward Harper's Ferry. Upon General Banks's accession to the command at Baltimore, the treasonable element of the population there, while believed to be very active in the furtherance of schemes for revolt, was certainly very quiet. Butler had fairly scotched the serpent of secession in that city; but under the lax rule of Cadwallader, it had revived. Yet the leaders were prudent, and the transference of the command to a new officer was a sufficient indication that the government was dissatisfied with the easy manner in which they had been dealt by, and they became cautious. But on June 27th they were surprised, and the whole people of the loyal states gratified, by an energetic act of the new commander. At three, A. M., on that day, George P. Kane, marshal of police of Baltimore, was arrested at his house, and imprisoned in Fort M'Henry. In explanation of this act, General Banks issued on the same day a proclamation, superseding Marshal Kane and the board of police, in which he said: " I desire to support the public authorities in all appropriate duties . . . . and in every municipal regulation and public statute consistent with the constitution and laws of the United States and of Maryland. But unlawful combinations of men, organized for resistance to such laws, that provide hidden deposits of arms and ammunition, encourage contraband traffic with men at war with the government, and, while enjoying its protection and privileges, stealthily await opportunity to combine their means and forces with those in rebellion against its authority, are not among the recognized or legal rights of any class of men, and cannot be permitted under any form of government whatever. Such combinations are well known to exist in this department. . . . The chief of police is not only believed to be cognizant of these facts, but in contravention of his duty, and in violation of law, he is, by direction or indirection, both witness and protector to the transactions and the parties engaged therein. Under such circumstances, the government cannot regard him otherwise than as the head of an armed force hostile to its authority, and acting in concert with its avowed enemies." For these reasons, Marshal Kane was superseded and held a prisoner; and Colonel Kenly, of the first Maryland regiment, was appointed provost-marshal of the city of Baltimore, "to superintend and cause to be executed the police laws." Against this action of General Banks the board of police protested, and pronounced it "an arbitrary exercise of military power, not warranted by any provision of the constitution or laws of the United States." They declared also that there was a suspension of the police law, and that the men of the police force were off duty, and thus in retaliation virtually invited a reign of lawlessness. General Banks, in response to this protest, published a letter of instruction to Marshal Kenly, by which he required him "to take especial notice that no opinion, resolution, or other act of the late board of commissioners, can operate to limit the effective force of the police law, or to discharge any officer engaged in its execution." Yet the police board, though thus superseded and dissolved by the military commandant, "continued their sessions daily, refused to recognize the officers and men selected by the provost-marshal for the protection of the city, and held subject to their orders the old police force, a large body of armed men, for some purpose not known to the government, and inconsistent with its peace and security." For the preservation of the public peace, therefore, General Banks caused the arrest, on July 1st, 1861, of all the members of the police board, whose head-quarters were found upon examination to resemble "in some respects a concealed arsenal;" and to anticipate any action of their adherents, he at the same time moved a portion of the force under his command, hitherto encamped beyond the city limits, into the city. On the 10th of July, General Banks appointed a permanent police marshal in the place of Colonel Kenly, and, trouble being no longer feared from the seces. sion plotters, ordered the military occupation to cease, and the regiments to occupy their former positions in the suburbs. Complete tranquillity was thus once again established in Baltimore.

Major-General Patterson, of the Pennsylvania volunteers, in command in the Valley of Virginia, was honorably discharged by general order, his term of service being expired, on July 19th. On the same day, General John A. Dix, of the United States army, was ordered to relieve General Banks in the command at Baltimore, and General Banks was ordered to assume command of the army under Patterson. His department was designated the department of the Shenandoah, with its head-quarters in the field. General Banks reached Harper's Ferry and assumed the command of his department, July 25th. This army, when the battle of Bull Run was fought, had numbered fourteen thousand effective men. But it was composed, in the greater part, of the Pennsylvania volunteers, enlisted for three months, whose terms expired about the period that General Banks was placed in command. He was thus left with only the skeleton of an army, to cover the approach to Washington most favorable for the rebels, and to hold in check all that portion of the rebel force which had not accompanied General Johnson to Manassas previous to the battle at Bull Run.

Immediately on his assumption of the command, General Banks withdrew his troops from Harper's Ferry to the Maryland side of the Potomac, and formed his camp in a strong position under the Maryland Heights, and near to Sandy Hook. There his force was rapidly organized, and increased by the addition of well-disciplined regiments, until it amounted in all to about twenty-five thousand men; and in this position he continued, still occupied with the organization and discipline of his force, up to the movement into Virginia, March, 1862.

Early in May, 1861, when the President had just called out seventy-five thousand men for three months, and long before the country at large realized the magnitude of the rebellion, Mr. Banks, then a simple citizen of Chicago, expressed a very strong opinion of the inadequacy of the measures taken by the government to put down the revolt. His words then spoken, and subsequently published by the "Chicago Tribune," are as follows:

"This rebellion cannot be put down by the force which the government has now called out. Seventy-five thousand militia will prove wholly inadequate to restore peace to the country. The government, and, he feared, the people of the loyal states, immensely underrated the strength and means which the rebel chiefs can command. This is a rebellion of the slave-power against a republican form of government. That political element which has been strong enough to rule this nation for fifty years, cannot be reduced to subjection to the constitution by a few regiments of militia. Before this gigantic slaveholders' conspiracy can be crushed, it will tax to the utmost the power and endurance of the nation. The people will have to put forth an effort which has no parallel in modern times. He regarded this as the most formidable as well as atrocious rebellion which has occurred since the middle ages. The Sepoy insurrection was no circumstance to it, either in strength or wickedness. The Sepoys did not revolt for the purpose of strangling free government and setting up a slave despotism, as the authors of the secession rebellion have done.

"The Sepoys were reduced to obedience in a few months by less than eighty thousand British troops. Four times that many will not suffice to crush out the slaveholders' revolt against the Union. If he was at the head of public affairs, he would call out five hundred thousand men for the war. He would charter every merchant steamer and ship fit for naval service. As soon as the army was equipped, and prepared to march, he would start one column of one hundred and fifty thousand men from Washington to Richmond. Simultaneously, he would move another column of one hundred thousand Western men down the Mississippi, to reach Memphis by the time the Eastern army got to Richmond. He would send a division of fifty thousand men from Louisville to Nashville, to

17

support and protect the Union men of central and eastern Tennessee, and the mountain country of Georgia, Alabama, and North Carolina. Before these columns moved, he would fit out an expedition by sea, and place fifty thousand soldiers aboard the fleet, to hover along the Southern coast from Charleston to Galveston. This would keep the rebels at home in the coast states, as they would be in constant dread of a visit to every port, not knowing where the fleet might land the army. This force on shipboard, Mr. Banks thought, would compel to remain in their own states four times the men in the expedition. It would be a movable column, which, by the aid of wind and steam, might be off Charleston to-day, and land at Savannah to-morrow. Hence its power and efficiency.

"The remaining one hundred and fifty thousand troops he would distribute in divisions at Washington, New York, St. Louis, Baltimore, and other points, to act as reserves and supports wherever the exigencies of the campaign might most need them. He would keep recruiting offices open wherever a regiment had been raised, to fill up the vacancies in the ranks caused by battle or sickness. He would call upon the people to organize a national home guard of half a million men, to take care of traitors in their midst, and to put their shoulders to the wheel for a final effort, if it were found that the first half-million were not able to crush out the foul rebellion.

"He calculated that Richmond, Nashville, and Memphis, could be occupied before the frosts of autumn, and that during the winter campaign the two main armies would move southward—one along the Atlantic slope, and the other down the Mississippi. By next spring, he thought, the stars and stripes might be waving over the Crescent city, and even Montgomery, the then capital of the rebels.   ᴵ

"When asked how he would procure the money necessary to equip and support so vast an army, he promptly replied: 'Open a national loan, as the Emperor Napoleon did, and appeal to the patriotism of the whole people; take all sums offered, from the widow's mite up to Astor's millions. The treasury would be abundantly supplied by the subscriptions of the masses. Only let the people see that the government is in real earnest in its purpose to put down the rebellion, and it will not call on Hercules for help in vain.'"

Such is a brief outline of the plan suggested by Major-General N. P. Banks, for the suppression of the slaveholders' rebellion.

MAJ. GEN. GEO. B. McCLELLAN. U.S.

GEORGE BRINTON McCLELLAN.

GEORGE BRINTON McCLELLAN was born in the city of Philadelphia, December 3d, 1826. He was the son of a physician, and was descended from Colonel McClellan of the Revolutionary army. At the age of sixteen he entered the United States Military Academy at West Point. In all the studies he maintained the second rank from the outset, and was graduated with the second rank in general merit in 1846. He was commissioned a second-lieutenant of engineers, July 1st, 1846. Congress, in the previous May, had authorized the organization of a company of sappers, miners, and pontoniers, and the recruits for this company were assembled at West Point. Lieutenant McClellan was attached to it, and assisted very actively in its drill and practical instruction for duty. Captain Swift and Lieutenant Gustavus W. Smith were his superior officers in the company, which sailed from West Point, September 24th. Ordered at first to report to General Taylor, the company went to Camargo, but was thence ordered to countermarch to Matamoras, and move with the column of General Patterson. Captain Swift was left in the hospital at Matamoras, and the only commissioned officers in the company were Lieutenants Smith and McClellan; and great praise was bestowed upon them by the engineer officer for the amount and excellence of their work done in this part of the Mexican war.

From Tampico the sappers and miners went to Vera Cruz, where, until the surrender of the castle, Lieutenant McClellan was engaged in the most severe duties, in opening paths and roads to facilitate the investment, in covering reconnoissances, and in the unceasing toil and hardship of the trenches; and his work was always done "with unsurpassed intelligence and zeal." Tribute is rendered in all the official reports to the services of this company and the efficiency of its two lieutenants on the march to Cerro Gordo, at Jalapa, and San Antonio. Before the battle of Contreras, Lieutenant McClellan had a horse shot under him by the Mexican pickets, and in that battle he served with Magruder's battery. General Twiggs, in his official report, says: "Lieutenant George B. McClellan, after Lieutenant Calendar was wounded, took charge of and managed the howitzer battery, with judgment and success, until it became so disabled as to require shelter. For Lieutenant McClellan's efficiency and gallantry in this affair, I present his name for the favorable consideration of the general-in-chief." General

Persifer F. Smith, in his report of all the actions at Churubusco and Contreras, says: "Lieutenant G. W. Smith, in command of the engineer company, and Lieutenant McClellan, his subaltern, distinguished themselves throughout the whole of the three actions. Nothing seemed to them too bold to be undertaken, or too difficult to be executed, and their services as engineers were as valuable as those they rendered in battle at the head of their gallant men." For "gallant and meritorious conduct in the battles of Contreras and Churubusco," McClellan was breveted first-lieutenant; and for "gallant and meritorious conduct in the battle of Molino del Rey," captain; but the latter brevet, through some delicacy toward others, he declined to accept. In the battle of Chepultepec he was one of "five lieutenants of engineers" who, in the words of Lieutenant-General Scott, "won the admiration of all about them;" and for his services on that day he was breveted captain. He was thus "on duty with the engineer company from its organization at West Point, in the siege of Vera Cruz, and in all the battles of General Scott's march to the city of Mexico."

Captain McClellan returned with his company, which reached West Point in June, 1847. In the next year he became its commander, and remained with it until 1851. During this time he translated from the French the manual of bayonet exercise, which has since become the text-book of the service. He superintended the construction of Fort Delaware in the fall of 1851, and in the spring of 1852 was assigned to duty in the expedition that explored Red River, and also served as an engineer upon some explorations in Texas.

Secretary of War Jefferson Davis, in 1853, committed to Captain McClellan an important and difficult survey of the Cascade range of mountains on the Pacific, with a view to the construction of the Pacific railroad. In his report the secretary says: "The examination of the approaches and passes, made by Captain McClellan of the corps of engineers, presents a reconnoissance of great value, and, though performed under adverse circumstances, exhibits all the information necessary to determine the practicability of this portion of the route, and reflects the highest credit on the capacity and resource of that officer." Besides the reports descriptive of the region surveyed, Captain McClellan also furnished a valuable collection of "Memoranda on Railways," the result of examinations made into the working of various railroads, to assist in determining the practicability of roads over the various routes.

In 1855, McClellan received a captaincy in the first United States cavalry, and in the same year was chosen as one of three officers to be sent on a military commission to Europe. He sailed, in company with Majors Delafield and Mordecai, in April, 1855, and proceeded to the Crimea and to northern Russia, to observe the war then in progress between Russia, England, and France; and subsequently visited every military establishment of interest on the continent and in

England. After an absence of two years, the commission returned, and the results of Captain McClellan's observations were embodied in a report to the secretary of war, published in 1857, "On the Organization of European Armies, and the Operations of the War"—a work which established the reputation of the young officer as a scientific soldier.

Upon receiving the offer of an important civil employment, that of vice-president and director of the Illinois Central Railroad, Captain McClellan resigned his position in the army, January 16th, 1857. His position on the Illinois Central Railroad he held for three years, when he was offered and accepted the presidency of the Ohio and Mississippi Railroad. This position he held when the war broke out.

When the state of Ohio began to marshal its forces in response to the President's call, McClellan was immediately chosen as the citizen of that state most fit to organize the volunteer regiments into an army. That patriotic state has therefore the honor of having brought to the front the man of the time; though Pennsylvania, through her governor, had also called upon the young captain, but vainly, to head her stout thousands as they were mustered for the war. Ohio's volunteers, thanks to the efficiency of the man chosen to lead them, became at once an army, and were ready to win battles, while those of some not less patriotic states were still raw recruits. On the 14th of May, General McClellan was appointed by the President a major-general in the United States army, and assigned to the command of the then newly created department of the Ohio, formed of the states of Ohio, Indiana, and Illinois, with his head-quarters at Cincinnati. Here he was still busy in the organization and equipment of the forces mustered in the various parts of his district, when the rebel forces from Eastern Virginia began offensive movements against the Western Virginians, who were faithful to the Union. Confederate troops occupied Philippi and Grafton, and began to burn bridges; and on May 25th, General McClellan ordered an advance against them of the first Virginia regiment, stationed at Wheeling, and of the fourteenth and sixteenth Ohio regiments, which crossed the Ohio respectively at Marietta and Bellaire. On the 26th, at night, the rebels fled precipitately from Grafton, and it was occupied by Colonel Kelly of the first Virginia, with his own regiment and the sixteenth Ohio, May 30th. Colonel Steedman, of the fourteenth Ohio, occupied Parkersburgh.

Simultaneously with his entrance into Virginia, General McClellan, in a proclamation to the people of Western Virginia, said: "The general government has long endured the machinations of a few factious rebels in your midst. Armed traitors have in vain endeavored to deter you from expressing your loyalty at the polls; having failed in this infamous attempt to deprive you of the exercise of your dearest rights, they now seek to inaugurate a reign of terror, and thus force you to yield to their schemes, and submit to the yoke of their traitorous conspiracy. . . . . Government has heretofore carefully abstained from sending troops across the Ohio, or even from posting them along its banks, although frequently urged by many of your prominent citizens to do so. It determined to await the result of the late election, desirous that no one might be able to say that the slightest effort had been made from this side to influence the free expression of your opinion. . . . . I have ordered troops to cross the river. They come as your friends and your brothers—as enemies only to the armed rebels who are preying upon you. . . . . All your rights shall be religiously respected." To his soldiers he said: "I place under the safeguard of your honor the persons and property of the Virginians. I know that you will respect their feelings and all their rights. Preserve the strictest discipline: remember that each one of you holds in his keeping the honor of Ohio and of the Union."

On June 2d, the Union troops at Grafton went forward to Philippi, on the Monongahela, twenty miles south of Grafton, which they reached at daylight on the next day, and attacked and drove out a body of rebels under Colonel Porterfield. Here they were joined, June 20th, by General McClellan, who on that day assumed command in person of the national forces in Western Virginia, and began more extensive operations against the enemy. Meantime the rebels made active preparations to resist. Henry A. Wise, formerly governor of Virginia, but appointed a general in the rebel army, took the field in the Kanawha region of Western Virginia, and, with the usual affectation of patriotism, called upon the people to "come to the defence of the commonwealth invaded and insulted by a ruthless and unnatural enemy;" while General Garnett, formerly of the United States army, occupied Laurel Hill and Rich Mountain, spurs of the Alleghany range, with ten thousand men.

General Cox was sent against Wise, and General McClellan advanced in person against Garnett. Beverly, in Randolph county, Virginia, is approached on the north by a road from Philippi, and on the west by a road from Buckhannon. Laurel Hill is upon the former road, and Rich Mountain upon the latter; and both roads, at the point where they cross the hills, were obstructed by Garnett's intrenchments. Garnett himself, with six thousand men, was at Laurel Hill, supposing doubtless that, as that point was nearest to Philippi, the attack would be made there. But General McClellan marched from Clarksburg, on the North-western Virginia Railroad, advanced directly toward Beverly by the Buckhannon road, and thus came upon the position at Rich Mountain. Colonel Pegram, Garnett's subordinate, held that place with four thousand men. At the foot of the hill, on the western slope, was a very strong work built of trees felled from the hill-side, filled in with earth, and furnished with artillery. Dense woods encircled it for a mile in every direction, and it could not have been carried from the front without great loss. On the top of the mountain was a smaller work, with two six-pounders. A sharp skirmish took place in front of the lower fort, July 10th; and on the 11th, at daylight, General Rosecrans, with four regiments, was sent around the southern slope of the mountain, to carry the small work above, and take the larger one in the rear. After an arduous march of eight miles, he reached the summit and carried the work, with but small loss. Meanwhile, General McClellan below had cut a road through the wood which surrounded the rebel battery, and had arranged a position for twelve guns, with which to participate in the attack to be made from above; but as soon as the rebels in the lower fort learned that the fort on the hill-top was taken, they abandoned their work, and fled in every direction. By this action the rebels lost six brass cannon, two hundred tents, sixty wagons, one hundred and fifty men in killed and wounded, and one hundred prisoners. Only six hundred men of the enemy retained any organization, and with these Colonel Pegram retreated toward Laurel Hill. General McClellan, by a rapid march, occupied Beverly.

Garnett, as soon as he learned of Pegram's rout at Rich Mountain, abandoned his intrenchments at Laurel Hill, and retreated toward Beverly; but the rapid occupation of that place by General McClellan cut off his retreat in that direction, and in great confusion he turned back and retreated toward St. George, in Tucker county, to the north-east of Laurel Hill. Thus ten thousand rebel troops from Eastern Virginia, Tennessee, Georgia, and South Carolina, were driven out of their intrenchments, with a loss to the Union forces of only eleven men killed and thirty-five wounded. On the 13th, Colonel Pegram surrendered what was left of his command (six hundred officers and men) prisoners, unconditionally.

Immediately upon the retreat of Garnett toward St. George, General Morris was ordered to follow him, and General Hill was ordered forward from Rawlesburg to intercept his retreat. General Garnett, finding himself pressed very closely by the brigade of General Morris, made a stand in an advantageous position at Carrick's Ford, on the Cheat River, eight miles south of St. George. There he was handsomely beaten by the seventh and ninth Indiana and the fourteenth Ohio regiments. General Garnett was killed, his army disorganized, and its whole baggage taken. Thus, by a series of brilliant movements, and in only twenty-four days after General McClellan had assumed the command, this portion of Western Virginia was freed, and the army that lately held it became a demoralized band of fugitives. In recognition of this first considerable success of the war, both houses of Congress, on June 16th, passed a joint resolution of thanks to General McClellan and the officers and soldiers under his command.

In an address to the "Soldiers of the Army of the West," dated subsequently to these battles, General McClellan said: "You have annihilated two armies, commanded by educated and experienced soldiers, intrenched in mountain fastnesses, and fortified at their leisure. You have taken five guns, twelve colors, fifteen hundred stand of arms, and one thousand prisoners, including more than forty officers. One of the second commanders of the rebels is a prisoner, the other lost his life on the field of battle. You have killed more than two hundred and fifty of the enemy, who has lost all his baggage and camp-equipage. All this has been accomplished with the loss of twenty brave men killed and sixty wounded on your part. You have proved that Union men, fighting for the preservation of our government, are more than a match for our misguided brothers. Soldiers! I have confidence in you, and I trust that you have learned to confide in me. Remember that discipline and subordination are qualities of equal value with courage."

Three days after the above order was issued, the national army that had been organized near Washington, under the eye of the veteran commander-in-chief, was defeated in the disastrous battle at Bull Run, and returned to the bank of the Potomac in a wild, disordered rout. Startled by this blow, the government first awoke to the great labor to be accomplished in putting down the rebellion. Regiments before refused, and all now offered, were immediately accepted, and it was determined to add at least one hundred thousand men to the Potomac army. General McClellan was ordered to Washington, to take command of this new force, and of the departments of Washington and Northeastern Virginia. He left Beverly June 23d, and arrived at the capital July 25th. His first order to the army was dated July 30th. In that he described the first practice he had observed "eminently prejudicial to good order and military discipline," and plainly declared that "it must be discontinued." Officers and soldiers were therefore strictly forbidden to leave their camps and quarters, except on important public business, and then not without written permission from the commander of the brigade to which they belonged. Washington was thus cleared of an army of loungers; and officers and soldiers, confined to their camps, found time to learn their respective duties.

On August 3d, General McClellan's appointment as a major-general in the United States army was confirmed by the Senate; and on August 20th, by general order, he assumed command of the army of the Potomac, and announced the officers of his staff. Lieutenant-General Scott was retired from active service November 1st, 1861, and on the same day General McClellan was appointed to succeed him as commander-in-chief of the armies of the United States. Both before and after this accession of authority, he labored without intermission, and with noble earnestness and simple purpose, to prepare for a proper discharge of its duties to the great army called out by the government. His many judicious orders in regulation of the actions of officers and soldiers, and the system of frequent reviews that he introduced, rendered it necessary that all should work to keep up with him, and gave some unity to the army.

After the retirement of the lieutenant-general, the whole military operations of the country came under the control of General McClellan; and, though it is not now possible to say how great a share we owe to him of the successes that crowned our arms in the beginning of the spring of 1862, yet by the admissions of the general officers most conspicuous in those actions it appears that they are all parts of one extensive plan of his arrangement. On March 11th, General McClellan took the field for active operations at the head of the army of the Potomac, and by the special order of the President was relieved from the command of the other departments.

18

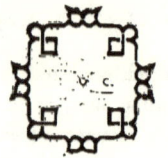

Col. WILLIAM SPRAGUE of R.I.

WILLIAM SPRAGUE.

WILLIAM SPRAGUE was born in Cranston, Rhode Island, on the 11th of September, 1830, and is therefore now thirty-one years of age. His father was Amasa Sprague. His grandfather, William Sprague, early engaged in cotton manufactures, and particularly in the business of calico-printing. He was among the first in the United States to attempt the latter. His works were erected in Cranston, about three miles from Providence, where he commenced with the most simple style of prints known as "indigo blues." William Sprague was associated in business with his sons Amasa and William, both of whom, being brought up in the mills and print-works, obtained a thorough knowledge of the business in all its details. Their cotton-mills were in Cranston, Johnston, and in the village of Natick; but the goods manufactured there were quite inadequate to furnish the supply for their calico-works, which were enlarged as their efforts were successful, and the demand for their goods increased.

William Sprague, the elder, died in 1836, when the entire business fell into the hands of his sons before mentioned, who then formed a new firm, under the name of A. and W. Sprague. The death of the father proved no check to the business; on the contrary, the new house continued to enlarge their works, and to erect new mills. Several, of large capacity, were erected at Natick; and soon after, the firm purchased two other mills, belonging to C. and W. Rhodes, which gave them the entire water-power of that place. But the Messrs. Sprague did not stop here, for they subsequently erected additional mills in the villages of Arctic and Quidneck; all were substantial structures of brick or stone, of four and five stories, with the usual dwelling-houses for the operatives, thereby forming populous villages.

Amasa died in the year 1843, leaving two sons, Amasa and William. The firm continued without change. The surviving partner, William, like most men of fortune and influence, was induced to enter political life. He first became a member of the general assembly of Rhode Island, and soon after was sent a Representative to Congress. Next, he was elected governor, and subsequently a Senator in Congress. The death of his brother Amasa, and his greatly increasing business, obliged him to relinquish the latter office. He now continued to devote his whole time to business, enlarging and extending his works, until the year 1856, when, after a very brief illness, his career was closed by death, at the age of fifty-six years, leaving one son, Byron.

At the time of the death of the first Governor Sprague, it was believed that, owing to the youth of his nephews Amasa and William, and of his son Byron, the great scheme he had laid out for erecting another cotton-mill, which should surpass any that the firm then owned, or any in the state, would be abandoned. Indeed, the business-friends of the young men strongly urged this step, under the impression that their eight large cotton-mills and extensive print-works would be as much as they could manage profitably. Most men, thus deprived of their long-experienced guide, and with a business so vast upon their hands, would gladly have reduced their responsibilities and curtailed their business; but our young men thought differently, even though (owing to the commercial crisis which followed soon after, in 1857) the prospects were any thing but favorable.

The firm was continued as before. William, the subject of this sketch, then but twenty-six years of age, determined to carry out all the plans of his uncle, in which determination his brother and cousin joined. The great cotton-mill at Baltic was erected and filled with machinery, large dams were constructed, and one hundred dwelling-houses were built, involving an expenditure of five hundred thousand dollars. This mill is built of stone, is one thousand feet in length, five stories high, and contains eighty thousand spindles.

Having thus given a brief sketch of the history of the firm of A. and W. Sprague during the three generations they have carried on the manufacturing and printing business, we shall now speak more particularly of the subject of this sketch, the present WILLIAM SPRAGUE, governor of the state of Rhode Island.

It has been stated that he was born in 1830. His education was confined to what could be obtained at the common school which he attended in his native village of Cranston, and in those of East Greenwich and Scituate, until he was thirteen years of age, when he was sent to the Irving Institute, at Tarrytown, in the state of New York, where he remained two years. Returning then, he was by his uncle placed in what is usually called the "factory store;" that is, the shop attached to the calico-works, in Cranston, where goods of all kinds are furnished to the operatives. Here William remained one year, when he was transferred to the counting-room of A. and W. Sprague, in Providence, where he did the work usually performed by the youngest boys, although this labor is now performed in most counting-houses by laboring men. Here our lad opened the office, made the fires, cleaned the lamps, swept out the office, and did such other drudgery as appertained to the station; all of which he performed in so satisfactory a manner, that after three years so employed he was promoted to the place of book-keeper. No young man ever felt the importance of his position more than William did, when, at the age of nineteen, he found himself book-keeper in the great establishment of his father and uncle. But a few years earlier he was dealing out tapes and buttons, pins and needles, molasses, oil, and tobacco, to the crowds of men, women, and children who, during the recess of their labors, came to make their purchases. Now, he was occupied in keeping accounts which amounted to hundreds of thousands of dollars. The sales of the house were wholly of packages of goods, and their purchases of hundreds of bales of cotton, or of large invoices of dye-stuffs.

William continued to fill the place of book-keeper, to the entire satisfaction of his uncle, for three years, during which time, by his constant attention, he made himself familiar with all the ramifications of their extensive business; so that, when he attained the age of twenty-two years, he relinquished his position at the books, and assumed that of an active participant in the concern. Here his active mind was constantly exercised; there was no portion of the business that did not come under his eye, and with which, from actual experience, he was not acquainted. Four years after (1856), his uncle died, when he was compelled to assume the whole weight of the business; and not content with this, as before stated, he finished the various projects which were commenced by his uncle. These were, the erection of their great Baltic cotton-mill, and the completion of the Providence, Hartford, and Fishkill Railroad, in which the firm were largely interested. It is now (1862) less than six years since the elder Governor Sprague died; and, large as the business then was, the concern has, chiefly under the direction of William, doubled its business, until it may now be said to be the largest calico establishment in the world. The firm now own and have in operation nine cotton-mills, the full capacity of which together is eight hundred thousand yards a week; while their printing establishment, when in full operation, is capable of turning out twenty-five thousand pieces, or about one million yards of prints, in the same time. It should be remarked that the firm sell their goods through their own houses, in the great markets of New York, Philadelphia, and Boston, in addition to their sales in Providence. Such is, in brief, a history of the business concerns of Messrs. A. and W. Sprague. We leave this, and shall now speak of the political and military career of the subject of our memoir.

Quite early in life, William manifested a strong passion for the military. When twelve years of age, he formed a company of forty boys, most of whom were older than himself; yet such was his influence among them, that he was chosen their captain. This was in 1842, a year memorable in the annals of Rhode Island as that of the insurrection, or, what is more generally known in the state, as the "Dorr War." A military spirit then prevailed throughout the state. Companies were everywhere organized, and constant drilling was kept up. This
19

was deemed necessary, not alone to suppress the insurrection, but for protection from attacks from without, which were threatened, particularly from New York. Our young soldier, not content with commanding his forty boys, resigned his place, compelled his youthful adherents to elect him governor, and then assumed to himself the appointment of his own officers. At this time the insurrectionists, under the command of Mr. Dorr, had assembled at Acote's Hill, in Chepachet, whither the state forces were advancing. Young Sprague, determined not to be outdone, also marched his band of young patriots toward Acote's Hill, which he might have reached in advance of the state troops, had not the regularly constituted authorities overtaken them when about half-way there, and turned them back.

In 1848, Mr. Sprague, then eighteen years of age, joined the Marine Artillery Company, in Providence, as a private. This company derives its name from having been originally formed by seafaring men; and, although its organization had long been kept up, the members scarcely drilled, or performed any duty beyond that of uniforming themselves and parading on public occasions. Mr. Sprague took a deep interest in this company, the members of which now determined to make it more efficient. He was soon promoted to the rank of lieutenant, and then to captain. In this position a wider field was opened to him, and, mainly through his exertions, the company increased in numbers and efficiency. In a few years he was elected lieutenant-colonel, and finally colonel, of the company. He had now reached the height of his ambition, the full command of a military company, and determined to make it as efficient as possible. Neither his time nor his money were spared; and, as he indulged in no sort of dissipation, amusement, or extravagance, his sole thoughts, when not in his counting-room, were devoted to his company, which he succeeded in making a full battery of light artillery.

In 1859, the cares of business had so much impaired the health of Mr. Sprague, that he felt himself compelled to visit Europe, for its recovery. But the earnest desire to witness the great events then transpiring in Italy, no doubt, had as much influence with him as the recovery of his health; but in the desire to witness some great battle he was disappointed, as the war was over before he reached Italy. Nevertheless, he visited all the recent battle-fields, as well as those made memorable in the wars of the first Napoleon. While in Italy, Mr. Sprague became acquainted with Garibaldi, and contributed liberally toward the fund then being raised for that distinguished patriot.

After an absence of seven months in Europe, Mr. Sprague returned, with his health restored, and received a warm welcome from his numerous friends. He arrived early in 1860, at a time when the state of Rhode Island was much agitated by the contending political parties, the Republican and the Democratic.

The former, in nominating its candidate for governor, had selected a gentleman whose political antecedents had been exceedingly ultra, being considered a strong abolitionist. This selection gave offence to a large majority of the Republican party, who thought that, in the then agitated state of the country upon the slavery question, a more conservative candidate should have been selected, and determined not to support his nomination. A convention was accordingly called of the conservative portion of the Republicans, which nominated Mr. Sprague, who, though a Republican, and opposed to the administration of President Buchanan, was very conservative. The Democratic party, anxious to defeat the gentleman nominated by the Republicans, readily came forward, nominated Mr. Sprague, and the whole conservative ticket, except that for attorney-general. The election took place. It was the most warmly contested of any that ever was held in the state, and resulted in the choice of Mr. Sprague. The following year (1861), Governor Sprague was re-elected, with little opposition. The result was a most happy one for the state, for there was no man more competent than its governor to carry it so successfully through the trying scenes connected with the rebellion. Few men in civil life had had a better military experience than the governor, who had been connected with one of the most active companies in the state for eleven years. His experience as a business man, and his command of a moneyed capital, were equally important in raising, equipping, and subsisting the large military force called out for the defence of the country and its constitution.

In February, 1861, while the Southern states, one after another, were passing ordinances of secession, and a determination was manifested to break up and destroy the Union, Governor Sprague visited Washington. He saw that a crisis was rapidly approaching in our affairs; that the states then in rebellion might attempt to take the capital; and that a large military force would be required there, at a very short notice, in order to thwart their plans. Knowing the patriotism of Rhode Island, and of the desire of the people to furnish every aid in their power in the emergency, Governor Sprague called upon Lieutenant-General Scott, made known to him the excellent organization and discipline of the military of his state, and tendered to him a full regiment of infantry and a battery of light artillery, in case they should be wanted. In conversation with President Lincoln, he made a similar offer. General Scott expressed his fears that the insurrectionary spirit shown by the South might culminate in something very serious; and further remarked that, should a war break out, and it should become necessary to put down the rebellion with arms, an army of at least three hundred thousand men would be required before a movement could be made against them with any prospect of success. On his return to Providence, finding matters growing worse, Governor Sprague sent Major Goddard, then a commissioned officer in the cavalry, to Washington, in order to lay before General Scott a fuller statement of the military resources of the state.

On the 11th of April, Governor Sprague addressed a letter to President Lincoln, of which the following is a copy:

"STATE OF RHODE ISLAND, EXECUTIVE DEPARTMENT,
PROVIDENCE, *April* 11*th*, 1861.

"SIR: At the time of the anticipated attack on Washington, previous to your inauguration, I had a messenger in constant communication with General Scott, giving him a minute detail of our military organization, and requesting him to make such demands for troops as the exigencies of the case should demand.

"I should not now be correctly representing the public sentiment of the people of this state, did I not assure you of their loyalty to the government of the Union, and of their anxiety to do their utmost to maintain it.

"I have just returned from New York, where I had an interview with Governor Corwin; and now take pleasure in saying that we have a battery of light artillery, six pieces, with horses and men complete, and a force of one thousand infantry, completely disciplined and equipped—unequalled, or at any rate not surpassed, by a similar number in any country—who would respond at short notice to the call of the government for the defence of the capital. The artillery especially, I imagine, would be very serviceable to take the place of a similar number required elsewhere. I am ready to accompany them.

"That God will grant his protecting care and guidance to you, sir, in your trying and difficult position, and a safe deliverance from our unhappy difficulties, is the constant prayer of your most obedient servant,

"WILLIAM SPRAGUE.

"To the President, Washington, D. C."

The attack of the seven thousand rebels, under General Beauregard, upon the seventy famished men, under Major Anderson, in Fort Sumter, took place on the 11th of April; and, as the news of this dastardly assault and beginning of the war of the rebellion was conveyed by telegraph to all parts of the Union, the people, with one accord, rose to arms. President Lincoln's proclamation, calling for seventy-five thousand men for the defence of Washington, reached Providence on the 15th, and was immediately promulgated. Governor Sprague, on his return from Washington, anticipating a call, had requested the officers of all the active military companies in the state to keep up their drills, and be ready at a moment's notice; so that, when the alarm was sounded through the President's proclamation, Rhode Island was ready to obey the call. On the 18th of April, three days after the proclamation was published, the first battery of light artillery, of six guns and one hundred and fifty men, under Colonel Tompkins newly clothed, completely equipped and officered, took their departure for the capital. Two days later (the 20th), the first battalion of the first regiment of infantry, seven hundred strong, under Colonel A. E. Burnside, with provisions for thirty days, followed. Governor Sprague accompanied the regiment in person. The following week, the second battalion, under Colonel Joseph S. Pitman, took its departure. The entire force of this regiment and battery numbered nearly fourteen hundred men. The first battalion, taking a steamer at New York, reached Annapolis in time to aid in saving the Constitution frigate from falling into the hands of the secessionists, who had already arranged their plans for taking her. From Annapolis they took up their line of march for Washington, and encamped in a beautiful grove near the city, which was occupied by the Rhode Island troops until the army of the Potomac advanced in March, 1862. It still bears the name of "Camp Sprague."

After remaining a few weeks with the regiment, during which time he was assiduously occupied in making arrangements for providing for the wants of officers and men, the governor returned to Rhode Island. During his absence new military companies were formed. Governor Sprague now took hold with vigor, and determined to form a second regiment. With this view, he appointed Major John S. Slocum, of the first regiment, colonel, and selected the most competent men for the other regimental and the company officers. He visited their armories every night, and by his presence, encouragement, and ardent zeal in the cause in which he had embarked, induced hundreds to come forward and join the ranks. The regiment was soon filled up, and, after remaining in camp a few weeks to perfect themselves in drill and marching, embarked for Washington, accompanied by Governor Sprague.

The governor remained with the Rhode Island troops most of the time, and accompanied them on their march with the army to Centreville on the 16th day of July, 1861. The battle of Bull Run took place on the 21st; and, as it is a matter of history, we shall enter into no details here. The two Rhode Island regiments, with the second battery of artillery, were among the foremost in this memorable fight, and, as is well known, suffered severely. No one was more prominent in the action than Governor Sprague. He was everywhere in the thickest of the fight; and when his horse was shot from under him by a cannon-ball, the governor seized a rifle from the grasp of a dead soldier, and, rushing forward, took his place among the soldiers, encouraging them by his presence and bravery. The two bullet-holes found in his clothes, after the battle, show that he did not shun danger.

On his return to Rhode Island, Governor Sprague did not relax in the least in his efforts to rouse the people to action. The President called for five hundred

20

thousand troops, and he was determined that his state should furnish her full quota. Enlistments for the new regiments of infantry and additional batteries of light artillery were pressed with vigor. The latter arm of the service having proved so effective in the battle of Bull Run, the governor now determined to raise a full regiment of ten batteries of six rifled guns, of one hundred and fifty men each, which have all gone forward. It is unnecessary to enter into details of these proceedings; we simply record the result. A third regiment of infantry, under Colonel N. W. Brown, went forward, and is now at Port Royal. A fourth, commanded by Colonel I. P. Rodman, and the first battalion of the fifth, accompanied General Burnside's expedition, and were engaged in the battles of Roanoke Island and Newbern. Besides these, there has been raised a regiment of cavalry, of which Colonel R. B. Lawton is in command. Other batteries of artillery are yet to be formed. The quota of five hundred thousand troops which Rhode Island is required to furnish is four thousand and fifty-seven. She has now (January, 1862) in the field about five thousand five hundred men, and is still sending on more to the seat of war. She has also furnished to the United States navy five hundred and eighty and to the regular army four hundred and twenty-five men. It may be added that Rhode Island also has a well-drilled home guard, four thousand strong.

Space does not admit of enlarging upon the family of Governor Sprague. His ancestor, Jonathan Sprague, is first noticed in Rhode Island history in 1681. He was for many years a member of the general assembly, and in 1703 was chosen speaker. By intermarriage the family is connected with Roger Williams, the founder of the state. The Rev. Dr. William B. Sprague, of Albany, and Charles Sprague, the well-known poet of Boston, are descendants of the Spragues of Rhode Island.

As an evidence that those who have most to do generally find time to do more, it is proper to state that Governor Sprague has other weighty cares and responsibilities besides those named, all of which he promptly attends to. As president of the Globe Bank, in Providence, where his firm are large stockholders, he is always at the board meetings, and scrutinizes every piece of paper presented for discount; and is as familiar with the standing of the business community as any of the directors. He is president of a Savings Bank, and a director in three of the Insurance Companies in Providence. Besides these, the governor is one of the board of visitors to the "Butler Hospital for the Insane," where he performs the regular round of duties required of every visitor, with as much care as he attends to the business of his counting-room.

HENRY B. HIDDEN.

THERE are poets who have produced but a single poem, orators of a single speech, and generals of a solitary battle; yet they are memorable. The conspicuous bravery which shone out with such lustre in the gallant charge of Lieutenant Hidden at Sangster's Station, was the single act in the brief career of this son of New York, but it was one which a grateful country will not let die. We need not apologize that he did not do more. The glorious privilege of dying for one's country is accorded to but few of only twenty-three years, and the legacy of such a death will be the inspiration of bards, illustration for orators, a theme for artists, and an example for heroes.

HENRY B. HIDDEN was born in the city of New York. He was the young-est son of Enoch and Louisa Hidden. His father was of New-England birth; his mother was born in New York, and a descendant from one of its oldest fami-lies—her great-grandfather, Thomas Ivers, being one of the "Tea-Party" in New York, and one of the committee of one hundred appointed by the people, May 1st, 1775.

It was truly said by Rev. Dr. Asa D. Smith, in his touching eulogy of the deceased, that "he was always a peculiar boy." In fact, he never passed through that phase of life so apt to be one of trial and uneasiness to parents, so disagree-able to acquaintances, so dangerous yet all-important to the individual himself— the interval between childhood and manhood, which may be called boyhood. Harry seemed to have overleaped this period, and assumed at once the character-istics of maturer life. And yet there was no assumption; he but eschewed the vices and aimed for the noble attributes of a man. Those who were familiar with him were not astonished at his death, for he seemed to be always emulous of commendable distinction; and they knew that he was anxious to find an opportunity to tread the path of honor, beset as it might be with dangers.

The most marked personal characteristic of young Hidden was his influence over all around him. When a boy at school, his teachers used to say to him: "It is all-important that you should be good, for all the boys will do as you say." This animal magnetism was conspicuous throughout his life. It was seen in his regiment, where the men loved him devotedly, would follow him to the death, and mourned his loss with the bitter tears wrung so hardly from the eyes of stern manhood. This species of magnetic attraction, which has characterized many distinguished men, would doubtless have been signally manifested in the after-life of young Hidden, had not his career been so speedily closed. This ascendency over schoolmates, associates, and strangers, was not obtained by any arrogant claim; for, on the contrary, Hidden was singularly modest an' rather retiring. He seemed not to desire, but rather to shrink from, conspicuousness, placing a modest estimate upon his own abilities. Early at the formation of his regiment, he might easily have had a captaincy, but intentionally avoided it, feeling his deficiency; and yet, by a week's longer life, he would have attained it by promotion.

Henry was educated with a view to a mercantile life, in several of the best schools in and around New York. He had, however, but barely entered upon the initiative, when, a favorable opportunity offering, he spent some six or eight months in the counting-room of a leading merchant in Havana, perfecting himself in the Spanish language, the main object of his going thither, and obtaining a knowledge of men and things which would have been of much service in after-life. On returning to his home, his opportunities for improvement were further advanced by the occasion of the sailing of the celebrated steam-frigate The General Admiral for Russia, in which he accompanied his brother-in-law, William H. Webb, the builder, to St. Petersburg, and afterward, during more than a year's travel over the principal states and kingdoms of Europe. Returning, he settled himself down to labor, not enervated by his life of ease and pleasure, entering a commercial house, with a certainty of speedy advance before him. This was not to be. With war's alarms, and treason in our midst, Hidden, or as he was soon called by his men, "gallant Harry," although before without any martial propensities, entered at once into the plan for getting up a cavalry corps in this city. The toils, fatigues, anxieties, and vexatious delays, which ushered into existence the Lincoln Cavalry, were felt by none more than by him. But it was a proud day for him when, mounted upon his thorough-bred stallion Chance, he accompanied his regiment to the steamer that took them from the city en route for Washington.

Six months or more in camp, never weary of drill, never fatigued with the tiresome delay in his mud-beleagured quarters, he waited, and the physical and moral growth of the man was consummated. His added inch of stature, and his increasing weight, made his five feet ten symmetrical, graceful, and enduring. Genial and friendly with all, his manner took a more thoughtful tone, and he seemed to see life in more serious aspects.

Finally, came the moment for action. The roads are again passable, and the long-expected advance is ordered. Right gladly did this incipient hero join his company on his first tour of duty. But two days after leaving the camp, spent in scouting through the woods, the morning of Sunday. March 9th, arrives. A summons from General Kearney orders Captain Stearns to detail his first-lieutenant, with five picked men, to unite with others for special duty. Reporting himself to the general, he is ordered to attend him as escort. We can almost feel how that young heart beats and his handsome features glow with enthusiasm with this unexpected honor. A few hours pass, when, from the knoll upon which they are standing, three men are seen upon the edge of the wood, about a quarter of a mile below them. General Kearney orders his guard to advance upon them "as foragers," with the design of capturing them. As the little band approach the spot, the men retreat; and suddenly a corps of infantry, one hundred and fifty or more, are disclosed in battle array. The guard have now proceeded too far, although to go on against such odds seems madness; but a safe retreat is impossible. "Will you follow me, men?" says the lieutenant, whose mind comprehends the danger, and is soon made up. "To the death!" is the unanimous reply. Dividing his little corps into two bands, Harry gives the order to charge, and these fourteen men are launched against the opposing hundred and fifty. Such a gallant dash is rarely seen. The barrels of the revolvers are soon emptied, and the swords cut a way through the yielding ranks. The rebels are dispersed: some, firing, flee; some throw down their arms; some cry for mercy, as the gallant band, uniting in their rear, gather in the prisoners, which equal themselves in number. As they return, attention is directed to one lying slightly wounded, and the lieutenant turns toward him to cut him down with his sabre; but he is arrested by the one next him, who says, "He has got enough, and we needn't trouble about him." So they left him, but had hardly rode on a dozen steps, when he whom they had just spared raises himself from the ground, and speeds the fatal bullet, which enters the back of the gallant hero in the flush of his maiden victory, and, going out under the chin, carries away with it the life of one so beautiful, so good, so noble.

He died without a struggle; for when Lieutenant Alexander, advancing to his support with a similar corps arrived, he was found about six yards from the spot where he was struck, lying upon his face as he fell, and with his blood-stained sword in his hand. Tenderly was he raised, and for the last time placed upon his own horse, by the men just now so fierce in battle, and borne to the camp. Here the regrets of his command, weeping like children, are mingled with execrations against him who had made such a cowardly assassination after the fight was over; and they promise that, in any future meeting with the First Maryland volunteers, their chivalrous leader will not be forgotten.

That bright morning was a sad day for the friends at home; and the telegram, briefly stating that "Harry B. Hidden was killed this morning, gallantly fighting for his country," was almost another bullet in the heart of his bereaved parents. Soon the daily press told how brave a youth had given his all for his country. General Kearney's order for the day, the eulogistic letters from his colonel, and the resolutions of condolence from the officers of his mess, attested to his merit; while later, the muffled drum, the solemn march of the military, the hearse with its nodding plumes and flag-enshrouded coffin, his champing steed restively following with empty saddle and draped spurs, slowly pass from the funeral rites in the crowded church, through the saddened throngs which line the streets, to his last resting-place, amid the umbrageous groves of Green-wood.

" Dulce et decorum est pro patria mori."

J. C. Fremont.

JOHN CHARLES FREMONT.

THE subject of this sketch was born at Savannah, in Georgia, January 21st, 1818. His father was a native of Lyons, and left France for St Domingo in 1798; but the ship in which he sailed, captured by an English cruiser, was taken into the British West Indies, whence the captive made his way to Norfolk, in Virginia. There he taught his native language for a livelihood, and eventually married the daughter of Colonel Thomas Whiting, of Gloucester county, a gentleman related by marriage to the family of Washington.

At the age of fifteen, young Fremont entered Charleston (S. C.) College. For some time he made rapid progress in his studies; but he fell in love, became inattentive to his collegiate duties, was frequently absent from his class, and for that cause was finally expelled. From his seventeenth to his twentieth year he was employed as an instructor in mathematics in various schools in Charleston, and as a practical surveyor. In 1833, he was appointed a teacher of mathematics on board the United States sloop-of-war Natchez, and made a cruise of two years and a half in that vessel. On his return, he declined the appointment of professor of mathematics in the navy, was employed as an engineer on the railway line between Augusta and Charleston, and subsequently. and until the fall of 1837, as an assistant engineer upon the preliminary survey for a railway between Charleston and Cincinnati. Fremont's part of the line lay in the mountain-passes between South Carolina and Tennessee. This work was suspended in the autumn, and the winter of 1837 was spent in making, with Captain Williams, of the United States army, a military reconnoissance of the mountains of Georgia, North Carolina, and Tennessee—a work performed in anticipation of hostilities with the Cherokee Indians. In the spring of 1838, he accompanied M. Nicollet, a man of science, employed by the United States government, to the upper Mississippi, and served as his principal assistant in the exploration of that year, and also in that of the next year, of the country between the Missouri and the British line; and afterward assisted in the preparation of the maps and report of the exploration. While upon this expedition, he was appointed, February 7th, 1838, a second-lieutenant in the corps of topographical engineers.

Before Nicollet's maps and report were completed, Fremont was ordered to explore the River Des Moines. After the execution of this service, he returned to Washington, and in October, 1841, married Jessie, the daughter of Thomas H. Benton, then United States Senator from Missouri.

While employed under Nicollet, Fremont had conceived the design of exploring the Far West, to facilitate its settlement, and open communication with the Pacific. As the first step toward this great labor, he applied for and obtained, in 1842, an order to explore the Missouri frontier as far as the Wind River Peak of the Rocky Mountains. He left the mouth of the Kansas River, June 10th, proceeded up the Platte River and its tributaries, through bands of hostile Indians, to the South Pass, which was carefully examined. Thence he proceeded to the Wind River Mountains, the loftiest peak of which he ascended, and on his return reached the mouth of the Kansas October 10th. His report was laid before Congress in the winter of 1842–'3. Humboldt praised it, and the London "Athenæum" pronounced it one of the most perfect productions of its kind.

Early in the spring of 1843, Fremont set out upon a second expedition, from which he did not return until August, 1844. His object in this expedition was to complete the survey of the line of communication between the state of Missouri and the tide-water region of the Columbia, which had never been examined or mapped by any geographer; and to explore the vast region to the south of the Columbia—the whole western slope of the Rocky Mountains—a territory almost unknown. He set out from Kansas City May 29th, and came in sight of Salt Lake September 6th. Eight months later, he reached Utah Lake, the southern limb of the Great Salt Lake, having completed a circuit of twelve degrees' diameter north and south, and ten degrees east and west. In the maps and report of this expedition, the Great Salt Lake, the Utah Lake, the Little Salt Lake, the Klamath Lake, the Sierra Nevada, the valleys of the Sacramento and San Joaquin, the Great Basin, the Three Parks—nearly all then unknown and desert regions, now the homes of multitudes of people—were revealed to the world. Nothing in the annals of human adventure can surpass the fortitude with which Fremont and his comrades met the hardships and dangers of this vast exploration. For this service he was breveted first-lieutenant and captain in January, 1845.

Captain Fremont set out on his third expedition in the spring of 1845. He crossed the Great Basin from the southern extremity of the Great Salt Lake, and reached California in December. From the authorities of that province he obtained permission to go to the valley of the San Joaquin, where he desired to procure supplies, and to recruit his force. At that time the relations between the United States and Mexico were critical; and, though the leave was granted for him to continue his exploration, it was almost immediately revoked, and he was peremptorily ordered to quit the country. In the condition of his men, this was impossible; and General Castro, the governor, mustered the forces of the province against him. Therefore, to be in a better condition to repel any attack,

Fremont took up a position on the Hawk's Peak, about thirty miles from Monterey, intrenched it, and with his command of sixty-two men awaited the Mexicans. Here he remained from the 7th till the 10th of March. General Castro did not approach, and Fremont abandoned his position, and commenced his march for Oregon. Several of his men, who desired to remain in the country, were discharged from service on the march. About the middle of May, 1846, when he had reached the northern shore of the great Tlamath Lake, and was within the limits of Oregon territory, he found his further progress in that direction obstructed by impassable snowy mountains, and by hostile Indians, who had been excited against him by General Castro; and Castro, he learned, was still advancing against him; and that the American settlers in the valley of the Sacramento were comprehended in the scheme of destruction meditated against his own party. At the same time, a messenger reached him with dispatches from Washington, in which he was directed to watch over the interests of the United States in California, as there was reason to apprehend that the province would be transferred to Great Britain. "Under these circumstances," says Secretary Marcy, "he determined to turn upon his Mexican pursuers, and seek safety for his own party and the American settlers, not merely in the defeat of Castro, but in the total overthrow of the Mexican authority in California, and the establishment of an independent government in that extensive department. It was on the 6th of June that this resolution was taken, and by the 5th of July it was carried into effect".... and "in the short space of sixty days from the first decisive movement, this conquest was achieved by a small body of men to an extent beyond their own expectations, for the Mexican authorities proclaimed it a conquest, not merely of the northern part, but of the whole province of the Californias."

California was thus virtually an independent province, and in the hands of the settler-conquerors, who immediately elected Fremont governor. Upon the arrival of the United States naval forces, under Stockton, Fremont co-operated with them, and his election as governor was recognized and ratified by Stockton. Subsequently, General Kearney, of the United States army, arrived in California, and claimed authority over the territory, and, as Fremont's superior in the national army, required his obedience to orders. His orders conflicted with those previously received from Commodore Stockton, and Fremont refused to obey them. This brought upon him the enmity of Kearney. Stockton received orders in the spring to turn the command over to Kearney, and that ended the dispute. Fremont, tried by court-martial for his share of the trouble, was found guilty of "mutiny," "disobedience of lawful orders," and "conduct to the prejudice of good order and military discipline," and was sentenced to be dismissed from the service. The President disapproved the decision of the court upon the

21

charge of mutiny, and remitted the penalty; but Fremont, indisposed to accept "mercy," resigned his commission, and started upon a winter expedition across the mountains, to remove the popular impression that the snow rendered them impassable. His intention was, to go from the Rio Grande to the Colorado, through the Cochatopee Pass; but, misled by his guide, he encountered a violent snow-storm while twelve thousand feet above the level of the sea. His expedition proved disastrous, but he finally demonstrated the existence of the pass, and that the route was practicable.

Upon his arrival in California, Fremont made his home on the Mariposas, a tract of land, about two hundred miles south-west from San Francisco, which he had purchased in 1847 for three thousand dollars. But he was not allowed to rest. Identified with all the great interests of California, and especially with the endeavor to exclude slavery from its constitution, he was chosen in December, 1849, to represent that state in the Senate of the United States, and was its first Senator. His senatorial career was brief. He had drawn the short term, and the protracted struggle upon the admission of his state left him but two weeks of his first session. In that time he offered bills to donate lands to settlers, to settle land-titles, to grant lands to the state for the purposes of education, to open a road across the continent, and for various other measures requisite in a new state. An attack of the Panama fever kept him from his seat throughout the next session.

By act of Congress, every claimant of title to land in California was required, at the discretion of the United States attorney-general, to sue for his title in person before three separate tribunals; and the attorney-general exercised his full authority in Fremont's case, though his title to the Mariposas was beyond doubt. One of the tribunals was in Washington, and Fremont was compelled to make the journey thither from California. He did so, and obtained his title. Investigation had demonstrated the mineral wealth of the Mariposas tract; and, upon the settlement of the title, Fremont was offered one million dollars for it by a London company of capitalists, and one hundred thousand dollars were deposited with Colonel Benton as a first payment. But Fremont refused to sell, and in 1852 went to Europe to negotiate for means to work the mines.

He returned in June, 1853, and in August set out to complete at his own expense the survey (abandoned in 1849) of the direct line for the Pacific road to San Francisco. Though this was also a winter expedition, and though the weather was extremely inclement, he found safe passes through a fine country all the way to San Francisco.

Though previously Fremont had not taken any active share in general politics, yet his known sympathy with the principles of the Republican party, and his career as a man associated with the great development of the Far West, brought him prominently before the Republican national convention which met at Philadelphia, June 17th, 1856, and that body unanimously nominated him as the candidate of the Republican party for the presidency. He was defeated in November by the election of James Buchanan, who received one hundred and seventy-four electoral votes from nineteen states; Fremont received one hundred and fourteen from eleven states, and his popular vote was one million. three hundred and forty-one thousand, five hundred and fourteen. In 1858, Mr. Fremont returned to California, made that state his residence, and there gave his whole attention to the management of his extensive Mariposas estate.

When the Southern disturbance became an open and aggressive war, Colonel Fremont was in Paris; but he determined immediately to return home, and reached Boston in the steamship Europa, June 27th, 1861. His arrival had been anticipated by his appointment as a major-general in the United States army; and on July 6th, upon the creation of the Western department, he was ordered to the command in it. This department comprised the state of Illinois, and the states and territories west of the Mississippi and east of the Rocky Mountains, including New Mexico, and head-quarters were fixed at St. Louis.

General Fremont reached his department and assumed the command, July 25th. Battles had then been fought at Booneville and Carthage, and nearly the whole force under Lyon was in and around Springfield, in daily expectation of attack from the large army known to be under M'Culloch and Price. Moreover, the federal army then in existence had been originally organized for three months' service: its time was now nearly expired; and in view of this, the rebel forces began to threaten along the whole line of operations in the department. Fremont had thus to hold a department against an active enemy, and had first to create an army. His difficulties were of immense magnitude; but he does not appear to have talked very much about them, nor to have taken the world at large into his confidence, and that caused more trouble still.

General Pillow, about the first of August, entered south-eastern Missouri at the head of a large rebel force; and, to meet this, General Fremont immediately organized an expedition of about eight regiments, which left St. Louis August 2d, and moved down the Mississippi to Cairo. Pillow was either alarmed by the force thus prepared to meet him, or his movement had been merely intended as a feint to cover the advance against Lyon in the south-western part of the state, for he withdrew without making any demonstration. Apparently, Fremont was beaten in this whole affair: for, by the actual movement made, he lost Lyon and Springfield; while, if he had moved to the assistance of Lyon, Pillow would doubtless have pressed his demonstration against Bird's Point and Cairo, and those places would probably have fallen into his hands.

Fremont's appointment as major-general was confirmed by the Senate on the 3d of August. On the 13th, he declared martial law in the "city and county

of St. Louis;" and at about the same time he began the construction of the very
extensive fortifications contemplated for the defence of that city. By his proclamation of August 81st, he extended the declaration of martial law throughout
Missouri, and "assumed the administrative powers of the state." This was made
necessary by "the helplessness of the civil authority." In the same document,
it is declared that "the property, real and personal, of all persons in the state of
Missouri, who shall take up arms against the United States, or who shall be
directly proven to have taken active part with their enemies in the field, is declared to be confiscated to the public use, and their slaves, if any they have, are
hereby declared free men." Against the extension of martial law over the state,
Hamilton R. Gamble, who had been elected governor upon the delinquency of
Governor Jackson, protested personally to the President; but the President was
disposed to leave the matter with General Fremont, and to "take no step backward;" yet by a public order of September 11th, the President qualified the slave
clause of General Fremont's proclamation, so that it should "not transcend the
provisions on the same subject contained in the act of Congress entitled 'an act
to confiscate property used for insurrectionary purposes.'" Very nearly at the
same time was first heard the rumor that General Fremont's conduct of affairs
in Missouri had not given satisfaction in Washington, and that he was to be
superseded.

After the battle at Wilson's Creek, and the consequent withdrawal of the
national forces from the south-western part of the state, it was completely over-
run by the united forces of M'Culloch, Rains, and Price, who extended their
operations as far north as the Missouri River, and approached St. Louis from the
direction of Springfield as near as Warsaw, on the Osage. Extensive preparations to rid the state of this invasion were made by General Fremont at St. Louis,
and subsequently at Jefferson City; and for this purpose he finally collected and
organized, though somewhat imperfectly, a force of thirty thousand men, which
was disposed in five divisions, commanded respectively by Generals Hunter,
Sigel, Asboth, M'Kinstry, and Pope. This force comprised twenty-five infantry
regiments. About five thousand cavalry made up the number, and it was furnished with thirty-six pieces of artillery. On the 14th of October, the whole
force took up its march—Asboth's and Hunter's commands from the camp at
Tipton, M'Kinstry's from Syracuse, Pope's from Booneville, and Sigel's from
Sedalia—for Warsaw, on the Osage.

Warsaw was reached on the 17th. There General Fremont halted to build
a bridge over the Osage, and passed that stream on the 22d. General Price, with
a force fully equal to the national army, retreated before Fremont as he advanced; but the latter pressed on, in the belief that he could overtake Price near
the Arkansas line, though his transportation was quite unequal to any very rapid

movement. Price was reported to have made a stand at Carthage, and Fremont occupied Springfield, October 27th. Price and M'Culloch were then certainly not far to the south, with a large force, and a battle became hourly more imminent. General Fremont devoted himself with intense earnestness to the work of preparation for the fight. Meantime, some excitement prevailed, as the possibility of his removal was talked over in the army, and rumors were current that it had already taken place. Fremont could not but be aware of these rumors; yet he worked on until Saturday, November 2d, when he received from a government messenger the President's unconditional order for him to relinquish the command to General Hunter. He did so, and left camp at Springfield for St. Louis on the 3d, having previously taken leave of the army in the following farewell order:

"SOLDIERS OF THE MISSISSIPPI ARMY: Agreeable to orders received this day, I take leave of you. Although our army has been of sudden growth, we have grown up together, and I have become familiar with the brave and generous spirits which you bring to the defence of your country, and which makes me anticipate for you a brilliant career. Continue as you have begun, and give to my successor the same cordial and enthusiastic support with which you have encouraged me. Emulate the splendid example which you have already before you, and let me remain, as I am, proud of the noble army which I have thus far labored to bring together.

"Soldiers, I regret to leave you. Most sincerely I thank you for the regard and confidence you have invariably shown me. I deeply regret that I shall not have the honor to lead you to the victory which you are just about to win; but I shall claim the right to share with you in the joy of every triumph, and trust always to be personally remembered by my companions in arms."

On the 11th of March, 1862, President Lincoln, having previously ordered a general movement of the land and naval forces of the United States, issued an order relieving General McClellan from the "other military departments" except the department of the Potomac, and creating the new departments of the "Mississippi" and the "Mountain department," assigning the command of the latter to General Fremont.

MR. ELY is one of those men who may be said to have become famous in a single day—a drive of twenty miles on a pleasant summer morning made him one of the "men of the time." He was the son of Charles Ely, and was born in the town of Lyme, New London county, Connecticut, on the 18th of February, 1815. He came from that branch of our national stock pre-eminently distinguished for its steadiness, its enterprise and perseverance, and which has given to the world its full proportion of eminent statesmen, merchants, lawyers, authors, adventurers, and heroes. From his earliest infancy the breezes of the ocean became, as it were, the guardian of his health; and one of the loveliest valleys in the world instilled into his mind an early love for the charms of nature. To these privileges were added all the advantages of a good common-school education.

While yet in his minority, a strong desire possessed Mr. Ely not only to go abroad, but to see what might be done in the way of obtaining a fortune. In December, 1835, he left his native place, and removed to the city of Rochester, New York, where he studied law, and was admitted to the bar of the supreme court and court of chancery of that state, in July, 1841. On the 30th of May, 1842, he married the daughter of the Honorable Joseph Field, late mayor of the city of Rochester. He entered upon the practice of his profession in that city, where he has ever since resided, and where he has followed his profession with eminent success, having accumulated a handsome fortune. In 1840, while yet a student at law, he was appointed clerk of the recorder's court of Rochester. Having subsequently taken some interest in politics, he was elected in 1858 a Representative in the thirty-sixth Congress from the famous and populous Monroe district of New York, serving as a member of the committee on claims. He was re-elected to the thirty-seventh Congress, and was placed at the head of the committee on invalid pensions; and it was while attending the first and extra session of this Congress that he became personally but unwittingly identified with the Great Rebellion.

The subsequent career of Mr. Ely, which resulted in the publication of the work entitled "Journal of Alfred Ely, a Prisoner of War in Richmond," and edited by Charles Lanman, is partially depicted in the introduction of that work, and may therefore with propriety be here reproduced. It is as follows:

"On the 18th of July, 1861, an encounter had occurred in Virginia between some of the Union troops and a portion of the rebel army, in which the thirteenth regiment of New York volunteers participated. Coming, as those men did, chiefly from the congressional district represented by the Honorable Alfred Ely, and as rumors had reached him that some of the soldiers in whom he felt a deep interest had been either killed or wounded in the action, he felt it to be his duty to visit the regiment and ascertain their exact condition. Under these circumstances, and to a certain extent induced by a common feeling of curiosity to witness the movements of an army in the field, he was with others induced to visit the scene of an expected combat. If the object which he contemplated should incur censure from any quarter, it cannot be questioned that he severely expiated the error.

"As a non-combatant, participating to no extent in the military operations, and accidentally becoming a spectator of the momentous scene at Bull Run, he found himself, before the day had closed, a prisoner of war. In company with many of our gallant officers and men, who had the misfortune to be captured on that occasion, some of whom bore honorable wounds, he was carried to the headquarters of the rebel general, thence transported to Richmond, and there confined in a prison for five weary months. During that time he saw much to interest his feelings in behalf of his brave and patriotic associates, and not a little to illustrate the character of the people under whose control it was their misfortune to be thrown.

"At an early period of this durance, Mr. Ely was impelled, by a variety of motives, to keep a journal of the events which transpired in and about his prison. Deprived of his accustomed employments, he found in this occupation some relief from *ennui*, and anticipated the period when, released from his captivity, the chronicle of these days and their experiences would afford him pleasure in the retrospect. It was with this view, therefore, that he commenced and continued his record. It never occurred to him to prepare a work for publication. Indeed, the restraint of a prison precluded the possibility of attempting any thing beyond a simple memorandum of daily events, and the performance of even this simple task was subjected to many difficulties and interruptions. The nature and extent of these difficulties will appear in the following pages.

"On his release from confinement and return to his friends, Mr. Ely found himself incessantly interrogated as to the events which had occurred, the treatment he had experienced, and the individuals with whom he had intercourse. His journal supplied ample responses to these various inquiries; and those to whom it was submitted concurring in urging him to publish it, he was induced to give his consent, believing that the unvarnished record of his prison-life would be acceptable, not only to his friends, but to many others in the North having relatives in the South enduring a similar fate to his, and that his reminiscences might throw some light on the hidden history of the Great Rebellion."

With regard to the merits and success of Mr. Ely's narrative, the writer may mention with propriety that it received the seal of public approbation. From the very nature of the case, no other man could have written just such a work, because no other man passed directly from a seat on the floor of Congress, over a bloody battle-field, into the close confinement of a prison. And as to his release, it only remains to be stated that he was exchanged by the rebels for the Honorable Charles J. Faulkner, late United States minister to France, who had been arrested and imprisoned at Fort Warren for infidelity to his government. His journey from Richmond to Washington, and hence to Rochester, was all that he could have desired, and will long be remembered by himself and family as the bright and cheerful sunshine which follows a night of gloom.

22

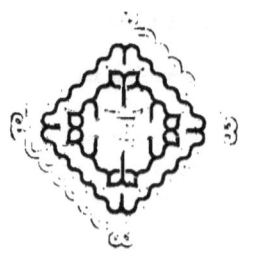

ABRAM DURYEA.

G ENERAL DURYEA was born in the city of New York, April 29th, 1815.
He is of French Huguenot descent, his ancestors having emigrated to
America on the revocation of the edict of Nantz by Louis XIV., to escape the
religious intolerance and persecutions of that reign. Young Duryea received a
liberal education, first at the High School in Crosby street, and finishing his
studies at the Grammar School of Columbia College. He was married in the
year 1838, to Caroline E. Allen, daughter of William Allen, Esq., by whom he
has four children, one son and three daughters; his son, J. Eugene, is now lieutenant-colonel of the second Maryland regiment.

General Duryea commenced business as a mahogany-merchant, in which
pursuit, by industry and perseverance, he has succeeded in realizing a fortune.
He commenced his military career as a private in the one hundred and forty-
second regiment, New York militia, Colonel Graham, and served as general guide,
quartermaster, and sergeant-major. In 1838, he joined the National Guard, 27th
regiment of artillery, doing duty in the ranks. Subsequently passing through
all the grades of non-commissioned officers with distinction, he at length obtained
his first commission, as second-lieutenant, in the year 1840. He was rapidly
promoted through the following grades, first-lieutenant, captain, major, and lieutenant-colonel, and on the 29th of January, 1847, succeeded to the command of
the famous seventh regiment.

During his term of service as lieutenant-colonel, he commanded a battery
of six guns. After an uninterrupted service of eleven years, by industry, military
and executive ability, he won for his regiment a world-wide reputation for efficiency, discipline, and moral bearing, not possessed by any other military body
in the country. He commanded the regiment in the memorable and bloody
riots at the Astor Place Opera House, which so effectually suppressed the rebellious element, that the regiment has ever since been a terror to all disturbers of
the public peace. He also subdued the terrible police riots at the City Hall, the
"Dead Rabbits," and sixth-ward riots, and in fact has been engaged in the suppression of every riot in the city of New York for the past twenty-one years.
He was the commanding officer at Camp Trumbull, New Haven; Camp Worth,
Kingston; in quarters at Newport, Rhode Island; and on two excursions to

Boston, in order to attend the Bunker Hill and Warren monuments celebrations; to which should be added the escort to the remains of President Monroe to Richmond, the regiment on their return visiting Mount Vernon, Washington, and Baltimore. On the 4th of July, 1859, he offered his resignation. On the intelligence reaching his command, it was received with deep regret. The regiment waited upon him in a body, with urgent solicitations for him to remain. All their efforts proved unavailing; he was inexorable. Colonel Duryea in his retirement was the recipient of compliments and testimonials such as no other officer has received. The merchants of New York presented him with an elegant service of silver, and his associates in arms a testimonial of surpassing beauty, a masterpiece of workmanship in silver, consisting of eleven massive pieces—a dinner-set—costing five thousand dollars.

Colonel Duryea remained in retirement until the breaking out of the present war, when he at once resolved to enter the field, and commenced to organize, discipline, and drill the distinguished fifth regiment of Zouaves. From his reputation as an officer, the ranks were quickly filled, and it was one of the first regiments in the field. After one month's instruction in garrison at Fort Schuyler, the regiment embarked on board the steamship Alabama for Fortress Monroe. On their arrival there, Colonel Duryea was placed in command of the troops at Camp Hamilton, as acting brigadier-general, his command consisting of the first, second, third, fifth, and twentieth regiments of New York, and Colonel Baker's California regiment, amounting to six thousand men. They were drilled in evolutions of the line, and outpost and picket duty. General Pierce having arrived, he was ordered to supersede Colonel Duryea, who therefore returned to his regiment. On the 9th of June, 1861, he received orders, through Generals Butler and Pierce, to advance on Little and Great Bethel, in which action the whole command distinguished itself for gallantry and bravery in front of a masked battery of great strength. On the retirement of General Pierce, Colonel Duryea was again placed in command as acting brigadier-general. Upon the disaster of Bull Run, a large portion of his force was ordered to reinforce Washington, and Colonel Baker was directed to assume command of the troops. Colonel Duryea again returned to his regiment. On the arrival of the troops at Baltimore, the fifth regiment was detained there, and encamped on Federal Hill, where they constructed a formidable and extensive fort.

On the 31st of August, the President of the United States appointed Colonel Duryea a brigadier-general, and placed him in command of one of the largest brigades in the service, near Baltimore. Few men in the country possess the united influence and skill to raise and discipline a large body of troops in so short a time as General Duryea. He brought the famous seventh regiment of New York to its unequalled discipline, so that over four hundred of the private soldiers have received commissions in the army of the United States. The celebrated Zouaves have contributed over a hundred officers in the present war. General Duryea has constantly distinguished himself by comprehensive skill, industry, and courage. His clear, well-known voice, ringing along the lines. inspires confidence and enthusiasm among the soldiers.

23

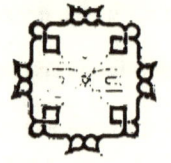

BRIG GEN J K F MANSFIELD U S A

JOSEPH K. F. MANSFIELD.

JOSEPH K. F. MANSFIELD, brigadier-general in the United States army, was born December 22d, 1803, in New Haven, Connecticut, where his first American ancestor of the name settled in 1640, just four years after they had landed at Boston, from Exeter, in Old England. His father, Henry S. Mansfield, was the son of Captain Stephen Mansfield. His mother was Mary Fenno, the daughter of Ephraim Fenno and Mary King, of Middletown, Connecticut, who, losing her husband by death at Santa Cruz, in the West Indies, moved with her family to her native village. Here the general, then an infant, and the youngest of six children, passed his earliest years, till in 1817, a mere lad of fourteen, he received a cadet's appointment, and entered the military academy at West Point. In this celebrated school of war, young Mansfield gave early promise of his future greatness. Such was his distinction, alike in military studies and military arts, that he passed through every grade of office in the cadet battalion, and during the last half-year acted as assistant professor in the department of natural philosophy. His prize drawings are still exhibited, and are almost unrivalled for their accuracy and beauty. He was graduated July 1st, 1822, a youth of nineteen, the youngest in years and the second in rank, and, had the decision been left to his classmates, would have won the first honors. Immediately after, he received a commission in the corps of engineers, and became a brevet second-lieutenant.

For the next two years we find him an assistant to the board of engineers, then assembled in the city of New York, and engaged in planning fortifications for the defence of the harbors and cities on the coast. From 1826 to 1828 he acted as assistant engineer, under Colonel De Russy, in the construction of Fort Hamilton, at the Narrows. From 1828 to 1830 he was engaged in the same capacity under General Gratiot, to whom the government had intrusted the building of Forts Monroe and Calhoun, at Old Point Comfort, Virginia. During the next sixteen years the young officer found a field worthy of his extraordinary talents and great experience, in the difficult science of military engineering. Fort Pulaski, at the mouth of the Savannah River, is a monument of his labors and genius as an architect. It is often spoken of as a model fortress, and would have proved impregnable to all but these latest missiles of war, which, by their prodigious weight and force, have baffled all the modern means of defence. In the midst of this great work he was often detached to duty at Charleston Harbor, Cape Fear River, and other points of national importance; and for these high professional services became, in 1838, captain of engineers.

In 1846, by our folly, if not our wickedness, we brought on the Mexican war. Captain Mansfield's abilities were at once recognized, and he was ordered to join General Taylor at Corpus Christi. Throughout the war he was the chief engineer of that distinguished commander, and possessed his fullest respect and confidence. While the army lay here encamped, Captain Mansfield, by order of the general, made a reconnoissance, survey, and map, of the whole Texan coast from Matagorda Bay to the Aransas River, a work which occupied him six weeks. The peaceful negotiations which, up to this time, had been pursued by the two governments, now seemed likely to fail, and General Taylor was ordered to advance to the Rio Grande. But the Mexicans resolved to meet him in force, and dispute the passage of the Arroyo Colorado; a purpose easily thwarted by Mansfield, who so quickly advanced and so skilfully planted his batteries, that the enemy withdrew without a contest.

Arriving at Point Isabel, General Taylor decided on that place as his chief military depot, and ordered Mansfield to plan its defence. Such was the engineer's promptness and energy, that in one half-day he had surveyed the ground, determined the key to the position, and traced a redoubt to cover it. Leaving a subaltern to complete the work, he hastened to rejoin his commander, now before Matamoras. His next task was truly a *vasta moles belli;* his orders being to erect a battery to command the town, and then to construct a fort to hold the position. The main army now fell back on Point Isabel. Mansfield was no longer to be a mere strategist and architect. With a small detachment of troops on guard, his garrison weak, his works unfinished, his materials to be brought often from points miles away, he must show that he can not only build forts, but defend them. The storm soon came. How he met it, let another tell: "Threatened in rear by light troops, bombarded in front by heavy batteries, day and night this devoted garrison fought and labored; and well did the genius of the engineer second the heroism of the troops. New resources met new difficulties; ingenuity supplied the want of material; and the army, as it came, shattered and bleeding, but victorious, from the plains of Palo Alto and Resaca de la Palma, saw the loved flag of the Union still flying defiant over the little garrison of Fort Brown." For his distinguished conduct in its defence, during a siege and bombardment of an entire week, Mansfield was breveted a major.

The next advance of the army was on Monterey, where Major Mansfield was ordered to make a reconnoissance around the city to the Saltillo road—a movement which he effected with energy and success, bringing in some of the enemy's pickets, and receiving the compliments of his commander. Acting on his report, the next morning General Taylor dispatched General Worth's division to the rear of the city, for the purpose of occupying the Saltillo road, and taking the works in the rear. On the second day, the major, supported by Colonel Garfield's command, was ordered to make a forced reconnoissance of the enemy's redoubt on our extreme left, and to take it if possible. The order was finely executed, and the redoubt taken. Early in the battle he was shot through the leg, but he still kept at his work all that day and part of the next, till the Bishop's Palace was taken, when his wounds compelled him to retire, and prostrated him for six weeks. But his cool and gallant conduct did not go unrewarded. In his reluctant confinement to the tent, he had the satisfaction of reflecting that he entered that field a major but left it a lieutenant-colonel. The battle of Buena Vista found him again ready for action.

This contest began on the 22d of February, 1847, with the light-armed troops, and lasted two days. As Santa Anna advanced, Colonel Mansfield spent all the first day in reconnoitring the enemy and the mountain-passes, and under orders of General Wool remained all night on the ground, while General Taylor returned seven miles to Saltillo. The next morning, the enemy commenced the fight with great spirit. Our left was defeated, driven back, and put to flight. At this moment, Colonel Mansfield rode forward, and, without waiting orders from General Wool, who was not in sight, assumed command, brought up Colonel Key's reserve regiment, and formed a new line, on which the unbroken troops fell back, formed anew, and saved the battle. For his services and gallantry, he was again promoted to the rank of colonel.

At the close of the war, Colonel Mansfield was assigned to duty at the fortifications in Boston Harbor, became a member of the board of engineers, and was often detached to superintend river improvements, &c., until in 1853 he was appointed inspector-general of the army, with the rank of colonel. In this high capacity he inspected the department of New Mexico once, California twice, and Texas twice, and had just returned from the latter field when he was summoned to the defence of Washington. Here, when the capital was filled with traitors and weak with fear, and when the spirit of the North was not as yet roused by one purpose and baptized in one blood—here General Mansfield protected the nation's heart when its life-beats seemed almost destined to cease. He fortified the city on every side, crowned the heights of Arlington, and took Alexandria. By his iron will, sleepless energy, constant industry, and his untiring courtesies to all under and around him in those perilous hours, called for the gratitude and honor of every American. But the fatal defeat at Manassas overshadowed and swept away on the tide of public shame and grief and fear all previous merit and demerits. The nation called for McClellan: *Sol surgit stellæque umbrantur.*

24

General Mansfield has since been put successively in command of Forts Monroe, Hatteras, Camp Hamilton, and Newport News, at which latter place he is said to have saved the Congress from the sad yet glorious fate of the Cumberland when the Merrimac assailed those mighty ships-of-war in the most signal naval battle recorded in history.

In private life, General Mansfield exhibits a pure and lofty character; kind and true to his family, noble to his relatives, generous to his friends, and just to all. In his native town he proves an exception to the proverb: "A prophet is not without honor save in his own country." A friend and helper of every good work, and especially a liberal patron of education, he seems to live above reproach. One intimate with him wonders that a man described by an eye-witness in the Mexican war as fierce and awful in battle, should be so kind and winsome in social life. It was this rare blending of promptness and courtesy which won for him the confidence of strangers, and the love of the troops successively marshalled at Washington. Perhaps this charm captivates our judgment when, with many others, we regret that one who never fought a battle without immediate promotion on the field, should not have been kept in a commanding position during this great national struggle. We will at least venture the opinion that if there had been no Mansfield to fortify the capital, there would have been no capital for McClellan to defend.

MAJ GEN JOHN A DIX USA

JOHN ADAMS DIX.

JOHN ADAMS DIX, son of Lieutenant-Colonel Timothy Dix, of the United States army, was born at Boscawen, New Hampshire, on the 24th of July, 1798. At a very early age he was sent to the academy at Salisbury, from which he was afterward transferred to the academy at Exeter, then under the direction of the celebrated Doctor Abbott, where he was the fellow-student of Doctor Jared Sparks, Honorable John G. Palfrey, the Peabodys, the Buckminsters, and others who have since acquired a just celebrity for their literary and scientific attainments. Early in 1811, while he was not yet fourteen years of age, he was transferred to a college at Montreal, where, under the direction of the Fathers of the Sulpician Order, he diligently pursued his studies until July, 1812, when, in consequence of the opening of hostilities between the United States and Great Britain, he was compelled to return to his own country.

After a short term of study at Boston, in December, 1812, young Dix was appointed a cadet in the army of the United States, and was ordered to Baltimore, where his father was then in command. His official duties were confined to an assistant clerkship to his father, in the recruiting service; and he was, fortunately, enabled to continue his studies, under the direction of the able faculty of St. Mary's College, a privilege which he gladly enjoyed. He was, at that time, a master of Spanish, a good Latin and Greek scholar, and well acquainted with mathematics. He spoke French fluently; and in every respect he was a highly-cultivated and scholarly young man.

In March, 1813, while on a visit to the city of Washington, the secretary of war offered him, without solicitation, the choice of a scholarship in the military academy at West Point, or an ensigncy in the army which was then about to take the field. He selected the latter, entered the fourteenth infantry, of which his father was then lieutenant-colonel, and immediately marched with his company to Sackett's Harbor, in New York.

In June, 1813, while yet in his fifteenth year, he was appointed adjutant of an independent battalion of nine companies, commanded by Major Upham, with which he descended the St. Lawrence, and participated in the perils and hardships of that unfortunate expedition.

His father having died in camp, in November, 1813, Lieutenant Dix sought and obtained leave of absence, and returned home for the purpose, if possible, of saving something from the wreck of his father's estate, which had become greatly, and, as it proved, hopelessly disordered, during the absence of the latter in the service of his country. The lieutenant was then but little more than fifteen years of age, and his situation was one of great embarrassment and difficulty. He had lost his father, by whose prudent counsels he had been guided, and with his mother and nine children—all but two younger than himself—he was thrown upon the world with no other means of support than his lieutenant's commission.

In August, 1814, he was transferred to the regiment of artillery of which Colonel Wallach was the commandant; and under the guidance of that gallant officer he continued several years, pursuing his studies in history and the classics whenever his duties enabled him to do so. In 1819, he was called into the military family of General Brown, as an aide-de-camp; and his leisure hours were spent in reading law, with a view of leaving the army at an early day.

In 1825, he was promoted to the command of a company in the third artillery; but his health having become impaired, he was compelled to ask for a leave of absence, and visited Cuba, where he passed the winter of 1825–'6. In the following summer, still in search of health, he visited Europe, and made an extended tour through the continent.

In 1826, Captain Dix married Catharine Morgan, adopted daughter of John I. Morgan, Esq., of the city of New York; and in December, 1828, he retired from the army, establishing himself soon afterward in Cooperstown, Otsego county, New York, in the practice of law. He also entered political life, and it was not long before he became one of the most active and influential members of the Democratic party in the interior of the state. In 1830, Governor Throop called him into the public service as adjutant-general, a post of duty which he filled with honor to himself and singular advantage to the militia of the state.

In January, 1833, he was chosen secretary of state of New York, and became, *ex officio*, superintendent of common schools, a regent of the university, a member of the canal board, and one of the commissioners of the canal fund. It was he who introduced and established school-district libraries; and his codification of the laws and decisions under which the common schools of the state are governed, is a monument to his industry and official integrity. As a regent of the university and a member of the canal boards, he also rendered very efficient services to the state; and he retired from office with well-earned honors.

In 1841, Mr. Dix was elected a member of the assembly of the state, from the county of Albany; and in the struggle which ensued concerning the financial policy of the state of New York, under the leadership of the sturdy Michael Hoffman, he took a very active part. In the extra session which followed, wherein the question of a division of the state into congressional districts was considered, and opposed with great skill and energy, Mr. Dix was again conspicuous; and in two very able speeches he urged an acquiescence in the measure, although at the same time he maintained that the interference of Congress in the matter was unnecessary and unauthorized.

In the fall of 1842, Mr. Dix went abroad, in consequence of the ill health of his wife; spending the winter in Madeira, and the following year in the southern countries of Europe. He returned to America in June, 1844, and in January, 1845, he was elected a Senator in the Congress of the United States, to fill the vacancy occasioned by the elevation of Silas Wright to the gubernatorial chair of the state. During the succeeding four years he was among the most useful members of that distinguished body; and, as chairman of the committee of commerce, he rendered very valuable services to his country. During his official term the annexation of Texas, the war with Mexico, the Oregon boundary, the French spoliations, and the right of Congress to prevent the extension of slavery into the territories, were the great subjects at issue; and on the latter question, especially, Mr. Dix took a decided and leading position, representing with great ability " *The Barnburners*" or free-soil Democrats of New York.

In the fall of 1848, Mr. Dix was the candidate of his party for governor of the state of New York; but, of course, he was not successful, and in March, 1849, he retired to private life. In 1853, he was appointed assistant treasurer of the United States, in New York; but soon afterward, having become dissatisfied with the official conduct of President Pierce, he resigned his office, and went abroad.

In May, 1860, Mr. Dix was appointed postmaster of the city of New York; and in January, 1861, when the public danger from the defection of the Southern states became manifest, he was summoned to Washington by President Buchanan, and on the 11th of that month succeeded Mr. Thomas as secretary of the treasury. On the 29th of January, he sent the justly celebrated telegraphic dispatch to Mr. William Hemphill Jones, whom he had previously sent to New Orleans, with orders to save, if possible, the revenue-cutters M'Clelland and Cass; and "*If any one attempts to haul down the American flag, shoot him on the spot!*" has since become one of the watchwords of our countrymen in their struggle with their rebellious brethren.

On the 6th of March, 1861, Mr. Dix retired from the treasury department, returning to his home in New York; and on the 20th of May, when the assault on Fort Sumter aroused the outraged North, he was called to preside at the immense meeting of the citizens of New York in Union Square, which had been convened to take measures for the defence of the constitution and the enforcement of the laws. "The Union Defence Committee," which was organized at that meeting, and on which so much depended in the earlier days of the struggle, called him to its head; and, as its chairman, he was one of the most active and intelligent of its members.

On the 6th of May, he was appointed a major-general in the volunteer service of New York; and, on the 14th of June, the President appointed him to a similar position in the army of the United States. On the 20th of July, having been appointed commandant of the department of Maryland, he was ordered to proceed to Baltimore, where he established his head-quarters.

Under his directions, the expedition to the county of Accomac, in Virginia, commanded by General Lockwood, was organized and successfully prosecuted; and his energetic and vigilant prosecution of his duties was displayed in the complete quiet which prevailed throughout his department.

In May, 1862, he was transferred to the command of the military department of Eastern Virginia; and established his head-quarters at Fortress Monroe, where he still remains.

The last civil duty which General Dix performed was as a member of the commission to consider the several cases of alleged treason among the rebel prisoners in the custody of the United States authorities.

General Dix possesses great energy of character; and he has always discharged the varied duties to which he has been called, with honor to himself and advantage to the country.

Major Gen. A. E. Burnside

AMBROSE EVERETT BURNSIDE.

AMBROSE EVERETT BURNSIDE was born at Liberty, Union county, Indiana, on the 23d day of May, 1824, and was, consequently, in the full prime of his early manhood when the War for the Union commenced. He is of the old blood that flowed in the veins of heroes at Bannockburn and Flodden Field, and which, in many a hotly-contested battle, has proved the Scotch to be among the best soldiers in the world.

His grand-parents were born in Scotland, but, removing to America near the close of the last century, settled in South Carolina. Here General Burnside's father was born, educated, and married. Following the profession of law, he acquired an eminent position, and enjoyed a profitable practice. After the war of 1812, the great fields of the West attracted the attention of the citizens of the old states. Mr. Burnside early felt the influence, and in the year 1821 he removed with his family to Liberty. We find him honorably and creditably filling the office of clerk, and afterward of judge of the circuit court, in his new home.

The son, AMBROSE, was carefully nurtured, and received his elementary education in the best schools of the neighborhood. He was admitted to the military academy at West Point in his eighteenth year, and was graduated in 1847, in the artillery, the fifteenth in rank, in a class numbering forty-seven members. In the following year he received a full second-lieutenancy, and was attached to the third regiment of artillery. During his stay at West Point, the war with Mexico commenced; and immediately upon his graduation, he proceeded to the scene of action. On his arrival at Vera Cruz, Lieutenant Burnside was put in command of an escort to a baggage-train, and sent into the interior. Although the route was in the nominal possession of the United States troops, the Mexicans, by a guerilla warfare, which they continually carried on, had succeeded in cutting off or disabling several trains that had previously been sent.

The duty was hazardous, and the post responsible; but the young lieutenant carried his small command through without injury, and manifested so much fidelity and skill as to win the commendation of his superior officers. Before the column to which Lieutenant Burnside joined himself could reach the capital, the battles in front of the city of Mexico had been fought, and the war was virtually finished. He was thus deprived of the opportunity which he desired of participating, to any great extent, in the active operations of the armies in the field. When peace was proclaimed, he was ordered to Fort Adams, Newport, Rhode Island, and was employed at that post until the spring of 1849. His natural refinement of manner, his urbane deportment, and his frank and manly bearing, gained him many friends, and here he laid the foundation of that remarkable esteem with which he is regarded in the state of Rhode Island.

In the year 1849, he was transferred from the agreeable duty of the post at Fort Adams, and ordered to New Mexico, to join Bragg's famous battery, of which he was now appointed first-lieutenant. It was found that the country was not favorable for the operations of light artillery. Bragg's command was reorganized as cavalry, and Lieutenant Burnside was put in charge of a company. The service was very exciting and perilous, but our lieutenant acquitted himself with such coolness and bravery as to receive warm encomium for his conduct. He reached New Mexico on the 1st of August, and immediately went into the field. On the 21st of that month, while scouring the country near Los Vegas, with a force of twenty-nine men, he saw a company of Indians, sixty or seventy-five strong, drawn up at the head of a ravine, prepared to dispute his progress. He immediately determined to attack them; and, after a single discharge of their rifles, his men, led by their gallant commander, charged with sabres, and swept the Apaches like chaff before them. In this brief and brilliant engagement, eighteen Indians were killed, nine were taken prisoners, forty horses were captured, and the whole band was effectually dispersed. The commander of the post, Captain Judd, complimented Burnside, in dispatches, in the highest terms, and recommended him for promotion.

In the winter of 1850-'51, we find Lieutenant Burnside acceptably filling the office of quartermaster of the boundary commission, then occupied in running the line between the United States and Mexico, as established by the treaty of peace negotiated by the two nations. In September, 1851, he was ordered across the plains of the Far West, as bearer of dispatches to the government. It was a duty requiring the utmost vigilance, prudence, and persistence. It was necessary that the dispatches which he bore should reach Washington at the earliest possible moment. With an escort of three men—one of whom was his faithful negro-servant, who has followed his fortunes for several years with singular devotion—he started on his difficult enterprise. Twelve hundred miles of wilderness, occupied by hostile Indians and wild beasts, lay between him and civilization. He accomplished the distance in seventeen days, meeting with many adventures and hair-breadth escapes upon the way. At one time a party of Indians was upon his trail for more than twenty-four hours, and he only escaped by taking advantage of the darkness of the night to double upon his pursuers. He fully accomplished the object of his mission, and received the thanks of the war department for his efficiency and success.

During his service in New Mexico, he had found that the carbine with which the troops were armed was a wholly inadequate weapon for the peculiar warfare of the plains. While upon his journey to Washington, he occupied his mind with an attempt to supply the defect. The result of his reflection and study was the invention of the new breech-loading rifle, which bears the name of its inventor, and seems a perfect weapon. Lieutenant Burnside was desirous that his own country should receive the benefit of his labors, and he offered to contract with the government for the manufacture of the arm. Pending negotiation, he returned to his former post at Newport. While here, on the 27th of April, 1852, he was married to Miss Mary Bishop, of Providence, a lady of great force of character and of most amiable disposition.

The expectation of a contract for the manufacture of the newly-invented rifle, and his marriage, decided Lieutenant Burnside to leave the service, and he resigned his commission. Removing to Bristol, he built a manufactory, and made all necessary arrangements for completing his business negotiations with the government. Unfortunately for him, the contract was not consummated; and, after three or four years of struggle and loss, Mr. Burnside became so deeply involved and embarrassed as to prevent any further progress in his adopted occupation. He was still more embarrassed by the action of John B. Floyd, who became secretary of war in 1857, and found himself compelled to withdraw entirely from the manufacture of arms. With characteristic high-mindedness, he gave up every thing which he possessed, including his patent, to his creditors; and, selling even his uniform and sword, sought to retrieve his fortunes at the West. He went to Chicago, April 27th, 1858, and obtained a situation as cashier in the land department of the Illinois Central Railroad. His old friend and schoolfellow, Captain George B. McClellan, occupied an honorable position in the same railroad company, and the two soldiers once more made their quarters together. Burnside, limiting his expenses to a certain amount, devoted the remainder of his salary to the payment of his debts; and when afterward he was enabled to free himself entirely from the claims of his creditors, his unblemished integrity in business was as conspicuous as his former gallantry in the field. In June, 1860, he was promoted to the office of treasurer of the railroad company.

The intelligence of the bombardment of Fort Sumter, and the proclamation of the President of the United States, awakened Mr. Burnside's patriotism, and he felt once more impelled to take the field. His country had given him his education, and he felt that to his country his life and services were due. His residence in Rhode Island had endeared him to the people of that gallant state, and he had already held the highest command of the state militia. When the first regiment of Rhode Island troops was offered to the secretary of war by the governor of that state, it was to him that all eyes turned for the command. He was appointed colonel, immediately closed his desk of business, and repaired to Providence. There he devoted his time to the organization and equipment of the regiment; and so effectively was the work performed, that on Thursday, April 18th, the light battery of six guns, and one hundred and fifty men, was embarked on board a steamer, and sailed to New York, on the way to Washington. On Saturday, the first detachment of the regiment, five hundred and forty-four officers and men—armed, uniformed, provisioned for a three weeks' campaign, and abundantly supplied with ammunition—left Providence by steamer. Transferred to the government transport Coatzocoalcos at New York, the command proceeded to Annapolis without delay, arriving on Wednesday, April 23d.

On Thursday morning the troops took up the line of march, and, bivouacking on the road, reached Annapolis Junction early on Friday morning. Taking cars at that point, they went on to Washington, reaching the capital at noon. The light battery, which had stopped at Easton, Pennsylvania, and the remainder of the regiment, arrived at Washington in the early part of the following week; and twelve hundred Rhode Island men, under the command of Colonel Burnside, were thus ready for any emergency. The regiment, under the thorough discipline of its commander, soon took high rank in the army for character and efficiency. Its camp, located in the northern suburbs of the city, became a favorite place of resort, and was considered a model of its kind. The excellent reputation which the regiment had acquired, was mainly due to the unwearied efforts and the unceasing vigilance of its colonel. In June, the regiment joined General Patterson's column, intended for the reduction of Harper's Ferry; but, on the evacuation of that place by the rebels, it was recalled to Washington, in anticipation of an attack upon the capital.

Upon the advance toward Manassas, in July, Colonel Burnside was placed in command of a brigade, consisting of four regiments and a battery, viz.: the first Rhode Island; the second Rhode Island, with its battery of light artillery, which had reached Washington in June; the second New Hampshire, which had also arrived in June; and the seventy-first New York, which had accompanied the Rhode Island troops on the march from Annapolis, in April. Colonel Burnside had been offered a brigadier-generalship upon his first arrival at Washington, but had declined it, on the ground of duty to his own regiment and state. But when it became necessary to organize the army, preparatory to an advance into Virginia, he did not hesitate to accept the post which was now pressed upon him. His brigade was joined to the division under Colonel David Hunter, and with the rest of the army left Washington on Tuesday, July 16th. The division bivouacked at Annandale, and on Wednesday, with Colonel Burnside's brigade in advance, pushed on to Fairfax Court House. On Thursday, the whole army encamped at Centreville, after a skirmish between a part of General Tyler's division and the rebels at Blackburn's Ford. On Sunday morning, July 21st, the army moved toward Manassas Junction.

In the disastrous battle of Bull Run, Colonel Burnside and his brigade were conspicuous for their bravery and steadiness. They were among the troops to whom that day's events brought no disgrace. Burnside's own regiment showed, by its gallantry and coolness, that its colonel's labors had produced the finest results. The other regiments of the brigade also proved what good soldiers could do in the hands of a brave and able officer. The battery of the second Rhode Island was most efficiently served, and the regiment itself was particularly distinguished for its gallantry. General M'Dowell had already complimented Colonel Burnside upon his command, and declared that he should rely upon the brigade in the time of action. Accordingly, in the flank movement toward Sudley's Ford, by Colonel Hunter's division, Burnside's brigade took the advance— the second Rhode Island regiment, under Colonel Slocum, a most gallant and accomplished officer, leading the column.

Soon after crossing Bull Run at Sudley's Ford, about half-past nine o'clock, A. M., the leading regiment was attacked by the enemy. Colonel Hunter, who was in advance, was wounded very early in the action; and Colonel Burnside, being in command of the troops till Colonel Porter, who was in the rear, came up, at once led the residue of his brigade forward, and, posting them most advantageously, succeeded in beating back the enemy's attack, and driving him from the part of the field where he had taken position. Colonel Porter's brigade was deployed to the right, and Colonel Heintzelman's division took post still farther upon the right. Colonel Burnside's brigade, assisted by Major Sykes's battalion of regulars, stood the brunt of the enemy's attack in complete order for nearly two hours, when, having completed the work assigned to it, with a loss of three hundred killed and wounded, and being relieved by Colonel Sherman's brigade, it was withdrawn to replenish its now exhausted supply of ammunition, and to await orders to renew the contest. But the order which came was not to advance, but to retreat. Colonel Burnside at once collected his brigade, formed his regiments in column by the side of the road, waited till the larger portion of the disorganized troops had passed, and with Major Sykes's battalion of regulars and Captain Arnold's regular battery in the rear, prepared to cover the retreat along the forest-path over which the division had marched in the morning.

The admirable disposition thus made by Colonel Burnside and Major Sykes, under General M'Dowell's direction, contributed greatly to the safety of the broken army in its perilous march through the woods. On emerging from the forest-path, the artillery passed to the front, and the infantry were left unprotected. The retreat continued in good order till the army reached the bridge on

the Warrenton turnpike, crossing Cub Run. Near this place, the rebels had
brought up a battery of artillery, a regiment or two of infantry, and a squadron
of cavalry, and attempted to cut off our defeated forces. They succeeded in obstructing the bridge sufficiently to prevent the passage of many baggage-wagons,
ambulances, and gun-carriages, and at this place the greatest loss of cannon by the
national troops occurred. When Colonel Burnside reached the bridge, it was in
such condition as to preclude the possibility of crossing, and he ordered the men to
ford the stream, and rally at Centreville. The scattered forces sought the camps
which they had left in the morning, and prepared to pass the night. General
M'Dowell soon sent orders to continue the retreat to Washington. The brigade
reached Long Bridge about seven o'clock on the morning of Monday, July 22d,
and two hours later entered Washington, in the order in which it had quitted
the city on the Tuesday previous. The regiments composing it immediately
marched to their respective camps. Colonel Burnside's bearing, in all the experience of the day and night, was all that could be expected of a man and a
soldier, and he at once attracted the attention of the country to his gallantry,
generalship, and skill.

The term of service for which the first Rhode Island regiment had enlisted,
expired on the day before the battle; but the regiment, having suffered little or
no demoralization, was ready to remain longer at Washington, if its services
should be required. Colonel Burnside was unwilling to return to Rhode Island
till he was assured that the capital was beyond danger of an attack. His officers
and men shared his feelings. But the war department had resolved upon a reorganization of the army, and the three months' regiments were all ordered to their
homes. The second regiment from Rhode Island, with its battery, was left in the
field; while the first returned to Providence, and was there mustered out of the
service of the United States. Colonel Burnside, with his regiment, received the
thanks of the general assembly of Rhode Island for the fidelity and bravery with
which he and they had performed their duties. Colonel Burnside's services were
also recognized by the general government, and he was at once promoted to the
rank of brigadier-general, his commission dating August 6th, 1862.

Immediately upon receiving his commission, General Burnside was summoned to Washington, to assist in reorganizing the forces in front of the capital.
He was employed in brigading the troops as they arrived, and assigning them
places of encampment. To his excellent judgment in this respect, and his great
executive skill, the efficiency of the army was to a great degree due, in those dark
days of the republic.

Later in the season, several expeditions were projected, to operate at different points upon the Southern coast. The most hazardous and difficult of these,
designed to effect a lodgement upon the dangerous shores of North Carolina, and,

carrying a force into the interior, in the rear of the rebel army in Virginia, to cut off communication with the South, was intrusted to the genius and ability of Burnside. For more than two months he was indefatigably employed at his head-quarters, in the city of New York, preparing for this important enterprise. The expedition finally set sail from Annapolis in the early part of January, 1862. Fifteen thousand men were embarked upon a large fleet of transports, and, convoyed by numerous gunboats, proceeded to the place of their destination. The route of the expedition lay through Hatteras Inlet into Albemarle Sound. It was a short voyage indeed, but a most perilous one. Cape Hatteras, noted for its storms, is the terror of every mariner whose course lies along the North American coast. The wintry season added to the dangers of the navigation. The expedition had hardly left the land-locked waters of Chesapeake Bay, when a most terrific storm burst upon the armada with frightful fury. The tortuous and shifting channel leading through the inlet into the sound was to be found and followed in the very teeth of the wind, when the storm was at its height. The inlet itself had been produced by the sea breaking across the narrow spit of sand from which Cape Hatteras projects, and the depth of the channel shifts and changes with the varying influence of the wind and tide. It was found, therefore, that several of the vessels which at New York had been certified to be of light draught, sufficient to pass through the channel, could not be got over the bar. The consequence was, that a large portion of the fleet was in imminent danger of shipwreck.

For nearly a week the storm continued, and the deplorable situation of affairs seemed to indicate the destruction of the entire expedition at the very threshold of its career. In this most trying crisis, General Burnside's admirable qualities shone forth in illustrious light. It is the universal testimony of all who were connected with this expedition, that the bearing of its brave commander was beyond all praise. He seemed to be omnipresent. Wherever the troops were to be rescued from their perilous position, wherever the danger was most threatening, wherever encouragement was needed, wherever help was most timely, there always appeared the general; and, by exertions beneath which any man with a less lofty purpose and a less persistent energy would have sunk exhausted, the expedition was brought to a safe anchorage within Albemarle Sound, and the forces landed in good order. Only a few vessels foundered, and two or three lives were lost by the accidental swamping of a life-boat. Encompassed by perils and threatened with disasters, General Burnside never lost his courage, his hope, and his faith. Buoyed up in the midst of misfortune by his unswerving trust in the care of a superintending Providence, he stood serene and unmoved at his post of duty, and conquered even the elements by an unwearied patience.

Harassed by the delays caused by the storm, active operations against the rebels could not at once be commenced. The plan agreed upon by General McClellan and the authorities at Washington was, to threaten Norfolk by an attack upon the rebel stronghold of Roanoke Island, before proceeding to the mainland. Every thing was prepared for this initial step by the first of February; and on the 5th of that month, the troops being embarked on board the transports (and the gunboats, under the command of Commodore L. M. Goldsborough, being ready to move), the whole fleet steamed slowly up toward the entrance of Albemarle Sound. On the 6th, the gunboats entered Croatan Sound, engaged the rebel fleet, and bombarded the water-batteries of the enemy on Roanoke Island. On the afternoon of the 7th, the troops were landed; and on the morning of the 8th, the attack was made upon the key of the position, a battery in the centre of the island. The battle lasted two hours, and resulted in the complete victory of the national forces, which placed in General Burnside's hands six forts and batteries, forty cannon, over two thousand prisoners of war, and three thousand stands of arms. The national loss was thirty-five killed and two hundred wounded.

Commodore Goldsborough immediately sent a fleet of gunboats up the Pasquotank and Chowan Rivers, by which the rebel gunboats were sunk, captured, or driven away; and Elizabeth City, Hertford, Edenton, and Plymouth, fell into the possession of the Union troops.

These brilliant successes were hailed with the utmost enthusiasm by the people of the North. Following swiftly upon the defeat of the rebels under General Zollicoffer at Mill Spring, Kentucky, they served to revive the spirits of the loyal men, and to assure them of greater victories to come. By none was the intelligence of Burnside's triumph more gratefully received than by the people of Rhode Island. The general assembly, which was in session, immediately voted General Burnside a sword in honor of the victory, and the thanks of the representatives of the people to the officers and men under his command. Massachusetts, through her legislature, expressed her gratitude. The Congress of the United States and the heads of the government acknowledged by their action their sense of the importance of this great success; and the President nominated General Burnside a major-general of volunteers. The Senate confirmed the nomination on the 18th of March, 1862.

Meanwhile, General Burnside was not idle. Releasing his prisoners by exchange, in order that the record of Bull Run might be thoroughly effaced, he prepared to make further advances upon the enemy's forces. In pursuance of the instructions of the general-in-chief, Burnside once more embarked his troops on the 6th of March, and made ready to strike another and more decisive blow. This time it was Newbern that was destined to feel the weight of his loyal hand. On Wednesday, March 12th, the expedition passed the scene of its first disasters;

on the morning of Thursday, the troops were landed at the mouth of Slocum's Creek, on the Neuse river, a distance of ten miles south of Newbern; and, in the afternoon of the same day, a fatiguing march of seven miles, flanked and protected by the gunboats in the river, brought them within a short distance of the enemy's intrenchments, passing one or two deserted batteries on the way. Here they bivouacked in the midst of a drenching rain; and early on the morning of Friday, March 14th, they were roused and prepared to make the attack.

The battle commenced about half-past seven o'clock, and continued for four hours. The enemy was strongly intrenched in batteries and rifle-pits, at least a mile in length, and bravely defended his works: But nothing could withstand the valor and endurance of our brave troops, and the consummate skill of their leader. The contest was decided, as at Roanoke, by a bayonet-charge, and the rebels fled in precipitate haste. They escaped by means of the bridges crossing the River Trent to Newbern, and retreated in disorder and panic by the railroad to Goldsborough. Our troops were prevented from following by the destruction of the bridges, which the rebels burnt as they retreated. The gunboats and transports were delayed by a dense fog, but, as soon as they came up, carried the troops across to the city. It was too late to overtake the flying foe, and only two hundred prisoners were captured.

By this success—hardly bought, indeed, by the loss of eighty-six killed, and four hundred and thirty-eight wounded—all the rebel intrenchments and batteries, mounting between fifty and sixty pieces of cannon, large quantities of stores, ammunition, arms, tents, and baggage, and the city of Newbern, came into the possession of the victorious and gallant chief. Two steamers, eight schooners, the water-batteries, and a considerable quantity of cotton, were the prizes of the naval portion of the expedition, under the command of Captain S. C. Rowan. The victory was complete, and the intelligence was received with heartfelt joy throughout the North. Some anxiety had been felt lest a part of the rebel army, which had evacuated Manassas the week previous, should march into North Carolina, and intercept Burnside on his way. The enthusiasm was heightened by the relief which his success had given, and the assurance of his safety, which was thus placed beyond question.

Continued victory seemed to wait upon his steps. General Burnside is a man who knows how to improve his successes; and as soon as Newbern had been reduced, an expedition was sent to Washington, to occupy that place. Beaufort also became an object for the general's victorious arms; and on Sunday, March 23d, General Parke's brigade peaceably took possession of Morehead City. opposite that town. Fort Macon was immediately summoned, and, upon the refusal of the officer in command to surrender, measures were immediately taken to force a capitulation. General Burnside repaired to the scene of operations, that he might personally superintend the investment of the place. Meanwhile, the enemy's forces were concentrating at Goldsborough and Kingston, threatening the recapture of Newbern. General Burnside did not allow his vigilance to relax in guarding the approaches to either place; and, leaving a sufficient force at Beaufort, he hastened back to Newbern, to fortify that important position. Every arrangement was made to give the foe a warm reception.

General Burnside's characteristics are finely illustrated in every act of his career. He is a man of eminent truthfulness and sincerity. Thoroughly beyond deceit or intrigue, above all jealousy or meanness, open-hearted as the day, and generous even to a fault, his genuine manhood shines through every part of his life. With a quick sense of honor, and the most conscientious regard for truth, he puts to shame all baseness and falsehood. The ways of his life never ran "in the corrupted currents" of the world, but always flow from the purest purposes to the truest results. With a quick perception of character, he is an adept in the difficult art of governing. He attracts and attaches all who approach him by the powerful magnetism of the simplicity of his character and the manliness of his bearing. He has a gentle heart, a clear mind, a guileless conscience, and a brave soul. A surpassing devotion to duty makes him superior to a wrongful intention. An unwearied energy gives vigor to his acts. An unswerving trust in God adorns his private and public life. Prudent without timidity, brave without rashness, religious without pretence, and wholly engaged in the great cause which has enlisted his powers, General Burnside nobly unites the best qualities of a soldier and a man.

In the care of his troops, in tender solicitude and untiring labors for their welfare, he is unsurpassed. When in command of his regiment, his sole thought seemed to be for the benefit of the men intrusted to his guidance. He gave a personal attention to all their needs. Always accessible to the humblest private in the ranks, he heard with unexampled patience the most trivial request or complaint, and replied to each with the necessary grave rebuke, the wise counsel, or the hopeful encouragement. In the camp he was a daily visitant to the hospital, the commissariat, the quarters of the men, that he might know, by his own inspection, the condition and necessities of all. On the road, he always marched on foot, that he might measure the endurance of his men by his own, and inspirit them by his example. In the bivouac, his own quarters were the last to be selected and the last to be prepared. In the field, his bearing was distinguished for coolness, courage, and self-possession, while his dispositions for battle insured the utmost efficiency of his command. He has carried these qualities to his higher positions; and thus, by their exercise, he awakens the sincerest enthusiasm, and inspires the most implicit confidence of his soldiers. From the lowest to the highest there is but one opinion and one voice.

FRAZAR AUGUSTUS STEARNS.

PROBABLY there has been no war in modern times in which so many have enlisted from a high sense of duty, as in this War of the Second American Revolution. The greater part of the thirty undergraduates and numerous recent graduates of Amherst College, who are in the army, were not only among the best scholars and the most consistent Christians in the institution, but they relinquished literary and scientific culture for the service of their country under the influence of patriotic and Christian motives.

This was eminently true of the young hero who fell fighting so bravely near the first gun captured from the enemy in the battle of Newbern. He was a Christian hero. He went to the war with the same conscientious persuasion of a call from God, with which the Christian missionary goes to preach the gospel to the heathen. He met danger and death on the field of battle in the same spirit of self-sacrificing devotion to a sacred cause, in which the martyr goes to the scaffold or the stake.

FRAZAR AUGUSTUS STEARNS, the second son of Reverend President Stearns, of Amherst College, was born in Cambridge, Massachusetts, on the 21st of June, 1840. He was, therefore, not yet twenty-two years of age at the time of his death. When a small boy, under the influence of parental teaching, and especially of the unconscious education of a Christian family, he was the subject of deep religious experiences, and, with the same decision of character with which in after-years he devoted himself to the service of his country, he signified repeatedly to his parents his desire to profess Christ before men; and having at length obtained their consent, he was received, at the age of twelve, into full communion in the church of which his father was pastor, and in which he had been baptized in infancy.

Educated chiefly in the common schools and the high school of Cambridge, after pursuing preparatory studies a little time at Phillips Academy, Andover, in August, 1857, he entered the freshman class in Amherst College.

In his boyhood, he was fond of youthful sports, without being addicted to the vices which are sometimes connected with them. He abhorred every thing that was low and mean, and never feared to express his indignation at vulgarity and profaneness. He refused to associate with boys who indulged in such habits,

26

and would part company under the most trying circumstances with those who used improper language. More instances than one might be related of such high moral courage in his early boyhood.

In college, his taste was for the mathematical and physical sciences rather than the classics; though when he rejoined the institution after an absence of two years occasioned by severe sickness, and after a voyage to India, from which he returned physically and mentally a new man, he took hold of Greek, and indeed of all his studies, with a resolution which would have made him a superior scholar. He excelled in writing and speaking, and won the first prize at the close of his sophomore year, in the prize declamation at commencement; though, with characteristic generosity, he insisted on giving it to a classmate, who was poor, and who from untoward circumstances had not a fair chance in the competition. He left college for the war, having completed only half of his academic course, but fully resolved, if his life was spared, to return and graduate.

The fall of Fort Sumter, which roused the nation from its slumbers, stirred young Stearns like the sound of a trumpet. On that dark and portentous Sunday, when so many ministers preached and so many congregations heard the word under the fearful foreboding that the flag of secession already darkened the capital, the ardent and generous young men of the college thought it no breach of the Sabbath to enroll a company to march, if needed, for the defence of Washington. At the head of this list of young patriot warriors was written the name of Frazar A. Stearns. With the passing away of immediate danger, ceased the call for immediate action, and the students consented to relinquish the proposed military company for a general drill of the college. But he never ceased to revolve the question of duty to his country; and after the disaster at Bull Run, he came to his father with the news, saying, "We have been beaten, and now there is a call for Frazar Stearns." His father, of course, counselled against precipitation, and expressed his belief that the time had not yet come for young men to enlist who were in a course of education. Frazar acquiesced for a season, but the fire still burned in his bones. As he conversed from time to time with his friends, his arguments grew clearer and his convictions became deeper, till at length his father and uncles—educated men and ministers of the gospel, who could not be carried away with a mere impulse of youthful enthusiasm—were constrained to feel that he had a call from God, which they dared not resist, and they gave him the hand, saying, "Frazar, if such are your motives, such your convictions of duty, go: and God be with you."

With rare thoughtfulness for one of his age, and with that unconscious foresight of the issue—which, when it does not take the form of a presentiment, often seems to foreshadow an early death—he arranged his letters and papers, made an inventory of all articles of value, and left written directions for their disposal if he should be killed in battle. He spent hours in conversation with his physician about the wounds and diseases of soldiers, their fatigues on the march, their dangers in the camp, and their exposures in battle, and went to the war with a knapsack of medicines and a stock of useful ideas as well as warm sympathies, fully resolved to be the medical and moral adviser as well as the military commander of the men who might be intrusted to his charge. Meanwhile, he had been most assiduously training himself in the use of the bayonet and the revolver, and in the sword-exercise, under the best teachers he could find in Amherst and in Boston.

Young Stearns entered the service with the commission of first-lieutenant in Company I, of the twenty-first regiment of Massachusetts volunteers. He had not long been stationed in Annapolis before General Reno offered him an appointment on his staff; but he declined the flattering offer, preferring an inferior station which brought him in more immediate contact with his men, whom he was intent on making better soldiers, better men, and, if possible, Christians, by his direct personal influence. In camp and on picket duty he was a rigid disciplinarian. Wherever *he* was, there was order and obedience. No man attempted more than once to disobey him. If his orders were not executed when given at second hand, he had only to give the word of command in person, and he met with instant obedience. In thorough drilling of his men, he was surpassed by no officer in the regiment. As military tactics had been his daily study and practice for months, so now, during the months which intervened before his regiment was called into actual service, he made it his daily business to train his soldiers to the prompt and perfect execution of every military movement which could be required of them. He knew his own place as a man "under authority," and kept it, occupied it, filled it to the full; and he expected his men to know and occupy and fill theirs. He expected every man to do his duty; but he expected no more subordination and obedience, no more self-denial or hardship from his men, than he was willing to submit to and did submit to himself, every day of his life. He ruled by example as well as by command. His character carried more weight than his office or even his personal presence.

He was considered a kind of prodigy at Annapolis. He was a soldier who never drank intoxicating drinks, nor used tobacco, nor swore, nor lost his temper; who always maintained his dignity, and yet always manifested the liveliest sympathy for the health, character, and happiness of all under his command. "There was not a religious service," so writes the chaplain of the regiment, "which he did not encourage. . . . . When I distributed among the men religious books, he was among the few officers who always received them gladly. His life was an example to officers and men. He was never angry, though often exceedingly tried. He never uttered a profane word. His language was gentle-

manly to all, and his bearing full of the dignity of a soldier and the affability of
a comrade and brother." Such dignity, combined with such courtesy and kindness, commanded at once respect and affection. The united influence of his
discipline and his example operated like a charm in the camp, producing not
only order and decorum, but manliness, and more or less of the manners of the
gentleman, if not also of the virtues of the Christian. He became, as might be
expected, a great favorite with the men; and when he was promoted to the
office of acting adjutant of the regiment, the superior officers vied with each
other in securing for him the appointment, and each claimed him as peculiarly
his own. He charmed also the families with whom he mingled freely during his
sojourn at and near the capital of Maryland, not more by his music, of which he
was a master, than by the rare dignity of his manners and the more rare excellence of his whole character. And when, at the embarkation of the regiment to
join the Burnside expedition, his noble form was seen marching at the head of
the lines, and then bowing reverently while his honored father (who had come to
take a last farewell of him) commended them to God in public prayer, he received
also the blessing and bore away the hearts of all who had known him there; as
was most affectingly manifested by the many and touching letters of condolence
which the bereaved parents received from those families after his too speedy
death.

Of his participation in the hardships, trials, battles, and victories of the
Burnside expedition; his patience, faith, and hope during the dreadful storm at
sea, and within the Straits of Hatteras; his constant exposure, steadfast courage,
repeated wounds, and hair-breadth escapes at Roanoke Island; and his brilliant
charge and heroic death in the hard-fought battle at Newbern—it is scarcely
necessary to write at length in this private memoir. The daring achievements
of that expedition, and the part which young Stearns bore in them, are no unim-
portant portion of the public history of the war; and this war will hold no unim-
portant place in the history of our country in coming centuries.

In the battle of Roanoke, the twenty-first regiment of Massachusetts volunteers, after lying on their arms through a sleepless and stormy night, and wading
and cutting their way through almost impenetrable swamps in the morning, were
under fire two hours and a half, flanked the enemy's battery and charged upon it
in the hottest of the fire, and were the first to plant the flag of Massachusetts and
the Union upon the fortifications.

In all these hardships and dangers, Adjutant Stearns was always leading the
men. Says Major Clark, in a private letter: "He was prostrated by a bullet
which struck the visor of his cap, but immediately sprang to his feet, the blood
streaming down his face, and rushed forward with his comrades to the charge
upon the battery. During the same terrific volley from the enemy, a rifle-ball

passed over his right shoulder and through his coat-collar, cutting a shallow wound, about three inches in length, on the back of his neck."—"The bullets whistled all around me," writes Adjutant Stearns himself, "the cannon-shots flew over me, and yet none hit me till the very last. Then, as if God wished to show me how kind he was to me, I was hit twice: first by a ball which passed within a quarter of an inch of my spine, made a little furrow in my neck, and passed through my shirt, vest, and overcoat; the other, a buckshot, entered my cap, passed through, and hit me on the right forehead. I immediately fell, half-stunned, but soon recovered, and was in the midst of it again. I never felt the wound till twenty-four hours after the battle, when it caused me some trouble for two or three days, but is now quite well. God grant I may see you all, dear ones, again, and that together we may thank him for preserving you from any harm, and me from the bullet and cannon-shot, and more still from the moral pestilence of camp-life! Pray for me that my faith may be strengthened, that my purposes may all be changed for righteousness. God grant this unhappy war may cease! He seems to be doing the work now, and I must hope that he will achieve the victory for us. But we must give him the credit. As when he told Gideon to leave most of his men behind, so now he seems to be working for us. He is our best Major-General, and where can the enemy find such an one, though educated at West Point, and trained by years of actual experience?"

After the battle, Adjutant Stearns was named with special honor in the reports of the major, the lieutenant-colonel commanding the regiment, and the general of the division.

The battle of Roanoke was fought on the 8th of February. On the 14th of March, the same troops were again engaged in the bloody fight at Newbern, with superior numbers, intrenched behind miles of fortifications bristling with cannon, and further protected by rifle-pits from approach on the flanks.

"Adjutant Stearns had never recovered entirely from the excessive fatigue and excitement through which he passed at Roanoke," so writes his friend and commanding officer, Colonel Clark—though, with characteristic self-forgetfulness, his own letters, all the while, make no mention of the fact to his friends—"and at the time of our landing here, he was scarcely fit to leave the ship. I advised him to remain behind, but he would not think of it." No sickness but that of absolute inability, was sufficient to keep him from the post of duty; and danger, so far from deterring, only beckoned him on to the thickest of the fight. Here, again, his regiment was the first to flank the rebel fortifications; and while the greater part of it was engaged in clearing the rifle-pits, two hundred men, with their gallant lieutenant-colonel (Clark) commanding at their head, penetrating along the line of the intrenchments, charged upon three thousand of the enemy, captured three of the mounted guns in succession, and, though afterward com-

27

pelled to fall back before overwhelming numbers, yet, reinforced by the fourth Rhode Island regiment, they returned to the charge, and swept all before them. Early in this fearful charge, near the first gun which was captured from the enemy, Adjutant Stearns fell, leading on his men, and himself fighting fearlessly against vastly superior numbers. A Minie ball, entering the right breast, passed directly through his body. He lived about two hours and a half, though most of the time unconscious—called for water twice—and, with uplifted hands, uttering for his last words the language of prayer, fell asleep.

The private who bore him off from the thickest of the battle, writes that he has "lost the best friend he had in the army;" and with something, perhaps, of the extravagance of his countrymen (for he was an Irishman), calls him "the star of the regiment, and the noblest soldier the world ever afforded, only too brave for his own good."

His admired and beloved colonel, his professor in college, and for years one of his most intimate friends, wept like a child when he heard that his friend, his pupil, his brother, his almost son, had been so suddenly snatched away from him. "We thought," he writes, "as he had been wounded and so narrowly escaped with his life on the 8th of February, we thought it would be the turn of some other officer to suffer before him. Alas! death loves a shining mark, and took from us the one most universally admired and most highly esteemed. He set us an almost perfect example in all his conduct. His faithfulness, efficiency, and bravery, were only surpassed by the spotless purity and complete correctness of his private life. He lived and died a Christian, in the full assurance of hope and faith. He fell while fighting gallantly, in the act of charging upon the enemy, in a most severely-contested battle, and on a field where the Union forces won a most glorious victory."

The chaplain speaks of his death as "our greatest loss at the battle of Newbern. He had the freshness and ardor of youth, with the courage of a veteran. The whole regiment mourn a brave officer lost, a loved brother dead."

General Burnside issued the following order:

"HEAD-QUARTERS, DEPARTMENT OF NORTH CAROLINA.

"Special Order No. 52.   "NEWBERN, *March* 16*th*, 1862.

"The commanding general directs that the six-pounder brass gun taken in the battery when Adjutant Stearns, of the twenty-first Massachusetts volunteers, met his death, while gallantly fighting at the battle of Newbern, shall be presented to his regiment, as a monument to the memory of a brave man.

"By command of Brigadier-General A. E. BURNSIDE.

"Lieutenant-Colonel CLARK, commanding.   LEWIS RICHMOND, Assist. Adj.-General."

The regiment voted to present the gun to the college of which Adjutant Stearns was a member, and of which his father is the president, to be deposited there as at once a monument to his bravery, and a just tribute to the patriotism and public spirit of the institution. It stands in the college library, bearing as an inscription the names of all the members of the regiment who lost their lives at Newbern, under the appropriate caption "DULCE ET DECORUM EST PRO PATRIA MORI."* It was one of the old United States guns, manufactured at Chicopee, Massachusetts, and carried South by the conspirators to arm the rebellion. By a just retribution, it returned to the section from which it was stolen.

The college classmate and fellow-soldier of Stearns, Lieutenant Sanderson, with whom he would often pass whole evenings in talking of their beloved college and home and friends, and especially of their home in heaven, and who, like him, had been wounded in the battle of Roanoke, had the melancholy satisfaction of accompanying his remains to the residence of his parents. An immense concourse from the college and the town, from the neighboring towns, and from various parts of the commonwealth and the country, assembled in the village church at the funeral, drawn by sympathy and a desire to do him honor; and a vast procession of students, citizens, and strangers followed the body to its last resting-place. Never before was there such a funeral in Amherst. "Precious in the sight of the Lord is the *death* of his saints." Precious also in the sight of the nation is the *death* of its patriotic, heroic, Christian young men. Sympathy for the "fallen brave," brought home by this war more or less directly to the hearts of the whole people, is enriching them with something of their heroism. In the mysterious providence and grace of God, the soil lately cursed with moral barrenness, or grown over with the rank weeds of selfishness, greed of gain, and political corruption, sown with their blood, is springing up into a plentiful harvest of patriotic, heroic, and Christian virtues.

It were quite superfluous to sketch the character of Adjutant Stearns. That character shone in every form and feature of his tall, erect, and manly person. It acted itself out, without disguise or concealment, in all the incidents of his short but noble and heroic life. It breathes in gentle yet lofty and earnest tones from his confidential letters to his friends. Perhaps courage and a high sense of honor were the most marked characteristics of his noble nature. None who knew him would hesitate to apply to him the title of "the knight without fear and without reproach." But the crown of all his excellences was, that he was a Christian. His patriotism was Christian patriotism; his chivalry, his heroism, were everywhere manifestly and distinctively Christian. This is sufficiently evident in his letter written after the battle of Roanoke, and copied in part on a former page. All his letters are in the same spirit. Let one or two more brief

---

* This was the motto of the military company organized in college, at the time of the fall of Fort Sumter.

extracts conclude this biographical sketch, and bear the impress of his own words, of his own fearless, generous, self-sacrificing spirit, on the minds of our readers:

ANNAPOLIS, *Sept. 25th.* "How can you terrify one who has made up his mind that his life is his country's; who can look *death* in the face, and expects it at every turn? If I can serve my country better by dying now than by living, I am ready to do it. Meantime, pray for me without ceasing, not that I may return safely, but that God may bless me spiritually."

ANNAPOLIS, *Oct. 6th.* "Oh, that I could see the country awake to their danger! that I could see them all on their knees in prayer to God to forgive their sins, and help them in the right! The war now before us is not unlike that of the Revolution. We must give not only our treasures and our sons, but ourselves. I want to see the whole country awake; it seems as though they were all dead or asleep. From all sides comes the cry, 'More men, more men— men of self-sacrificing spirit, men who know how to die!'"

ROANOKE ISLAND, *March 9th,* the evening before the expedition set sail for Newbern. "These are horrible times, when every man's hand is against his neighbor. But I have hope. Let the North pray more. Let them give the glory to God, and not to men, and these days which are rolling by shall be full of glorious victories, which are soon, very soon, to bring a peace."

EPHRAIM E. ELLSWORTH.

EPHRAIM ELMER ELLSWORTH, of the eleventh New York volunteers (New York Fire Zouaves), was born at Mechanicsville, a small village in the towns of Stillwater and Halfmoon, in the county of Saratoga, New York, on the 23d of April, 1837.

The distress which swept over the country in consequence of the financial difficulties of the times, ingulfed the parents of the infant in poverty immediately after his birth, and the earlier years of his life were spent in witnessing the buffeting of fortune by his parents, and in sharing their trials. At an early age the science of war arrested his attention; and with great difficulty, and at great sacrifices, he fitted himself for a cadetship at West Point; but the want of political influence in the poor and friendless boy, rendered all his endeavors unavailing, and blasted all his hopes.

Disappointed, but without desponding, while yet a lad he turned from the home of his childhood, and from the aged couple whom he loved, to seek and to secure his own fortune by his own unaided efforts; and after spending some time in Troy, and in the city of New York, he established himself as a patent-agent in the thriving city of Chicago, Illinois. Notwithstanding the promise of success, to which his diligence and attention entitled him, he was again doomed to disappointment, through the fraudulent practices of one in whom he had confided; and he commenced the study of the law, supporting himself meanwhile by copying, during the hours which are usually appropriated to repose.

During this diversified career, young Ellsworth never lost sight of the military of the country, or wholly abandoned his earlier purposes. He witnessed the sad effects of imperfect militia laws, inefficiently administered by incompetent officers; and he aspired to the honor of being instrumental in elevating the standard of military discipline in the local militia of the United States. With this view, he carefully examined the different systems of tactics which had been published in the United States, and having become satisfied that the habits and tastes of the people were better adapted to the discipline and manœuvres of light infantry, he adopted Hardee's modifications of the French Zouave system as a basis; and from that he constructed a new and peculiar system, differing somewhat from any which had been before in use. His next step was to organize a

28

model corps, with which to test the newly-formed system, and through which to introduce it to the notice of the country. A band of respectable, temperate, and athletic young men responded to his invitation; and on the 4th of May, 1859, were organized, under his direction, the well-known United States Zouaves of the city of Chicago. Adopting the most rigid of the codes of temperance, the use of intoxicating drinks or tobacco, in any form or at any time, was made cause for immediate expulsion; and the most laborious modes of exercise were practised to habituate the young city-bred recruits, to the arduous duties attending a tour of active duty in the field. Heavily-laden knapsacks, prolonged drills, in quick and double-quick time, and other artificial means, were regularly and systematically employed, to inure the men to fatigue; while, at the same time, the greatest attention was paid to the practice of the manual, to the promptitude and precision of the facings, and to the celerity of the different movements. After having spent about a year in the training of this company of light troops —the rising fame of which gradually extended from one extremity of the Union to the other—Captain Ellsworth entered it, in competition for a stand of colors, which had been off'red for the best-drilled company of citizen soldiery, by the United States Agricultural Association at the annual exhibition; and the young commander enjoyed the pleasure of carrying away with his company all the honors, as well as the coveted prize for which he had contended.

This triumph, heralded through the press, increased the measure of Captain Ellsworth's fame; and, in July, 1860, the Zouaves made a tour to the East, for the purpose of testing their efficiency with that of the justly celebrated commands in Boston, New York, and other principal cities of the seaboard states, and of giving them an opportunity to compete with them for the custody of the prize.

The novel character of their uniform, combined with the equally novel system of tactics which they used, and their apparent indifference to the greatest amount of overwhelming labor and fatigue, insured for the Zouaves the most enthusiastic welcome wherever they went; and after a long absence they returned to their western homes, laden with well-earned honors, freely bestowed on them by the multitudes who witnessed their drills and parades.

Immediately after his return to Chicago, so great was the military enthusiasm which prevailed among the young men of that city, a volunteer regiment was organized, and the command tendered to Captain Ellsworth, which he promptly accepted. Without any unnecessary delay, he proceeded to instruct his new command; and soon afterward he tendered it to the newly-elected governor of the state, for active duty, whenever its services might be required.

In the Presidential election of 1860, Captain Ellsworth took an active part in behalf of Mr. Lincoln; and when that gentleman proceeded to Washington in the following spring, for the purpose of assuming the responsible duties of his office, he accompanied him as one of his party of escort.

Soon afterward he received a commission as lieutenant in the regular service, preliminary to his entrance into the department of war, as the head of the proposed bureau of the militia ; but the opening of hostilities in the South, by the attack on Fort Sumter, which aroused the hitherto dormant energies of the North, also liberated Ellsworth from the monotony of bureau service, and secured his more useful services, as a disciplinarian, to his outraged country.

He had long known the peculiar characteristics of the firemen of the city of New York, and had coveted an opportunity to employ them in the particular service to which he had devoted himself. As soon as possible, therefore, after the publication of the President's proclamation, calling for seventy-five thousand men from the militia of the several states, Colonel Ellsworth proceeded to New York and organized a regiment from among the firemen of that city Ten companies were filled within two days after the opening of the rolls ; and with his whole soul resting on the work, he immediately proceeded to instruct his men in the primary branches of their military education. The peculiarly winning manners of the colonel instantly gained for him the affections of his men, and he acquired perfect control of them, notwithstanding the remarkable impatience of control which so strongly marked their character.

On the 29th of April, all things requisite having been provided, the regiment prepared to move to the city of Washington. Stands of colors were presented to it with appropriate addresses, by the fire department, by Mrs. Augusta Astor—the accomplished lady of John Jacob Astor, Jr., and by the ladies at the Astor House ; when, under an escort of upwards of five thousand firemen in uniform, it proceeded to the foot of Canal street, and embarked on board the steamship Baltic, bound for Annapolis, Maryland.

On its arrival at Annapolis, the regiment moved forward to Washington ; and on the 2d of May, it entered that city, amid an ovation which was equalled only by that which attended its departure from New York. The hall of representatives, in the Capitol, was set apart for the quarters of the regiment ; and there it remained for several days. The colonel, meanwhile, employing his time in the instruction of his command in the duties of their new profession.

On the 23d of May, orders were received by Colonel Ellsworth to hold his command in readiness to move into Virginia in the following night ; and at a late hour on that day, he called his men around him and addressed them in his familiar and affectionate style, in the following words :

" Boys, no doubt you felt surprised on hearing my orders to be in readiness at a moment's notice, but I will explain all as far as I am allowed.

" Yesterday forenoon I understood that a movement was to be made against

Alexandria. Of course, I was on the *qui vive*. I went to see General Mansfield, the commander at Washington, and told him that I would consider it as a personal affront if he would not allow us to have the right of the line, which is our own, as the first volunteer regiment sworn in for the war.

"All that I can tell you is, to prepare yourselves for a nice little sail, and, at the end of it, a skirmish.

"Go to your tents, lie down and take your rest till two o'clock, when the boat arrives, and we go forward to victory or death.

"When we reach the place of destination, act as men; do nothing to shame the regiment; show the enemy that you are men, as well as soldiers; and that you will treat them with kindness until they force you to use violence. I want to kill them with kindness.

"Go to your tents, and do as I tell you."

He then proceeded to his quarters, and addressed a letter to his bethrothed, and the following to his parents:

"HEAD-QUARTERS, FIRST ZOUAVES, CAMP LINCOLN,
"WASHINGTON, *May* 23*d*.

"MY DEAR FATHER AND MOTHER: The regiment is to move across the river to-night. We have no means of knowing what reception we are to meet with. I am inclined to the opinion that our entrance into the city of Alexandria will be hotly contested, as I am informed that a large force have arrived there to-day. Should that happen, my dear parents. it may be my lot to be injured in some manner.

"Whatever may happen, cherish the consolation that I was engaged in the performance of a sacred duty; and to-night, thinking over the probabilities of the morrow, and the occurrences of the past, I am perfectly content to accept whatever my fortune may be, confident that He who noteth even the fall of a sparrow, will have some purpose even in the fate of one like me.

"My darling and ever-loved parents, good-by. God bless, protect, and care for you.   ELMER."

During the night, as has been intimated, the Zouaves embarked on the steamers Baltimore and Mount Vernon, and, preceded by the steam sloop-of-war Pawnee, they advanced down the Potomac to the city of Alexandria, for the purpose of co-operating in a proposed attack on that city. The Pawnee had already summoned the town to surrender when the Zouaves reached it; and as the two transports approached the wharf, the enemy's sentinels discharged their pieces in the air and retired.

Immediately afterward the regiment debarked, company E, Captain Leveridge, having been the first to go ashore, and it was immediately formed in line on the street facing the river. After having detailed company E to occupy and destroy the railroad track leading to Richmond, for the purpose of cutting off the enemy's communication, he took Lieutenant Winser and a file of men, and, in person, proceeded to cut off the telegraph wires leading from the city. They marched in double-quick time, and had proceeded only a short distance, when the attention of Colonel Ellsworth was attracted to a large secession flag, which floated from the roof of the Marshall House, a hotel kept by J. W. Jackson. Colonel Ellsworth, notwithstanding the weakness of his party, and his want of adequate support, immediately undertook to remove the obnoxious ensign; and for that purpose he entered the hotel, demanding from a man whom he met in the hall—"Who put that flag up?" and received as an answer, "I don't know; I am a boarder here."

The party immediately proceeded to the roof of the building, and the colonel cut down the colors. As they were returning, they were met in one of the halls of the building by the same person who had previously stated that he was a boarder—who was, in fact, the landlord of the hotel—who, meanwhile, had armed himself with a double-barrelled gun. Rushing forward, he aimed at Colonel Ellsworth's breast, which was observed by Francis E. Brownell, a private of company A, who was one of the party. Before the latter succeeded in throwing up the gun, one barrel was discharged, the contents of which entered the colonel's breast, instantly killing him. He dropped forward with that heavy, horrible, headlong weight which always comes of sudden death inflicted in this manner. His assailant then turned to give the contents of the other barrel to Brownell; but at that moment, the ball from Brownell's rifle was sent into his forehead; and, for the purpose of insuring the retributive deed of justice, the young Zouave followed up his fire with an energetic thrust with his sabre-bayonet, which passed through the body of the assailant, and he, also, fell to the floor, perfectly dead.

There is little doubt that Jackson acted on the impulse of the moment, without meditation, and not expecting co-operation. Considering that his house had been invaded, he determined to punish what, in his passion, he thought to be an intrusion on his rights. On the other hand, Colonel Ellsworth unnecessarily exposed himself, without sufficient support, in the heart of an enemy's town; and ventured, with unaccountable rashness, with a squad of men, to do that which required a regiment for its execution.

The body of Colonel Ellsworth, after remaining at the Marshall house a short time, was removed to the navy-yard, at Washington, whence it was carried to the executive mansion. After lying in state in the east room for several hours, the remains were again removed, with every possible demonstration of respect, to the railroad station; and on the entire route, from Washington to Mechanicsville, where the remains were interred, the funeral train was received by throngs of anxious and sorrowful spectators.

The intelligence of Colonel Ellsworth's death, as it was received throughout the extended country, excited the sympathies of all classes for his aged parents; and Brownell, his faithful avenger, was honored with the most marked attentions.

GIDEON WELLES.

THE subject of this sketch is a native of Glastenbury, in the state of Connecticut, where he was born in July, 1802. In early life, he applied his energies to the study of law, first in the office of Thomas S. Williams, the chief-justice of Connecticut, and subsequently under the direction of William W. Ellsworth. He entered upon the editorial duties of the *Hartford Times*, in January, 1826, and in the following year, was elected to the legislature of his native state. Upon the breaking up of the Republican and Federal parties about this time, he, with other influential and well-known men, aided in the organization of the Democratic party, which lent its support to Andrew Jackson, and finally elevated him to the presidency of the United States.

Mr. Welles continued in the editorial department of the *Hartford Times*, until near the termination of Jackson's administration, and was one of its principal contributors until the repeal of the Missouri compromise. He was repeatedly elected to the state legislature of Connecticut, until the year 1835, at which time he received from the General Assembly the appointment of comptroller of the state.

On the election of John M. Niles to the Senate of the United States, Mr. Welles was selected to succeed him in the post-office at Hartford. Here he remained until 1841. The following year he was elected comptroller of the state by the people (that office having been made elective by an alteration of the constitution of the state), and continued in that position until 1844. His administration of the duties of this office was distinguished by ability, and was eminently satisfactory to the people whom he served. From 1846 until 1849, Mr. Welles occupied a prominent place in one of the offices in the navy department at Washington, continuing therein until, by a change of law, civilians were excluded from all naval bureaus in the departments of the United States.

On the adjustment of the financial questions during the administration of President Polk, says a cotemporary, Mr. Welles considered the mission of the old parties at an end—nothing but their organizations and the prejudices and antagonisms engendered remaining. In the mean time, new questions arising relating to the territorial policy of the federal government as connected therewith, Mr. Welles, adhering to his original principles, maintained the Jeffersonian doctrine, that slavery was the creature of local law, and should not be extended into the territories through the agency or instrumentality of the government. On the repeal of the Missouri compromise, followed by the Kansas aggressions, rendering the institution of a new party organization necessary, the Republican party sprung into existence. Sympathizing in this movement, Mr. Welles took an early and active part in Connecticut, and was, in 1856, the candidate of the Republican party for governor of that state.

From the day of its inception, Mr. Welles threw his whole energy and power into the Republican movement. In 1856 he was appointed by the convention in Philadelphia a member of the Republican National Committee, and, as one of its executive members from its commencement, was chairman of the Connecticut delegation to the convention which met at Chicago, Illinois, and nominated Mr. Lincoln for the presidency.

For many years Mr. Welles has been an active and prolific political writer, and his essays have largely contributed to lend interest to many of the leading journals, and character to the politics of the country. Among these papers, beside those of Connecticut, have been the *Globe* and *Union* at Washington, and the *Evening Post* at New York. The series of articles on the history of nullification, which appeared in the *Evening Post*, exhibit in a very marked manner his historical knowledge and statesmanship.

In March, 1861, on the accession of Abraham Lincoln to the presidency, Mr. Welles was tendered the office of secretary of the navy, and on the 7th of that month, he was confirmed by the United States Senate. This recognition of his eminent abilities, profound sagacity, and stanch, unyielding Republicanism, was a source of the highest gratification to his personal friends in Connecticut, as well as to the people of the country. "It is not invidious in this connection," says a writer, "to remark that his friends are not inclined to boast of the out-going secretary, twice deliberately censured by the House of Representatives; but they have an immovable certainty of conviction that at the expiration of his term, Mr. Welles will return to Connecticut with the universal testimony that he has discharged his duties with spotless integrity, unwearying industry, unshaken firmness, and unimpeachable patriotism."

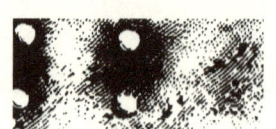

THEODORE WINTHROP.

THEODORE WINTHROP, who fell in the battle of Great Bethel, Virginia,
June 10th, 1861, was born in New Haven, Connecticut, September 21st,
1828. He was a lineal descendant of the first John Winthrop, who in 1630 led
out from England one of the noblest of the many Puritan colonies, and became
himself governor of the commonwealth of Massachusetts. In the next generation we find the second John Winthrop joining the Connecticut colony, soon
raised to its chief magistracy, and in 1665 procuring for her from the crown that
charter of privileges which became the herald and nurse of her future independence, and which, in 1688, she held against the threats and baits of the throne
and its royal representative. Thus Winthrop died to maintain the rights now
and ever supported by his ancestors. It was then the colony against the founder.
It is now the country against the state. The one was a protest of a mature
daughter against a false and cruel mother: the other is a protest of the head and
heart and soul against the hand or foot which would be separated from the nour-
ishing body of which it is a living member. Later still the family furnished yet
another governor, and have in every succeeding generation shared her protection
and dignities.

Major Winthrop's father was Francis Bayard Winthrop, a gentleman of
wealth and education, who was graduated from Yale College in 1804, and died
at his residence in New Haven in 1841. His mother is a grand-daughter of
President Dwight, and a sister of President Wolsey—the latter almost a syno-
nym for scholarship, manners and a Christianized Roman virtue. Thus Winthrop's very name is pervaded with New England virtues and memories—an
aristocratic name, if one can bring himself to utter a term so fraught with meanness, pride, and tyranny, so hateful to a Christian republican; for, in spite of all
levelling, social theories, blood is character. The Edwardses, the Dwights, the
Wolseys, and the Winthrops, did meet in the antecedent blood of Theodore
Winthrop, the soldier, and went to mould and inspire the future hero. We are
each the resultant of past forces; and not only the looks and tones, the habits
and traits of our fathers, but their spirit, their sentiment, and their "faith un-
feigned," leave their invisible, silent deposits in our veins.

As a boy, Major Winthrop is described as fair and pale in feature, but not

29

sickly, delicate in frame, neat in habits, quick and rather precocious in studies. He entered Yale from the well-known school of Messrs. French, of New Haven, and was graduated with the class of 1848. At first he seemed indifferent to literary success; but about the middle of his course his spirit received a mighty momentum, as if a new soul possessed him. Always highly reflective beyond his years, the thought that he was the eldest son, and must sustain the ancestral honors by his personal character and deeds, together with the solemn shadow of life which falls heavily on every sensible and conscientious youth as he passes on through college, awoke him to the intensest activity. The result of this discipline of thought was soon evinced in his sharing the honor, though not the prize, of the senior Berkleian with one classmate, and in his wresting, by severe competition, from another prominent scholar, the Clark scholarship, then for the first time put on a foundation. This contest placed him on perhaps the most honorable list which Yale presents, the "Scholars of the House;" and was more significant of power, since the ordeal was new. The later "Biennial" had not been inaugurated.

Soon after graduation, Winthrop, with Rutledge of South Carolina, and others, formed the first class in the "School of Philosophy and Arts;" a department generously established the year previous, and opening before the youthful scholar a broader range of studies worthy of his best ambition. As the winter wore away, Winthrop's mind proved of a finer grain than had been suspected. He loved metaphysics, and, without remarkable talent for logical inquiry, entered with keen and penetrative sagacity into the vast questions of the infinite, and the unknown, and the phenomenal—the *vasta semina rerum* which will loom up around the chaotic mind of youth. Winthrop seems then to have had a clear, neat, keen intellect, and to have been earnest and tender in spirit, manly in tastes, noble in resolves, high-bred in manners, and showing that poetic refinement and almost ethereal delicacy of sentiment which usually go with the fine organism of the Saxon.

But this severe mental work, added to private literary studies, proved too much for his frame. His physicians told him he must travel. Giving up the plans of theology, literature, and law, which he had successively formed in choosing a profession, he embarked in July, 1849, for Europe. By his journal, we find him arriving at London, August 28th; in Paris, November 23d; and at Rome, January 9th. With eyes, ears, and pen continually busy, he spends February in traversing eastern Italy, March in Greece, April in northern Italy, and, after tramping in a sturdy pedestrian tour through Germany and Switzerland, returns to Paris in September. To enter and mingle thus in the historic glories of the Old World, was a privilege longed for from childhood; and yet his itineraries show that travel cultured and broadened his observing mind only to sadden it. In London, at the outset of his journey, he writes, "I am half-dead in body and mind;" and at Paris, at its close, he bitterly exclaims on his birth-day, "Life at present offers me no hope." This subtle, pervasive melancholy was due less to disease than the fine structure of his mind. Nothing can exceed the sufferings of a gifted youth who is conscious of power, yet unable to gauge that power, determine its true field, and realize it in action. He longs to traverse the sea of life where his companions have wandered before him, hearing in the distance its tumultuous waves, each crested with hopes yet dark below, the grave of many projects. Full of allusions to death, he dreads it not. It is the premature decay of mental health, this dying before one has half lived or even begun to live, that cast down his high and regnant soul. In his last years, philosophy, religion, and worldly knowledge, brought him to a "serene and upper air," which no such fears could disturb. In Greece alone he becomes buoyant and elastic. It was sacred ground, where heroes called to his classic mind from every hill and stream and valley; a land pervaded with high resolves, long since made good in history. He, too, could become all he wished; for, to a true heart, a clear purpose is more inspiring even than achievement.

In April, 1851, three months after his return, Mr. Winthrop entered the Pacific Mail Steamship Company, at the invitation of W. H. Aspinwall, Esq., whose acquaintance he had made in Europe. His diaries show him still alive to poetry, metaphysics, criticisms; still wrestling with the problem of the life of the body and the higher life of the soul. In one place he says strongly: "Men die for three reasons; because they have, or cannot, or will not, achieve their destiny. As for me, I *would* belong to the first class; but, finding myself in the third, prefer, even with a shock to my pride, to be ranked in the second, and pray that the fruitless struggle may be soon ended." He fears that he cannot realize a perfect manhood; and yet who would have thought that such pensiveness could underlie so much life, action, and noble feeling?

In September, Mr. Winthrop recrossed the Atlantic, to place Mr. Aspinwall's son and nephew at school in Switzerland, and, after revisiting some of the more interesting portions of Germany, enters upon his old duties in January, 1852. The ensuing autumn finds him in Panama, in the employment of the steamship company, and almost well and happy. The tropics, where physical life is most intense, varied, and perfect, is a new world. Every thing invites and promises adventure. The spirit of travel is strong upon him, and he cannot be quiet. Nature speaks, and he is her child, and must ever listen with reverence and joy to her many voices. After often traversing the Isthmus with the treasure-parties, he returned home by San Francisco. Here the observer, poet, thinker, is busy. The mines of California, the filthy delusions of Utah, sickness at the Dalles of the Columbia, the hospitalities of Governor Ogden of the Hudson's Bay Company, perils from treacherous Indians, the wilderness, the desert, and the mountains, crowd his note-book with thrilling incident and vivid pictures. These are partly embodied in "John Brent," and a volume of Sketches, yet to be published.

He returns to the counting-room in November; but his heart and fancy are still abroad. Accordingly, in January, 1854, with Mr. Aspinwall's consent, he joins Lieutenant Strain's expedition to prospect for a ship-canal among the Sierras of the Isthmus, and would have perished from hardships had he not wandered from his party and been forced to make his way back to the ship. Returning to New York, he began in March the study of law in the office of Charles Tracy, Esq.; and after his admission to the bar, in 1855, remained with him as clerk another year.

The following summer finds him travelling in Maine with Church the artist, and under their mutual inspiration he drinks in nature with the soul of a poet and the eye of a painter. He returned to enter the political campaign of 1856. Long since a Republican in heart and by scholarship, he canvassed for Fremont in Pennsylvania, entering with all his energies into that conflict between slaveocracy and liberty of which the present civil war is the bloody consummation. America, to use his own strong words, seemed—

> "A noble land to stride athwart and wake
> All its myriads up to noble thought;
> Deep sleep of thousand hearts to break,
> Till great deliverance is wrought!"

After the issue, he established himself in law at St. Louis; but the climate and life not suiting, he returned in July, 1858, to find at last his true calling—the pleasing, perilous field of literature and authorship. Never did a writer use more conscientious energy. He studied, read, wrote, and rewrote, mastered botany, and travelled by every method; so that the thought, the quotation, the style, the features, might be perfect—coming ever near the face and heart of his great teacher, Nature. "The March of the Seventh New York Regiment to Washington," and "Love and Skates," two well-known contributions to the *Atlantic Monthly,* "Cecil Dreeme," "John Brent," and "Edwin Brothertoft," are already published; while a volume of travels is promised—but a small portion of the embryo novels, tales, essays, and poems, which shine among his papers. The prelude has become, with his deeds, the whole drama. "John Brent" especially abounds in masterly single pictures of scenes and characters; while all his works are marked by a clear, neat, antithetic style, and sublimed by just, warm, nobly humane sentiments. Here and there we find a broad generalization, showing that fine philosophy which the deeper novelist always draws from.

But, at the fall of Sumter, Winthrop dropped the pen and grasped the sword. The acts which followed all know. He joined the seventh regiment at New York; marched with it to Washington; became a member of General Butler's staff, as aid and military secretary, at Fortress Monroe; and aided in planning the attack on the batteries at Great Bethel, where, on the disastrous 10th of June, he fell in the van, his firm wiry form erect, waving his sword, and calling his comrades on into the very jaws of death.

And yet he did not die, he cannot die. The brave, like the good, die never. He lives—destined to be an inspiring historic name of the war.

But Winthrop's life and death are best sung by himself, in his own poems:

> " March we must, ever wearily,
> March we will; true men will be true.....
>   " Mine be a life
> Of struggle and endurance, and a *free*
> *Dash at the fates* which front us terribly!
> Certain bliss, yet nobler effort still!
> Grander duties, gemmed with finer joys.—
> He sleeps! Ah, well! not on some field
> Where victor charge and victor shout,
> Ringing through feeble pulses, pealed
> As when a falchion smites a shield,
> And dying hearts, too happy, yield
> Their life with conquering pæans out!"

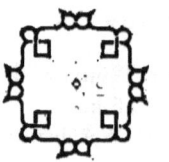

FREDERICK W. LANDER.

AT a moment of peculiar peril, the nation was called upon to lament the death of one of her bravest chiefs. In the midst of the smoke and tumult of battle, she paused to twine the cypress-leaf with the laurel she had given him.

Brigadier-General FREDERICK W. LANDER was born at Salem, Massachusetts, in the year 1823. Like Putnam, Stark, and Marion, he was born a soldier: the profession of arms was a passion with him from his youth, and, though the graduate of no military academy, he will be remembered among the very ablest of those great-hearted gentlemen who have made themselves the bulwark of the American republic.

General Lander's name was first brought prominently before the American people in connection with the exploration for a wagon-road to the Pacific, several years since. By referring to the state papers, it will be seen how admirably he performed his arduous labors. His official report to the department proves him to have possessed fine literary as well as scientific attainments. He would have been a poet of no ordinary power, if he had not been so thoroughly a soldier.

At the breaking out of the present rebellion, he was assigned by General McClellan, then in Western Virginia, a position on his staff. In Lander's cool daring throughout that successful campaign, particularly at Philippa and Rich Mountain, was the ring of the true metal. The people listened to it with hope. Upon General McClellan's appointment to the command of the army of the Potomac, General Lander accompanied him, and proved an invaluable auxiliary in putting fresh strength into the half-demoralized and dispirited forces. Shortly afterward, the government dispatched him upon secret service; he accomplished the delicate task with credit to his own discernment, and to the entire satisfaction of the President.

On his return from the foreign mission, he was immediately placed in command of a brigade in General Banks's division; and at the affair at Edwards's Ferry, on the 22d of October, 1861, he was for the first time wounded, receiving a musket-ball in the leg while gallantly leading his men. He was no holiday hero. He shared the dangers of the battle with his humblest private.

The wound was of such a serious nature, that he was obliged to relinquish his command for several weeks. How patiently he endured the mere physical suffering, and how he chafed under the galling necessity that kept him a prisoner in a sick-room, when his country needed him so much, is known to those whose privilege it was to nurse him during that dark period.

In person, General Lander was a type of strength and masculine beauty. Tall of stature, with a countenance that indicated the possession of that impartial integrity and nobleness which we associate with the ancient Greek character, he was warm and loyal in his friendships, but cold and severe to every shape of wrong. His wild frontier experiences had given him something of the imperturbability of an Indian warrior. It has been said that he was insensible to peril. He was more than that. No eye was quicker than his to detect danger, but he had that lofty moral courage which taught him to scorn it judiciously. His men revered and loved him. The corps which was enlisted in his native city formed his body-guard, and followed him to Western Virginia under a pledge to Mrs. Lander that they would never leave him upon the field of battle. In case of defeat, this devoted band had sworn to die with him. Some four years since, General Lander was married to Miss J. M. Davenport, the distinguished tragedienne, and a most accomplished lady.

Before General Lander had fairly recovered from the effects of his wound, he again took the field. He assumed the command of the national forces at Romney, Virginia. A movement on the part of the rebel General Jackson, threatening to outflank his troops, rendered it expedient for him to evacuate the position. It was his fate to give us but one more instance of his indomitable energy and valor. Having discovered that there was a rebel camp at Blooming Gap, he marched his four thousand men a distance of thirty-two miles, and completely surprised the enemy, capturing no less than seventeen commissioned officers and fifty privates. The general, with one of his aides-de-camp, Lieutenant Fitz-James O'Brien, dashed in among them, and demanded their surrender, some two minutes before the Union lines reached the spot. The secretary of war complimented General Lander in the following letter:

"WAR DEPARTMENT, WASHINGTON, *February 17th,* 1862.

"The President directs me to say that he has observed with pleasure the activity and enterprise manifested by yourself and the officers and the soldiers of your command. You have shown how much may be done in the worst weather and worst roads, by a spirited officer at the head of a small force of brave men unwilling to waste life in camp when the enemies of their country are within reach.

"Your brilliant success is a happy presage of what may be expected when the army of the Potomac shall be led to the field by their gallant general.

"EDWIN M. STANTON, *Secretary of War.*

"To Brigadier-General F. W. LANDER."

The knightly exploit, however, was not without its price. The terrible march irritated the wound, which had never ceased to be painful, and brought on a complication of diseases. At Camp Chase, on the 2d of March, 1862, this gallant spirit passed

> "To where beyond these voices there is peace."

He was buried with all the honors that a sorrowful and grateful nation could bestow. His name will be woven forever with the annals of the land he loved. "History will preserve the record of his life and character, and romance will delight in portraying a figure so striking, a nature so noble, and a career so gallant."[*]

Such is the brief story of a man whose love of country was so pure and beautiful, whose heart was so full of all kindly and chivalric qualities, that, at firesides where he had never been, women wept for him as if he were their brother; and old men said of him, as though he were their son, "LANDER IS DEAD!"

---

[*] General McClellan, in Order No. 86, announcing Lander's death to the army of the Potomac.

30

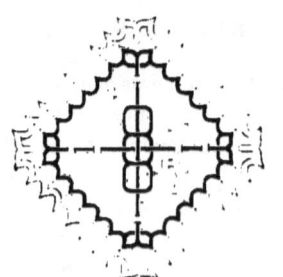

WILLIAM STARKE ROSECRANS.

WILLIAM STARKE ROSECRANS was born in Kingston, Delaware county, Ohio, December 6th, 1819. His father emigrated to Ohio from the Wyoming valley, in 1808. His mother, Jemima Hopkins, was the daughter of a Revolutionary soldier. His early life was passed in close application to study, and in his eighteenth year he entered the United States military academy at West Point; whence he graduated, third in mathematics and fifth in general merit, in 1842. He received the brevet of second-lieutenant of engineers, July 1st; served that year at Fortress Monroe as first assistant-engineer, under command of Lieutenant-Colonel R. E. De Russey; and was ordered to duty at West Point, in September, 1843, as assistant professor of engineering. From August, 1844, until August, 1845, he served as assistant professor of natural and experimental philosophy at the military academy, and in 1845, '46, and '47, in the engineering department as assistant and first assistant professor. He also served as post-quartermaster at West Point for some months.

In 1847, Lieutenant Rosecrans was assigned to duty at Newport, Rhode Island, to reconstruct the large military wharves destroyed by a storm—an appointment regarded as an official recognition of his great ability as an engineer. Here he remained until 1852, when he was charged with the survey (made under act of Congress) of New-Bedford harbor, Taunton River, and Providence harbor. From April till November, 1853, he served as constructing engineer at the Washington navy-yard, when, on account of ill health, he tendered his resignation to the secretary of war, Jefferson Davis. His resignation was not accepted; but he was given leave of absence, with the understanding that if, upon the expiration of the leave, the resignation was insisted upon, it would be accepted. In April, 1854, therefore, Lieutenant Rosecrans again tendered his resignation, and retired from the service.

For the next year he occupied an office in Cincinnati, as consulting engineer and architect; and in June, 1855, became president of the Canal-Coal Company, and superintended its work on Coal River, Virginia, where it was engaged in the construction of locks and dams, and in the endeavor to effect slack-water navigation. This position he relinquished to assume control of the business of the Cincinnati Coal-Oil Company, in which he was directly interested.

When General McClellan was placed at the head of the Ohio volunteers, he appointed Rosecrans acting chief engineer, with the rank of major; and the legislature of Ohio soon after created, purposely for him, and with the rank of colonel, the office of chief engineer of the state. Governor Dennison appointed him, June 10th, colonel of the twenty-third regiment Ohio volunteers, and in that capacity he went to Washington, and arranged for the payment and maintenance of the troops from his state.

Colonel Rosecrans was appointed a brigadier-general of the United States army, June 20th, 1861. Placed at the head of a brigade, composed of the eighth and tenth Indiana and the seventeenth and nineteenth Ohio regiments, he participated in the earliest advance into Western Virginia; was in command at Parkersburg; proceeded thence to Grafton, and by Buckhannon, with the other part of McClellan's force to Rich Mountain, where a portion of the rebel General Garnett's force, variously stated at two and four thousand, and commanded by Colonel Pegram, were intrenched at the foot of the hill, on the western slope. Before this position some of General Rosecrans's men had a sharp skirmish with the enemy on the 10th of July, and it was then discovered that their work at the foot of the hill was a very strong one, and was in a position well chosen for defence; it was also learned that they had a much less considerable work on the summit of the hill. It was therefore arranged that, while General McClellan made his preparations to attack the larger work in front, General Rosecrans with his brigade should reach the rear of the rebels, carry their work on the summit of the hill, and participate from that side in the attack on the main fort.

In pursuance of this plan, General Rosecrans left his camp at Roaring Run, two miles west of Rich Mountain, at daylight on July 11th, and advanced by a pathless route through the woods along the south-western slope of the mountain. Compelled very often to cut the way, and even to build a road for the artillery, their progress was necessarily slow. Much rain had previously fallen, and the bushes were still very wet; this, with the cold, and the toilsome march, made the service an unusually severe one. Yet they pressed on, silently and resolutely, and, after a circuit of eight miles, reached a point on the road in the enemy's rear, at three P. M. Although this movement had been projected as a surprise, the enemy was aware of it, and prepared: yet, after a hard fight of three quarters of an hour, he was driven out, and his position taken.

This success decided the fortunes of the rebels at Rich Mountain; for those in the work at the foot of the mountain abandoned their position in the night, and retreated to Laurel Hill. Nearly all the killed and wounded of the Union men at this place were in General Rosecrans's brigade. General McClellan immediately pushed on to Beverly, to cut off the retreat of the force at Laurel Hill; while General Rosecrans, passed on the road, followed at leisure: and other portions of McClellan's command went toward Laurel Hill, and followed the retreat of Garnett to Carrick's Ford.

Immediately after the destruction of the rebel force at Rich Mountain and Laurel Hill, General McClellan began to make active preparations to co-operate with General Cox, on the Kanawha, against the rebels under Wise; but the preparations were delayed by news of the national defeat at Bull Run. McClellan was ordered to Washington; and his army, then at Beverly, was counter-marched to Webster, a few miles south of Grafton, where he left it, July 23d, and the command of the department of the Ohio devolved upon General Rosecrans.

Preparations for the campaign on the Kanawha were continued, but they were now retarded by the necessity for the reorganization of the army, which was composed in a great degree of men enlisted for three months. Meantime, head-quarters were established at Clarksburg; and from that place, on August 20th, General Rosecrans issued an address to the loyal inhabitants of Western Virginia. "Contrary to your interests and your wishes," he said, "the Confeder-ates "have brought war upon your soil. . . . . Between submission to them, and subjugation or expulsion, they leave you no alternative. They have set neigh-bor against neighbor, and friend against friend; they have introduced among you warfare only known among savages. In violation of the laws of nations and humanity, they have proclaimed that private citizens may and ought to make war. Under this bloody code, peaceful citizens, unarmed travellers, and single soldiers, have been shot down, and even the wounded and defenceless have been killed; scalping their victims is all that is wanting to make their war-fare like that which, seventy or eighty years ago, was waged by the Indians against the white race on this very ground. You have no alternative left you but to unite as one man in the defence of your homes, for the restoration of law and order, or be subjugated, or expelled from the soil. I therefore earnestly exhort you to take the most prompt and vigorous measures to put a stop to neighborhood and private wars. . . . . Citizens of Western Virginia, your fate is mainly in your own hands. If you allow yourselves to be trampled under foot by hordes of disturbers, plunderers, and murderers, your land will become a desolation. If you stand firm for law and order, and maintain your rights, you may dwell together peacefully and happily as in former days."

General Rosecrans marched from Clarksburg, August 31st, and once more put himself at the head of his army for active operations. On the 10th of Sep-tember, he reached the rebel intrenchments in front of Carnifex Ferry, and, after a slight skirmish, succeeded in routing General Floyd, and capturing "a few prisoners, two stand of colors, a considerable quantity of arms," together with some military stores.

31

Soon after this action, he established his head-quarters at Wheeling, and commenced preparations for the campaign that was to be opened in the following spring; but in March, 1862, on the creation of the "Mountain Department," and the appointment of General Fremont to its command, General Rosecrans was relieved from duty in Western Virginia, and repaired to Washington, preparatory to entering the field at the West.

Your obedient servant
Benj. F. Butler

BENJAMIN F. BUTLER.

L ITERATURE and Art are the children of Peace. Diplomacy, strategy, and valor, flourish only in the shadow of turbulent events. It is only amid the angry clashing of antagonistic interests, that such men as the subject of this sketch develop and achieve distinction.

BENJAMIN F. BUTLER was born in Deerfield, New Hampshire, on the 5th of November, 1818. His father, John Butler, who served in some capacity in the War of 1812, was of Irish descent. Young Butler's boyhood was passed at Lowell, Massachusetts, where he attended the High School, preparatory to becoming a student at the Exeter Academy. He graduated with honors at Waterville College, studied law in the office of William Smith, Esq., and was admitted to the bar in 1840.

Butler at once plunged into law and politics, pursuing both with equal ardor, and displaying the adroitness and energy which have always characterized him. He speedily made his mark in Middlesex as one of the prominent men of the county. He espoused the most desperate causes, and became, in court, the leader of forlorn-hopes. His singular fertility in expedients, and success in defending rather awkward suits, brought him, in time, a more respectable *clientele*, and he soon won the reputation of being the ablest criminal lawyer in the state.

In 1853, Butler was nominated for the legislature, and elected; in 1858, he was elected to the senate; in 1860, we find him playing a prominent *rôle* as delegate to the Charleston and Baltimore conventions, fulfilling the mission with his usual tact and skill.

During all these years, the combative lawyer and politician had been taking lessons in "the school of the soldier." Butler had always possessed and evinced a taste for military life. In 1840, he was a private in the Lowell City Guards, now immortalized by their share in the memorable conflict at Baltimore, on the 19th of April, 1861. In 1857, he was appointed brigadier-general in the state militia. Destiny was preparing him for his subsequent career. The hour was approaching when his alert brain and strong hand were to be worth untold gold.

In the month of April, 1861, General Butler was one of the earliest to respond to the call of President Lincoln for volunteers, keenly appreciating the important aspect of affairs, and not unmindful, possibly, of the opportunity afforded for military distinction. He eagerly availed himself of it. With a single regiment, the Massachusetts eighth, he marched into Maryland, embarked on board a steamer, made a descent upon Annapolis, then the enemy's country, and held it. The war department immediately created the department of Annapolis, extending to within seven miles of Washington, and including Baltimore. General Butler was installed commander, with the rank of major-general.

He was equal to the emergency. He strengthened his exposed position in all possible ways, setting his soldiers—the *ci-devant* blacksmiths and jacks-of-all-trades—to construct locomotives, build bridges, and make railroads. He took possession of the Relay House, fortifying himself there with the Massachusetts sixth, the New York eighth, and Cook's Boston battery, controlling the great channel of communication between the insurgents in Baltimore and the rebels at Harper's Ferry. He seized the famous steam-gun, and turned it on the enemy. General Butler then marched into Baltimore, accompanied by the two regiments and the battery mentioned; intrenched himself on the highest point of land, overlooking the whole city; issued his proclamation of protection to all loyalists; arrested traitors; seized arms and munitions of war; and rode through the perilous streets at the head of a single company of the gallant Massachusetts sixth, which the mob had so grievously assaulted only three weeks before. His campaign here was a brilliant one in every respect.

In pursuance of Special Order No. 9, dated at Fortress Monroe, the headquarters of the department of Virginia, August 20th, 1861, General Butler assumed command of the volunteer forces in that vicinity. While occupying this post, the lamentable affair at Little Bethel, and the more disastrous repulse at Big Bethel, occurred, and General Butler was superseded by General Wool.

On the 1st day of the following September, the war department "authorized Major-General B. F. Butler to raise, organize, arm, uniform, and equip a volunteer force for the war, in the New England states, not exceeding six regiments." Two days later, the war department authorized him "to fit out and prepare such troops in New England as he may judge fit for the purpose, to make an expedition along the eastern shore of Virginia," etc., etc. In carrying out these plans, a series of embarrassing conflicts arose between General Butler and Governor Andrew. Much bitter feeling was generated. Recruiting was retarded in consequence, and delay followed delay. This is neither the tme nor the place to more than allude to the unfortunate controversy.

At length, on the 20th of February, 1862, General Butler left Boston for Ship Island, in Mississippi Sound, at which destination he arrived on the 23d of March, with a force of fifteen thousand men, to attack New Orleans. Leaving Ship Island on the 17th of April, with a portion of his command, he went up the Mississippi, and, after the surrender of Forts Jackson and St. Philip, proceeded to New Orleans, which city he entered with twenty-five hundred men on the evening of the 1st of May.

Here General Butler again loomed up as the man for the hour. His executive ability, his ready wit, decision, unflinching justice, and, in short, all the peculiar powers of his mind, came into play. That he should have made some false steps, where so many perplexing claims came in contact, does not admit of surprise. No man could have done better, few so well. General Butler's course in New Orleans was, from the first, necessarily a stringent one. He suppressed *The Delta* and *The Bee*, for advocating destruction of produce; arrested several British subjects, for affording aid to the rebels; seized a large amount of specie belonging to the enemy, in the office of the consul for the Netherlands; stopped the circulation of confederate paper-money; distributed among the suffering poor the provisions intended for the support of the Southern army; levied a tax on rebel sympathizers; gave care and protection to Mrs. Beauregard, whom he found in the house of Mr. Slidell; and issued that celebrated and characteristic proclamation respecting active female traitors, which at once extirpated a most annoying nuisance.* He found the city demoralized. He shaped order out of chaos.

---

* Sympathizers with the South claimed to be greatly outraged by this order. The English press became eloquently vituperative on the subject; and General Butler was induced to explain, in a private letter, the motives which constrained him to issue the proclamation. The following is the general's characteristic epistle:

"HEAD-QUARTERS, DEPARTMENT OF THE GULF, NEW ORLEANS, July 2d, 1862.

"MY DEAR SIR: I am as jealous of the good opinion of my friends as I am careless of the slanders of my enemies, and your kind expressions in regard to Order No. 28 lead me to say a word to you on the subject.

"That it ever could have been so misconceived as it has been by some portions of the Northern press is wonderful, and would lead one to exclaim with the Jew, 'O Father Abraham, what these Christians are, whose own hard dealings teaches them suspect the thoughts of others!'

"What was the state of things to which the woman order applied?

"We were two thousand five hundred men in a city seven miles long by two to four wide, of a hundred and fifty thousand inhabitants—all hostile, bitter, defiant, explosive—standing literally on a magazine; a spark only needed for destruction. The devil had entered the hearts of the women of this town (you know seven of them chose Mary Magdalen for a residence), to stir up strife in every way possible. Every opprobrious epithet, every insulting gesture was made by these bejewelled, beerinolined, and laced creatures, calling themselves ladies, toward my soldiers and officers, from the windows of houses and in the streets. How long do you suppose our flesh and blood could have stood this without retort? That would lead to disturbances and riot, from which we must clear the streets with artillery; and then a howl that we murdered these fine women! I had arrested the men who hurrahed for Beauregard. Could I arrest the women? No. What was to be done? No order could be made save one that would execute itself. With anxious, careful thought I hit upon this: 'Women who insult my soldiers are to be regarded and treated as common women plying their vocation.'

"Pray, how do you treat a common woman plying her vocation in the streets? You pass her by unheeded. She cannot insult you! As a gentleman, you can and will take no notice of her. If she

32

He has been the government's faithful servant, and his services will link his name forever with that of the Crescent City. It was a fortunate day for New Orleans when "Picayune Butler came to town." He still retains the post, and the people who hate him can hardly help liking him!

As a man, General Butler is of a warm, impulsive temperament, generous, combative, and brusque. As a politician, he is earnest and formidable. As an advocate, he has never ranked with the leaders of the Massachusetts bar, though his success as a criminal lawyer is, perhaps, without parallel. As an orator, he is fluent and effective, but seldom eloquent. He is apt at reading character, and sometimes applies his knowledge with consummate shrewdness. As a soldier, he has evinced many very high qualities: he has undertaken and performed various onerous duties with such *éclat*, that none but his most ungenerous political adversaries can withhold their commendation.

speaks, her words are not opprobrious. It is only when she becomes a continuous and positive nuisance that you call a watchman and give her in charge to him.

"But some of the Northern editors seem to think that whenever one meets such a woman, one must stop her, talk with her, insult her, or hold dalliance with her; and so from their own conduct they construed my order.

"The editor of the *Boston Courier* may so deal with common women, and out of the abundance of the heart his mouth may speak; but so do not I.

"Why, these she-adders of New Orleans themselves were at once shamed into propriety of conduct by the order; and, from that day, no woman has either insulted or annoyed any live soldier or officer, and of a certainty no soldier has insulted any woman.

"When I passed through Baltimore, on the 23d of February last, members of my staff were insulted by the gestures of the ladies (?) there. Not so in New Orleans.

"One of the worst possible of all these women showed disrespect to the remains of gallant young De Kay; and you will see her punishment—a copy of the order of which I enclose—is at once a vindication and a construction of my order.

"I can only say that I would issue it again under like circumstances. Again thanking you for your kind interest, I am truly your friend,

"BENJAMIN F. BUTLER, *Major-General commanding*."

HON. CHARLES SUMNER.

CHARLES SUMNER.

CHARLES SUMNER was born in Boston, Massachusetts, January 6th, 1811. His grandfather, Major Job Sumner, was an officer of the Revolutionary army; and his father, Charles Pinckney Sumner, a lawyer by profession, and an accomplished gentleman of the old school, held during the latter part of his life the responsible position of sheriff of Suffolk county, which comprises the city of Boston.

At ten years of age, Charles Sumner was placed in the public Latin school of Boston, the best preparatory institution for classical training in New England, and, during the five years that he remained there, gave abundant evidences of industry and ability. Of naturally studious habits, he devoted much of his leisure time to reading history, of which he was passionately fond, and often arose before daylight to peruse Hume, Gibbon, and other favorite authors. At the age of fifteen, he entered Harvard College, where he was graduated in 1830, holding a respectable rank in his class, though one by no means commensurate with his natural abilities. More interested in the general improvement of his mind than in the acquisition of academical honors, he deviated from the pre-scribed curriculum whenever it was opposed to his plans or tastes, and pursued an independent course of reading in classical and general literature. Having devoted another year to private reading in his favorite studies, he entered in 1831 the Law School at Cambridge, where, under the instruction of Professors Ashmun and Greenleaf, and Justice Story, he acquired a profound knowledge of judicial science. Not content with the information to be gained from the ordinary text-books, he explored the curious learning of the old year-books, made himself familiar with the voluminous reports of the English and American courts, and neglected no opportunity to trace the principles of law to their sources.

While still a student, he contributed articles to the *American Jurist*, a law quarterly published in Boston, which attracted attention by their marked ability and learning. Subsequently, he became the editor of this periodical, and it is a fact creditable to his early acquirements that several of his contributions have been cited as authorities by Justice Story. With each of the distinguished jurists above mentioned he was on terms of cordial intimacy; and Justice Story, down to the time of his death, in 1845, was his warm friend and admirer.

Leaving the Law School in 1834, Mr. Sumner passed a few months in the office of Benjamin Rand, in Boston, with a view of learning the forms of practice; and in the same year was admitted to the bar, at Worcester. He immediately commenced practice in Boston, where his reputation for learning and forensic ability secured him a warm welcome from the members of his profession, and offers to enter lucrative law partnerships, which he declined, preferring to make no engagements which should interfere with a long-cherished plan of making a European tour. In addition to his large practice, he assumed the duties of reporter of the United States circuit court, in which capacity he published three volumes of cases, known as "Sumner's Reports," and comprising chiefly the decisions of Justice Story; and during the absence of the latter at Washington, he filled his place for three winters at the Cambridge Law School, by appointment of the university authorities—a significant proof of the estimation in which his abilities were held. His lectures on constitutional law and the law of nations were prepared with much labor, and greatly enhanced his reputation. Amid these absorbing pursuits he found time to edit "Dunlap's Treatise on Admiralty Practice," left unfinished by the author, and to which he added a copious appendix, containing many practical forms and precedents of pleadings, since adopted in our admiralty courts, and an index, the whole making a larger amount of matter than the original treatise.

In 1837, having in the preceding year declined flattering offers of a professorship at Cambridge, Mr. Sumner turned aside from the temptations and emoluments of professional life, to make his contemplated visit to Europe, where he remained until 1840. Carrying to foreign lands his enthusiasm for his profession, he made a special study in Paris of the celebrated Code Napoleon, both in its essential principles and forms of procedure, with which his previous studies in civil law had made him tolerably familiar. In England, where he remained nearly a year, his opportunities for meeting society in all its forms were such as are rarely accorded to American travellers. Bench and bar vied with each other in paying attentions to him; and in private circles, as well as in Westminster Hall—where, on more than one occasion, at the invitation of the judges, he sat by their side at trials—his reception was most gratifying. As an evidence of the impression which his extensive learning and accomplishments produced upon an eminent English jurist, it is related that, several years after his return to America, during the hearing in an insurance question before the court of exchequer, one of the counsel having cited an American case, Baron Parke (since created Lord Wensleydale, the ablest perhaps of the English judges of the time) asked him what book he quoted. He replied, "Sumner's Reports." Baron Rolfe inquired, "Is that the Mr. Sumner who was once in England?" and, upon receiving a reply in the affirmative, Baron Parke observed, "We shall not consider it entitled to less attention, because reported by a gentleman whom we all knew and respected."

In Germany, Mr. Sumner made the acquaintance of Savigny, Mittermaier, and other eminent civilians, and of such distinguished characters as Humboldt, Carl Ritter the geographer, and Ranke the historian of popes; and here, as elsewhere in Europe, he was frequently consulted by writers on the law of nations. At the request of Mr. Cass, then minister to France, he prepared a defence of the American claim in the North-eastern Boundary controversy, which was published in Galignani's Paris *Messenger*; and he also conceived the idea of writing a "History of the Law of Nations," a task which he finally relinquished to Mr. Wheaton, whom he had consulted on the subject.

After a brief residence in Italy, where he studied art and general literature, Mr. Sumner returned in 1840 to Boston, and resumed the practice of his profession, though to a more moderate extent than formerly, his attention being now much occupied with subjects connected with social and political ethics, and kindred topics. His love of law as a science, however, showed no diminution; and in 1844–'46, he produced an edition of "Vesey's Reports," in twenty volumes, enriched with numerous notes, and with what was a novelty in a work of the kind, biographical illustrations of the text.

Though previously known as a graceful and impressive speaker, it was not until 1845 that the full effect of Mr. Sumner's oratory was appreciated by a public assembly; and not until then, it may be added, did the orator exhibit that lofty moral courage which he has since illustrated on innumerable occasions, as the advocate of principles which he believes to be right, in defiance of an adverse public opinion. On the 4th of July of that year, he delivered before the municipal authorities of Boston an oration on "The True Grandeur of Nations," in which he exhibited the war system as the old ordeal by battle, a relic of middle-age barbarism retained by international law as the arbiter of justice between nations; and portrayed, in contrast, the blessings of peace. The doctrine was not then, and is not now, popular; and, while the enunciation of it gained him warm friends and admirers, others received the speaker's sentiments with distrust or open ridicule. None, however, could deny the persuasive charm of his elocution, the finish and elegance of the diction, and the finely-conceived classical and historical illustrations with which many of his passages were enriched. Justice Story, though dissenting from some of his views, declared that certain parts of his discourse were "such as befit an exalted mind and an enlarged benevolence," and resembled, in their manly moral enthusiasm, the great efforts of Sir James Mackintosh. From Chancellor Kent and other distinguished men he received equally strong tokens of approbation. In England, the oration was republished in five or six different forms, and met with a ready sale. Richard Cobden, in a letter to the author, called it "the most noble contribution of any modern writer to the cause of peace;" and the venerable poet Rogers wrote to him, "Every pulse of my heart beats in accordance with yours on the subject." His oration before the Phi Beta Kappa Society of Harvard University, in August, 1846, entitled "The Scholar, the Jurist, the Artist, and the Philanthropist," excited equal admiration; and John Quincy Adams offered as a sentiment, at the annual dinner of the society, "The memory of the scholar, the jurist, the artist, and the philanthropist, and—not the memory, but the long life of the kindred spirit who has this day embalmed them all." Writing to the orator shortly afterward, on the success of his performance, he observed, in allusion to the approaching close of his own career: "I see you have a mission to perform. I look from Pisgah to the promised land—you must enter upon it." How fully the injunction of the aged statesman has been obeyed, Mr. Sumner's life attests. Thenceforth he frequently appeared before public bodies and literary associations as the earnest and eloquent advocate of philanthropic measures; and the two volumes of his "Orations and Speeches," published in 1850, contain noble specimens of national oratory.

Previous to 1845, Mr. Sumner had kept aloof from politics, his tastes being averse to the rough experiences and demoralizing influences to which the professed politician must too often accustom himself, and inclining wholly to those studies which can be pursued in the peaceful walks of private life. "The strife of parties," to use his own words, "had seemed ignoble to him." He had always, however, borne his testimony against slavery; and upon the agitation, in 1845, of the question of the annexation of Texas, which involved the extension of slave-territory within the Union, he came promptly forward as an opponent of the measure. His speech on this subject, before a popular convention held in Faneuil Hall, in Boston, in that year, is one of the most brilliant and pointed he ever delivered.

In the autumn of 1845, the Dane professorship of law in the Cambridge Law School became vacant by the death of Justice Story; and it was supposed, in accordance with the expressed desire of the late incumbent, that Mr. Sumner would be appointed his successor. If that recommendation were not sufficient, the declaration of Chancellor Kent that he was "the only person in the country competent to succeed Story," might have been entitled to some weight with those having the appointment. It was, however, never offered to him—a proof that the estimation in which he had been held a few years previous had for some reason declined. The extreme views expressed by him on questions of public interest which had then begun to agitate the community, probably alarmed the conservatism of many who had been his admirers, and weighed against him. It is certain, however, that his social status with a portion of the community thenceforth became impaired; though it may be doubted whether, in the generous support which the expression of his sentiments brought him from many to whom he had been previously unknown, he suffered any material loss of position.

Having once embarked in the crusade against the extension of the slave-power, Mr. Sumner delivered in September, 1846, an address before the Whig state convention of Massachusetts, "On the Anti-Slavery Duties of the Whig Party;" and in the succeeding month he published a letter of rebuke to the Honorable Robert C. Winthrop, then a representative in Congress from Massachusetts, for his vote in favor of the war with Mexico. He refused to allow himself to be put forward as a rival candidate to that gentleman in the impending election, but supported Mr. Samuel G. Howe, who was nominated in that capacity, and in a speech, delivered during the canvass, opposed the Mexican war and all supplies for its prosecution. These acts, instigated by a clear conviction of the demands which duty imposed, alienated him from many old friends, and made his position an isolated and in many respects an unpleasant one. He still adhered, however, to the Whig party, with which he had always acted, and as late as September, 1847, was a delegate to the state convention; but after the schism in the Whig ranks, in 1848, which resulted in the formation of the Free-Soil party, he attached himself to the latter organization, and during the presidential canvass of 1848 was an earnest advocate of the election of Van Buren and Adams.

In 1850, the Whig party lost its ascendency in Massachusetts; and upon the legislature elected in that year, and which contained an opposition majority composed of Democratic and Free-Soil members, devolved the choice of a Senator in Congress to succeed Mr. Webster. Mr. Sumner, in opposition to his often-expressed wishes to avoid official life, was nominated for the office by the members of his party, Mr. Winthrop being the candidate of the Whigs; and after an exciting contest, prolonged by his refusal to give any pledge as to his future course, beyond what was implied in his past acts, he was, on April 24th, 1851, elected by a coalition between the Free-Soilers and Democrats. This result, the first substantial triumph of the Anti-Slavery party in Massachusetts, was appropriately celebrated in many places.

Mr. Sumner's first important speech in Congress was directed against the fugitive-slave law of 1850, which he denounced as unconstitutional, tyrannical, and cruel. On this occasion he laid down the well-known formula that "freedom is national, and slavery sectional," which has since been adopted by his party as their rule of political action. He participated with earnestness in the debates on the repeal of the Missouri Compromise, and on the Kansas troubles; and, upon the formation of the Republican party, in 1855-'56, he became, with the great body of the Free-Soilers, identified with it.

On May 19th and 20th, Mr. Sumner delivered in the Senate the celebrated speech, subsequently published under the title of "The Crime against Kansas," the most elaborate and masterly of any of his political efforts up to that time, but which greatly incensed certain of the Southern members. It was determined that the man who had so fearlessly and eloquently attacked the institutions of the South should be silenced by force, if arguments were unavailing; and on May 22d, shortly after the adjournment of the Senate, while Mr. Sumner was sitting at his desk, absorbed in writing, Preston S. Brooks, one of the representatives from South Carolina, entered the Senate-chamber, attended by Mr. Keitt, also of South Carolina, and Mr. Edmundson, of Virginia, and with a heavy gutta-percha cane struck the offending Senator repeated blows over the head, from the effects of which he almost immediately fell to the floor insensible. The excitement throughout the country, in consequence of this outrage, is too fresh in the public mind to need more than a passing allusion. It became a powerful element in the succeeding presidential canvass, and perceptibly widened the breach between the North and the South. A resolution for the expulsion of Brooks was almost immediately introduced into the House of Representatives, but failed of receiving the requisite two-thirds vote. The severe illness which followed the assault prevented Mr. Sumner from taking any part in the public affairs during the succeeding summer and winter; and in March, 1857, his health was so seriously impaired, that he was induced, by the advice of his physicians, to make a visit to Europe. Previous to his departure, the legislature of Massachusetts afforded him a gratifying proof of their esteem and confidence by re-electing him a United States Senator for another full term—the vote being unanimous in the senate, and almost so in the house of representatives, containing several hundred members. In the autumn of the same year, he returned to the United States; but his health being still too much impaired to admit of the resumption of his legislative duties, he went abroad again in May, 1858, and for more than a year was subjected to a course of medical treatment, which caused the most acute suffering, but which restored him to his legislative duties in the winter of 1859-'60, in comparative vigor.

As if to show that the attempt to crush the utterance of his opinions had inspired him to renewed efforts in the anti-slavery cause, his first speech after his recovery was an eloquent exposition of the demoralizing influences of slavery, subsequently widely distributed in pamphlet form, under the title of "The Barbarism of Slavery." He spoke frequently in favor of the Republican candidates during the presidential canvass of 1860; and, in the memorable session of 1860-'61, maintained a stern opposition to all compromises with or concessions to the seceding states as a means of restoring them to the Union. With all patriotic statesmen, he has urged the vigorous prosecution of the war against the rebellious states, and, as might be supposed from his previous course, is in favor of making emancipation an element in the contest. Emancipation he has repeatedly declared to be the speediest, if not the only mode, of bringing the war to a close; and he justifies that measure on moral, historical, and particularly on constitutional grounds. One of Mr. Sumner's last great efforts was a speech delivered in the Senate, on January 9th, 1862, on the question of the rendition of Mason and Slidell, which he advocated on principles of international law always previously insisted upon by the United States government.

In addition to the publications already mentioned, Mr. Sumner has a work on "White Slavery in the Barbary States" (Boston, 1853), expanded from a lecture; and an additional volume of speeches, entitled "Recent Speeches and Addresses" (1856).

Though past fifty, Mr. Sumner gives little evidence of the approach of old age. His tall and well-knit figure has lost none of its erectness; and his features, when lighted up by enthusiasm, or during the relaxations of social intercourse, have a youthfulness of appearance which seems hardly in keeping with the gravity supposed to pertain to the senatorial office. In personal appearance, as well as in the luxuriance and elaborate finish of his style, he has been compared to Edmund Burke. "For depth and accuracy of thought," says an eminent British critic, "for fulness of historical information, and for a species of gigantic morality, which treads all sophistry under foot, and rushes at once to the right conclusion, we know not a single orator speaking the English tongue who ranks as his superior. He combines to a remarkable extent the peculiar features of our British emancipationists, the perseverance of Granville Sharp, the knowledge of Brougham, the enthusiasm of Wilberforce, and a courage which, as he is still a young man, may be expected to tell powerfully on the destinies of the republic."

33

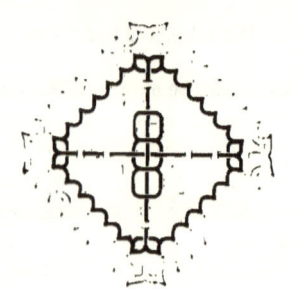

HENRY WAGER HALLECK.

A N ancestry good, honest, and reputable, removed alike from the dazzling heights of a public career, with its jealousies, hostilities, and temptations, and from the ignominy of a low and obscure birth, may justly be accounted a fortunate circumstance in any man's lineage. This good fortune General Halleck enjoys.

The Hallecks claim as their ancestor Peter Halleck, of Southold, Suffolk county, Long Island, a descendant of the lords of Alnwick Castle, which Fitz-Greene Halleck, a relative of the general, has so finely described. The name in England was originally Hallyoak, and is now written there Hulliock, Hallock, and Halleck. In this country the Hallocks and Hallecks both trace their lineage to the same ancestor. Honorable Joseph Halleck, the general's father, settled in the early part of the present century in Western, a small town on the Mohawk River, in Oneida county, a few miles west of Utica, where he married Miss Wager, the daughter of Henry Wager, a German, the near neighbor and personal friend of Baron Steuben, who, still hale and hearty, though one hundred years old, has lived to see his grandson commander-in-chief of the armies of the United States.

In this little town of Western, HENRY WAGER HALLECK was born in 1816. We have been able to learn but little of his early childhood. He is represented, by those who recollect him, as a studious, manly boy, with a decided predilection for mathematical studies. When fifteen or sixteen years of age, he left home, and, after consulting an uncle, then resident at Syracuse, went to Hudson, and commenced a course of preparation for college at the Hudson Academy, entering his name as Henry Wager. The cause of his dropping his last name is uncertain. After spending nearly three years in the academy at Hudson, where he acquitted himself with honor and reputation as a student, he entered Union College in 1834; and the following year, receiving through his uncle's influence a cadet appointment at West Point, joined his class there, resuming his full name. He was somewhat older than most of the cadets of his class, having attained his nineteenth year when he received his appointment.

It is sufficient evidence of his diligence and ability, that in the class of 1839, consisting of thirty-one members, and in many respects one of the most remarkable classes which have graduated at the academy, young Halleck held the third rank. Immediately after his graduation he was appointed second-lieutenant of engineers, without any delay of brevet rank. In 1840, he was assistant professor of engineering at the academy, and in 1841 became assistant to the chief-engineer, General Totten, at Washington. Soon after, he was assigned to the charge of the construction of the fortifications of New York harbor, in which employment he continued till 1844. In 1841. his "Papers on Practical Engineering, No. 1," were published by the engineer department; and the same year he prepared a "Practical Treatise on Bitumen and its Uses." In 1843, Union College conferred on him the honorary degree of A. M. In 1844, Congress published his "Report on Military Defences."

In January, 1845, he was promoted to a first-lieutenancy, during his absence from the country; having obtained a furlough and sailed for Europe in the autumn of 1844, to observe what progress European nations had made in military science. Through the friendship of Marshal Bertrand, he was introduced to Marshal Soult, then war minister of Louis Philippe, and received from him full authority to examine every thing of a military character in France. His investigations were extended to several other of the continental powers. Returning to this country in the summer of 1845, he was requested by the committee of the Lowell Institute, Boston, to deliver a course of lectures on the subject of "Military Science and Art." These lectures, which give evidence of high scientific and literary ability, were published in 1846, the author having prefixed an elaborate introduction on the "Justifiableness of War."

The commencement of the Mexican War recalled Lieutenant Halleck to his professional duties. He took part in the battle of Palo Alto, and immediately after that action was sent to California and the Pacific coast, where he served during the war in both a military and civil capacity. He was in the engagements of Palos Prietas, Urias, San Antonio, and Todos Santos. At San Antonio he marched, with about thirty mounted volunteers, one hundred and twenty miles in twenty-eight hours, surprised the enemy's garrison of several hundred men, rescued two naval officers and several marines who were prisoners-of-war, and captured the enemy's flag, two Mexican officers, and the governor's archives, the governor himself barely escaping in his night-clothes. At Todos Santos he led into action the main body of Colonel Burton's forces. When Commodore Shubrick attacked Mazatlan, Halleck acted as his aid, and afterward as chief of staff and lieutenant-governor of the city. While engaged in these duties, he planned and directed the construction of the fortifications at that place. For his services on those occasions he was breveted captain.

In 1847-'8-'9, under the military governments of General Kearney and Governors Mason and Riley, Captain Halleck was secretary of state in California.

When the convention met in 1849, to form a constitution for the future state of California, he was one of the leading members of that body and of the drafting-committee, and the constitution was almost entirely his work. It was at his suggestion also that a convention was called, to relieve Congress and General Taylor's administration from the difficulties in which they were involved by the Free-Soil and Pro-Slavery parties of 1849. From 1847 to 1850, Captain Halleck also directed and superintended the entire collection of the public revenues in California, amounting to several millions of dollars, and examined and audited all the accounts before they were forwarded to Washington. The importers denied the legality of these collections, and the secretary of the treasury, Honorable Robert J. Walker, doubted their authority; but Captain Halleck was subsequently sustained, in his interpretation of the law, by the Supreme Court of the United States.

From 1850 to 1854, Captain Halleck served in California as judge-advocate, a member of the Pacific board of engineers, and inspector of lighthouses. In July, 1853, he received his commission as captain of engineers. In August, 1854, he resigned his commission, and entered upon the practice of law, for the study of which he had managed to find time during his singularly busy career as a soldier; and the same year he published a carefully-compiled translation of "The Mining-Laws of Spain and Mexico." His legal abilities soon brought him an extensive and lucrative practice; and, as the senior partner of the great law-firm of Halleck, Peachy, and Billings, in San Francisco, he was rapidly accumulating a large fortune, to which his position of director-general of the New Almaden quicksilver-mines also contributed. In 1860, he published a translation of "De Foz on the Law of Mines;" and in December of that year accepted the appointment of major-general of militia, and reorganized the militia of California. Early in 1861, he was offered by the governor a seat in the supreme court of the state, but declined the honor.

In the spring of 1861, he published an elaborate work, on which he had long been engaged, entitled "International Law and the Laws of War," which has received from competent critics the highest commendation.

Qualities and abilities such as those of General Halleck were too rare in the army of the United States—are, indeed, too rare in the army of any country— for the nation to spare him from its service in its hour of trial; and in August, 1861, the President, at the suggestion of Lieutenant-General Scott, nominated him as major-general in the regular army. He accepted, and his commission bore date August 17th, 1861. Arranging his business as rapidly as possible, he left California about the first of October, and arrived in New York the latter part of the same month. After an interview with the President and General Scott (who had determined to retire from the active command of the army), he was assigned to the command of the Western department, and on the 11th of November relieved General Hunter, at St. Louis, who had temporarily succeeded General Fremont.

General Halleck's energy and great executive ability were soon felt in every department of the vast army which rapidly gathered at the West. Contractors were looked after; bridge-burners and marauders promptly and severely punished; levies made on the property of wealthy secessionists, for the support of the families of Unionists whom they or their friends had plundered; troops raised, equipped, drilled, and sent off to the different points where they were required, in large numbers; and the people led to feel that they had at the head of affairs a general who fully understood the wants of his department, and had the capacity to supply them.

On the 20th of November, 1861, General Halleck issued the following order:

"HEAD-QUARTERS, DEPARTMENT OF MISSOURI, ST. LOUIS, *November 20th*, 1861.

"GENERAL ORDERS, No. 3.—1. It has been represented that important information respecting the numbers and condition of our forces is conveyed to the enemy by means of fugitive slaves who are admitted within our lines. In order to remedy this evil, it is directed that no such persons be hereafter permitted to enter the lines of any camp, or of any forces on the march, and that any within such lines be immediately excluded therefrom.

"2. The general commanding wishes to impress upon all officers in command of posts, and troops in the field, the importance of preventing unauthorized persons of every description from entering and leaving our lines, and of observing the greatest precaution in the employment of agents and clerks in confidential positions.

"By order of Major-General HALLECK.

"WILLIAM McMICHAEL, Assistant-Adjutant General."

General Halleck was severely blamed for this order. It is hardly probable that, at a later date, when the value of the information received from fugitive slaves was better understood, and the probability of their falling into the hands of the rebels (if driven from our lines) ascertained, he would have issued it; but at the time when it was promulgated, only nine days after he reached St. Louis, and under the influences by which he was surrounded, he, no doubt, honestly believed it to be necessary, to prevent the enemy from being informed of what was transpiring within our lines. During the latter part of his administration of the Western department, Order No. 3 was substantially a dead letter. The matter was brought up in Congress, and Honorable F. P. Blair, member from the St. Louis district, wrote to General Halleck for an explanation. The general made the following reply:

"To Honorable F. P. BLAIR, Washington:

"DEAR COLONEL: Yours of the 4th instant is just received. Order No. 3 was, in my mind, clearly a military necessity. Unauthorized persons, black or white, free or slave, must be kept out of our camps, unless we are willing to publish to the enemy every thing we do or intend to do.

"It was a military and not a political order.

"I am willing to carry out any lawful instructions in regard to fugitive slaves which my superiors may give me, and to enforce any law which Congress may pass; but I cannot make law, and will not violate it.

"You know my private opinion on the policy of enacting a law confiscating the slave-property of rebels in arms. If Congress shall pass it, you may be certain I shall enforce it.

"Yours truly, H. W. HALLECK.'

The successful progress of the war in the West, and the prompt massing of troops against the strong points of the enemy, which resulted in the capture of Forts Henry and Donelson; the evacuation of Bowling Green, Columbus, and Nashville, culminating in the bloody and hard-fought field of Shiloh—gave the strongest testimony to the comprehensive intellect and extraordinary executive ability of the commander of the Western department. After the last-named battle, he assumed the command of the army in person, and, after a siege of nearly two months, compelled the rebels to evacuate Corinth, and break up in disorder. The capture of Island Number Ten, of Huntsville, Alabama, and the line of the Memphis and Charleston railroad, and finally of Memphis itself, for a time paralyzed the power of the rebels in the West.

The disastrous result of the attempt to effect a change of base in the army of the Potomac, at the close of June and the beginning of July, 1862, convinced the President of the necessity of having at the capital a general of the highest military skill, who should be capable of performing the duties of commander-in-chief of all the army-corps which were in the field, and who could direct the necessary combinations for efficient and successful warfare, and thus relieve the overtasked officials of the war department, and at the same time bring the war to a more speedy termination. Among the numerous generals in command, none possessed the qualifications needed to the same degree as Major-General Halleck; and after consultation with General Scott, the President summoned him to Washington, and, by an order bearing date July 11th, but not promulgated till July 23d, 1862, assigned him to the command of the whole land-forces of the United States, as general-in-chief.

General Halleck entered upon his new duties about the 25th of July, and, as soon as possible, visited the camp of the army of the Potomac, at Harrison's

Landing. A survey of the condition of affairs satisfied him of the necessity of the withdrawal of that army from the peninsula, although this involved the raising of the siege of Richmond. He accordingly ordered General McClellan to remove his force (except General Keyes's corps, which was to be left at Fortress Monroe), as speedily as could be done consistently with the safety of the troops, to Alexandria, on the Potomac, seven miles below Washington, the point from which he had embarked for the disastrous campaign on the peninsula. Meanwhile, he ordered General Pope to advance toward Gordonsville, and threaten Richmond from that direction, in order to create a diversion which should prevent the enemy from attacking General McClellan's rear in force. The two armies, once consolidated, could move forward on Richmond, in connection with Burnside's corps, then at Fredericksburg, with irresistible power.

The plan was an admirable one, and, had it been carried out as General Halleck designed, must have given us speedy possession of Virginia; but the delay incident to the removal of so large a force compelled General Pope to retreat north of the Rappahannock; and, during the subsequent delays and misunderstandings, his army was outflanked and compelled to fall back to the fortifications around Washington—the junction of the two forces not being effected till after the defeat of August 30th, 1862.

It is under these circumstances, which will so thoroughly test the great qualities of a commander, that we are called to leave our record of General Halleck's career: but though the clouds lower more darkly over our country than at any previous period of its history, we feel confident that the man is equal to the emergency; that his vigorous intellect and his military skill will soon educe order from the present confusion; and, if his efforts are not thwarted by the incompetency of subordinate generals, we may hope soon to see victory again perch upon our banners.

In stature, General Halleck is somewhat below the medium height; he is straight, active, well formed, and his gait and manner betoken the energetic soldier. His forehead is ample; his eye a clear, brilliant hazel, of great penetrating power; and, though his general expression is stern, his mouth indicates that he possesses a vein of humor. He has no fondness for fine clothes, and during his Western campaign was oftener seen in citizen's dress than in uniform. When he appeared in full military dress, he seemed not at ease; and, though a good rider—as, indeed, he ought to be, after his Californian experiences—he never appears worse than when in full dress, reviewing his troops.

The love of order, promptness in dispatching business, and a capacity for comprehending the whole of a subject at a glance, are General Halleck's most marked characteristics. That he possesses some eccentricities, all who know him will readily admit. He is at times brusque almost to incivility; utterly intolernnt of bores, whom he dismisses without ceremony; and neglectful of those little arts by which so many men, of far less calibre, gain popularity. That he scorns to seek, and never won it with his soldiers, who, however, had the greatest respect for his intellectual capacity. His thoughtful pacings in front of his tent at Corinth, with his thumbs in the armholes of his vest, and his felt hat on the back of his head, and inclining upward at an angle of forty-five degrees, were often watched by the soldiers, who always concluded, and generally correctly, that "Old Brains," the *soubriquet* by which he was most commonly known in the camp, was solving some new problem, or preparing for some new movement to thwart and confound the enemy.

These traits show conclusively what is the work to which General Halleck is best adapted. His qualities are not those which win the admiration and rouse the enthusiasm of an army; he is not, and does not aim to be, a dashing commander; but his strong common sense, his thorough knowledge of military science and military law, and his comprehensive and grasping intellect, qualify him, beyond any other man connected with the national armies, to fill successfully, and with signal advantage to the country, the post to which he has been called by the President.

34

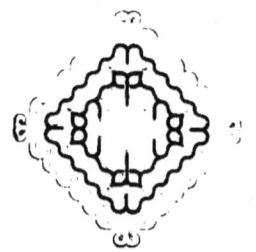

JOSEPH HOLT.

JOSEPH HOLT was born in Breckenridge county, Kentucky, in 1807. By his own energy and industry he was enabled to obtain a good education, which was completed at St. Joseph's College, Bardstown, and at Centre College, Danville. In 1828, he commenced the practice of law, in Elizabethtown, Kentucky, whence in the winter of 1831-'32 he removed to Louisville. Establishing himself in the latter place, he was elected a delegate to a Democratic convention held in Harrodsburg, in which capacity he delivered a speech of great power and eloquence, thereby confirming his reputation as one of the most promising young orators of the West. He was not, however, diverted from his professional labors by the *éclat* which this effort gained him ; and upon receiving, early in 1833, the appointment of commonwealth's attorney for the Jefferson circuit, which included the city of Louisville, he entered upon the discharge of his official duties with an energy and ability which won the commendations of his most ardent political opponents. Never unprepared for trial, never disconcerted by any unexpected turn which a case might take during the progress of the trial, he aimed only at securing convictions, in which it is said he scarcely ever failed ; and he frequently astonished both bench and bar by forensic addresses not unworthy to be compared with the early efforts of Clay, Crittenden, and other Kentucky orators. On one occasion, Judge Rowan, the leader of the Kentucky bar, and a contemporary of the great Western lawyers, characterized his address to the jury as "the finest specimen of legal eloquence he had ever heard."

In 1835, much against the wishes of the people of Louisville, who very generally petitioned for his reappointment as prosecuting attorney, Mr. Holt removed to Port Gibson, Mississippi, whence in the following spring he went to Vicksburg. Here he entered upon a large and lucrative practice, and was brought into frequent competition with the leading advocates of the Southern bar. Sargeant S. Prentiss, the brilliant rhetorician of Mississippi, was his chief antagonist, and in their forensic contests Mr. Holt acquitted himself with decided ability. Having acquired an ample fortune by his professional labors, he returned, in 1842, to Louisville. In 1848, he visited Europe and the East, for the benefit of his health, and, upon his return to Louisville, resumed the practice of law. At the accession of Mr. Buchanan to the presidency, he was appointed commissioner of patents, and took up his residence in Washington. Two years later, upon the death of A. V. Brown, he was transferred to the post-office department, the duties of which he discharged until the resignation of John B. Floyd, when he succeeded him as secretary of war.

The gloom and anxiety which then weighed upon the public mind, had recently become intensified by the belief that persons high in office were plotting to overthrow the government; and the retirement from office of Mr. Cass, followed by that of Floyd, seemed to indicate that the cabinet were too much divided in sentiment, or too seriously implicated in treasonable acts, to admit of any vigorous action for the preservation of the Union. Under these circumstances, the appointment of Mr. Holt, a man of approved integrity and courage, and a devoted friend of the Union, was very instrumental in restoring public confidence; and, during the brief term in which he administered the affairs of the war department, he became known to the loyal portion of the country as one who would perform his duty in any emergency.

Mr. Holt retired from office upon the accession of Mr. Lincoln, with an enhanced reputation for administrative ability, and forthwith employed his efforts to awaken a spirit of patriotism in the lukewarm citizens of his own state. The policy of "neutrality," which the border states would fain have adopted as their rule of action in the impending struggle, he emphatically denounced; and in a letter, written on May 31st, to J. F. Speed, of Kentucky, on the duty of that state in the crisis, he laid bare, in eloquent language, the fallacy of neutrality; vindicated the right of the federal executive to send troops into or through any state, to suppress rebellion; and showed that the crimes of the rebel leaders were such as no government could afford to overlook, and that their pretence of wishing "to be let alone" was a patent absurdity. "The ordeal through which we are passing," he said, "must involve immense suffering and losses for us all, but the expenditure of not merely hundreds of millions, but of billions of treasure, will be well made, if the result will be the preservation of our institutions."

On July 13th, Mr. Holt delivered an impressive address at Louisville, on the same subject; and in the following September, at the invitation of the New York Chamber of Commerce, he appeared before a large meeting in that city.

After the removal of General Fremont from the command of the military department of the West, Mr. Holt was appointed one of a committee of three to examine and decide upon claims brought against that department prior to October 14th, 1861, in which duty he was busily occupied until March, 1862, when the committee presented its report. In the succeeding September, he was appointed judge-advocate general of the army, an office of peculiar responsibility, and one which his extended professional training has well qualified him to fill.

GEORGE ARCHIBALD McCALL.

GEORGE ARCHIBALD McCALL, now brigadier-general of volunteers in the army of the United States, was born in Philadelphia, March 16th, 1802, and, after receiving his early education in the schools of his native city, entered the United States military academy at West Point, in 1818, just after it had received that thorough reorganization which has made it one of the finest military schools in the world. He was graduated, and received his commission as second-lieutenant in the first regiment of infantry, in 1822; and was transferred, the same year, to the fourth regiment of infantry. In 1831, he was selected by General E. P. Gaines as one of his aides-de-camp, and served on his staff in that capacity, and as assistant-adjutant general of the Western department, till 1836, when he was promoted to the rank of captain in his regiment.

During the Florida War, Captain McCall served with his company against the Indians, and was recommended by the late General W. J. Worth for a major's brevet, for gallant conduct at the battle of Pelahlikaha, in these terms: "He will do more honor to the rank, than the rank can confer on him." The brevet, so justly won, was at this time withheld; but, though modest merit may be ignored for a time, it will eventually meet its reward.

At the commencement of the Mexican War, McCall was still serving as captain; but his "gallant and distinguished conduct" on the fields of Palo Alto and Resaca de la Palma, in 1846, brought him the brevets of major and lieutenant-colonel; and the citizens of Philadelphia, in token of their approval of his valor, presented him with an elegant and costly sword. Soon after these battles he was appointed assistant-adjutant general, which staff appointment he retained until promoted major of the third infantry, in 1847. In June, 1850, he was in command of his regiment in New Mexico, when he received from President Taylor the appointment of inspector-general of the United States army, with the rank of colonel of cavalry. He served in this capacity until April 29th, 1853, when, on account of impaired health, he resigned his commission, and retired to his country residence in Chester county, Pennsylvania, where he remained till the spring of 1861.

Immediately after the bombardment of Fort Sumter, Colonel McCall was called upon by Governor Curtin to organize a corps of fifteen thousand men, to

35

be styled the Pennsylvania volunteer reserve corps, who, by act of the legislature, were ordered for the defence of the state frontier. He obeyed the summons with alacrity; organized twelve regiments of infantry, one of artillery, one of cavalry, and one of rifles; and in two months marched to Washington at the head of this fine corps. It was soon after converted into a division of three brigades, and under his command (he having meanwhile received a commission as brigadier-general of volunteers, from the federal government) joined the army of the Potomac. Here, during the autumn and winter of 1861, they occupied the post of danger, being stationed from six to ten miles west of Washington.

In December, 1861, General McCall learned, through his scouts, that the rebels proposed making a foray in force, in the vicinity of Dranesville, Virginia, eleven miles in front of his camp, about the 20th of the month. On the morning of that day he marched out, with the determination of giving them battle, should they appear. The information proved to be correct. The enemy, under the command of General Stuart, having been apprised of his approach, occupied a position on the heights in front of Dranesville, and at once opened upon McCall's advancing column with their artillery. General McCall ordered his guns forward, and at once returned the fire. The line of battle was then formed, and, after a well-contested action of an hour and a half, the enemy were routed, and fled in disorder, leaving many of their dead and wounded on the field. The loss of the rebels in killed and wounded was about two hundred and fifty; that of General McCall's force nineteen killed and sixty-two wounded. The troops engaged on each side were about equal, numbering not far from three thousand, comprising infantry and cavalry, and a battery of four guns on either side.

General McCall was not again engaged in a battle until June 26th, 1862. when his Pennsylvania reserves, seven thousand in number, were attacked at Mechanicsville, in front of Richmond, by a rebel force fourteen thousand strong, under the command of their ablest general, Robert E. Lee. General McCall's position was a strong one, and was bravely defended. For five hours the enemy assailed it, attacking repeatedly and with the utmost determination, but each time they were driven back with great slaughter, until night closed the scene. The loss of the rebels, by their own showing, did not fall short of two thousand killed and wounded; the fortieth North Carolina regiment having left one-half and the first Georgia three-fourths of their men on the field, according to their own published statements. The loss sustained by General McCall's division was thirty-three killed and one hundred and fifty wounded.

At daylight the next morning (June 27th), General McCall received orders from General McClellan to withdraw to the rear of Gaines's Mills, about five miles distant. This movement, always a most difficult one to accomplish in the presence of an enemy, was so successfully completed, under fire, in the course of three hours, and was effected so regularly and gradually, that the foe was not aware of the fact till some time after the firing on the national side had ceased, and the division was on its march. The dead were buried, the wounded sent away, and not a gun or a knapsack left behind on the ground so gallantly maintained. The same afternoon, the enemy, reinforced to the number of fifty thousand men, pressed hard upon General Porter's corps of twenty-two thousand, with which the Pennsylvania reserves were temporarily serving, and compelled him, after four hours' hard fighting, to fall back across the Chickahominy. In this severe struggle General McCall's horse was twice wounded, but he and his troops received the praise of the commanding general for their steadfastness under a most galling and destructive fire.

On the 30th of June, during that memorable retreat toward the James River, General McCall's division was ordered to halt at the crossing of the Turkey Bridge and New Market roads, and defend the immense wagon-train which was trailing slowly on toward the James River. His division had been reduced to about six thousand; and he was required to stand at bay, and protect this train against General Lee, who advanced with Longstreet's and Hill's divisions, numbering from eighteen to twenty thousand men. The odds were very great, but retreat was impossible; so, fighting desperately, he maintained his position till nightfall, and, though the object was accomplished with a fearful loss of brave men, yet he secured the safe passage of the train, whose loss would have perilled the lives of a still greater number.

At the close of the day, having silenced the fire of the rebels on the left and centre, General McCall brought up about five hundred men, his entire reserve, to oppose the enemy, who still kept up a scattering fire on the extreme right. The night was dark, and all his staff were either killed or put *hors du combat* by the loss of their horses; of his personal escort, composed of one officer and twenty cavalry soldiers, but one corporal and one private remained. Halting the battalion which he had brought up, in rear of the line of battle first occupied, and having no aide-de-camp, he rode forward about one hundred yards, to ascertain whether any of his men were still in front, and in the darkness found himself surrounded by the soldiers of the forty-seventh Virginia regiment, who were drawn up under some trees, and who at once made him prisoner. He was kept in prison and in close confinement at Richmond for six weeks, when, having been exchanged, he returned to his home in Chester county, for the benefit of his health, which had been sadly impaired by his imprisonment. On the 26th of August, the citizens of the county presented him a superb sword, as a testimony of their approval of his conduct while in command of the Pennsylvania reserves: the address at the presentation being made by Honorable John Hickman.

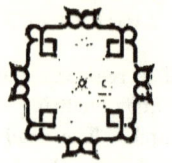

JOHN ALBION ANDREW.

JOHN ALBION ANDREW, governor of Massachusetts, was born in Windham, Cumberland county, Maine, May 31st, 1818. The family of Andrew is one of the oldest in New England, its immediate ancestor having arrived among the early settlers, and has been connected by marriage with many of the colonial worthies, including Francis Higginson, the founder and pastor of the first church in Massachusetts Bay, from whom the subject of this memoir is directly descended.

Entering Bowdoin College at the age of fifteen, he was graduated in 1837, and soon after commenced the study of law in Boston, where in 1840 he was admitted to the bar. To an enthusiasm for his profession he added a pleasing address, an exuberant flow of language, variety and force of expression, and that sympathetic quality, so useful to an advocate, which identifies him with the cause of his client. With these advantages, it is not surprising that he soon became a successful *nisi-prius* lawyer, and, as he gained in years and experience, an advocate before juries second only to Rufus Choate, the great leader of the Boston bar. But, though securing his full share of professional practice and emoluments, it was in arguments on questions of political significance before the state and federal courts that he gained most distinction; and there have been few cases of late years in the Massachusetts courts involving such questions in which he has not appeared or been consulted as counsel.

In 1854, Mr. Andrew appeared for the parties indicted for an attempt to rescue the fugitive slave Burns, and succeeded in quashing the indictment. In the following year, he defended the British consul at Boston against a charge of violating the neutrality laws. In 1856, he was concerned in an application to Judge Curtis, of the United States Supreme Court, for a writ of *habeas corpus* to test the legality of the imprisonment of certain free-state men in Kansas; and in 1859, he was instrumental in procuring counsel for the defence of John Brown, in Virginia. In the last-mentioned case he took a peculiar interest, and besides procuring the release of Hyatt and Sanborn, who were arrested by the United States marshal for Massachusetts, for refusing to appear before Senator Mason's committee of investigation, he was himself examined by that committee. In obedience to his views of professional propriety, he has also occasionally been retained in cases abhorrent to his sympathies and well-defined opinions—a no-

86

table instance being the case of the slave-yacht Wanderer, which in 1860 he defended against a claim for forfeiture on the part of the government.

Though always interested in political matters, Mr. Andrew for many years persistently declined to make any engagements or assume any connections which would interfere with his legal duties; and it was not until 1858 that he would consent to become a candidate for office. In that year he was elected one of the members from Boston to the Massachusetts house of representatives, where his eminent talents in debate suggested him as a leader of the party in power, to which was opposed a vigorous minority led by Caleb Cushing, the attorney-general of the United States under President Pierce.

A Whig until 1848, then a Free-Soiler, and since 1855 a member of the Republican party, Mr. Andrew brought to this important position a thorough knowledge of the prominent political topics of the day, and a self-command and fluency of speech—the results of twenty years of professional training—which proved of great benefit to his party. But though gaining distinction as a parliamentary leader, he gladly resumed the practice of his profession at the close of the session, and declined a renomination to the legislature. With equal firmness he declined to permit his name to be submitted to the Republican convention in 1859 as a candidate for nomination as governor, or to accept the office of judge of the superior court of Massachusetts tendered to him in the same year by Governor Banks.

In the spring of 1860, however, Mr. Andrew headed the delegation sent from Massachusetts to the Republican convention which met at Chicago to nominate a candidate for the presidency, and cast his vote for Mr. Seward until the final ballot, when he voted for Mr. Lincoln. Upon returning to Massachusetts, he accepted the Republican nomination for governor, and after an animated canvass, in which he spoke in every county in the state, was elected by the largest popular vote ever cast for a governor of Massachusetts, his majority over all other candidates being nearly forty thousand.

The clouds which portended the outbreak of the Great Rebellion of 1861 were beginning to gather on the horizon at the time of Governor Andrew's inauguration, and he entered upon his office with the apprehension that the federal government would be compelled to assert its rights by force, and with the determination to make military preparations for the approaching emergency. In his inaugural address he recommended that "the dormant militia, or some considerable portion of it, now simply enrolled and not organized nor subject to drill, be placed on a footing of activity," in order that Massachusetts might "be ready, without inconvenient delay, to contribute her share of force in any exigency of public danger;" and his first administrative act was to send a messenger to the capitals of several of the New England states, for the purpose of laying before their governors suggestions having a similar end in view. He soon after communicated to General Scott, at Washington, a plan for dispatching the militia of Massachusetts to that city, in the event of any disturbance arising out of the official declaration of the vote for President. It is worthy of note that in this plan the possibility of the obstruction of the route through Baltimore was anticipated, and the advance by way of Annapolis suggested. The available disciplined militia of the commonwealth at that time did not exceed five thousand men, a body sufficient for any local exigencies likely to arise : and the legislature, less apprehensive than Governor Andrew of the necessity of appealing to arms, were unwilling to enlarge this force by calling into service any considerable number of the enrolled but unorganized militia. The governor, however, amid much opposition, ordered all company commanders of the organized militia to report the number of men in their respective commands incapable of responding at once to any call the President might make upon them, in order that their places might be filled " by men ready for any public exigency which might arise, whenever called upon." Soon afterward, he entered into contracts for complete equipments for two thousand of these troops.

In the midst of these preparations the rebel batteries opened upon Fort Sumter, and on the morning of April 15th a requisition from the war department for two regiments from Massachusetts reached Governor Andrew. With the promptness of their forefathers, the minute-men of the Revolution, the troops began on the same day to assemble from many different points at Faneuil Hall ; and within a week, instead of the two regiments called for, five regiments of infantry, a battalion of riflemen, and a battery of light artillery, were collected at Washington, Annapolis, or Fortress Monroe, or were far advanced on their way thither. The wise foresight of Governor Andrew in preparing the commonwealth to respond in this crisis with alacrity, and in a manner becoming her ancient reputation for patriotism, was duly acknowledged by the people ; and the banks rendered their testimony to his high integrity by placing at his disposal voluntary loans to the amount of six and a half millions of dollars, to be expended at his discretion, the legislature having failed to provide funds for the emergency. An agent was immediately dispatched to Europe, to purchase arms; steamers, loaded with munitions and reinforcements, were sent to the Potomac; and Massachusetts troops were among the first to reach Washington by sea as they had been by land. Throwing aside party prejudices, the governor selected as the commander of the troops his unsuccessful Democratic competitor for the office of governor, an act which tended to produce a unanimity of feeling and purpose throughout the commonwealth, and to disappoint an expectation fondly cherished by the rebel leaders that political animosities would prevent the North from acting with any degree of vigor in the struggle.

Nor did Governor Andrew stop short with these measures. In response to his stirring appeals, thirteen thousand men were under arms in Massachusetts before the middle of May, 1861, for whose enlistment he made himself personally responsible. The government, distrusting the dimensions which the rebellion was about to assume, accepted less than half the number, and advised the governor to disband the rest. The latter, confident that every man he had called out would be needed, laid the subject before an extra session of the Massachusetts legislature, convened on May 14th, in a message of great eloquence, which was widely read and admired; and an act was passed, authorizing five thousand troops to be placed in camps, at the expense of the commonwealth, to await the requisition of the President.

The disastrous defeat at Bull Run, in July, having brought the administration to realize the necessity of increasing the number of the federal forces in the field, Governor Andrew again received a recognition of his foresight, in the demand upon Massachusetts for a larger quota of men than had been offered and refused in May. With his customary energy, he proceeded to organize additional regiments, all of which were ready to march or in the field by the beginning of winter, and have since rendered efficient service in many parts of the country.

Upward of four millions of dollars were expended in the equipment of the Massachusetts contingent during the first year of the war; and no stronger testimony to the integrity of Governor Andrew's administration can be adduced than the report (in April, 1862) of a legislative committee, appointed to investigate the manner in which these funds had been disbursed, and which contained no allegation of improper conduct on the part of any person connected with the government.

During the latter part of 1861, Governor Andrew was brought into temporary collision with Major-General Butler, of the United States volunteers, who fixed his head-quarters in Boston, and assumed to enlist and organize volunteers, and appoint officers—a proceeding which the governor opposed with ability and success as an encroachment upon his official prerogative.

In November, 1861, he was re-elected governor by a vote of sixty-five thousand two hundred and fifty-one, to thirty-one thousand eight hundred and ninety-two for all others. He responded with alacrity to the call of the President in May, 1862, for militia regiments to protect Washington, when threatened by the rebel General Jackson, although the troops collected by him for this emergency were to a very limited extent called into the service; and during the succeeding summer and autumn his time was almost constantly employed in preparing for the field the additional troops, both volunteers and militia, which Massachusetts was called upon to furnish to the general government. In this service, as on other occasions, he has made repeated visits to Washington and other places, held conferences with governors of states, and performed a multi-tude of important duties. At the Republican state convention held September 10th, 1862, he was for the third time nominated for governor, with every pros-pect of being re-elected by a large vote.

Governor Andrew is in the prime of manhood, of middle stature, and an erect and somewhat portly figure. His head is square in shape, well developed, and covered with short, curly hair; and his features indicate vivacity and intel-ligence, the mouth being expressive of decision and firmness. In private life he is much esteemed for amiability and active benevolence.

Robert Anderson

ROBERT ANDERSON.

IN the history of the Southern Conspiracy, General ROBERT ANDERSON must hold a distinguished place, being the first federal officer against whom the fatal thought of rebellion took voice in the throat of a cannon; and though his shattered health has constrained him to play no further part in the tragedy which he opened with such brilliancy, his loyalty to "old glory," his wise courage and Christian firmness, in that one hour of peril, will ever keep his name honored and revered among the American people.

General Anderson came from a patriotic and military family. His father, Captain Richard C. Anderson, was the man whose little band surprised an outpost of the Hessians at Trenton, on the night prior to the decisive battle of that place—an attack which the Hessian commander, Colonel Rahl, then on the lookout for Washington, construed to be the whole assault against which he had been warned. General Washington met Anderson retreating with his company, and was very indignant at what they had done, fearing it would prepare the enemy for their advance in force. The result, however, proved the contrary, and Anderson was then complimented on the exploit. Captain Anderson served with Washington throughout the New Jersey campaign.

The subject of this sketch is a native of the state of Kentucky. The blood of a brave soldier ran in his veins, and displayed itself in his early desire to adopt the profession of arms. Passing over young Anderson's preliminary studies and scholastic successes, we find him, in 1832, acting inspector-general of Illinois volunteers in the Black Hawk War. He filled this situation, with credit to himself, from May until the ensuing October. In the following June, 1833, he was made first-lieutenant. From 1835 to 1837 he occupied the responsible post of assistant instructor and inspector at the United States military academy. He was assigned to the staff of General Winfield Scott as aide-de-camp in 1838; and in 1839 published his "Instructions for Field Artillery, Horse and Foot, arranged for the Service of the United States"—a handbook of great practical value.

Lieutenant Anderson's services during the Indian troubles were acknowledged by a brevet captaincy, April 2d, 1838. In July of the same year, he was made assistant adjutant-general, with the rank of captain, which he subsequently relinquished on being promoted to a captaincy in his own regiment. the third artillery.

In March, 1847, he was with his regiment in the army of General Scott, and took part in the siege of Vera Cruz; being one of the officers to whom was intrusted, by Colonel Bankhead, the command of the batteries. This duty he accomplished with signal skill and gallantry. He remained with the army until its triumphant entry into the Mexican capital the following September.

During the operations in the valley of Mexico, Captain Anderson was attached to the brigade of General Garland, which formed a portion of General Worth's division. In the attack on El Molino del Rey, September 8th, Anderson was severely wounded. His admirable conduct under the circumstances was the theme of praise on the part of his men and superior officers. Captain Burke, his immediate commander, in his dispatch of September 9th, says: "Captain Robert Anderson (acting field-officer) behaved with great heroism on this occasion. Even after receiving a severe and painful wound, he continued at the head of the column, regardless of pain and self-preservation, and setting a handsome example to his men of coolness, energy, and courage." General Garland speaks of him as being "with some few others the very first to enter the strong position of El Molino;" and adds that "Brevet-Major Buchanan, fourth infantry, Captain Robert Anderson, third artillery, and Lieutenant Sedgwick, second artillery, appear to have been particularly distinguished for their gallant defence of the captured works." In addition to this testimony, General Worth directed the attention of the secretary of war to the part he had taken in the action. He was made brevet-major, his commission dating from the day of the battle.

In the year 1851. he was promoted to the full rank of major, in the first artillery. It was while holding this rank, and in command of the garrison of Fort Moultrie, that the storm which has so devastated this fair land first gathered strength and broke upon us.

On the 20th day of December, 1860, the state of South Carolina declared itself out of the Union. The event was celebrated in numerous Southern towns and cities by the firing of salutes, military parades, and secession speeches. At New Orleans, a bust of Calhoun was exhibited, decorated with a cockade; and at Memphis the citizens burned Senator Andrew Johnson in effigy. The plague of disloyalty overspread the entire South. In the mean time, while the commissioners from South Carolina and the plotting members of Congress from the border states were complicating matters with a timid and vacillating President, Major Anderson found himself, with less than a hundred men, shut up in an untenable fort, his own government fearing to send him reinforcements. Cut off from aid or supplies, menaced on every side, the deep murmurs of war growing louder and more threatening, the position of Major Anderson and his handful of men became imminent in the extreme. At this juncture of affairs, the brave soldier gave us an illustration of his forethought and sagacity.

One sunny morning, crowds of anxious people fringed the wharves of Charleston, watching the mysterious curls of smoke that rose lazily from the ramparts of Fort Moultrie, and floated off seaward—smoke from the burning gun-carriages.

On the night previous, Major Anderson had quietly removed his men and stores to Fort Sumter, the strongest of the Charleston fortifications, and the key of its defences. The deserted guns of Moultrie were spiked, and the carriages burned to cinders. The evacuation of the fort commenced a little after sunset. The men were ordered to hold themselves in readiness, with their knapsacks packed, at a second's notice; but up to the moment of their leaving they had no idea of abandoning the post. They were reviewed on parade, and then ordered to two schooners lying in the vicinity. The garrison flag unwound itself to the morning over Sumter.

The rage of the South at this unexpected strategic manœuvre, was equalled in its intenseness only by the thrill of joy which ran through the North. Major Anderson and his command were safe, for the time being, and treason disconcerted. "Major Robert Anderson," says the *Charleston Courier*, bitterly, "has achieved the unenviable distinction of opening civil war between American citizens, by an act of gross breach of faith." The sequel proved his prudence. Having all the forts of the harbor under his charge, he had, necessarily, the right to occupy whatever post he deemed expedient. He did his duty, and he did it well. His course was sustained in the House of Representatives, January 7th, 1861.

Before the first burst of indignation had subsided, Fort Moultrie was taken possession of by the South Carolinians, and carefully put into a state of defence. The rebel convention ordered immense fortifications to be built in and about Charleston harbor, to resist any reinforcements that might be sent to Major Anderson. Strong redoubts were thrown up on Morris' and James' Islands, and Forts Moultrie, Johnson, and Castle Pinckney, stood ready to belch flame and iron on the devoted little garrison. Sumter was invested: no ship could approach the place in the teeth of those sullen batteries.

On the 8th of April, information having been given by the United States government to the authorities of Charleston, that they desired to send supplies to Fort Sumter on an unarmed transport, they were informed that the vessel would be fired upon and not allowed to enter the port. The United States government then officially advised the insurgents that supplies would be sent to Major Anderson, peaceably if possible, otherwise by force. Lieutenant Talbot, attached to the garrison of Fort Sumter, and bearer of this dispatch, was not permitted to

37

proceed to his post. The steamer Star of the West was signalled at the entrance of the harbor on the morning of the 9th. She displayed the United States flag, but was fired into, repeatedly, from Morris' Island battery. Her course was then altered, and she again put out to sea.

A formidable floating battery, constructed and manned at Charleston, was taken out of dock on the evening of the 10th, and anchored in a cove near Sullivan's Island. About seven thousand troops now crowded the earthworks and forts, under command of General G. T. Beauregard. The report that a fleet lay off the bay, waiting for a favorable tide to enter the harbor and relieve the fort, caused the greatest excitement in Charleston.

On the afternoon of April 11th, Colonel Chestnut and Major Lee, aids to General Beauregard, conveyed to Fort Sumter the demand that Major Anderson should evacuate that fort. Major Anderson refused to accede to the demand. On being waited on by a second deputation (April 12, 1 A. M.), desiring him to state what time he would evacuate, and to stipulate not to fire upon the batteries in the mean time, Major Anderson replied that he would evacuate at the noon of the 15th, if not previously otherwise ordered, or not supplied, and that he would not in the meanwhile open his fire unless compelled by some hostile act against his fort or the flag of his government. At 3.30 A. M., the officers who received this answer notified Major Anderson that the batteries under command of General Beauregard, would open on Fort Sumter in one hour, and immediately left. The sentinels on Sumter were then ordered in from the parapets, the posterns closed, and the men directed not to leave the bomb-proofs until summoned by the drum. The garrison had but two days' rations.

At 4.30 Friday morning, fire was opened upon Fort Sumter from Fort Moultrie, and soon after from the batteries on Mount Pleasant and Cummings' Point, then from an unsuspected masked battery of heavy columbiads on Sullivan's Island. It soon became evident that no part of the beleagured fort was without the range of the enemy's guns. A rim of scarlet fire encircled it. Meanwhile the undaunted little band of seventy true men, took breakfast quietly at the regular hour, reserving their fire until 7 A. M., when they opened their lower tier of guns upon Fort Moultrie, the iron battery on Cummings' Point, the two works on Sullivan's Island, and the floating battery, simultaneously. When the first relief went to work, the enthusiasm of the men was so great that the second and third reliefs could not be kept from the guns. The rebel iron battery was of immense strength, and our balls glanced from it like hail-stones. Fort Moultrie, however, stood the cannonading badly, a great many of our shells taking effect in the embrasures. Shells from every point burst against the various walls of Sumter, and the fire upon the parapet became so terrific that Major Anderson refused to allow the men to work the barbette guns. There were no cartridge-bags, and the men were set to making them out of shirts. Fire broke out in the barracks three times, and was extinguished. Meals were served at the guns. At 6 P. M. the fire from Sumter ceased. Fire was kept up by the enemy during the night, at intervals of twenty-five minutes.

At daybreak the following morning the bombardment recommenced. Fort Sumter resumed operations at 7 A. M. An hour afterward the officers' quarters took fire from a shell, and it was necessary to detach nearly all the men from the guns to stop the conflagration. Shells from Moultrie and Morris' Island now fell faster than ever. The effect of the enemy's shot, on the officers' quarters in particular, was terrible. One tower was so completely demolished that not one brick was left standing upon another. The main gates were blown away, and the walls considerably weakened. Fearful that they might crack, and a shell pierce the magazine, ninety-six barrels of powder were emptied into the sea; finally the magazine had to be closed; the material for cartridges was exhausted, and the garrison was left destitute of any means to continue the contest. The men had eaten the last biscuit thirty-six hours before. They were nearly stifled by the dense, livid smoke from the burning buildings, lying prostrate on the ground with wet handkerchiefs over their mouths and eyes. The crashing of the shot, the bursting of the shells, the falling of the masonry, and the mad roaring of the flames, made a pandemonium of the place. Strangely enough, but four men had been injured, thus far, and those only slightly.

Toward the close of the day, ex-Senator Wigfall suddenly made his appearance at an embrasure with a white handkerchief on the point of a sword, and begged to see Major Anderson, asserting that he came from General Beauregard.

"Well, sir!" said Major Anderson, confronting him.

General Wigfall, in an excited manner, then demanded to know on what terms Major Anderson would evacuate the position. The major informed him that General Beauregard was already advised of the terms. "Then, sir," said Wigfall, "the fort is ours." "On those conditions," replied Major Anderson. During this interview the firing from Moultrie and Sullivan's Island had not ceased, though General Wigfall timidly displayed a white flag at an embrasure facing the batteries. Wigfall retired.

A short time afterward a deputation, consisting of Senator Chestnut, Roger A. Pryor, and two others, came from General Beauregard, and had an interview with Major Anderson: it then turned out that the officious Wigfall had "acted on his own hook," without any authority whatever from his commanding general. After a protracted consultation and a second deputation, Major Anderson agreed to evacuate Fort Sumter the next day. This was Saturday evening. That night the garrison took what rest it could. Next morning the Isabel anchored near the fort to receive the gallant little band. The terms of evacuation were that the garrison should take all its individual and company property; that they should march out with their side and other arms with all the honors, in their own way, and at their own time; that they should salute their flag and take it with them.

With their tattered flag flying, and the band playing national airs, these seventy heroes marched out of Fort Sumter. Seventy to seven thousand!

Major Anderson's heroic conduct had drawn all loyal hearts toward him, and it was the wish of the country that he should immediately be invested with some important command. He was made a brigadier-general, and sent to Kentucky to superintend the raising of troops in that state. But the terrible ordeal through which he had just passed, and the results of hardships undergone in Mexico, unfitted him for active duty. Since then, General Anderson has resided in New York City.

A tall, elderly gentleman in undress uniform, leading a little child by the hand, is often seen passing slowly along Broadway. His fine, intellectual face is the index to the genuine goodness and nobility of his heart. Though men of noisier name meet you at each corner, your eyes follow pleasantly after this one —Robert Anderson.

COM. S. F. DUPONT U. S. N.

SAMUEL FRANCIS DU PONT.

SAMUEL FRANCIS DU PONT, rear-admiral in the United States navy, was born at Bergen Point, New Jersey, September 27th, 1803. His grandfather, Pierre Samuel Du Pont de Nemours, well known in French history as a political economist, and a representative in the Chamber of Notables and the States-General, emigrated to America with his two sons, Victor and E. S. Du Pont, at the close of the year 1799. The elder of these resided in the state of New York until 1809, when he removed with his family to the neighborhood of Wilmington, Delaware, of which state his son, Admiral Du Pont, is a resident and citizen. The latter was, in 1815, when but twelve years of age, commissioned by President Madison a midshipman in the United States navy; and it is an interesting fact that Mr. Jefferson, alluding to the appointment in a letter to his grandfather, expressed the hope that he might live to be an admiral. He sailed on his first cruise in 1817, on board the Franklin, seventy-four, under Commodore Stewart, and thenceforth for many years performed the ordinary routine duties of his profession, which, owing to the peaceful relations subsisting between the United States and foreign powers, were of no special importance. He, however, showed himself an active and able officer, in whatever capacity employed, and saw a fair proportion of sea-service.

In 1845, being then a commander, Du Pont was ordered to the Pacific, in command of the frigate Congress, bearing the broad pennant of Commodore Stockton, and was on the California coast at the commencement of the war with Mexico. He was soon after put in command of the sloop-of-war Cyane, and, in the varied and difficult service which fell to his lot, acquitted himself with prudence and gallantry, taking a conspicuous part in the conquest of Lower California. Four different commodores commanding on that station testified to the faithful manner in which he discharged his duties, and the secretary of the navy added the unqualified approval of his department.

Early in February, 1848, Commander Du Pont, while lying off La Paz, ascertained that a brother-officer, Lieutenant Heywood, with four midshipmen and a few marines, was beleaguered in the mission-house of San José by an overpowering force of Mexicans under Colonel Piñeda. He immediately sailed for the latter place, landed on the 15th of the month a force of one hundred and two men of all ranks, and, defeating and dispersing the besiegers, who outnumbered him four or five to one, rescued the hard-pressed but dauntless little band of his countrymen. "I want words," wrote Commodore Shubrick, the commanding officer of the station, "to express my sense of the gallant conduct of these officers, but feel that I am perfectly safe in saying that the annals of war cannot furnish instances of greater coolness, of more indomitable perseverance, of more conspicuous bravery, and of sounder judgment."

In 1856, Du Pont attained the rank of captain, and in the succeeding year was placed in command of the steam-frigate Minnesota, which conveyed Mr. Reed, the American minister, to China. Arriving during the Anglo-French war with the Chinese, he was one of the first who visited Canton after its bombardment, and was also an eye-witness of the capture by the allies of the forts at the mouth of the Peiho River. He returned to the United States in 1859, having extended his cruise to Japan and the coast of southern Asia, and on January 1st, 1861, was appointed to the command of the Philadelphia navy-yard.

The outbreak of the Southern Rebellion found Du Pont on the active list of captains, and with a reputation for professional capacity and fidelity of which the government was not slow to avail itself. As a means of crushing the naval power of the rebels, and cutting them off effectually from supplies, it was early determined to occupy one or more important points on the Southern coast, where the blockading squadrons or cruisers of the government might resort for shelter or supplies, or rendezvous for expeditions; and to Captain Du Pont was intrusted the selection of such a place. After consultation between Mr. Fox, assistant secretary of the navy, and himself, the harbor of Port Royal, on the coast of South Carolina, was fixed upon; and during the summer and autumn of 1861, preparations for a joint naval and military expedition thither were vigorously but quietly pursued. The land-forces, under the command of General Thomas W. Sherman, assembled at Annapolis, whence on October 21st they were conveyed in transports to Fortress Monroe, to join the fleet of war-vessels under Commodore Du Pont with which they were intended to co-operate. On the 29th, the whole fleet, numbering upward of fifty sail, weighed anchor and stood out to sea, led by the steam-frigate Wabash, bearing the broad pennant of Commodore Du Pont, as commander of the South Atlantic blockading squadron. On the afternoon of November 1st, a heavy gale set in, which increased in violence during the night, and raged with fury until the next evening, dispersing the fleet in all directions, and causing the loss of several transports and a quantity of material. On Monday, the 4th, the greater part of the fleet had assembled off Port Royal bar, which lies ten miles seaward, and is about two miles in width; and the small steamer Vixen was immediately dispatched to find the channel, and replace the buoys removed by the rebels. This having been accomplished early in the afternoon of the same day, the gunboats and lighter transports were immediately sent forward, dispersing a fleet of small rebel steamers, under Commodore Tatnall; and a reconnoissance discovered that Hilton Head and Bay Point, commanding the entrance to Port Royal harbor, called Broad River, which is here about two and a half miles wide, were protected by works of great strength, scientifically constructed, and mounted with guns of heavy calibre. Fort Walker, on Hilton Head, at the southerly entrance of the river, mounted twenty-three pieces, many of which were rifled, and was the defence mainly relied upon for the protection of the harbor. The works on Bay Point comprised Fort Beauregard mounting fifteen guns, and a battery of four guns about half a mile distant.

On Tuesday morning, the 5th, the Wabash crossed the bar, followed by the frigate Susquehanna and the larger transports; and another reconnoissance, made by the gunboats, satisfied the commodore of the superiority of Fort Walker, against which he determined to direct his chief efforts. Wednesday being a stormy day, the attack upon the forts was deferred until Thursday morning, the 7th.

The plan was, for the ships to steam in a circle or ellipse between the forts, running close to Hilton Head as they came down the river, and pouring broadsides into Fort Walker; and, on their return, attacking in a similar manner Fort Beauregard. The squadron was drawn up in two columns, the larger being headed by the Wabash, and at half-past nine in the morning stood into Broad River, and moved up past Fort Beauregard. At a few minutes before ten the action became general, and for four hours a continuous stream of shot and shell was poured upon the rebel forts. The Wabash, directed by Commodore Du Pont in person, was carried by the soundings as close to the shore as possible, the engines working with barely enough power to give her steerage-way, and proceeded with such deliberation, that but three circuits were accomplished during the fight. At the same time her signals were given as regularly as on an ordinary occasion. Her heavy guns played with terrible effect upon the enemy, and she was herself a prominent target for the guns of either fort. The commodore estimated that he saved a hundred lives by keeping under way and bearing in close, and subsequently stated that he never conceived of such a fire as that of the Wabash in her second turn. She also bore in great measure the brunt of the enemy's fire; as, after the first circuit, the small gunboats took their positions at discretion, and the Susquehanna and Bienville were her only companions. At two o'clock, the enemy's fire began to slacken, and he was soon discovered in rapid flight from Fort Walker toward a neighboring wood. At half-past two, the work was occupied by a party from the Wabash, and on the succeeding morning Fort Beauregard was found deserted by its garrison. The casualties of the fleet were eight killed and twenty-three wounded; and the rebel loss is supposed to have amounted to between one and two hundred. In the hurry of their flight they also abandoned every thing but their muskets. This victory, the most considerable gained since the defeat at Bull Run, excited universal enthusiasm throughout the loyal states, and contributed very materially to restore confidence in the ability of the government to crush the rebellion, as well as to increase the *éclat* which had attended the naval operations in the war.

Commodore Du Pont immediately took active measures to follow up his success; and his fleet has since been busily employed in expeditions along the coast, or in co-operating with the land-forces under General Sherman and the other military officers. During the year that he has commanded the South Atlantic blockading squadron, the vigilance of his subordinates has very materially checked the violations of the blockade so frequent in the early part of the war, and numerous captures of valuable vessels and cargoes have added to the resources of the government. In August, 1862, he was nominated by the President one of the seven rear-admirals on the active list authorized to be appointed by act of Congress.

Apart from his sea-service, which covers a period of nearly a quarter of a century, Admiral Du Pont has been employed on shore in numerous important public duties requiring the exercise of high professional knowledge and experience. He was one of the officers consulted by Mr. Bancroft, when secretary of the navy, in regard to the formation of a naval school; and a member of the board which organized the academy at Annapolis on its subsequent efficient footing. He has also served on boards convened for the purpose of making codes of rules and regulations for the government of the service, for the examination of midshipmen, and similar purposes, and was for three years a prominent member of the lighthouse board, taking an active part in the creation of the present system for lighting the coast. He also performed the unwelcome duties of a member of the naval retiring board of 1855. More important than any of these services, perhaps, were his investigations with reference to the introduction of floating batteries for coast defence, which were embodied in a report esteemed of so much value, that it has been republished separately, and very generally consulted by officers of the engineer-corps. The late Lieutenant-General Sir Howard Douglas, the chief English authority on the subject, in a recent edition of his standard work on gunnery, has cited its opinions and conclusions with respect, and styles it "an admirable work." The private as well as the public career of Admiral Du Pont is without reproach. "No man," said Mr. Clayton, of Delaware, in the United States Senate, in allusion to his services, "is more beloved or honored by his brother-officers in the navy, or more respected as an accomplished officer, sailor, and gentleman. No man living stands in higher repute wherever he is known."

COL EDWARD D BAKER

EDWARD D. BAKER.

THE death of a soldier in honorable warfare, on a well-fought field, is an event so intimately connected with his calling, that the mind is always more or less prepared for the calamity, however sudden may be its approach. Choice has made him "seek renown even in the jaws of danger and of death," and chance holds the scales in which his fate is weighed. But when one who has gained distinction in the peaceful walks of civil life, whose eloquent voice has moved multitudes to enthusiasm or to tears, and who has taken the sword from motives of patriotism only, is cut off in the midst of fame and usefulness, fighting in the ranks of a loyal army, the community receives a shock from which it does not readily recover, refusing for a time to be comforted. Such was the feeling occasioned by the death of Colonel Baker, who, at the call of a betrayed and threatened country, forsook his seat in the halls of the national legislature for the field of battle, and there "foremost fighting, fell."

EDWARD D. BAKER, late a Senator of the United States from Oregon, and colonel of the first California regiment, was born in London, England, on the 24th day of February, in the year 1811. His father, Edward Baker, a member of the Society of Friends, was a man of education and refinement; and his mother's brother, Captain Dickinson, of the royal navy, was one of the heroes of Trafalgar, where he fought under Lord Collingwood. In 1815, the elder Baker removed with his family to Philadelphia, whence ten years later he made a further migration to Illinois, and settling in the pleasant town of Belleville, in St. Clair county, established there an academy for boys, on what was then called the Lancasterian plan of instruction. Here his son Edward, a handsome and intelligent boy, received his principal education, giving even then many indications of the brilliant talents he was destined to develop in mature life. Not content with his prescribed studies, he would devour whatever books came within his reach, storing his mind with almost every thing which the wide range of literature embraced. To great industry, energy, and perseverance, he united a memory almost superhuman; and such were his powers of concentration, that the hasty perusal of a book would enable him to repeat *verbatim* whole pages of it. Hence the ready and almost inexhaustible fund of varied knowledge which in after-life astonished those who knew the circumstances of his childhood, and which contributed in no slight degree to his success as a public speaker. As an illustration of the ambition for public life which even then began to stir him, it is related that a friend surprised him one day weeping bitterly over a volume which he was perusing, and asked him what book it was that so affected him. "The Contitution of the United States," was the reply. "I find that no foreigner can be President, and I am of English birth."

At the age of eighteen, young Baker removed to Carrollton, in Greene county, where he obtained a deputy clerkship in the county court; and in the intervals of his office labors applied himself with diligence to the study of law, which he determined to make his profession. Before reaching his majority he was admitted to the bar, after a highly creditable examination, and commenced practice in Carrollton. Possessing a practical knowledge of the details of his profession remarkable in so young a man, he soon showed also powers of oratory which placed him high as an advocate, at the very head of the bar in his circuit, and gave him a considerable reputation outside the courts of law.

About 1832–'33, a noted revival took place among the Christians or Campbellite Baptists in Illinois, under the influence of which Mr. Baker became a convert to the doctrines of the sect. Impressed with the belief that his abilities as a public speaker ought to be employed in the service of religion, he regularly devoted his Sundays, and such other time as he could spare from professional duties, to preaching; and in this course he persevered for several years, with high reputation as a pulpit orator.

In 1838, finding Carrollton too limited a field for his forensic powers, Mr. Baker removed to Springfield, then recently created the capital of the state, and immediately embarked in a lucrative practice. Among the many distinguished men with whom he then entered into competition were President Lincoln, the late Senator Douglas, Senators Trumbull and McDougal (the latter now of California), General Shields, and Colonel Bissell, not one of whom equalled him in the ready flow, the brilliancy, or the pathos, of his eloquence. In respect to voice, grace of delivery, and the other outward attributes of the orator, he far surpassed all of his contemporaries. These qualities suggested him as an aspirant for political honors; and in 1844, having previously held a seat in both houses of the state legislature, he was elected by the Whigs to represent the Springfield district (the only one in the state controlled by that party) in the twenty-ninth Congress, which met in the succeeding year. He was rapidly making himself known as one of the leaders of that body, when the Mexican War broke out; and, unable to resist the fascinations of a military career, he obtained permission from President Polk to raise a regiment in Illinois for the relief of General Taylor. Within two weeks it was recruited, equipped, and on the way to New Orleans, being the first one embarked from north of the Ohio. On the

Rio Grande he was dangerously wounded in the neck, in repressing a mutiny in a Mississippi regiment, and in consequence was unable to participate in the hard-fought battles of Monterey and Buena Vista.

Having resumed his seat in Congress for a few months, Colonel Baker re-joined his regiment before Vera Cruz, and marched with the army under Scott for Mexico. At Cerro Gordo his regiment, which formed part of the brigade of General Shields, took a prominent part in the assault upon the enemy's works; and upon the fall of Shields, severely wounded, Colonel Baker, assuming the command of the brigade, led it forward with a gallantry and dash which greatly contributed to the success of the day, and elicited the warm commendation of Generals Scott and Twiggs, and other high officers.

The term for which his men had enlisted having expired soon afterward, Colonel Baker returned home in the summer of 1847, and claimed from his friends a renomination to Congress. Being disappointed in this, he removed immediately to the Galena district, which for many years had been under the control of the Democrats, and taking the stump as a candidate in 1848, con-ducted an exciting canvass with a vigor and ability surpassing any of his previ-ous efforts. The result was, his election to Congress by a large majority. He served through his term, with credit; but his mind, unsettled by the excitements of military life, was revolving schemes of adventure or political power in the newly-acquired possessions of the republic on the Pacific coast—the El Dorado of the West, toward which so many were already directing longing eyes. In 1852, he removed with his family to California, whither his reputation had pre-ceded him, and, settling in San Francisco, he at once built up a large practice, and by common consent was acknowledged to be the most eloquent speaker in the state. The death of Senator Broderick in a duel, under circumstances which made it certain that a deep-laid plot had been conceived to murder him for his bold denunciations of slavery and the corrupt practices of the administration, afforded a memorable instance of the oratorical powers of Colonel Baker; and his address, delivered over the body of the deceased, aroused in a vast audience, collected in the principal square of San Francisco, the wildest emotions of grief. "Never, perhaps," says one who was present on the occasion, "was eloquence more thrilling; never certainly was it better adapted to the temper of its listen-ers. The merits of the eulogy divided public encomiums with the virtues of the deceased, and the orator became invested with the dead Senator's political for-tunes."

But California was at that time too thoroughly under the control of the Democratic party to enable Colonel Baker, who had become associated with the Republicans, to enter the political arena with any prospect of success; and in 1859, having in the previous year been defeated as Republican candidate for

Congress in the San Francisco district, he removed to Oregon, and was elected a United States Senator for the term expiring March 4th, 1865. He also stumped the state vigorously for Lincoln in the presidential campaign of that year, and, in consequence of divisions among the Democrats, secured the electoral vote of Oregon for the Republican candidate. His eloquent voice was first heard in the Senate-chamber in the eventful session of 1860–'61; and his speech in reply to Senator Benjamin, of Louisiana, showed the quality of his genius. "Perhaps," said Senator Sumner, in his eulogy on Colonel Baker, delivered in the Senate on December 10th, 1861, "the argument against the sophism of secession was never better arranged and combined, or more simply popularized for the general apprehension. That speech at once passed into the permanent literature of the country, while it gave to its author an assured position in this body." On another occasion, he had a parliamentary contest with Senator Breckenridge, not then expelled from his seat, "meeting the polished traitor everywhere with weapons keener and brighter than his own."

The outbreak of the Rebellion found Colonel Baker no lukewarm friend of the Union. He threw himself, heart and soul, into the contest: and at the great Union mass meeting held in New York after the fall of Fort Sumter, his kindling eloquence stirred the multitude like the sound of a trumpet. "It may cost us seven thousand five hundred lives to crush this rebellion," he said; "it may be seventy-five thousand lives; it may be seven hundred and fifty thousand. What then? We have them! The blood of every loyal citizen of this government is dear to me; my sons and theirs—young men grown up beneath my eye and care—are here: they are all dear to me; but if the organization, the destiny, the renown, the glory, freedom of a constitutional government, the only hope of a free people demand it, let them all go!"

Colonel Baker immediately recruited, chiefly in New York and Philadelphia, a regiment of three years' volunteers, which, in grateful remembrance of the state where he had passed the last ten years of his life, he called the first California regiment. With this he took the field during the summer of 1861, still retaining his seat in the Senate, and holding under consideration the offer of a brigadier-generalship, and subsequently of a major-generalship, tendered him by the President; neither of which he was willing to accept, if it should prove incompatible with his legislative functions.

The autumn found Colonel Baker stationed with his regiment on the upper Potomac, near Edwards's Ferry, and within the department commanded by General Stone. On the 21st of October, in obedience to orders from that officer, he led a battalion of his regiment across the river, at Conrad's Ferry, to Ball's Bluff, on the Virginia shore, for the purpose of supporting reconnoissances made above and below under the general direction of Stone. Here he assumed command of all the national troops, about twenty-one hundred in number, which had effected a landing. The butchery of that devoted band, surrounded by an unseen and numerous enemy, is more familiar to the public than the causes which brought about the catastrophe, and which perhaps will never be known. In the midst of imminent danger, Colonel Baker was courageous and collected; and although . impressed with a presentiment, which he had expressed on previous occasions, that he should meet his death during this campaign, he spared no effort to encourage his men. At length the enemy showed a disposition to leave their cover in the woods. Colonel Baker ordered his thinned ranks to charge them, and, while cheering on his men, fell pierced by nine bullets. He expired instantly, dying as his generous and self-sacrificing spirit could have wished—

> "In some good cause, not his own,
> And like a warrior overthrown. . . . .
> Whose eyes are dim with glorious tears
> When, soiled with noble dust, he hears
> His country's war-song thrill his ears!"

His body was recovered, and, after being honored by imposing funeral ceremonies in Washington and New York, was conveyed to San Francisco for interment. The public mourning along the Pacific sea-board, where he was best known and appreciated, is a sufficient evidence of the regard he had inspired in the hearts of his countrymen.

CHARLES WILKES.

CHARLES WILKES was born in New York city, in 1801, entered the navy as midshipman in 1818, and during the next two years cruised under Commodore McDonough in the Mediterranean. He was then sent to the Pacific station with Commodore Stewart, under whom he obtained the command of a tender; and in 1830 was placed in charge of the depot of charts and instruments at Washington. This was long before the establishment of the National Observatory, or indeed of any building of the kind, in the United States; and Lieutenant Wilkes has the honor of being the first in the United States to make observations with fixed astronomical instruments—unless his claim be disputed by Yale College, where a telescope was erected the same year. His instruments were mounted on stone piers, in his own garden; and such was the opposition at that time to any thing like a national observatory, that he was not permitted to enclose them by a permanent structure.

The ability with which Lieutenant Wilkes discharged the duties of this post, and his services in the surveys of Newport harbor and of George's Bank, raised him so high in the opinion of his superior officers, that in the spring of 1838 he was appointed to organize and command a government Exploring Expedition around the world; the first of the kind that ever left these shores. The vessels consisted of the sloops-of-war Vincennes and Peacock, brig Porpoise, storeship Relief, and tenders Sea-Gull and Flying-Fish.

On the 18th of August, 1838, they sailed from Hampton Roads for Madeira, and thence by way of Cape Verde Islands and Rio de Janeiro to Orange harbor, Terra del Fuego, where the whole squadron was at anchor by the month of February, 1839. The Vincennes was left here, while Lieutenant Wilkes with the other vessels set out on a cruise to the antarctic region. Little was accomplished, owing to the lateness of the season, and the lack of proper equipments. In the latter part of May, the Vincennes, Peacock, Porpoise, and Flying-Fish, were together in Valparaiso harbor, waiting in vain for the arrival of the Sea-Gull. She was last seen in a gale on the 28th of April, and since that time nothing has been heard from the gallant little vessel or her seventeen officers and men. A visit to Callao (whence the storeship Relief, proving from her bad sailing-qualities more of a hinderance than a help, was sent home) gave the officers of the expedition an opportunity to replenish their stores; and in July they crossed over to the Paumotee Group, or Cloud of Islands—Tahiti, Upolu, the Samoan Islands, and New South Wales. At Tahiti they had hardly cast anchor, before the principal chiefs crowded around them in boats to solicit the washing of the white men's dirty linen—a business which proved to be one of the prerogatives of the queen and the highest nobility.

On the 26th of December, leaving Sydney, they spread sail for another visit to the unknown Southern Polar Seas, and on the 16th of January, 1840, discovered the great Antarctic Continent, whose existence had hitherto not even been suspected. Lieutenant Wilkes himself received the discovery with doubt and hesitation, and did not venture to record it in his journal until three days after his most experienced officers were fully assured of its reality. Both French and English navigators soon afterward confirmed it. Until the end of the month the little squadron coasted along the icy shore of this new-found continent, exposed to the most fearful dangers, and driven by fierce gales through clusters of icebergs, while the snow fell so fast and thick, that they could see but a few yards ahead. On the night of the 28th, "we were swiftly dashing on," writes Lieutenant Wilkes, "for I felt it necessary to keep the ship under rapid way through the water, to enable her to steer and work quickly. Suddenly many voices cried out, 'Ice ahead!' then, 'On the weather-bow!' and again, 'On the lee-bow and abeam!' All hope of escape seemed in a moment to vanish; return we could not, as large ice-islands had just been passed to leeward; so we dashed on, expecting every moment the crash. The ship, in an instant, from having her lee-guns under water, rose upright; and so close were we passing to leeward of one of these huge islands, that our trysails were almost thrown aback by the eddy wind. . . . . As we proceeded, a glimmering of hope arose, for we accidentally had hit upon a clear passage between two large ice-islands, which in fine weather we should not dare to have ventured through. The suspense endured while making our way between them was intense, but of short duration; and my spirits rose as I heard the whistling of the gale grow louder and louder before us, as we emerged from the passage. We had escaped an awful death, and were again tempest-tossed."

During the ensuing summer, the squadron found constant occupation in visiting and exploring New Zealand, the Friendly Isles, and the Feejee Group; in the last of which a tragical affair occurred during the latter part of July, at the island of Malolo, where Lieutenant Underwood and Midshipman Wilkes Henry, the commander's nephew, were murdered by the natives. Lieutenant Wilkes determined to punish this outrage with exemplary severity. There were two towns, Snalib and Arro, situated upon opposite sides of the island. A force of seventy officers and men, under the command of Lieutenant Cadwalader Ringgold, was sent to destroy them both, while Lieutenant Wilkes remained with a boat-party to cut off the escape of the natives, and protect the ships. Arro was burned with little difficulty, but Sualib was strongly fortified with ditches, a palisade, and a parapet of earth; and here the savages prepared for a stubborn resistance. Men, women, and children, took part in the defence, darting spears and arrows, and opening a fire of musketry, which did little damage—partly, no doubt, in consequence of their practice of putting charges into their guns in proportion to the size of the person at whom they intend to shoot. A rocket at last struck the thatched roof of one of the houses, and in a moment the whole town was in a blaze. In an hour nothing was left of Sualib but a heap of ashes. The Americans now drew off to the ships, bearing a number of prisoners, and leaving fifty-seven of the Feejeeans dead or mortally wounded. On their own side, not a life was lost. The next day they landed again, for the purpose of receiving the submission of the natives. "Toward four o'clock," says Lieutenant Wilkes, "the sound of distant wailings was heard, which gradually drew nearer and nearer. At the same time the natives were seen passing over the hills toward us, giving an effect to the whole scene which will long be borne in my memory. They at length reached the foot of the hill, but would come no farther, until assured that their submission would be received. On receiving this assurance, they wound upward, and in a short time about forty men appeared, crouching on their hands and knees, and occasionally stopping to utter piteous moans and wailings. When within thirty feet of us, they stopped; and an old man, their leader, in the most piteous manner begged pardon."

After a survey of various other islands in the Pacific, and a toilsome expedition to the summit of the volcano of Mouna Loa, in Hawaii, Lieutenant Wilkes crossed over to the western shore of North America, made some interesting explorations in California and Oregon, and then sailed for Singapore, whence on the 26th of February, 1842, the squadron got under way for their homeward voyage. On the 10th of June, they anchored in New York harbor.

Lieutenant Wilkes was almost immediately rewarded by his promotion to the rank of commander; but notwithstanding the valuable results of the expedition, and the effective manner in which with very inadequate means he had carried out his instructions, his conduct during the four years' cruise did not pass unquestioned. In August, he was arraigned before a naval court-martial, on board the North Carolina, at New York, on eleven charges, and, after a trial of three weeks, was acquitted of all except a technical violation of the laws of the navy, in the punishment of certain deserters from his squadron. For this, in which there can be little question that he was perfectly excusable, he was sentenced to a reprimand. He was now employed for several years in preparing for the press his "Narrative of the United States Exploring Expedition," which

40

appeared in 1845; and in 1849, he published an account of his observations in California and Oregon, under the title of "Western America." In 1855, he was promoted to the rank of captain.

He was engaged in no other important sea-service until 1861, when he was ordered to the West Indies, in the steam-frigate San Jacinto, to look after the privateer Sumter. Touching at Cienfuegos, on the island of Cuba, he there learned that Messrs. James M. Mason and John Slidell, the rebel commissioners to England and France, had escaped from Charleston on the steamer Theodora, and were then at Havana, with their families and suites, preparing to embark for England. Captain Wilkes at once went in pursuit of the Theodora, but, failing to come up with her, ran to the eastward, to the narrowest part of the Bahama Channel, for the purpose of intercepting the British mail-steamer Trent, on which the confederate emissaries had taken passage. On the 8th of November the Trent hove in sight. The San Jacinto beat to quarters, two boats were manned and armed, the guns were brought to bear upon the steamer, and, as she approached, a shot and then a shell were fired across her bow. As soon as she hove to, Lieutenant Fairfax boarded her, and demanded the surrender of Messrs. Mason and Slidell, and their secretaries, McFarland and Eustis. The demand was refused; but the gentlemen in question were recognized, and, after a faint show of resistance, were brought off by force. Captain Wilkes at once proceeded to Hampton Roads, and there received orders to refit at Charlestown, and transfer his prisoners to Fort Warren, in Boston harbor. His prompt and decisive action awakened the liveliest popular enthusiasm. He was honored with a public banquet in Boston, and the secretary of the navy, in his next official report, warmly commended his conduct; but the President subsequently disavowed the seizure, on account of informality, and surrendered Messrs. Slidell and Mason at the demand of the British government.

When the navy was reorganized in the summer of 1862, Captain Wilkes was placed first on the list of commodores, and about the same time was assigned to the command of the gunboat flotilla in the James River. Shortly afterward, he was appointed acting rear-admiral, and sent to the West Indies in command of a squadron, to protect American commerce.

Commodore Wilkes is a member of the American Association for the Advancement of Science, before which he read in 1855 a paper on the "Theory of the Winds," which was published the next year; and is the author of the volume on Meteorology, in the series forming the elaborate official report of his Exploring Expedition. In 1848, he received the gold medal of the London Geographical Society.

JOHN POPE.

JOHN POPE was born in the state of Kentucky, March 12th, 1823. His father, Governor Nathaniel Pope, of Virginia, emigrated to Kentucky in the early part of the present century, and, during the infancy of his son, removed with his family to Kaskaskia, Illinois. He was a delegate to Congress from Illinois before its organization as a state, and was subsequently for many years United States district judge, an office which he filled with eminent ability and fidelity. After receiving a careful preliminary education, young Pope was admitted in 1838 a cadet in the West Point military academy, where he was graduated in 1842, standing high in a class which numbered among its members Generals Rosecrans and Doubleday of the Union army, and the rebel Generals Gustavus W. Smith, Lovell, Longstreet, Van Dorn, and others. In July of the same year he was commissioned brevet second-lieutenant in the corps of topographical engineers. Upon the breaking out of the war with Mexico, he was attached to the army under General Taylor, and for "gallant and meritorious" conduct at the battle of Monterey was breveted a first-lieutenant, his commission bearing date September 23d, 1846. For "highly gallant and meritorious conduct" on the hard-fought field of Buena Vista he was breveted a captain, his commission being dated February 23d, 1847; and at the conclusion of the war, the state of Illinois testified its sense of the importance of his services by presenting him with a sword.

Thenceforth for many years Captain Pope was chiefly employed, in common with other officers of engineers, on the surveying and exploring expeditions which have opened to travel and emigration the vast and comparatively unknown regions lying between the valley of the Mississippi and the Pacific Ocean. In 1849, he conducted an expedition into the northern portions of Minnesota, and demonstrated the practicability of navigating the Red River of the North with steamers, for which service he received a vote of thanks from the territorial legislature.

After several years' service in New Mexico, Captain Pope was, in 1853, appointed to command one of the six expeditions organized by the war department, under an act of Congress, to ascertain the most practicable route for a railroad from the Mississippi to the Pacific, and was directed to explore the thirty-second parallel from Red River to the Rio Grande.   His survey, completed in the summer of 1854, was stated by Jefferson Davis, then secretary of war, to have been "creditably performed under the most disadvantageous circumstances."   In connection with this enterprise he explored, in 1855-'56, the *Llano Estacado*, or Staked Plain, in Texas and New Mexico, and made some experiments in Artesian-well boring, with a view to determine the feasibility of obtaining a supply of water for railroad or other purposes.   In July, 1856, he was advanced to the full rank of captain, and during the next three years his time was principally occupied with engineering duties in the Western military department.

Obtaining a leave of absence for the year 1860, Captain Pope entered zealously into the presidential canvass, and was a warm supporter of Mr. Lincoln. When the clouds of civil war began to gather on the horizon, he was not backward to proclaim the necessity of vigorous measures on the part of the government to maintain the integrity of the Union; expressing opinions which, if contrary to the etiquette of the service, as understood by some members of his profession, were nevertheless eminently patriotic, and, amid the positive defection of many of the regular army officers and the apparent lukewarmness of others, were gratefully received by the people of the loyal states.   For some severe strictures on the temporizing policy of President Buchanan, to which he gave utterance in a lecture on fortifications, delivered in Cincinnati, in February, 1861, he was court-martialled by order of the President; but by the advice of Mr. Holt, secretary of war, the matter was dropped, the government having matters of graver import to occupy its attention.   Captain Pope accordingly resumed his command in the engineer corps, and was one of the officers detailed by the war department to escort President Lincoln to Washington.

On May 3d, 1861, the President issued a call for forty-two thousand volunteers to serve for three years or the war; and on the 17th of the month, Captain Pope was commissioned a brigadier-general in that force, and appointed to a command in Northern Missouri, then swarming with secession sympathizers, who, at the instigation of the traitor governor, Jackson, were obstructing railroad travel, and committing depredations on private property.   On July 19th, he issued a proclamation to the people of North Missouri, warning them against unlawful combinations, and during the next few weeks prosecuted a vigorous war against bridge-burners and guerillas, who soon discovered that General Pope's department was no place for their operations.   After the arrival of General Halleck at St. Louis, in November, as commander-in-chief of the Western department, General Pope was detailed to active duty in Central Missouri; and on December 18th, in co-operation with General Jefferson C. Davis, he surprised and captured at Blackwater nearly two thousand rebel recruits for Price's army. Then, marching rapidly upon Shawnee Mound, he succeeded in the brief space of ten days in driving the rebel forces completely out of that part of the country. These services, widely and gratefully acknowledged by the public, suggested him to General Halleck as a competent officer to command the army of the Mississippi, destined to co-operate, with the opening of the spring, in the general movement of the Western troops against the enemy.

On the 23d of February, 1862, General Pope assumed command of a well-appointed army at Commerce, Missouri, and a few days later marched upon New Madrid, where a force of ten thousand rebels, under General Jefferson Thompson, was intrenched in a strong position, defended by many heavy guns, and covered by a fleet of gunboats. During a delay occasioned by the failure to receive his siege-guns from Cairo, he dispatched a portion of his force to Point Pleasant, twelve miles below New Madrid, thus establishing an efficient blockade of the Mississippi, and preventing the arrival of supplies to the rebels from below. At sunset, on the 12th of March, the siege-guns arrived; on the same night they were placed in battery, within eight hundred yards of the enemy's main work; and at daylight, on the 13th, a heavy fire was opened. The enemy withstood the attack during the day, but on the night of the 13th precipitately abandoned their works, and took refuge on the other side of the river, leaving upward of sixty guns, several thousand small-arms, and equipments, stores, and munitions, of the value of nearly a million of dollars.

The rebels, however, still occupied Island Number Ten, commanding the river above New Madrid; and General Pope, being without the means of transporting his troops to the Kentucky shore, could not immediately pursue his advantage. On the 17th, Flag-Officer Foote, with his flotilla of gunboats and mortar-boats, opened fire upon Island Number Ten from above; but the work proving of far greater strength than he had anticipated, it became evident that, without the assistance of a land-force, operating on the other side of the river, the siege might be protracted for months. But General Pope had no transports, to cross the river below the island; and the inundated state of the country rendered it difficult, if not impossible, to march his troops to the vicinity of the flotilla. Availing himself, in this emergency, of the suggestion of General Schuyler Hamilton, one of his generals of division, he ordered a canal twelve miles long to be cut across the neck of land formed by a bend in the river opposite the island, with a view of floating transports down it to his assistance. The work was completed within three weeks, and on the 7th of April a number of transports and gunboats passed through. The embarkation of troops at New Madrid was commenced on the same day, and on the evening of the 9th nine thousand Union soldiers were landed on the Kentucky shore. The enemy at once surrendered their costly works on Island Number Ten, with an immense amount of material of war; and Pope, pushing on a division, under General Paine, to Tiptonville, succeeded in capturing upward of five thousand retreating rebels, including three generals, seven colonels, and several hundred inferior officers, together with an immense amount of spoils. For these successes he was promoted to be a major-general, his commission dating from March 21st.

Flushed with victory, and with the applause of the country ringing in his ears, General Pope proceeded down the Mississippi, to attack Fort Pillow, but was arrested in his course by an order from General Halleck, directing him to repair with his troops to Pittsburg Landing. Within five days after receiving the order, his entire force was at Hamburg, four miles from Pittsburg, occupying a position on the extreme left of the Union line. He received the command of one of the three grand divisions into which General Halleck divided his army, and showed characteristic activity in the sharp actions which preceded the withdrawal of the enemy into his defensive works at Corinth; succeeding on one occasion, by a brilliant piece of strategy, in capturing a considerable number of prisoners. After the evacuation of Corinth, on May 30th, he pursued the retreating army under General Beauregard down the Mobile railroad, securing many prisoners and large quantities of munitions; and while engaged in this duty, he was summoned by the President to Washington, and appointed to the command of the "army of Virginia," comprising the combined corps of Generals Fremont, Banks, and McDowell, then stationed along the Potomac, and in front of Washington. These officers were all his seniors in rank, but, in the opinion of the President, the exigencies of the service demanded that he should be placed over them.

Before General Pope could commence the organization of his command, the series of reverses before Richmond, consequent upon General McClellan's transferring his base of operations to the James River, brought dismay to the government and people, and rendered necessary an entire change in the plans of the campaign. On the 14th of July, the new general issued an address to his troops, breathing the most ardent spirit of enterprise; and on the 29th—the President having in the mean time decided to remove the army of McClellan from the peninsula—he took the field in person, establishing his head-quarters at Warrenton, Virginia. As the readiest means of diverting the attention of the enemy from McClellan, Pope was ordered to make a demonstration in force upon Richmond; and immediately a forward movement, which had been preceded by several dashing cavalry reconnoissances, was commenced by his whole army. Reconnoitring parties crossed the Rapidan River, and pushed forward to Orange Court-House and other points; and on August 9th, the corps of General Banks fought a well-contested battle with the rebels under Jackson at Cedar Mountain. The latter fell back on the 11th, and Pope immediately brought his whole force up to the line of the Rapidan. Under cover of these movements, the army of McClellan evacuated its position at Harrison's Landing on the 14th and 15th, without mo-lestation, and the enemy at once prepared to fall upon and crush Pope before reinforcements could reach him.

On the 17th and 18th, Pope withdrew his whole army behind the Rappa-hannock, and, being in too feeble force to defend that line, subsequently fell back as far as Warrenton, in the expectation that a portion of McClellan's troops would meet him there, or be within supporting distance. A rebel corps under Jackson meanwhile made a flank movement on Pope's right, and, passing through Thor-oughfare Gap, took possession of the old defensive works at Manassas, which Pope supposed had been occupied, in accordance with his orders, by two divisions of McClellan's army. The contrary proving to be the case, Pope marched rapidly in three columns toward Manassas; and on the 28th, 29th, and 30th, a series of desperate battles was fought, resulting in the discomfiture of the federal forces, who retired across Bull Run to the strong position of Centreville. The advan-tage on the 28th and 29th rested with the federal troops; and General Pope has asserted, in his official dispatch, that if General Fitz-John Porter had attacked the enemy in flank on the latter day, as he had been ordered to do, Jackson would have been utterly routed before the rebel reinforcements under Lee could reach him. On the evening of that day the junction of the enemy's forces was effected, and the defeat of Pope, confronted on the 30th by superior numbers, was the consequence. The army subsequently retired in good order to Washington; and on September 3d, General Pope was at his own request relieved of his com-mand—having first, in a well-written dispatch, stated what he claimed to have been the obstacles to his success. He also preferred charges of insubordination against three of McClellan's generals, and demanded a court of inquiry, which was granted. At the special request of General McClellan, proceedings were stayed; and the public are accordingly for the present unable to form a correct judgment with regard to the facts connected with the late battles before Wash-ington, and the motives of the principal actors in them.

General Pope was immediately assigned to the command of the department of the North-west, where he is now engaged in protecting the inhabitants from threatened attacks of the Indian tribes.

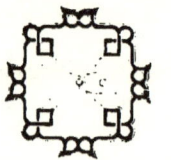

S. H. Stringham

SILAS HORTON STRINGHAM.

WE have never had occasion to feel the blush of shame tingle our cheeks when reference was made to our American navy. From that daring series of exploits, which made the name of John Paul Jones immortal; through all the years of the War of 1812–1815, when the cross of St. George was so often compulsorily lowered before the Stars and Stripes, that British tars found small comfort in singing "Britannia rules the Waves;" alike on the Atlantic, Pacific, and Indian Oceans, the Arctic and the Antarctic Seas, the gallant officers of our navy have maintained its fair fame and prowess against all comers. Among those to whom the nation's flag has been thus intrusted, and who have maintained it in unsullied purity, is the subject of this memoir.

SILAS HORTON STRINGHAM is a native of New York, having been born in Middletown, Orange county, on the 7th of November, 1798. He entered the navy as a midshipman in his thirteenth year, and was ordered, immediately on receiving his commission, to the frigate President, Commodore John Rodgers, then lying in Hampton Roads.

There were already signs of the coming storm; and for the next four years, during which he was attached to the President, the young midshipman found naval life no holiday sport. On the 16th of May, 1811, occurred that memorable fight between the President and the English corvette Little Belt, which was one of the immediate causes of the War of 1812. The chastisement which the English vessel received, and which caused such exasperation on the part of the British government, though but a just return for the unwarrantable insolence displayed by British officers in the case of the Chesapeake, was, as the event proved, the result of a misunderstanding. The President had also a running fight in June, 1812, with the Belvidere, a British frigate; but the enemy was fleeter than the President, and made her escape. In 1814, the President was transferred to Commodore Decatur, and young Stringham with the rest of the officers was assigned to the Guerriere, on which he served for a year, when he was ordered to the brig Spark, one of the vessels of Commodore Decatur's Algerine squadron. The Spark did not long remain in the Mediterranean. After convoying two prizes to Algiers, she joined Commodore Bainbridge's squadron, and returned with it to the United States in November, 1815.

41

The Spark returned to the Mediterranean the ensuing spring, but of her former officers all except Stringham were transferred to other ships. The morning after their arrival at Gibraltar, a heavy south-east gale sprung up, and a French brig, coming into the harbor, capsized. Captain Gamble, of the Spark, immediately called for volunteers to go to the help of the perishing crew and passengers of the French vessel. Young Stringham was the first to volunteer, and lowering a small boat, with six seamen, started on his perilous excursion. He reached the brig in safety, and succeeded in rescuing five persons from her; but the gale being so severe as to render their return to the Spark impossible, the boat was headed for the Algesiras shore, but before reaching it was capsized, and one of his own crew and two of the rescued Frenchmen were drowned; the rest succeeded in swimming to land. On board the Spark it was believed that all were drowned, and the flag at half-mast, and the minute-guns fired in honor of the supposed deceased, indicated the sorrow of their comrades at their loss; but on the subsidence of the storm, they regained their vessel, where they were received with hearty welcome.

In 1817, Lieutenant Stringham was transferred to the sloop-of-war Erie, and in the fall of 1818, to the Peacock, which soon afterward returned to the United States. After a few months at home, he was ordered to the Cyane sloop-of-war, in the autumn of 1819. The first duty assigned to the Cyane, after he joined her, was the convoying of the ship Elizabeth, which carried to the African coast the first settlers to the future republic of Liberia. After their arrival on the coast, and while stationed off the Gallinas River, each lieutenant was put in command of a boat, to board a number of vessels supposed to be slavers. Lieutenant Stringham captured two—the Endymion, of Baltimore, and the Esperanza, a Spanish vessel; and, obtaining permission from his commander, took' one of these vessels and captured two schooners, the Plattsburg and the Science, also engaged in the slave-trade. He was then made prize-commodore, and brought his four prizes to New York, where they were condemned.

In 1821, he was ordered to the Hornet, as first-lieutenant, and assigned to the West India station; and during his service on that station, the Hornet captured a notorious pirate-ship and a slaver. The former was sent to Norfolk, and the latter to New Orleans, for condemnation. In 1822, Lieutenant Stringham returned to New York, and in the autumn of the next year was ordered to the Cyane, as first-lieutenant, under Commodore Creighton. In the spring of 1824, the Cyane took the American minister to France to his destination, and then joined the Mediterranean squadron, of which she formed a part till the autumn of 1825. There was no opportunity during this cruise for the display of the courage which is exhibited on the battle-field or in the horrors of a sea-fight; but the young lieutenant showed a higher and nobler courage, by leaping into the sea and saving two men who had fallen overboard, and were in imminent danger of drowning.

The next four years were spent at the Brooklyn navy-yard, where he was actively engaged in fitting out war-vessels. In 1829, he was assigned to the Peacock, sent on the sad duty of searching for the missing sloop-of-war Hornet, on board of which he had formerly been an officer. She was supposed to have been lost near Tampico, in the Gulf of Mexico, but the most careful search failed to discover any traces of her. After some time spent in this search, Lieutenant Stringham was appointed by Commodore Elliott to the command of the Falmouth, and ordered to Carthagena. The Falmouth returned to New York in 1830.

The next five years were spent by Lieutenant Stringham in shore-service, and in 1835 he was ordered to the command of the sloop-of-war John Adams, then in the Mediterranean squadron. While in this squadron, his vessel being stationed at Malaga, he saved the Orestes, an English man-of-war, from being wrecked in the harbor, and rendered valuable assistance both to her and her consort, which was also seriously crippled. Having taken their mails and part of their stores to Barcelona, he was there instrumental in assisting a third English man-of-war, which had gone ashore near that city.

In 1837, Lieutenant Stringham returned to New York, and was immediately appointed second in command at the Brooklyn navy-yard; and with the exception of a cruise in the brig Porpoise, to look for the "long, low, black schooner," whose appearance had excited so much alarm in the mercantile marine, he remained attached to the navy-yard till 1842. In 1841, he was one of the board appointed to test the merits of the Stevens elongated shell. In 1842, he was ordered to the razee Independence; and, in the spring of 1843, appointed commander of the Brooklyn navy-yard, where he remained till 1846.

The commencement of the Mexican War called him at once into active service. He was ordered to the Ohio ship-of-the-line, and sailed from Boston for Vera Cruz, stopping at Hampton Roads on his way. He took an active part in the bombardment of the fortress of San Juan de Ulloa. After the reduction of the fort, the Ohio was ordered to return to New York, and on her way called at Havana, being the first American ship-of-the-line which had ever entered that port.

On his return to New York, Captain Stringham received Honorable David Tod (now governor of Ohio), the minister to Brazil, on board his ship, and proceeded at once to Rio Janeiro, where he was put in command of the squadron, and, when relieved by the arrival of Commodore Storer, returned to New York. In 1851, he was made commander of the Norfolk navy-yard, and in April, 1852, assigned to the command of the Mediterranean squadron, and hoisted his flag, as commodore, on the Cumberland frigate. He remained in command of the squadron till July, 1855, when he returned to the United States, and was assigned to the command of the Charlestown navy-yard, which he held till May, 1859. In March, 1861, he was ordered to Washington, as a member of a naval court-martial, and on special duty, and while there was appointed flag-officer of the Atlantic blockading squadron, and ordered to the Minnesota as his flag-ship. In May, this squadron was divided, and his cruising-ground extended from Key West to the Chesapeake Bay.

In the summer of 1861, Commodore Stringham was honored with the preparation of the first of those combined naval and military expeditions which have crowned the American navy with such glory; and in his case, as in most of the others, the success has been almost exclusively due to the action of the navy. On the 26th of August, the fleet, consisting of the Minnesota, Captain Van Brunt; the Wabash, Captain Mercer; the Monticello, Commander Gillis; the Pawnee, Commander Rowan; and the Harriet Lane, Captain Faunce, sailed from Hampton Roads for Hatteras Inlet. The Susquehanna steam-frigate and the Cumberland sailing-frigate were ordered also to join the expedition, which they did the next day. There were also a number of chartered steamers, transports, &c., which carried the troops intended to take part in the expedition. About four o'clock, P. M., on Tuesday, August 27th, the fleet arrived off Hatteras Inlet, where were two forts—Fort Hatteras, mounting ten cannon, and Fort Clark, mounting five—the two manned by about seven hundred confederate troops, under the command of Samuel F. Barron, formerly a captain in the United States navy, but at that time acting secretary of the navy of the confederate states, assisted by a colonel and major of the "Confederate Volunteers."

At daylight, on the morning of the 28th of August, the arrangements were made for an attack upon the forts, and the bombardment of Fort Clark was continued till half-past one P. M., when both forts hauled down their flags, and the garrison of Fort Clark escaped to Fort Hatteras. The fleet ceased firing, and the Monticello was sent into the inlet, to discover whether the forts intended to surrender. When she had approached within six hundred yards of Fort Hatteras, the occupants of that fort commenced firing upon her, and inflicted serious injuries upon her hull. Perceiving this, Flag-Officer Stringham came to her assistance with the Wabash, Susquehanna, and Minnesota, and soon drove the garrison into their bomb-proof, and compelled them to cease firing. The next morning, at eight o'clock, the fleet renewed its fire upon Fort Hatteras, dropping almost every shell from their heavy guns inside the fort. At ten minutes past eleven, a white flag was displayed from the fort; and the preliminaries having been agreed upon, the garrison, consisting of seven hundred and fifteen men, surrendered to Flag-Officer Stringham and General Benjamin F. Butler, who commanded the land-forces. Besides the prisoners, the fruits of this victory were—the possession of two forts; one thousand stand of arms; seventy-five kegs of powder; five stand of colors; thirty-one cannon, including one ten-inch columbiad; a brig, loaded with cotton; a sloop, laden with provisions and stores; two light boats; one hundred and fifty bags of coffee, &c. Not a man belonging to the fleet was killed.

For this brilliant affair, Flag-Officer Stringham received the thanks of the government. On the 23d of September, 1861, he was, at his own request, relieved from his command. In August, 1862, he was made a rear-admiral, on the retired list, and in August and September was president of the naval commission to locate a new navy-yard.

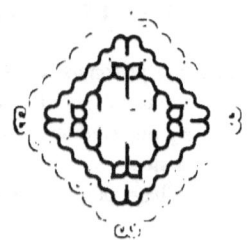

ANDREW HULL FOOTE.

ANDREW HULL FOOTE was born in New Haven, Connecticut, September 12th, 1806. His father, Samuel A. Foote, well known in the political history of Connecticut in the early part of the present century, as a member of the legislature and governor of the state, served also several terms in Congress; and was in 1830 the mover, in the United States Senate, of the resolution commonly known as "Foote's resolution on the public lands," which gave rise to the celebrated debate between Daniel Webster and Robert Y. Hayne.

Young Foote was intended by his parents for one of the learned professions, but exhibiting a strong inclination for a sea-life, he was allowed, in December, 1822, to enter the navy as acting midshipman, and made his first cruise in the schooner Grampus, Commander Gregory, which formed part of the squadron under Commodore Porter, dispatched in 1823 to the West Indies, to chastise the pirates who infested those waters and preyed upon American commerce. Having participated with credit in this dangerous service, he obtained a midshipman's warrant, and in 1824 joined the Pacific squadron under Commodore Hull. In 1827, he passed his examination for passed-midshipman; in 1830, he was commissioned a lieutenant; and in 1833, he was ordered to join the Delaware, seventy-four, bearing the broad pennant of Commodore Patterson, as flag-lieutenant of the Mediterranean squadron. During his service on this station he visited every accessible place of historic interest, and with a party of brother-officers explored many parts of Egypt and the Holy Land, extending his journey to the Dead Sea and the adjacent regions. In 1838, he was appointed first-lieutenant of the sloop-of-war John Adams, in which he accompanied Commodore Read in his voyage of circumnavigation, participating in the attack upon the towns of Quallahbattoo and Abuckie, in the island of Sumatra, which had become a noted rendezvous of pirates; and rendering effectual service to the American missionaries at Honolulu, in obtaining the publication of their defence, and in supporting them against the false charges of the French commander, La Place.

From 1841 until 1843, Lieutenant Foote was stationed at the Naval Asylum, in Philadelphia, where his efforts were beneficially directed to ameliorate and elevate the condition of the inmates. A consistent advocate, from his youth upward, of total abstinence from spirituous liquors, he had not failed during his experience of sea-life to observe the demoralizing influence upon sailors of an habitual indulgence in drinking, even when it did not produce intoxication. Waiving for the time any notice of the plea, so frequently urged, that the severe labors and hardships imposed upon the sailor compel him to resort to grog as a stimulant (which he did not believe, his opinion being that "whiskey-rations are evil, and only evil, and that continually"), he maintained that the case of the retired pensioner differed essentially from that of the sailor on active duty, and that the former would be happier and better without his grog. With admirable address, he prevailed upon many of the "old salts" under his charge to take the temperance pledge, and to the surprise of the incredulous carried out his predictions to the letter, the institution showing a marked improvement in discipline and order during the period that he was connected with it. The reform thus commenced twenty years ago, by an earnest advocate of total abstinence, has since been extended to the entire service, and in the estimation of experienced persons will greatly raise the standard of its *personnel.*

On his next cruise, which he made in the frigate Cumberland, in 1843–'45, as first-lieutenant, Foote tested his theory of the benefits of total abstinence upon a sea-going crew, whom he succeeded in persuading to give up their grog. The spirit-room was accordingly emptied of its contents; and the improvement in the moral as well as the physical condition of the men was perceptible in the high order of discipline soon attained, and which made the Cumberland a model ship. Nor did Lieutenant Foote stop here. Having established sobriety and order in the ship, he directed his attention to the religious instruction of the crew, and delivered weekly a Sunday lecture on the berth-deck, at which nearly two hundred of the men voluntarily attended. Many of them also took part in prayer-meetings which usually succeeded the lecture.

Soon after returning home, Lieutenant Foote was ordered to the Charlestown navy-yard, where he discharged the duties of executive officer during the Mexican War, being prevented from participating in that struggle by a species of ophthalmia contracted in Egypt. In October, 1849, he was assigned to the command of the brig Perry, and ordered to join the American squadron under Commodore Gregory on the coast of Africa. The suppression of the slave-trade was the special service assigned to him, and the British squadron cruising in the same waters found no more earnest or efficient co-operator. Several slavers were captured and condemned; and the trade was, in fact, broken up along a considerable portion of the coast—a result so satisfactory to the American government, that Lieutenant Foote received from the naval department an official recognition of his services. This compliment was doubly earned from the fact that, while engaging in every effort to put down the nefarious traffic in human flesh, he had rigidly kept in view, in his communications with the British authorities, the great principle of the War of 1812, maintaining that "the deck of an American vessel under its flag is the territory of the United States, and that no other authority but that of the United States could ever be allowed to exercise jurisdiction over it." It is worthy of note also that during this cruise of two and a half years, not a drop of grog was served out to the crew, and not an officer or man was for any lengthened period on the sick-list (although the station is notoriously unhealthy), or was lost or disabled. Lieutenant Foote subsequently embodied his observations and reflections on this cruise in an interesting volume entitled "Africa and the American Flag," which contains a general survey of the African continent in its physical, historical, and social relations, with remarks on the progress of colonization and the blighting influence of the slave-trade. Returning home in 1852, he was promoted to be a commander, and appointed executive officer at the Naval Asylum, at which post he remained about a year.

His next important service was on the "Naval Retiring Board," composed of fifteen of the most competent officers of the navy, to whom was assigned the ungracious task of reporting the names of those of their brother-officers who were incapacitated by age or other causes from discharging their duties, in order that their places might be filled by younger and better men. It may be doubted whether the government could have employed a more faithful or conscientious person in this service; and the fact that President Pierce subsequently reinstated many officers whose incompetency had been reported by the board, in no respect affects the action of Commander Foote and his associates, who simply performed a duty imposed upon them by Congress.

In 1856, he was placed in command of the sloop-of-war Portsmouth, and ordered to proceed to the China station. Arriving at Canton in October, just previous to the commencement of hostilities between the English and Chinese, he landed an armed force in the city for the protection of the American residents, whom, in view of the threatening aspect of affairs, he advised to remove their property. His boat, carrying the American flag at her stern, having been fired upon from the Canton barrier forts while he was engaged in this duty, he received, after urgent solicitation, permission from Commodore Armstrong, his commanding officer, to vindicate the honor of the flag by attack upon the forts. The Levant was ordered to support the Portsmouth, but grounded in coming up the river, so that the latter vessel was compelled to bear the brunt of the attack alone. Anchoring under a heavy fire at the distance of four hundred and ninety yards from the nearest fort, she succeeded, in less than two and a half hours. in silencing all the forts, four in number; and on the next day, November 21st, in company with the Levant, she renewed the attack with great effect. A breach having been made in the nearest fort, which was the strongest of all, Commander Foote landed with a force of two hundred and eighty sailors and marines, and

42

carried the work by assault. Within the next two days the remaining forts were stormed in the face of a galling fire from the enemy; and on the 24th, the American flag waved over all of them. The forts were massive granite structures, with walls seven feet thick, mounting one hundred and seventy-six guns, and were garrisoned by five thousand men, of whom upward of four hundred were killed and wounded. The American loss did not exceed forty. This gallant series of actions took place within sight of the British and French squadrons, and greatly enhanced the reputation of the American navy as a ready and efficient vindicator of the national flag. The foreign officers and correspondents of the English newspapers spoke in high praise of the conduct of Commander Foote and his men; and as the Portsmouth and Levant dropped down the river past the British squadron, the admiral, Sir Michael Seymour, ordered the rigging of the ship to be manned, while the crew greeted the American vessels with loud cheers, and the band played "Hail Columbia" and "Yankee Doodle." The effect of the capture of the forts was, to cause the American flag to be thenceforth respected by the Chinese, and to open the way for the treaty made in the succeeding year by Mr. Reed. Commander Foote subsequently visited Japan and Siam, on important business in behalf of his government, and after a cruise of two years returned in June, 1858, to the United States.

The outbreak of the Rebellion found Commander Foote stationed at the Brooklyn navy-yard as executive officer, in which capacity he aided in fitting out many vessels of the blockading squadron. In July, 1861, he received his captain's commission; and in the September following he was appointed to succeed Commander Rodgers as flag-officer of the flotilla fitting out in the Western waters to co-operate with the land-forces in opposing the rebels in that part of the country. The obstacles with which he had to contend in prosecuting this work were numerous and vexatious; and in the absence of the means and appliances which are always at hand in the government ship-yards, he was obliged to tax his constructive genius to the utmost in order to keep pace with the public expectation, working day and night with unflagging energy. "The most difficult and arduous work of my life," he wrote to a friend several months afterward, "has been the improvising of the flotilla which, under God, has been so efficient in repressing rebellion, and in protecting loyal interests upon the magnificent rivers of the West. My other acts are more than appreciated—this probably never will be." The obstacles were nevertheless overcome with a skill and promptness surprising to all who were unacquainted with the man and with the native energy of his character, and long before active military operations commenced in the West, every one of the vessels comprising the flotilla was completed, and awaiting its crew and armament.

Early in February, 1862, the long-expected advance against the enemy commenced with an attack on Fort Henry, an important position on the Tennessee River; and to Flag-Officer Foote was assigned the privilege of opening the campaign, and of demonstrating the efficiency of the flotilla in whose equipment he had labored so assiduously. His fleet of gunboats, seven in number, of which four were iron-clad, entered the Tennessee River on the 5th of February, with the design of co-operating with a large land-force, under General Grant, in the reduction of the fort; but the troops not arriving on the ground in season, Foote opened fire, at about noon of the 6th, with the gunboats alone, and after a spirited action of two hours, in which his vessels were pretty roughly handled, compelled the rebel General Tilghman to make an unconditional surrender. About twenty large guns and an immense amount of munitions fell into the hands of the federal commander. The prisoners numbered only about sixty, comprising the remnant of the garrison; a rebel force of five thousand men, encamped outside the fort, having been dispersed by shots from the fleet during the progress of the fight. The Cincinnati, the flag-officer's ship, was hit thirty-one times; but the casualties of the fleet, with the exception of the Essex (which received a shot in her boiler, whereby twenty-nine officers and men were injured), were slight.

Having transferred the fort and prisoners to General Grant, who arrived on the ground an hour after the surrender, Flag-Officer Foote returned to Cairo, and a few days later sailed for the Cumberland River, to assist the land-forces in an attack upon Fort Donelson, a work of great size and strength, mounting many heavy guns on the water-side. At three o'clock P. M., on the 14th of February, the fleet moved up to the attack, which for an hour and a quarter was conducted with great vigor on both sides, and would have resulted in the capture of the fort, had not the St. Louis, Foote's flag-ship, and the Louisville, become unmanageable, by having their steering apparatus shot away, and drifted out of the fire. The enemy immediately returned to the guns from which they had been driven, and the remaining vessels were obliged to haul off, somewhat the worse for the encounter. The St. Louis alone received sixty-one shots, and among the wounded was her gallant commander, who was severely injured in the ankle by the fragment of a sixty-four-pound shot. With no thought of his own suffering, though moving with great difficulty upon crutches, he proceeded up the river in his flagship immediately after the surrender of the fort to the land-forces under General Grant, took possession of Clarksville without firing a gun, and destroyed the Tennessee Iron-Works, which had been used for the manufacture of iron plates for rebel steamers.

After a brief respite at Cairo, Foote sailed down the Mississippi with his flotilla, greatly increased in efficiency by the addition of the mortar-boats, whose construction he had also superintended. The enemy evacuated their strong positions at Columbus and Hickman previous to his approach, influenced doubtless by the wholesome terror which the gunboats (the "iron hell-hounds," as General Pillow called them) had inspired among them; and on March 17th was commenced the famous siege of Island Number Ten. Through all the tedious episodes of that investment, Foote remained faithfully at his post; although, from exertion and excitement, his wound grew daily more painful, until it was with the utmost difficulty he could ascend the deck of his ship. At length, on the 8th of April, the enemy, assailed in front by the flotilla and in the rear by the troops under General Pope (who after long delay had been conveyed across the Mississippi in boats), surrendered their works, and the flotilla was at liberty to proceed to new conquests. But so debilitated had Flag-Officer Foote become during the interval, that, in the opinion of his medical advisers, retirement for a season from active service could alone preserve his life. Under these circumstances, he reluctantly applied to the government for a leave of absence, and early in May turned over his command to Captain Davis in an appropriate address to his men, in which he was several times completely overcome by emotion.

His return to his home, in New Haven, was one continuous ovation, and all along the route enthusiastic crowds greeted him with shouts of approval. Public receptions, which he invariably declined, were tendered to him in almost every city through which he passed. "I should be as able to renew the fight with my flotilla," he wrote, in reply to the invitation of a committee of the citizens of Cleveland, "as to be the recipient of your numerous favors; and I know too well the intelligent citizens of Cleveland to doubt for a moment that they would deem this my paramount duty." A few weeks of rest restored him to health; but the opening of the Mississippi, which he had so brilliantly commenced, having by that time been so nearly accomplished, that the result was in no doubt, he was called to other duties of not less importance, and on the nomination of the President, which was confirmed by the Senate, was appointed chief of the bureau of equipment and recruiting, under the new organization of the navy. Of this office he is still the incumbent. He was also, though one of the youngest captains in point of rank in the navy, selected by the President—with the entire approbation of the people—as one of the seven rear-admirals on the active list authorized by the act of Congress.

Thus much for the public services of Admiral Foote. In the peaceful walks of private life, he has shown the same strict sense of duty, the same energy in all good works, and withal a modesty characteristic of the true hero. Frank and unassuming in his manners, he is noted for his active philanthropy, his unobtrusive piety, and his endeavors to elevate the moral condition of his race; and has repeatedly vindicated his sincerity, in addresses at the religious anniversaries of our large cities. His religion is of too earnest a stamp to be repressed or weakened by ridicule, and on more than one occasion he has publicly shown how deeply it is ingrained in his character. The often-repeated anecdote of his Sunday discourse at Cairo is one which history delights to treasure, and is too characteristic of the man to be omitted here. He had just returned from the capture of Fort Henry; and in the fulfilment of a duty, with which, if possible, he never permitted any circumstances to interfere, he attended the regular services at the Presbyterian church in Cairo. The preacher, for some reason, was absent, and the congregation were about to leave, when Flag-Officer Foote arose and approached the desk. At the appearance of the weather-beaten veteran, fresh from his recent victory, "like a servant of the Lord, with his Bible and his sword,' the congregation were with difficulty restrained from breaking into applause. He checked them with a look, and, the first murmur of surprise having subsided, offered an impressive prayer, to which he added an extempore sermon. The commander who, emerging from the smoke and roar of a great battle, could stand before the people in the character of a preacher of the gospel, will be acknowledged a worthy descendant of the "men who fought and prayed"—the founders of religious and political liberty in New England.

The orders of Admiral Foote upon assuming command of the flotilla, enjoining a rigid observance of Sunday, and an avoidance, by both officers and men, of profane swearing and intemperance, are conceived in the same spirit which prompted his action on the above occasion, and stamp him as one who believes that religion and morals are not the least effective agents in making good sailors. Among the popular heroes whom the war has produced, no one is more honored or trusted; and while such men survive in active duty, the early fame of the American navy will be fully sustained.

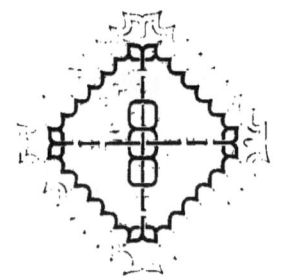